The Canada Project

a novel

By Claudia Cattaneo

 FriesenPress

One Printers Way
Altona, MB R0G 0B0
Canada

www.friesenpress.com

ISBN
978-1-03-913720-2 (Hardcover)
978-1-03-913719-6(Paperback)
978-1-03-913721-9 (eBook)

1. FICTION, THRILLERS, POLITICAL

Distributed to the trade by The Ingram Book Company

"It is open to every man to choose the direction of his striving and every man may take comfort from the fine saying that the search for truth is more precious than its possession."

Albert Einstein

This book is dedicated to the tens of thousands of Albertans who lost their livelihoods as a result of the campaign to shut down the oilsands industry

Chapter 1

John Hess. Elise was in a pub, nursing a glass of Chianti, when she first heard his name. It came up in a public relations pitch at the end of a long news day. It remained stuck in her head, haunting her like an irritating echo from her subconscious, teasing her to pay attention, presaging something big.

"You should do a profile on him," suggested Peter Persic, John's public relations man.

Too much work for little upside, Elise thought, chasing away the echo.

"He's working on a new strategy, a big one," Peter insisted.

She was still unconvinced. To her, John Hess did not seem big enough for the prime time she represented.

"You'll get an exclusive," Peter added, emphasizing the word *exclusive*, as if dangling a huge, special, one-time offer that Elise would be a fool to refuse. "He wants to talk to you because you understand the business. Plus, he has great respect for your paper. But if you are not interested, I'll offer it to someone else," he said, implying his bidding was over.

Peter knew – or thought he knew – how to get a reporter's attention. He'd been a news director at a Calgary TV station before crossing over to the oil business, which immediately doubled his salary in exchange for pushing corporate propaganda. Overweight and gregarious, he was wearing an expensive suit and a fresh haircut to show he'd done well as a corporate mouthpiece after years of slugging it out in the media trenches, pushing sob stories and trashing oil leaders like the one who was now paying his wage.

Elise had heard such pitches before, of course, in the same place. Many had turned out well. But even more had not and cost her precious time.

She decided to take the interview, as a second glass of Chianti clouded her usually sharp news judgement, mostly because she was competitive and didn't want someone else to get a scoop. Plus, she needed new story ideas. The pressure to fill the newspaper, that bottomless pit, never stopped.

Peter, his job done, picked up the tab and walked over to a group of oil people he knew.

Elise finished up her wine and watched the crowd surrounding her – the people were loud, enthusiastic, boastful. An oil gusher had been announced. She overheard talk about the money that would be made, especially by the insiders.

O'Reilly Pub, a popular Calgary restaurant and bar, was owned and patronized by oil types who needed a home away from home to meet with friends and investors. Faded photos of Hollywood celebrities and of Alberta notables who had paid a visit filled the walls, alongside plaques featuring Irish sayings – oddly appropriate for a rough-and-tumble place like Calgary – like: "May you be at the gates of heaven an hour before the devil knows you're dead!"

Imported wine from a well-stocked cellar and locally brewed beer flowed freely, often washing down tasty Alberta rib-eye steaks, the pub's specialty.

O'Reilly was also an unofficial press club where reporters like Elise and oilpatch spin doctors with big expense accounts talked shop and traded gossip about who was on the take, who was on his way up and, occasionally, who was on his way down. The scuttlebutt often made the rounds before those in question even knew it.

Everyone knew the rules. Journalists worked off the record and looked for leads. Flacks — as PR men and women were known — developed press connections they hoped to milk. Their corporate bonuses depended on cultivating strategic relationships, and the business media was at the top of their lists. Favourable press coverage could bring big rewards, especially in big papers, as it could influence big investors and big hedge funds, preferably based in New York. It led to their bosses' recognition and promotions – and competitors' envy. Of course, flacks and their masters always took credit when the coverage was good, and blamed media incompetence when it was not. A few still believed that any press was good press.

Elise got up and joined Peter again. He was chatting with an influential stock analyst. She was tired, but before she went home, she wanted to confirm she would do the interview.

"How soon is Hess available to do this?" Elise asked the PR man.

"I'll tell him to expect your call," Peter said, already imagining a favourable article above the fold. "Try him after five thirty p.m. tomorrow. His executive assistant will have left for the day, and he will personally pick up the phone."

Elise didn't know much about John Hess. Back at the office the following day, she scoured news archives and a preliminary picture emerged: A securities lawyer and a geologist, he found fossil fuel deposits, made oil and gas deals, and raised huge amounts of cash.

She looked up his corporate biography, which she knew offered what he wanted others to know. Groomed to perfection, she thought. Husband, athlete, philanthropist, volunteer, member of the right clubs and of the right circles. He attended the right schools, was awarded the right scholarships, got the right internships, won the right first jobs, was promoted to the right first executive roles, and then led successful startups. He supported the right charities, was appointed to the right boards, served on the right political advisory panels. He's such a shining example of how to gain, retain, and expand power that Machiavelli could have learned a thing or two, she concluded.

She solicited gossip from her sources, hoping to find juicier nuggets. One of the oilman's former partners, speaking off the record in a phone interview, admitting both respect and jealousy, said John had been well rewarded for making the most of oil prices' highs and lows. He was a billionaire on paper before the age of billionaires, drove a Bentley, and travelled the world on his company's buttery-leather-seat jet. He golfed in exclusive clubs and bought his wife big diamonds. He had a weakness for expensive art, Italian suits, and fine wines, the man said. "But when the occasion demands, John does the redneck like a pro," the former partner said with a laugh. "He owns steel-toed boots, a hardhat and, when he must, sleeps in portable housing at his drilling sites alongside his crew. He says that's where he gets the best sleep."

A broker, who claimed to be one of John's close friends, confided that there was plenty of greedy money prepared to back him, particularly at the bottom of the oil-price cycle or at the start of a new company, when shares were handed out for pennies in advance of their market debut. "No one else has his track record of value creation," the broker said over coffee, not for attribution. "My clients have done well by investing in John's companies."

A Wall Street banker had a different take. John Hess – tall, blond, patrician – fit the description of the blue-eyed sheik well, he said to Elise over the phone. "He's as astute and greedy as his white-robed counterpart in the Arabian Gulf, only a friendly Canadian. While the Arabs hire cheap labour from the Third World to produce their oil, use oil money to oppress their people and to fund wars, the Canadians, of which John is a leading example, are eager beavers who invent their own oilfield technologies, work on their own projects, are highly regulated, and are transparent."

A long-time conservative politician, eager to cultivate his own relationship with Elise, talked up John's contributions to Alberta. "He's a top oil entrepreneur. We'd be poorer without him. Oil and gas are disgusting words among the political left, but few other industries create so much wealth, so quickly, so regularly, for so many who know how to ride the booms and busts. John knows how to do it more than anyone I know. You can quote me on that," the stout man said over beer. They were in a dark, run-down bar he liked to call his second office.

"Off the record, governments know and understand the racket," he continued, ordering another round on Elise's tab. "They play along because they need industry's royalties and taxes to pay for the services voters expect, or for the handouts to voters that keep them in power. Politicians court oil barons to fund their election campaigns, and John Hess is no exception. They make pilgrimages to their glass towers on a regular basis to ensure their relationships are well oiled and current.

"That's where they lay their cards on those shiny boardroom tables," he continued, half inebriated. "Quid-pro-quos are discussed and arranged. Strategies are shared. Perhaps jobs for sons and daughters are suggested, you know, to tighten the bond. That's how business is done, not just in oil but in every part of the economy and of the political spectrum. Elites looking after each other to ensure self-preservation. Better the devil you know than the one you don't – or the angel who doesn't owe you a favour, right?" the politician said, grinning, ordering more beer.

"Sure, there are oil price busts," he continued, as Elise soaked up his words, though not the beer, even if they strayed from the topic she was interested in. "They are usually kicked off by the volatile Arabs to suppress new competition, but they come and go because everyone knows the Arabs can't live without the world's oil money. Besides, Canadian oilmen know how to read the OPEC oil cartel's tea leaves better than most. They send their own observers to its meetings, build relationships, show deference, and learn."

Elise was intrigued but had nagging second thoughts about meeting John. She was worried the CEO wasn't well-known enough outside Calgary's oil circles, that he was too small league by North American standards to justify her attention, and that any story on John Hess would be too promotional. Too many people were saying too many good things, and she suspected she was being managed. Peter had done his homework, she concluded. The feeling was stuck in her gut.

She opted for a middle ground. She'd do the interview and store the information for a later day. She needed to meet more industry people, anyway. She got the go-ahead from her editor to meet him in person – no obligation to write. She would waste the oilman's time, but not her own.

But John had his own media strategy and was playing hard to get. He postponed the interview numerous times, claiming to have too much on the go. He finally confirmed an hour-long meeting with Elise for the next Tuesday morning in his office.

Chapter 2

CALGARY, ALBERTA, FEBRUARY 2000

Elise knew the ten-minute walk from her editorial bureau to John's office in the downtown area would be a struggle. It was February, and Calgary was at its wintry worst. Snow was falling hard, the roads were coated with ice, and the temperature was a biting minus 35° Celsius, nearly matching that in the Canadian Arctic. Located a short drive from the eastern wall of the Canadian Rockies, the city was far south of the North Pole, but winters could be frigid because of its elevation – 3,500 feet above sea level – and because there were no obstacles in the open prairie to hold back cold fronts.

The deep freeze came with a silver lining for its oilpatch, one reason it shrugged off the blasts of Arctic air as a temporary inconvenience. Cold usually meant higher oil and gas prices due to higher winter heating demand, which in turn strengthened Canadian energy stock prices.

Elise estimated it would take her an hour to hear John out. If he turned out to be as bland and as scripted as she suspected, she had enough time left in her day to chase another lead. She already had an eye on a story about stock-market manipulation that seemed to hold promise, especially if her sources were as solid as she thought.

This would allow her to fulfill her obligation to Peter just in case she might need him in the future, and to keep her competitors at bay. Peter had been a good and reliable source, particularly about industry gossip. She needed to keep that pipeline open and flowing. One of her golden rules was that news leads could come from anyone, anywhere, anytime, and Peter had been such a good asset his phone number was seared in her memory.

For the interview, she wore a warm wool pant suit and her thick fur coat – at such freezing temperatures, even the bleeding hearts in the anti-fur movement preferred to stay quiet and out of the way.

By the time Elise arrived, her hands and feet were frozen, her nostrils were stuck together, her cheeks were close to being permanently damaged by frostbite, and her eyebrows were frosted. She cursed Calgary's winters. She entered the lobby of the black glass tower that housed John's company, Hunter Exploration, and kicked the snow from her boots. His office was on the 39th floor. She'd heard it was a desirable address that had housed some of the industry's most storied oil companies at one time or another. Some had disappeared because of takeovers, others during price busts. She took off her coat on the smooth elevator ride up and walked into a large, dark-wood-paneled lobby.

"I am sorry, but Mr. Hess is in an important meeting," Sheila, his executive assistant, sighed. She was one of the many large-chested faux blondes that oilmen liked to keep on display, along with white orchids, bronze cowboy sculptures, Canadian Indigenous art, and historic oil-industry paraphernalia.

"If you come back in an hour, he'll be available to talk to you. Otherwise, we can reschedule. We can try something in a month."

Elise was disappointed. She turned and noticed a well-known investment banker slipping into a boardroom for a meeting during what should have been her time.

So, that's what's going on, she thought. I'm dispensable.

Elise was tempted to walk away and cancel the whole thing. She felt the charade for a marginal interview had dragged on long enough. But after talking up the oilman to her editor, she felt obligated to follow through. She knew her bosses didn't care about her bruised ego, just about getting stories and more stories. She killed the idle hour at a nearby coffee shop, sucking up the snub, then took the elevator up to the 39th floor for a second time.

John was in the lobby when she returned, making small talk with the assistant. He smiled at Elise, asked to take her coat, hung it in a closet, then extended his hand.

"John Hess," he said. "It's a pleasure to meet you. Call me John. I apologize for the misunderstanding. I must have made a mistake. I should have let Sheila handle the appointment."

Elise decided not to dwell on the delay and instead offered her hand. She decided to do the interview and get out. She'd wasted enough time.

"Elise Chamonter with the *Journal*. Nice to meet you," she said, projecting confidence. She was proud of her career and showed it openly. She belonged to the world's best-known, most influential business paper. She'd earned her job fair and square.

"I've heard a lot about you," John said, looking uneasy as he sized her up, taken by Elise's beautiful face and intense, intelligent brown eyes.

Elise followed him through a hallway to his large corner office overlooking the Rocky Mountains. The snowstorm was winding down and sunshine erupted across the horizon, highlighting the jagged mountain peaks at the end of the prairies.

She looked around and noticed Group of Seven art. Then her gaze landed on a large painting portraying the discovery of the Leduc field, Alberta's first major commercial oil discovery, in a small boardroom separated from John's office by a glass wall. Made in 1947, the field was found after 133 dry holes and launched Alberta's commercial oil industry. It reminded her that the Canadian oil business was not for the faint of heart.

Geological maps of Western Canada were pinned up on a wall. A big, thick screen displaying stock and commodity prices was mounted on another wall and provided live coverage of the day's market news. An ornate antique desk in the centre dominated the room. Elise looked for but didn't see family photos.

John wore his age well, Elise thought. He was in his early fifties, sported a golden golf tan and walked elegantly, like a feline at the top of the food chain. A nicely tailored black suit, a yellow silk tie, bleached white teeth, and smoothness around his eyes suggested regular maintenance.

They sat down on comfortable leather chairs around a coffee table where several newspapers, including her own, were displayed like a hand of giant playing cards.

"Thank you for agreeing to see me. Mr. Persic, Peter, was very persuasive," Elise said politely, smiling to put the interviewee at ease. "Peter said you are working on a new strategy. Can you tell me about it?" She switched on her tape recorder while flipping open her small notebook, in case she needed a backup.

"We have created a lot of shareholder value since we started the company, and we are now working on a great new play in British Columbia," John said, referring to a region in Canada's Northwest that was getting market attention and was one of Hunter's latest exploration targets.

"If we're successful, it will take us to the next level as an oil and gas company. We have accumulated a large spread of land in the main fairway, and we like the rocks. But I can't be more specific about the potential because I don't want to tip off my competitors. We are still working on it."

"How could it change the company?" Elise asked, hoping for more information that wasn't already widely available on investor presentations, which she had reviewed.

"I can tell you that we are very excited about it and that we have started some exploratory drilling to size up the resource," John responded. "We will have more to say in our next investor presentation."

"Can you tell me a bit about yourself?" Elise asked. "When did you start in the oil business?"

"Soon after university," he said. "I liked the opportunity. I wanted to work in Alberta because it rewards entrepreneurs."

Elise kept asking questions, and John kept offering what seemed to her like previously rehearsed answers. It was obvious that he didn't want to be there. The oilman was not the confident maverick she had expected. His voice was strong, but his words were not his own. He gave up little of himself. His large blue eyes were as icy as that morning's blizzard.

Elise tried unsuccessfully to find out more about his background, his interests, his mentors. He stuck to his lines, as if nothing bad had ever happened to him to penetrate his phony smile. No setbacks. No failures. No pain. At times he looked at her with a sensual gaze that made her feel uncomfortable.

He seemed out of his depth, like a poor version of his reputation, Elise thought. She even felt a bit sorry for him. Promoters were common in the oil industry, and she was beginning to wonder if John was one of them. She was disappointed.

After an hour, they wrapped up the meeting and walked together to the elevator. Suddenly, his eyes became lively, and he seemed relieved.

Elise decided during the walk back to the office to write an article after all, almost out of pity. She had enough to do a piece, though not a great one. She offered to phone him back to double check facts, trying to build a relationship. She hoped a nice story could pay off in the future and turn him into a source.

A few days later the article made the front page, above the fold. She was surprised it got big play and was pleased with the story in the end, even if it was too promotional and didn't write itself. She had to work hard to make John look like he had deserved any coverage at all. Other sources, some of them suggested by Peter, provided more information, helping her build a fuller picture.

Peter was ecstatic when the article appeared. He met with John first thing on the morning of publication.

"Nicely played, Peter," John said, grateful that his first media interview had gone so well. "You are good at this. Your coaching helped. I'll keep it in mind at bonus time. I am glad everyone stepped up and made me look so good."

"I told you we could pull it off," Peter said. "Earned media is worth the effort. The article will come in handy in your upcoming meetings with investors."

"We can use it in our presentations," John proposed. "The board will be delighted, too. And timing was perfect if our program in the North is as good as we think it is."

John had his own reasons to be pleased but didn't share them. His strategy had proven successful. He had disregarded Elise's schedule to throw her off balance. He had projected helplessness to win her sympathy. He said the bare minimum while getting others to say what he wanted to see in print.

John knew he did not impress Elise, but Elise impressed him. She could be useful, he thought, imagining how such a connection could help him get what he wanted.

A few days later, Elise sat behind her desk in her editorial office, chasing another news lead, when the phone rang.

"Thank you for the nice story," John said, seeming so friendly Elise barely recognized the cold fish who had recently stood before her. "I received dozens of calls about it. My board is thrilled. You did a great job of capturing our strategy."

"Thank you for the interview. I'm glad it worked out," Elise said politely, distracted by another market play that was beginning to get noticed. It was known as the oilsands and was in the Athabasca region of northeast Alberta.

"I'd like to take you out for lunch some time, as a token of my appreciation," John proposed. "Maybe you can tell me more about you and about how the media works. I'm afraid I am not used to being interviewed. I never had to do it. I could use some advice."

Elise was surprised by the invitation and started wondering if John had an angle.

She knew it was unusual for the CEO of a prominent company to have lunch with a reporter, even one as well-known as she was, unaccompanied by public relations staff. CEOs kept their distance. Partly it was arrogance, partly it was self-preservation. Regulations were hard on executives with loose lips. To avoid passing on inside information, oil CEOs kept their contact with the real world to a minimum. It made them dependent on their inner circle for information, Elise had heard, which often led to bad judgement calls about controversial stuff, such as environmental policy or Indigenous issues.

Elise agreed to the lunch date. High-level inside sources were worth a lot in her business, she decided, and John seemed like one worth cultivating.

When she arrived at O'Reilly a week later at noon, the oilman was already waiting, sitting at a table for two in a secluded area against a wall, way at the back.

He was no longer the icy executive Elise had interviewed. He had a friendly smile. He looked relaxed. A dusty blue tie matched the shade of his eyes. They greeted each other warmly and the conversation flowed easily, jumping from one topic to another.

John explained to Elise his company's growth strategy in detail, supporting his points by drawing charts on paper napkins. He spoke about his beliefs about the market's next big things, why he loved the oil and gas business and the company he created. Elise was fascinated. She was surprised by the transformation. She wished she'd met the real John Hess the first time around.

"I'm a deal junkie," he confessed, looking at her like she was his new best friend. "I don't get as involved with finding oil and gas as most people believe. I hire the best technical people and give them the support and rewards to motivate them. I prefer to focus on the big picture."

He offered to show her photos and maps of his core holdings. He suggested new story ideas they could work on together in the future.

Elise spoke about her recent move to Calgary, her recent personal loss, her passion for journalism.

She thought it felt more like a date than a business meeting. She became concerned about his intentions. Working together? Is he flirting with me? She wondered. Or is he just buttering me up for more good press? Either way, it's not happening.

"I wish you had told me all this stuff during the interview," Elise complained, ignoring the undercurrent.

She didn't know how to tell him that her first story on him was a one-off deal, that she was not his friend, and that any follow-ups would have to be newsworthy. She hated promotional stuff. Her reputation was on the line. Puff pieces were beneath her and bad for her brand as a serious investigative journalist. She gave him a chance he didn't deserve, and now she expected him to deliver something in return that really warranted news coverage.

"I would have done a much better job on your profile if I could have included your views about the market, or the anecdote you just mentioned about your early days as a salesman," Elise said. "People love to read the stories of successful people like you."

"What I just told you is not for public consumption," he said. "That was just me saying too much. I shouldn't have done that."

John picked up the tab and paid it without looking at it. They walked toward the exit, turning a few heads. They were running late, and the lunch-time crowd had thinned. From the restaurant's vestibule, John had noticed a parking ticket was sitting on the windshield of his Bentley and shook his head, looking annoyed.

And then it happened, that gesture of no return. John helped Elise put on her coat at the door and caressed her chin with his hand. Elise didn't know if it was an accident or if he was coming on to her. She lost her composure and lowered her eyes, hoping the caress was unintended, that he wasn't just another powerful man trying to control her.

He looked at her with the same intensity he had shown during the interview.

Something jolted inside her. Her knees weakened. A warm feeling rushed through her. Elise snapped back. Suddenly she was glad her business lunch with John was over. She knew she had to tread carefully. He was the type of man who didn't play by the rules of professional conduct – but she had to. She needed her job. She needed boundaries. Her readers expected boundaries. Scrap him as a source, she thought. She would not be used. She walked away.

Chapter 3

CALGARY, ALBERTA, FEBRUARY 2000

Elise was sliding into midlife with none of the big, exciting plans she had anticipated. Her husband had passed away, ravaged by a cancer that took over his body with the speed of an Alberta-forest fire. Dr. Julien Chamonter had left her a small fortune to live well for the rest of her life and to fund their children's education. But she felt too broken to enjoy it. They had built a fairy-tale life together, and now it was gone. And she still needed – wanted – to work. She had always paid her way. She had to make the world a more truthful place.

Julien had been an up-and-coming cardiologist who'd moved to New York from Switzerland to be with Elise.

Brooklyn-born and raised, Elise was the granddaughter of Italian immigrants. She attended journalism school at Columbia and graduated at the top of her class, which led to a graduate finance degree at Harvard, and then a job at the *Journal* right out of school.

She was a classic beauty, with shoulder-length auburn hair and dazzling brown eyes. She met Julien at a medical conference where she was interviewing doctors for a feature about pharmaceutical companies and their conflicts of interest with health practitioners.

Julien was careful with Elise's questions – he didn't tell her he was in New York on a routine drug-company junket – but not about feeling attracted to her. The son of a prominent surgeon in Geneva, he told her he had a job interview lined up, too. He liked the idea of spreading his wings in the New World, so he could work with the best, he said, then asked her out for dinner.

She took him to Little Italy. They fell in love between antipasto and tiramisu.

They were married a year later and made New York their home.

Twins showed up a year after that – a boy and a girl. The couple's jobs were demanding, but they travelled extensively as a family, shuttling regularly from New York, where Elise's parents babysat on demand, to Switzerland, where Julien's parents filled in during holidays. They had a wide circle of friends on both sides of the ocean. They enjoyed their lives to the fullest. Their love for each other had been pure and unconditional.

Julien died the same way he lived – in a hurry. His fight with pancreatic cancer lasted just shy of three months. She cursed the long shifts he had worked at the hospital before he got sick, which she believed had made him physically weak. She resented him for leaving her to fend for herself so soon after her parents were killed instantly in a car accident while on their way to Florida for a vacation. The double-whammy of loss felt like rogue waves slamming into her, one after the other, dragging her deep into the abyss.

Everything in New York reminded her of her best and of her darkest hours. Her future seemed like a black box. She thought of suicide often. She needed a new scene and a new life.

When her newspaper advertised a job in Calgary for an energy correspondent, she raised her hand. She wanted a new start, away from the darkness. She rented out her Park Avenue flat to a work colleague, bid farewell to her friends, hugged her kids as they moved into their university dorms for the first time, and aimed her Subaru station wagon straight north to Toronto, and then west on the TransCanada Highway toward the Canadian Rockies, where she'd never been.

It's just a short-term gig, she told herself, her children, and her friends. She would fly back so often her twins would barely notice she was gone. The new job would not be a step up. It meant starting over and learning a new beat. But she needed it as much as the paper needed to fill it.

One step at a time, she told herself during the long, lonely drive, past the turquoise lakes and the gold canola fields, the grain elevators and the railway crossings, knowing every inch forward would be difficult. Sadness was always just a memory away.

The sun was shining high in the sky when Elise got her first glimpse of the Calgary skyline through her car window. The city sprouted from the green foothills like a glittering glass fortress. The contrast of past and future intrigued her.

Elise rented a modern condo in the city's core with views of the mountains and embraced her new job. Before long, she hit the area's ski slopes, so white and powdery and close to the sky she felt close to God and to Julien. Her children joined her during school breaks. New friends filled the space in between.

The oil and natural gas industry turned out to be more interesting than Elise had anticipated. It had drama, greed, conflict, sex, and a colourful cast of characters, she said to her bosses back in the newsroom. It had been marginalized by big media for too long, overshadowed by sexier parts of the economy like technology and finance. Perhaps energy wasn't well known because so many of the key decisions were made far away, in Riyadh or Houston or Aberdeen, she argued, feeling excited once again about the stories she wanted to write. Or because policy makers didn't really care about meddling with energy, provided it was cheap and available.

But the world was waking up to the realization that fossil fuels were running out, and most remaining deposits were concentrated in the Middle East, Russia, Venezuela, or Western Canada. The first three were controlled by governments that used their energy for political leverage, at best, or as a weapon, at worst, and were risky for private investors. Western Canada, as the location of the only remaining investable deposits, was getting the market's attention.

Elise was joined in the new energy powerhouse by many other reporters, the oil lobby, the public relations industry, the investment community, the banks, and the environmental movement, transforming the city into a crossroad to the world.

Elise's mandate was to build the energy beat so global investors who read the *Journal* were informed about key events and key people in Western Canada. She would be their boots on the ground, like a war correspondent filing dispatches from the front.

She was expected to write about the good and the bad, the facts and the context, the winners and the losers, the spoken and the unspoken.

Her content had to be accurate and based on information from respected sources. She had to be fair.

Her newspaper demanded such discipline from all its writers and contributors, building on centuries of journalism evolution, to honour the special standing it enjoyed in developed societies. The expectations were so high, and the rules so firm, the result was journalism that was trusted to reflect the first draft of history.

There was no activism. There was no judgement about which truth was more important and which had to be suppressed.

The journalism that Elise was expected to deliver was about pursuing all truths for all people.

Chapter 4

CALGARY, ALBERTA, AND DAWSON CREEK, BRITISH COLUMBIA, MARCH 2000

John was on his way back to his office when his new mobile phone rang.

"John, we're getting close," Mike Beck, his drilling manager, said with anticipation. John loved hearing from Mike. They had known each other since the beginning of their careers, when John was a wellsite geologist, and Mike was a roughneck. He missed those times, when they worked together in the North, and spent their free time observing wildlife, or staying up until midnight to watch the northern lights bounce from one end of the night sky to the other, or meeting with Indigenous people and hearing their timeless wisdom about life.

"We should have some firmer results overnight," Mike said. "We're trying to keep things tight, but it's hard. There are dozens of oil scouts right outside the lease. They're pests. They won't leave us alone."

"It's best if we talk in person," John said. "I will come to see you tomorrow. I don't trust this phone. We can't afford a leak."

John hung up and asked his assistant to book the jet and the helicopter for an early morning run to the field. He asked his exploration chief, Drew Little, to join him at 6:00 a.m. the next day at the hangar. He was excited. His gut told him he was about to strike a company-building gusher, that his expensive bet would finally pay off. To-do items filled his mind. He needed to review his plan to get all the land around the well under his control. He needed to firm up drilling plans. He needed to tighten the information flow until he was prepared to make an announcement.

John summoned Peter to his office. "I'd like you to prepare a news release about our drilling program in British Columbia. Keep it general for now. A lot of background and some context about the region. We may have something to announce. I expect maximum confidentiality on this one. Too many of our competitors are looking over our shoulders."

When Peter left, John looked at the screen above his desk and shook his head. His company's stock had jumped, and a big volume of shares were changing hands.

Oh no, he said to himself, suspecting rumours of a big find were already all over the Street. He knew it meant a substantial increase in his net worth, but he was troubled: the stock's behaviour showed once again that information was leaking.

John felt alone. He was concerned about the way the business was evolving. Thoughts about getting out while he was still ahead, perhaps selling to one of his rivals, starting fresh, both personally and professionally, were tempting him more and more.

Too much was changing. It used to be about looking for the best places to drill, the excitement of a successful discovery, ingenuity and initiative, people wrestling with mother nature and harvesting one of her most precious offerings – energy – so they could bring progress and prosperity to the masses.

Now, it was all about activist investors, corporate fights, and arguing with foreign green activists about the merits of fossil fuels.

His landline rang, jolting him back to reality.

"Hi John. It's Fred Mitchell from Tristar Capital in New York. We heard you are on the cusp of announcing a big one," he said.

"I'm sorry. Who's this and how did you get my number?"

"It's Fred Mitchell. I'm with one of the largest hedge funds on Wall Street. We spoke last fall at a conference. We're betting on your company because our sources tell us your drilling results in Northeast British Columbia are spectacular. When will you news release this?"

"What you are saying is premature," John responded. "We have nothing to announce at this moment." The CEO hung up, annoyed, and asked his assistant to screen his calls.

He looked up at his screen and noticed that his company's stock was still trading heavily, but its rise had stalled.

John was the largest shareholder of Hunter Exploration. He owned a third. The company had a value in the market of $4 billion, making it one of the largest Canadian independent oil and gas producers. It had great assets and a great workforce. John had built the company up from scratch, one of a handful he'd started after graduating from law school. He was worth half a billion when he was still in his thirties. His first love had been geology, but there were few steady jobs in the industry after he earned his degree from the University of Alberta. Commodity prices were weak, and companies were laying off staff. He took out another student loan and signed up to do law at the University of Toronto, where he specialized in securities and corporate tax. The additional education eventually served him well. He offered the full package: he was as astute at finding hydrocarbons as he was at putting together tax-effective deals. He understood rocks and he understood greed. They were the oil and gas industry's two most important ingredients. When he was young and idealistic, he also liked that oil was a surrogate for political power. Oil won wars and powered economies. Lack of it meant being beholden to those who had it.

The flight to Dawson Creek took just over an hour. It was a sunny but cold March day. A mantel of fresh snow covered the landscape. Spring was days away, but the North had not noticed.

John saw seismic lines from the airplane's oblong windows. His company had cut the lines through the forest the previous summer to generate seismic data so his geophysicists could map the prospect and pick the best drilling locations. The precursors of something big, he thought, feeling good about the work.

He spotted a cluster of shacks linked together by dirt roads, puffing plumes of smoke. They housed one of the local First Nations, his project's closest neighbours. He'd visited them a few times to get to know them and avoid opposition. They were a poor, restless band, governed by an elderly matriarch. They lived off the land, on farming, hunting, and government cheques, as far as he knew. Social problems were rampant – alcoholism, suicide, unemployment. Yet the people were fiercely protective of fish and wildlife. They told him on many occasions they were worried a discovery would bring an end to their way of life, such as it was. He'd assured them it would mean a path to prosperity for them and for their children, who could get jobs on rigs, building pipelines, and providing land-clearing services. He encouraged them to set up their own businesses.

They asked for a share of his company's revenue. He was drilling on their traditional lands, after all, which they had occupied for millennia. He said he'd think about it.

John knew he couldn't – wouldn't – share his bounty if one was found. He liked and respected them, and wanted to help them, but band members had no legal standing, in his view, to make such demands. As for jobs, he was prepared to do his part, but they had few useful skills and a poor work ethic. He hired in town when he needed to get the job done. Business was business, and his main obligation was to his shareholders, who wouldn't have approved of giveaways to Indigenous bands after risking so much of their own capital on exploration. His board would have questioned his sanity.

Besides, there was nothing that the band could do to stop his project. He'd done his homework. Everyone who mattered was looked after. He had purchased tickets at political fundraisers, hired the children of bureaucrats, donated funds to build community facilities, and sponsored events. It wasn't bribery, per se. But it made the people in decision-making roles beholden to him, and it worked most of the time.

John stepped off the airplane and walked briskly to a helicopter that was ready to fly him to the field. He put on his noise-cancelling earphones and his thoughts drifted to Elise. She was different from the women he knew. She seemed sincere, uncompromised – which was rare in the circles he frequented – and he admired her quiet confidence. She was smart and was interested in him and his work. Few women wanted to know about the oil business. Most simply wanted oilmen, their fast life, and their big bucks. And that suited most oil types just fine. He was one of them.

Elise scared him, too. He didn't know how to relate to a woman so accomplished and so well known. Columbia, Harvard, the *Journal*?

He regretted making that clumsy move on her, thinking he could charm her and make her a useful ally. Elise was too powerful in her own right to keep her under his thumb. She would not be loyal to him. She was not like the others who liked to have sex with him but accepted he was married to Claire. Stay away from her, he whispered to himself, as his helicopter prepared for landing.

Claire. His wife was a Calgary society fixture. She was in her early fifties, but her Barbie-doll looks had held up well, aided by plastic surgery, a strict diet, and a personal trainer.

An elementary school teacher by training, she didn't work a day in her life. She didn't have to. Her parents were oil pioneers and left her a substantial trust fund that made her financially independent and allowed her to enjoy a carefree life. She was an A-lister at big social events where her designer outfits would be admired.

That's how they met. They were at a charity ball. He had big ambitions but no money and no connections. She had money and connections, but no husband. It was a match made in heaven – at first. They had a fairy-tale wedding and honeymooned in Polynesia.

Then, reality. He was too busy building his companies to pay much attention to matters of the heart. At times, he regretted the marriage. He knew he should try harder to love her.

What stopped him, then, from being happier with her? He had asked himself often. Heavy thoughts churned in his head, one contradicting the other. He blamed Claire for their inability to have children. For being frivolous and spoiled. For being cold. For spending lavishly on her friends. For galivanting on the corporate jet – his company's corporate jet – on trips to Europe, which could get him in trouble with his board. He resented Claire for showing no interest in his work, although she acted as if she owned his company, which was not untrue.

He had considered a divorce, but it would cost him a fortune. He'd done the math. She could claim more than half his net worth and cause him to lose control of his company. She could hang him out to dry in the press over his many indiscretions.

He knew she knew about his affairs during business trips and after business hours. And yet she accepted him. He'd given her a good life, and he always returned home when it mattered. They had reached an understanding, like many of the wealthy couples they knew.

But she was not enough. John needed other women to feel confident with men. He needed the thrill of the mid-afternoon escapade to release the stresses of his job. Other men did drugs and alcohol. He did good sex. He was built for affairs. A rake and proud of it. What was the point of being as handsome, as rich, as powerful as he was if he couldn't capitalize on it? In the past kings deemed it their right. He deemed it a perk that everyone in his circle exploited, but never acknowledged. Affairs were like Swiss bank accounts, or off-book transactions. CEOs like him shared their playbooks, privately, and occasionally looked out for each other.

John dreaded the day when he would be too old to be attractive. What would he do then to satisfy his cravings? So far, so good. Women were chasing him. They were shameless; reckless, even, he thought. They were so eager to hook a big fish he usually had multiple affairs at once.

He outplayed his mistresses by vetting them like he vetted business partners. He liked them married, with promising careers, with reputations to protect, so they'd have as much to lose as he did in case things soured.

He did not make promises he couldn't – wouldn't – keep. He developed elaborate routines to string his women along. He never offered gifts. He didn't leave compromising messages. He got them to tell him about their secrets in case he needed leverage. He immediately got rid of evidence – hotel keys, stray hair, clothes. He'd managed to keep it all discreet, though he knew he was vulnerable to gossip. He kept a low profile and employed professionals to protect his public image.

What about Elise? He found himself madly, strangely attracted to her. He daydreamed about a relationship, until she told him she was a widow. Strike one. She was still single. Strike two. She had children. Strike three. As a journalist, she was harder to manipulate. Strike four. He resolved to keep her at a safe distance and use her to his advantage. Case closed.

The helicopter landed. John zipped up his down-filled parka, put on gloves and a wool toque, and jumped out. He crouched forward and ran toward the perimeter of the landing pad. The blades spun noisily above him, blowing the fresh snow to the sidelines.

Mike was waiting for him, donning a similar parka, sunglasses, and a fur hat. Drew was right behind him.

"How are you, my friend?" John said, patting the tall, hefty man on the back.

"Outstanding today," Mike said, grinning.

"How's the drilling?" John asked.

"We tested last night. This well is a monster. We need to move ahead as quickly as possible with our program and drill five more wells on lands we own. We need to secure all the leases around us that we can still capture. It's hard to tell at this point how big this pool is. My guess is that it's bigger than anything we have seen in Western Canada."

"That big? How soon do we have to drill the next wells?" John asked, smiling.

"As soon as we can if we want to stay dominant. All our major competitors hold land around us. They haven't done anything with it for decades, but they'll ramp up when they find out about this. Watch them try to scoop us at the next land auction."

"What are you calling the discovery?" John asked. He always looked forward to the names Mike picked for their discoveries. He admired Mike, who was a big reader, for having a way with words.

"Ladyfern."

John loved it. Lady ferns were the stalwarts of the forest. His Ladyfern would be the stalwart of his company.

The giant pool of natural gas had eluded explorers for decades. Some of the world's largest companies had searched for a big reservoir in the area, spending tens of millions drilling in the wilderness between Alaska and Alberta. Hunter had bought the lands for a song from one of the global players that had stopped trying, tired of ending up with dry holes, threats, and court actions from First Nations, on top of getting stuck in swampy terrain in the summer that made it impossible to move equipment, and Artic cold in the winter that made drilling an agony.

But instincts and extensive geological interpretation told John the marshes were hiding a prize. It made no sense to him that Alberta would be so rich in oil and natural gas, while the province across the provincial boundary had nothing to offer.

The first five wells were dry. His shareholders thought he was crazy to try a sixth. But he persevered. He knew that a sixth dry hole would kill his stock. Six had been his lucky number. He had to keep going.

Part of his confidence came from Indigenous stories. They were built on thousands of years of wisdom, knowledge of the land, perhaps clairvoyance. He was not naïve, but he sensed there was truth to them.

Chief Anne Proudfoot, the neighbouring First Nation's senior leader, had told him that a 'dreamer' had predicted the coming of large-scale industry development decades ago and warned against giant snakes and huge matchsticks lighting the sky.

"Prepare yourself. This is coming," the dreamer said to her tribe. "Make sure you understand. Hang on to your culture and your roots, because if you don't do it, you will become lost. And fight for your rights. This is our land."

Chief Anne begged John to look after the environment during one of the many chief-to-chief talks the two had held. He pledged to her that he would do his best. He believed in running a clean shop. His Ladyfern drilling program used the best practices and was the costliest he'd ever done, he assured her.

"Can we keep this quiet?" John asked Mike.

"We'll try," the drilling manager said. "We're being watched, though. See those trucks?" He pointed to a dozen parked outside the lease.

Some were pickups. Some were fifth wheelers. They'd been there for days, he told John. The only time the oil scouts would get out was to relieve themselves in the bush. Occasionally they drove off for a few hours to fill up their fuel tanks and buy booze. For the most part, they watched activity on Hunter's rig with binoculars, eavesdropped on mobile phone conversations with spy-worthy gear, and reported back to those who hired them.

"Yes, I see them," John said, shaking his head.

"They are working for our competitors. There are freelancers, too. But there is nothing we can do to stop them," Mike said.

John was angry. They were stealing from him. He loved a lot of things about his industry, but not how nasty it got when money was on the line. Everyone always went too far.

"We need to tighten security," John suggested, entering one of the trailers adjacent to the rig that housed his roughnecks and the operation's control centre.

"I'll make sure that all our phone lines are secure. Offer extra incentives to staff to keep this tight."

While rubbing his hands to warm up, John peeked from a frosted window and noticed the rig's slippery floor. Roughnecks in heavy suits, hard hats, and protective glasses were pushing pipe deep inside the earth, their coveralls soaked with drilling mud. Ignoring the cold, they were in a hurry to complete the well. Spring breakup, when the frozen land became a swamp, was just around the corner, ending the Canadian drilling season until winter returned, when the earth would be frozen again.

One of the work site's new recruits sauntered in. Andrew was a high school dropout looking for fast bucks to start his own business. He'd heard the tail end of the conversation and perked up. He recognized John from a photo he saw in the news.

"Mr. Hess, pleased to meet you," the young man said cordially, removing his hard hat and wiping ice and dirt off his face.

"It's freezing out there," he said to Mike. "I'm glad I'm off for a few days. I logged a lot of overtime and I'd like to go back home. Can I please have my cheque?"

"Thanks, Andrew," Mike said, handing him a small envelope. "Don't spend it all at once. And please – keep your mouth shut."

The roughneck helped himself to a warm cup of coffee, put his hard hat and thick gloves back on, and took off, slamming the trailer's door behind him. Two hours later, all cleaned up and drinking beer at his favourite pub, he doubled his pay. A scout freelancing for Plains Exploration asked him for an update. Andrew bragged that something big was happening, because none other than John Hess had shown up at his rig, and even shook his hand.

Chapter 5

CALGARY, ALBERTA, MARCH 2000

On the executive floor of Plains' cream-marbled tower, Susan Scott watched the computer screen in front of her. Her stock was sinking at about the same speed as Hunter Exploration's stock was surging. She was concerned. Investors were trading one for the other, she heard from her staff. They had picked up rumours about John Hess's company making a giant discovery. In contrast, her company had nothing to brag about, and much to worry about, because of trouble brewing in Peru.

She couldn't stand it anymore. She was tired of giving excuses for her stock's weakness to investors and the board of directors. How could she tell them the truth – that Plains had grown too fat, too bureaucratic, too far flung, and too complacent to keep up with a nimble exploration company like Hunter? It was hard to cut fat, or to get people to give up pay and perks that had become obscene – club memberships, hockey tickets, bonuses. As lazy as her employees were, she couldn't afford to lose them. Labour was scarce, and she needed a large staff to justify her high rank.

She looked at her corner office. It was larger than most people's homes. She'd selected her decor with one goal in mind – to convey power. The public part of the suite had dark walls and a dark mahogany desk, a matching wall unit where she kept her files, a closet for emergency suits and makeup, a picture of her husband during happier times, a table with six chairs for small conferences, and plenty of expensive art. Cut flowers were refreshed regularly.

Susan's favourite spot was a private area tucked behind French doors with a fireplace and a leather couch. She'd spent many nights there, stealing a few hours of sleep between late-night and early-morning meetings.

She loved it. It was the only place where she truly felt at home, and she'd do anything to protect it. Then she felt anxiety rush from her heart to her head as she realized that a weak stock price could lead to a change in strategy and then budget cuts, which meant giving up her prized sponsorships, including the coming ballet season that she supported with company money. She had been doing all the right things to win an award that she had long coveted for exemplary leadership in the arts.

Her distaste for Hunter was personal, too. John had snubbed her more than once. Most recently she tried a bit too hard to charm him when they were both attending an industry conference. He looked at her with disdain so obvious she felt humiliated. She knew he was open to affairs. She could have used a side fling to spice up her life – maybe collect some valuable information, too.

And she could have used better intelligence. Plains had a big land position near Hunter's rumoured find, but no activity. Instead, her company had purchased lands in Peru that remained unloved by the market, despite good drilling success and decent revenue prospects. High-profile opposition from an obscure environmental group had made them so toxic her company couldn't even give them away.

Susan had downplayed the importance of the eco-radicals, as she called them, to the company's board. She promised their overblown accusations of environmental destruction in the Amazon would never stick. They would go broke, or lose interest, and Plains would outlast them, she said.

But the attacks had continued and gotten louder. Awful things about Plains were posted all over the internet. Untrue things that Plains was unable to stop – not even legally. She'd considered a lawsuit, but to what end? The activists would have put her company on trial, generating more bad publicity.

"The chairman of the board is on the phone," Pat, her executive assistant, told her, making her even more anxious. "He seems upset."

"I'm on it," Susan said.

"Hello, George," she said sweetly, kicking off her shoes under her desk, a reflex that helped her calm down when anticipating stressful conversations.

"Can you please explain to me what is going on?" George Irving asked.

"I don't like the rumours on the street. Why is John Hess making these big discoveries while we are spending all that cash and treading water in

South America? Why aren't we all over this thing? Don't we have a lot of land up in Northern British Columbia?"

"Well, Peru is part of the strategy that the board approved, George. We were going for a big international expansion to become a Canadian international energy champion. We were going head-to-head with the majors – remember? – to get American market attention. We didn't have the capital to do both Peru and BC. Northeast BC has been a wasteland for decades. Plus, the government there is such a mess, and we didn't want to deal with First Nations. Too risky."

"Right," the chairman said, losing his cool. "And now Peru is proving to be riskier. We approved the strategy that *you* proposed. What else were we supposed to do? Plus, I heard John did it all with two hundred and fifty million. You blow fifty million on art sponsorships every year. What's the upside in that?"

"We'll take a look at BC again," Susan promised, hoping that the natural-gas exploration guys hadn't been fired yet to free up funds so the Peru operation could be built up. "We have a lot of land in BC. If there are discoveries to be made, we'll make them, or we will find a way to buy our way into the play."

"We need a strategy for the next board meeting," the chairman said, and slammed down the phone.

It was 8:00 p.m. and Susan was still in the office. She was exhausted. She'd missed another family dinner. Her husband had stopped expecting her to come home. Her team was still in the office, too. They always had to wait for her to leave so they could leave work themselves. It was one of her unwritten rules, and breaking it meant banishment to dead-end roles, or even dismissal. Getting ahead in Susan's fiefdom meant fourteen-hour workdays, seven days a week, regardless of whether there was work to do. No one ever left until she was out the door.

As an executive vice-president for corporate affairs and secretary to the board of directors, she had created a pink ghetto within a male-dominated industry. She ruled her department like a medieval queen ruled her court. She hired and promoted many unattached women because they were easier to control and worked harder for less. She meddled in their personal lives.

She told them how to speak and how to dress. She knew they wouldn't complain. If they dared, she'd fire them. She ruled with impunity. She knew no male would dare question a woman about how she ran her department of women.

Susan felt she'd earned the right to be mean. The older she got, the meaner her ways. She'd worked hard to get to the top. She used her power to ensure she'd never lose it – particularly not to other women. There was little room for women at the top in the oilpatch. It might as well be her up there. She also knew she'd never be the CEO. The industry would never promote a female to the top job, particularly one that rose from the 'softer' side of the business, the one where there were no engineers and geologists. But Susan was the next best thing – or the next worst thing. It was well known that she was the de facto leader of the company because she ran the president himself.

Susan Scott began her climb using the oldest trick in the book. A few years back, she travelled regularly with David Anderson to meet investors. He was the finance chief, and she was an investor relations assistant. Her credentials were unimpressive, but she was pretty enough and had killer legs, which she showed off by wearing short skirts and the highest heels she could handle without losing her balance.

Zurich, London, New York. No trip was too marginal to hop on one of the jets from the company's fleet. They stayed at luxurious hotels and stretched their jaunts over weekends – at shareholders' expense. Before long, they were sleeping together more than they were sleeping with their spouses. When her boss tried to put an end to it, concerned an affair could derail his career, Susan blackmailed him. She knew the board liked him and that he was on the fast track to the top. She also knew that he was under her manicured thumb. As he rose, she demanded – and got – promotions. When he became CEO, she landed with him on the executive floor. He gave her control of a good part of the company, including handing her responsibility for relations with analysts and investors, the board, the government, and the media. Few knew it, but she was also put in charge of corporate spying, which meant a big discretionary budget to dig up dirt on competitors, and on anyone else she deemed interesting, including her fellow executives.

Susan rang her assistant. "I'd like to meet with my team leaders tomorrow at seven thirty a.m. sharp," she said. "Send out invitations."

By the time her employees were able to leave the building, it was pitch black and late in the evening. They were angry but knew they couldn't complain. To the outside world, they were well paid, pampered oilpatch workers. Inside, they were grunts who loathed their jobs and everything their company stood for. But they were trapped. Quitting was out of the question. They'd become so dependent on their outsized paycheques and golden handcuffs, or their stock options, they couldn't afford to leave.

As usual, Susan took a private elevator to the executive garage. She hopped into her gas-guzzling, eight-seat SUV and drove the four blocks to her downtown condo overlooking the Bow River. She crashed there when she needed a real bed, and when she was too tired to drive to her new mansion on an acreage in the city's western outskirts on the way to the Rocky Mountains. It had been her husband's idea when they still cared for each other. Now they mostly lived separate lives.

She walked past the building security and took another private elevator to the 14th floor. She entered her bedroom, took off her jacket and assessed herself in her mirror. She was pleased with what she saw. She had a nice figure for a fifty-something who rarely exercised. A mane of unruly chestnut hair draped over her shoulders. She sat down on her bed, smoked a joint and switched on the TV to watch the late-night news.

How naïve, she thought, as the anchorwoman wrapped up a political news story about the prime minister's latest staff shuffle due to the resignation of a female advisor. It was presented as a health issue. She knew better. Her lobbyists in the capital had told her the woman had slept with the big guy himself and now she was being sidelined because they feared a leak to the media about the affair. A big payout and a non-disclosure agreement were surely part of the deal.

Four hours later she woke up, still dressed. She was an efficient sleeper. She showered, put on a tight pant suit, and by 5:00 a.m. she was back in her office, ready for another power play.

A large bouquet of flowers greeted her on her desk, deposited overnight by corporate security. "Thank you for your donation to the women's shelter. We couldn't have done it without you," read the handwritten note. She didn't remember donating to that cause. It must have come from one of her staff. No matter. It would be good for her image. She made a note to ask her assistant to send a thank-you card to the charity.

When her four most senior employees gathered around her conference table, fresh coffee in hand, the sky was still dark. A snowstorm was starting.

Susan opened the meeting by summing up the company's stock dilemma – as if they weren't already aware – and looked at each one of them in the eye to convey urgency, as if their lives depended more than ever on the performance of Plains' stock.

"We need to do something big, shake things up," she said. "Our international expansion is getting too little profile, while analysts are knocking us for missing out on natural gas in BC. They compare us to Hunter and don't like how we stack up."

"We can issue a news release about our new reserves in Peru and the play's big potential," said her investor-relations vice president. "We're also long overdue for an analyst tour. We could take them all to New York City for an investor presentation. We could take them to Broadway and show them a very good time."

"How about we take some reporters to view our play in Peru?" another senior team member, her chief spokesman, proposed. "Some have been asking us if we are open to the idea."

Susan thought about the pitches. "They're good ideas," she said. "But we must also play up our holdings in BC and get Hunter's find to rub off good publicity on us. Let's check with our gas guys to see if they're locking up any free land. We could choke Hunter's growth."

The market opened for trading. Plains' stock was continuing to slide. Faces around the table were glum. Susan offered hockey tickets to lighten the mood.

She had another idea but kept it to herself. When her group eventually dissolved, she dialed her security consultant.

"I want you to start monitoring all conversations between Hess and his field people, on top of the stuff that we are already doing," she told him. "Report to me daily."

She loved that part of the job. No one else in the corporation had the balls for espionage. She was a natural. She'd learned the craft many years ago when she worked for the federal government abroad. Digging up dirt may have been unethical in the corporate world, but it wasn't illegal – for the most part. It gave her an edge.

She knew that to maintain her power she needed information, particularly of the sensitive kind, so she collected it and stored it in her secret files. It was disguised in her budget under 'corporate consultants.' The president knew about it, but what could he do? She had her own secret file on David Anderson, just as she knew he had one on her.

Like everyone else in Calgary, Elise was watching Hunter's stock's big climb. It gained 20 percent since her latest story on Hunter appeared, which was significant since it was based on mere rumour.

"Can you look into what is going on?" her editor asked over the phone. "Wall Street is noticing. Either they hit a big one, or someone is trying to take them over."

Elise's first call was to John. She had tried to get a hold of him several times to discuss progress in his operation in BC. No response.

Clearly, John Hess's MO is all about him calling me when it suits him, not about me calling him, she realized. Elise was disappointed. She felt used. She trashed his business card and notes from her interview with him. She was done with John Hess.

She picked up the phone and tried the usual analysts, competitors, and observers, but they offered few usable facts. The best she could come up with was speculation that Hunter Exploration had hit a gusher unequalled in Western Canada. It was all kept under wraps while the company secured land around it, the sources told her. Some investors were making a killing, first by fueling the speculation and the stock's climb, then by shorting it due to lack of information.

"We do not comment on rumours or speculation," Peter had told her a hundred times, relishing the power that came with withholding information and keeping the media on a tight leash.

Elise wrote a quick story and moved on. Other stories were breaking, and she had a big trip coming up to Peru, organized by Plains Exploration. She was surprised they offered it to her as an exclusive, no strings attached. They even proposed to arrange all the interviews she needed, which she declined. Too much control. She had pitched the idea to Plains several times, but previously they had seemed unenthusiastic. Their operations there were mired in controversy and were a drag on their stock. Analysts and investors were urging them to exit. Shareholders were appalled with environmentalists' portrayal of the company as a corrupt, foreign polluter that profited from the exploitation of the local Indigenous communities and were destroying the Amazon.

Elise was excited she was offered a seat on a crew plane that shuttled Plains' workers weekly from Calgary to their field operations in Peru. She hoped the trip would help her fill some information gaps. She also knew it would be yet another challenging assignment, with poor security and few comforts. Since it wasn't a commercial flight, she would have to find a way to pay the company back for the junket, perhaps through a charitable donation. It was *Journal* policy. She picked the food bank.

Chapter 6

AMAZON FOREST AND LIMA, PERU, APRIL 2000

The snow was finally beginning to melt across the Canadian Prairies when Elise boarded Plains' chartered plane at the company's corporate hangar adjacent to Calgary's airport. The sun was just rising. Alberta's sky was coming alive with hues of red, pink, and orange.

She found her seat near the back of the cabin, next to a young rig worker. Her carry-on was packed with photo and recording equipment. In her checked bag, she stuffed long-sleeved shirts and a generous bucket hat for the jungle, strong insect repellent to protect her from malaria, energy bars, and dried fruit and nuts in case food wasn't available or edible.

The aircraft took off and Elise looked from the jet's window at the clouds below, as she often did when she went on a risky assignment. She chased away fears of kidnapping, which she knew was a risk where she was going.

Out-of-town jobs gave her an opportunity to regroup and reflect on her life. Thoughts of John were bothering her. If something is too good to be true, it usually is, she reminded herself, wondering again why he behaved the way he did with her. Hot and cold. She was offended that he hadn't returned any of her phone calls. She reminded herself that she was done with John Hess, that she needed to back up and find new industry insiders that she could count on.

She pulled out her notebook and listed questions she needed to find answers for during her assignment. She envisioned a nice, long feature. She knew Plains had organized the trip because it hoped for good publicity – or at least an impartial look at their operations. She had her own agenda. She wanted to get to the bottom of the controversy over Plains' environmental and Indigenous practices.

Was the company really causing environmental damage? Was it threatening the Indigenous way of life? The green organization Amazon Fighters, which orchestrated the international campaign using the internet to try and force Plains out of the country, was publicizing photos of oil spills in the forest, crying Indigenous children, street protests, and of company executives meeting with the leaders of Peru's government. But where was the evidence that the images portrayed were of Plains' operations? They could have shown the operations of any oil company, Elise thought. Yet loaded words like 'murderers,' 'polluters,' and 'corruption' were splattered all over the photos in red ink. Elise had never seen such an aggressive attack on a corporate reputation. In her experience, Canadian companies were respectful of the environment, particularly compared to South American companies, but she accepted she didn't know enough and thought it best to keep an open mind.

Elise re-read research materials on the country and its oil industry. Peru was not a big oil producer, but its government was offering incentives to attract foreign capital, such as generous taxation and lax regulations. Plains had recently entered the country through an expensive acquisition.

The potential for oil discoveries was good, but fields were in the jungle, far from infrastructure like roads and airports. There was risk to the country's environment from oilfield waste and tree cutting, which scared away local species. Pipelines had to be built in difficult terrain that would be hard to reach in case of a spill. The local population, mostly Indigenous people with few skills, was poor and neglected, much like Canada's own First Nations.

Food was served by a sleepy flight attendant. Elise tried to start a conversation with the young man beside her, who'd woken up from a nap. She reckoned he was in his early twenties. He wore a baseball cap, sweatpants, and a hoodie. With Nordic blond hair and blue eyes, tall and well built, he could have been a model, she thought. Instead, he seemed humble and rough around the edges, like so many Alberta and Saskatchewan farm kids who worked on oil rigs to earn their first money. He took the job to pay for a new pickup truck and a down payment for farmland he coveted, she pried out of him.

"How long have you worked in Peru?" Elise asked.

"Since they started drilling in the fall."

"How do you like it there?"

"It's okay, I guess. They pay us good money and the shifts are not too bad. I work two weeks, then I'm back home for two. I stay out of trouble and inside our camp. There are lots of people who don't like us there, though," the kid revealed, feeling comfortable talking to Elise, despite the fact she was a reporter.

"Really? That's interesting. Why don't they like you?" Elise asked, leaning in to catch every word. The cabin was noisy. A group of workers near the front was laughing hard while playing cards.

"It's because the greens are telling the locals that we're polluting their lands and stealing their resources. I heard they're paying them off to oppose us. It's a shame. They're liars. We are bringing the Natives to the drilling site to show them what we do, how we protect the jungle. We drilled a water well in town, and that made us some friends. We're building a new school. We have the skills and the materials, and it's nice to help. They're good people – like our own Indigenous people. Everything helps, but I don't know if it's enough."

"What's your name?" Elise asked.

"I'd rather not be in your story," the young man said. "It could get me in trouble."

"Sure," Elise responded. "Don't worry about it."

After an eight-hour flight, the plane landed on a new landing strip built by the company near the drilling operation. Passengers climbed down the staircase on the tarmac toward a small terminal. *Made in Alberta*, said a large logo displayed near the entrance of the temporary structure. Inside there was a rugged waiting area for the rig workers and a comfortable lounge for high-level visitors, like Peruvian government officials who kept a watchful eye on the Canadians, and company brass.

Fresh coffee, cookies, pop, and water bottles were displayed on a counter in the waiting area. Outside, around the terminal and along the landing strip, hundreds of Peruvian soldiers, armed with machine guns, protected the operation.

Overcome by the humid heat, Elise picked up some water, collected her luggage, and walked to a van where Gordon Wilson, Plains' top media-relations guy, was waiting for her. She assumed he was instructed by Susan

Scott, his boss, to accompany her everywhere she went, inside and outside the project, and to monitor all her interviews. She liked Gordon – he was always helpful, knowledgeable, not too promotional. He knew she had a job to do and helped without telling her what to write. He had worked as a print reporter earlier in his career, so he understood her needs, then switched to the corporate side.

They shared the van with four soldiers. She was invited to sit up front, between the driver and Gordon, who was sweating profusely. Two soldiers sat in the middle seats, and the remaining two took the back. All guns were pointed outward. Elise had been in rough places before, but never with so many weapons. Gordon told her they were necessary because of the recent kidnapping of Plains' contract workers by a guerrilla group, an incident that briefly made the news.

"Don't worry," Gordon assured her. "We won't let it happen again. We have increased our security. These people are the best of the best. They will look after us."

The van drove on a dirt road for half an hour, through a patch of jungle and then to a checkpoint at the entrance of a drilling operation. Vegetation had been cleared and several towering rigs were actively drilling, piercing the Amazon's silence with loud, mechanical blows.

There were more soldiers on the perimeter of the site. It was late in the day, and Elise was escorted to a small private room in a complex of trailers that was lined up neatly in a clearing and displayed the same *Made-in-Alberta* logo. Her room was clean and tidy, with a single bed, a shower, a night table, and a desk. She suspected she was the only woman at the site.

As she lay in the small bed, she felt uneasy. She realized she was in a foreign country, with no protection but what was offered by the company, at risk of being kidnapped, with limited phone access. Would her boss organize a rescue if she got in trouble? Probably not, she thought. Newspapers talked a good talk about the importance of a free press, but she knew they did not have the money to protect their staff. Yet she still pursued difficult and often thankless assignments because of the personal satisfaction she got from getting to the bottom of things and sharing with the world what she found. Elise snacked on her energy bars, drank bottled water, and fell asleep.

The next day, Elise woke early after a restless night. Chin up, she told herself. No time for fear. She showered and dressed quickly, sprayed her clothing with insect repellent, put on her hat, and exited the housing complex. She joined staff for a hearty breakfast. Then she took out her notebook, tape recorder, and camera and walked around the project. Gordon and a handful of guards followed a few steps behind. She introduced herself to staff and asked them questions about the potential of the oilfield, environmental practices, and efforts to establish good relations with the local Indigenous communities. Most were from Alberta, a few were from Peru, and all were sticking to prepared answers. They told her they were heartbroken about the bad publicity spread by the activists. In their minds, they were aiding a poor country to find new revenue to improve its standard of living.

The temperature was rising quickly. Elise felt sweat dampen her clothes. She climbed onto the van with her entourage to the nearest village to get another perspective. The town hall was modest but clean. Tables were adorned with flowers pots, and the walls with children's paintings. She found Jose, the mayor, in a small office. Plains' logo was emblazoned on his desk. It's a gift from the company, he said, shaking her hand.

"Is the company a good neighbour?" Elise asked the elderly Indigenous man with wrinkled, dark skin. She was grateful for the ceiling fan spinning above them.

"Yes," the man said through an interpreter provided by Plains, even though Elise understood Spanish well. "We have been waiting for years for the government to build us a school and to help us with clean water. They ignore us because we're too far away and our votes are insignificant to them. Plains helped us. Now we have a water well, and soon we will have a school. In fact, we are in the process of hiring a teacher."

"That's great to hear," Elise said. "But tell me. Is the company polluting the environment?"

"No. No. No," the mayor said, shaking his head. "That's just propaganda from Amazon Fighters. Plains is better than our country's state oil company. They are showing us how to drill for oil the right way. Our own company, they have dumped waste all around us for years. They don't listen to us."

"And those activists, they raise money from Hollywood and then come here to tell us what to do and how to live our lives," the mayor continued. "They tell us that they don't want more fossil fuels. They don't want foreign oil companies. That's their fight, not ours. They tried to recruit us. They offered us bribes. Some in other villages took them. But in our village, we don't like what they do. We don't want them around here. We need money, fuel, jobs."

"Is there no room for improvement for Plains?" Elise asked.

"Plains is not perfect," the mayor said. "They could hire more people from the village, for sure, but so far, we are happy with the company. We hope they stay for a long time. We like it that the Canadians come to see us in the village. We consider them friends."

Elise thanked Jose for making the time to meet her and handed him her business card. "Call collect if anything else comes to mind," she said, and took his picture.

Elise liked the mayor. He seemed sincere. She returned to the van, where her minders were waiting. As they drove away, back toward the jungle, she noticed rows of shacks on both sides of the main road. In a nearby field, children were kicking a football with a red Canadian maple leaf printed on it.

The van stopped at a lodge with a panoramic view of the jungle. The restaurant was favoured by Plains' staff. There were only two choices on the menu: beans or chicken, with a side of rice. Elise found herself in a lively conversation with more oil company employees over lunch about the challenges of operating in the jungle, security issues, and environmental practices. Three government officials who flew in at Plains' request joined her after the meal. They wanted her to know that Peru was open for business and that they were favourably impressed with Plains. It was the first foreign company to operate under new, tighter environmental regulations, they told her. Plains was doing a good job in a difficult environment, they assured her.

Elise recorded as much as she could in her notes and on her tape recorder. She was puzzled by the information generated by the Amazon Fighters. Who was telling the truth? Was she missing something? Was she being misled? Most likely, she concluded, Plains was glossing over the environmental impact of its operations. But Amazon Fighters' portrayal of environmental devastation and human rights abuses was an absurd exaggeration.

Elise did a dozen more interviews during the rest of the day. She spoke to more employees. She spoke to more local officials. She spoke to Indigenous people. She spoke to teachers. The message was consistent: Plains was doing good work in what had been a neglected, remote, impoverished area of Peru.

It was evening by the time Elise returned to her room in the trailer near Plains' drilling operation. Early the next day, after another uncomfortable night, she packed her belongings and re-joined Plains' crew for a short flight back to Lima, where the plane would pick up a group of oil executives before returning to Canada.

"I have another interview lined up for tomorrow, in Lima," she told Gordon before climbing off the plane.

"With Amazon Fighters, right?" he asked.

"Yes," she responded.

"I would have been very surprised if you didn't. Are you flying back commercial?"

"Yes. In a couple of days."

"Good luck. Let me know if you need anything else from us," he said.

Elise collected her bags, exited the airport, hailed a taxi, and asked the driver to take her to a hotel located just outside the historic downtown. As they approached the city, Elise noticed a large landfill. Smoke billowed from burning garbage. A stream rushed through it. Children picked plastic bottles and anything else they found of value. Elise wondered why Amazon Fighters spent so much effort to shut down Plains' operations in the remote jungle, while ignoring environmental degradation right there. This was obviously immediately harmful to the local population.

She took a mental note to ask Erika Bernstein, the leader of the group in Peru who had agreed to meet her.

Elise checked into her hotel and crashed on a comfortable, large bed. She woke up the following morning and reviewed her notes. Then she listed issues that she needed Erika to address. The activist had proposed to meet for lunch near the municipal building. It was Elise's first encounter with an environmentalist. She was excited to hear her side of the story.

She found Erika in a rustic eatery near a vast square crowded with tourists, sitting at a table for two. They shook hands. Elise took the seat across from her, pulled her notebook and tape recorder out of her bag, and observed the short, wiry woman. With a knitted skull cap, matted hair, flowing skirt, and fabric purse hanging by her hip, Erika looked like an ageing hippy. But her mannerism, her good posture, her confidence, suggested a privileged upbringing. They should have had lots in common, Elise thought. They came from similar places – Erika was from New Jersey. They were probably the same age. Instead, they couldn't be more different. She was a representative of the establishment, while Erika was committed to disrupting it.

Elise thanked Erika for responding to her interview request so promptly.

"Glad to be of assistance. Is this your first time in Peru?" the activist asked.

"I have been here before, on holidays," Elise said. "But it's the first time I got to see an oil operation in the jungle. I was impressed."

"It's a bad project," Erika shot back. "We can't continue to rely on fossil fuels. The pipeline they are building is an environmental disaster. The company is dumping waste all over that beautiful region. We should be investing in renewable energy, not more oil production that destroys such a rich ecosystem. Besides, that oil is heavy and hard to refine. Plains is not welcome here."

Elise was surprised by how quickly Erika got to the point but pressed on. "Have you seen their operation?" she asked.

"No. I don't want to be influenced by their propaganda."

"How do you know that they are dumping waste in the jungle?" Elise asked. "I saw their project. It's clean and it uses the highest environmental standards. I spoke to many people on the ground." Elise proceeded to sum up what she heard from the workers and the community.

Erika laughed. "You've been brainwashed. Our activists have seen dirty water, pools of oil, discarded equipment. They are contaminating rivers and drinking water."

"But Plains has only been drilling for a few months. How do you know for sure this is their waste, and not someone else's – for example, the state oil company's?" Elise asked, hoping Erika would move past her prepared lines.

"We don't know for sure," Erika admitted. "But it doesn't matter. They should not be here. We want them out of the country – and we want all foreign oil companies to take notice that the people of Peru do not welcome the oil business."

"So, Plains is being targeted regardless of whether they cause the environmental damage you claim they are responsible for?" Elise asked.

The question lingered as a waiter came by and took their order. He cracked a joke, hoping to defuse the tension. The loud conversation was raising eyebrows in nearby tables.

"Plains is being singled out to show what happens to the reputation of an oil company that produces fossil fuels in the Amazon," Erika told Elise. "You can quote me on that."

Elise sensed Erika was becoming irritated with her questions but pressed the activist to answer one more. "Why are you so concerned about Plains, and not by the mountains of garbage that are dumped near the city? It looks like a major environmental disaster to me that is very dangerous for the people who live there."

"We don't like that either," Erika responded. "But our focus is on fossil fuels. We have limited funding. We deploy our money where we can have the biggest impact. Plains is giving us the international visibility and leverage we need to keep building our campaign."

They finished their lunch, and Elise asked for the bill. She tried to end the interview respectfully.

"I appreciate your input," she said.

"And I appreciate your interest. I hope your story warns your readers that if they continue to invest in Plains, we will continue to hold them accountable for contributing to environmental destruction."

Erika stood up and shook Elise's hand. Elise walked back to her hotel through the crowded streets. She was disturbed by Erika's words. If her cause is just, why is she being dishonest about Plains? she asked herself.

When Elise's lengthy feature appeared two weeks later in the print and online edition of her newspaper, Erika accused her on the Amazon Fighters website of being too soft on the company. She phoned competing media to criticize the *Journal* for taking a corporate junket to Peru and for ignoring her side of the story.

Elise couldn't believe it. She had paid her way and had receipts for all her travel expenses. She had put herself at risk to see the company's operations. She had met with Erika and heard what she had to say but had included only few quotes because she didn't consider the activist to be a credible source. Her facts didn't line up.

Elise was beginning to understand why oil and gas companies, no matter how diligent, faced an uphill battle defending their business against such campaigns. She was distressed by Erika's lies about her. She discussed the situation with her editor, but he wasn't worried. He argued that readers trusted the *Journal* more than the activists, and that the feature was widely read because it represented the first independent reporting into Plains' activities in Peru.

Elise lightened up after receiving messages from Plains' workers in Peru.

"Thank you for your accurate reporting," said one.

"It's about time someone took on those liars," said another.

In her office, Susan Scott folded her copy of the *Journal* and smiled. The reporting on the project wasn't all positive, but positive enough that the company's stock had stopped sliding. Analysts were asking the company to arrange a similar tour of Plains' Peruvian project so they could see the operation for themselves.

Susan took pleasure, too, in the Amazon Fighters' attacks on Elise. She'd been her useful idiot. She didn't like Elise; she was too influential. Susan needed Elise's wings to be clipped before all that attention got to her head.

Chapter 7

DAWSON CREEK, BRITISH COLUMBIA, AUGUST 2000

Summer was already fading in Western Canada. Elise was struggling to get back to work after vacationing with her children on Canada's East Coast when Peter Persic phoned her. Hunter Exploration was organizing a media trip to its Ladyfern field. He told Elise she was first on his media list.

"How nice," Elise responded. "Not interested."

"Why?" the PR man asked, though he was not surprised.

"I gave you guys lots of exposure just a few months ago and got the cold shoulder when I needed you. It's a two-way street, remember? Not a one-way street in your direction. Besides, I am working on other things," she said.

Peter knew his boss had avoided Elise, but not why, and had advised against it. Elise was too influential to ignore, he told him at a rowdy Calgary Stampede party at the oilman's house. "We worked hard to build that relationship, we can't impair it now," he said. John had nodded.

A few days later Elise received another call from Hunter. This time John was on the line.

"Elise, we really need you to participate in this trip. Some of our company's top experts on the area's geology are coming along. The BC energy minister will also be there. I will make it worthwhile," he said, acting as if not a day had gone by since they had that lunch many months ago, or as if he hadn't ignored Elise's phone calls.

As far as Elise was concerned, the Ladyfern story was old news. Other competing media had covered it. She broke the news. She didn't follow the news.

"I don't see the point," Elise replied. "What's the story? A free trip to the tundra? Another story on Ladyfern? They've been done. Besides, we wrote about you just a few months ago, and the market seems to have moved on to bigger things, like the oilsands. And we are not allowed to take junkets from oil companies. It's against our policy."

"I will be there, too," John insisted. "I will be available to answer all your questions. I will be completely honest with you. I need you to come."

Elise pondered the request. There were several seconds of dead air. She could tell that he was uneasy. He was used to getting his way, not pleading. Good, she thought. It's time someone stood up to him.

She was still miffed by the way he had snubbed her despite making lots of promises. Besides, she didn't see a story and didn't want to be used again for a promotional piece that could damage her reputation. The last thing she needed was to be seen as champion for oil, or for John Hess.

"I will need to discuss it with my editor and get his permission. I need your word that I will get a lot of face time with you and your experts," she said. "Otherwise, I'm going to take a rain check."

"Okay. You won't be disappointed," John said, and hung up.

August was a slow month for financial news, so Elise's editor asked her to join the Ladyfern tour, even if it meant a wasted workday.

"Just do the time," the editor suggested. "Look for new leads and take photos." He reminded her to donate an amount equivalent to the cost of the flight to a charity. Elise agreed and suggested that he keep his expectations low.

On the day of the tour, a dozen people, mostly reporters from trade publications, met at the city's private airport terminal just before dawn. The waiting area was buzzing with oil workers lined up to get on their rides. Rows of jets parked outside a hangar were warming their engines. Some were luxurious and used exclusively by company executives for business trips, and, it was rumoured, for personal trips to second or third homes. Others were bush planes impatient to fly workers across the North, to places like Dawson Creek, Fort McMurray, Inuvik and Tuktoyaktuk.

Elise, still sleepy from waking up at 3:30 a.m., poured steaming black coffee into a paper cup and waited for the call to board.

John appeared from nowhere and walked up to her with a bright smile, ignoring everyone else in the room. She was embarrassed to be singled out for special attention in front of her media peers and hid her face behind the coffee cup.

"I am so glad you could make it," he said, sporting expensive khakis and a cashmere V-neck sweater, his idea of casual work wear.

"Yes, I hope it's a worthwhile trip and that you can tell us about your program up there," Elise said half-heartedly, noticing other reporters' curious glances.

They boarded the plane. He took the seat facing her. No way, she thought. He should know better than to be so obvious. She worried the rest of the passengers would be gossiping about them.

Elise wore a short-sleeved cotton shirt, khakis, and a light suede jacket. She checked her shirt buttons to ensure they were done up to her neck. She started a conversation with her seat partner, a senior technical expert at Hunter, about northeastern BC and its oil and gas history. John stared at her, surprised she was avoiding him. The flight took an hour, then two helicopters took turns ferrying the group to the discovery site, located a half-hour away.

It was a beautiful late-summer day. The forest was lush and beginning to show shades of yellow and red. A series of lakes were scattered through the region like broken mirrors reflecting the deep blue sky. The odd dirt road here and there, and freshly cut seismic lines that sliced the wilderness, were signs civilization was moving in.

Elise's group was whisked to one of the trailers surrounding a drilling rig and was asked to wait. John walked up to Elise and attempted small talk.

"I liked your story about Plains in Peru," he said. "You should have told me you were going there. I know some well-connected people who could have given you more background."

"Really? I tried to get a hold of you a few times, but you didn't respond. I was disappointed," Elise snapped back.

"Oh, I'm sorry," John lied. "I have so much on the go that I often don't get to respond to calls until weeks later. I don't mean to be rude. I just forget."

What a bunch of manure, Elise thought, but didn't say it because she knew she had nothing to gain from being unpleasant.

"I get it," she said. "So much to do, so little time."

John walked briskly to an outdoor podium and asked others to follow him. Government bureaucrats, elders from the nearest First Nation in full regalia, and the energy minister gathered around him.

"Thank you all for joining us here today in this beautiful part of Northern British Columbia," he said, looking directly at Elise. Cameras began rolling and photographers snapped pictures. Elise took out her notebook and tape recorder. The late-summer day was unusually mild, the sun bright and warm, and the wilderness in the background provided a stunning backdrop.

"We worked hard at Hunter to make this special day happen," he continued. "Earlier this year, we made a very significant discovery in this location. It's so large it will support thousands of new jobs in Canada, good-paying jobs for years to come." The crowd applauded.

"It will provide new reserves of natural gas to fuel the North American economy. It will result in billions in new tax and royalty revenue for the provincial economy. And it will mean a better way of life for the Bearspaw Nation, our esteemed neighbour to the north. Thanks to this discovery, we can make a five-million-dollar contribution to build the Bearspaw Community Centre, where a dozen young people will be employed, and elders will enjoy recreational activities and comfortable meeting rooms." He looked at Chief Anne Proudfoot, a petite woman dressed in full regalia who was standing beside him, smiling. More applause.

"As I mentioned, we made a great discovery. We have not been able to disclose its size because we didn't have a good understanding of it until now. Meanwhile, we purchased land around us and concluded negotiations with the provincial government for a new fiscal regime. The minister will speak about that later.

"We can finally announce that the Ladyfern field contains at least one trillion cubic feet of natural gas, making it the biggest discovery of natural gas in Canada in the last fifteen years. We will start producing as soon as we complete our pipelines. We expect to peak at a rate of one billion cubic feet a day, after all drilling is finished. Ladyfern will double the size of Hunter. This is a huge day for our company, for our shareholders, and for this community." Enthusiastic applause.

Elise knew a scoop when she heard one. She didn't wait for the minister to talk. John had delivered after all. She rushed to the nearest trailer, found a phone to dial her editor, and summed up the highlights. The discovery was important because natural gas in North America had become scarce, pushing prices to crushing levels. Ladyfern would help protect consumers from further increases, she told him.

"How soon can you file?" her editor asked.

"How about a couple of paragraphs with the main points in five minutes, and a full story in an hour?"

"Sounds good. Are there any other reporters there?"

"Yes, but they are all from the trade press, so they won't write for a few days. Looks like we have a *Journal* exclusive."

Elise placed her boxy computer on an unoccupied desk and started writing. It was hard to report accurately on deadline, but she cherished the pressure. The initial paragraphs went live online almost immediately, grabbing the market's attention. It was noon by the time she finished her full story, with all the details readers would want to know.

Within an hour, Hunter stock soared to a record. By early afternoon, John was on the phone with competing media scrambling to match Elise's work. She didn't care. The scoop was hers, and her story would keep her paper ahead of competitors.

After her job was done, she joined a tour of the natural gas field and took pictures. John stayed beside her the entire time. He was already aware about her story – his assistant had told him about the highlights on his mobile phone – and was pleased with the market's response. His net worth had increased by hundreds of millions.

In the early evening, Hunter hosted a dinner at the site, catered by the camp's cooks, and Elise relaxed and enjoyed the northern air.

It was dark when she boarded the plane to return to Calgary. John again took the seat facing her. The seat next to her was empty. John attempted to start a conversation. This time he got her attention.

"What did your late husband do?" he asked, picking up where they left off at lunch months earlier.

"He was a cardiologist."

"What happened?"

"Pancreatic cancer. He left me quickly," Elise said, her eyes watering, as they always did when she thought about him.

"How old are your children?"

"They are nineteen, twins, a boy and a girl. We are very close, but they like their independence, too."

"Are they in school?"

"They are both at Columbia, my first university. My son is in pre-med. He wants to follow in his father's footsteps. My daughter is interested in public policy, for now, then we'll see. She's a good writer, and I wouldn't be surprised if she ends up in the media, like me."

"And then?"

"They're both hard-working students," Elise continued. "They want to get into Harvard for graduate degrees. They are very motivated to live up to their father's high expectations. He was a loving dad, but also a hard task master when it came to school."

Elise answered his questions uneasily. She was wary of sharing too much about herself to a source – any source. She knew personal information could be misused and abused. She didn't know the oilman enough to trust him.

"How long will you be posted here?" John asked.

"I don't know," Elise said. "I suppose as long as my newspaper needs me in Calgary."

It was Elise's turn to make conversation. "What about you. Are you married?" she asked. She already knew the answer since she'd researched him well but wanted to hear his response.

"Yes. I have been for more than twenty-five years."

"Do you have children?"

"No. We didn't get around to having them when we were young, and before we knew it, we were too old and too busy to have a family. Frankly, I don't think we would have been good parents. I have a busy life – I work fourteen-hour days most of the time, often weekends too – and Claire has a lot on the go. She sits on several boards and manages her family's affairs."

"Do you two do anything besides work?" Elise asked. She was curious to find out more about John's wife. He hadn't mentioned Claire before.

"We are both golfers. We go to the club when we can. We have a cabin in the mountains. We love to hike and to ski. That's what we do together," John said. Elise nodded, feeling a tad jealous.

Hunter's jet landed in Calgary and John looked at Elise one last time. He couldn't help himself; he was captivated by her intelligent, striking face. The attraction he felt was primal and forbidden, like Dante's longing for his Beatrice.

Elise was unsure how to relate to him. She was forty-four years old and hadn't loved anyone but her late husband. She'd always considered herself a one-man woman. After Julien's death, she resolved to never marry again. She didn't want anyone to take the special place that Julien had – would always have – in her heart. Julien had been an exceptional man. He was so confident in himself that he had encouraged her to be herself, to be the mistress of her own life. The men she'd been involved with before Julien had wanted to own her, one way or the other.

She certainly didn't want to get involved with a married man, particularly one as manipulative as John. He was the kind of man who cheated because he could, and stayed married because he had to, Elise concluded.

"Thanks for joining us," John said, shaking Elise's hand.

"Thanks for the scoop," Elise responded. As she rushed back to her car, she saw him watching her from the terminal building, like he wasn't ready to let her go.

Chapter 8

CALGARY, ALBERTA, JANUARY 2001

Hunter Exploration's day in the sun didn't last. The rush to buy land near the discovery area intensified after its Ladyfern announcement. Within months, competing companies locked up all the exploration rights they could get their hands on. Some were big and established, like Plains. Some were startups that assembled land for the sole purpose of flipping it at a big profit to the highest bidder.

The craftiest buyers improved their odds of making the best land picks by using their oil scouts – shadowy figures who collected information they could sell for cash. They gleaned it from the oddest sources: a gas flare could be a sign that a hydrocarbon pool was struck, trucks transporting casing pipe to the lease could mean a well was not a dry hole, the length of pipe used downhole could provide an indication of the depth of a well. They intercepted mobile phone calls, used wire taps, took photos. Some exploited personal and business connections or developed friendships with rig workers.

The land rush soon led to dozens of rigs pounding the muskeg on behalf of a multitude of companies near Hunter's project. The services industry was booming, selling everything from seismic data to hotel rooms. Pipeline companies were making money building new pipelines to connect the discovery to bigger pipeline networks. Governments collected new royalties and taxes.

But costs were also running up, profits were getting squeezed, and John Hess was worried that his big find could be drained prematurely by his competitors, barely a year after he found it.

Before long, analysts were speculating that the massive reservoir, which stretched underneath seventy square miles of swamp and forest and was only accessible for drilling during the winter when everything was frozen, was so large it was a geological anomaly. That meant there was probably no further growth potential in the area.

John rang Elise and offered her an interview. He wanted to warn all those with a stake in Ladyfern about the dangers of producing it too aggressively. Elise jumped on it. With gas scarce, Ladyfern had become big international news.

When they met in his office on a weekday afternoon, both Elise and John stuck to business.

"Is there a danger that Ladyfern will deplete sooner than you expected?" Elise asked.

"I have tried to come to an agreement with the other operators," the oilman complained. "That area has become a circus. We haven't been able to find common ground, so it will continue to be a free-for-all, unfortunately. We're throwing a lot of gas in the market and depressing our prices."

"What does this mean for Hunter?" Elise asked, noticing dark shadows under the oilman's eyes.

"Hunter pushed hard. All companies recognized that when you get into something competitive like that, value is destroyed. We are destroying the reservoir, too, by producing it so quickly. I feel a bit robbed," John admitted.

At Plains, Susan Scott was savouring every moment. After a year in the board's bad books, she was back on top and Plains' stock was soaring, while Hunter was tanking. She had been the most intransigent of the oil executives representing the Ladyfern producers – Plains had the second-largest operation after Hunter – that drilling should continue unrestrained.

Sure, costs were rising, but the Plains' executive argued to her competitors that the quick payoff was worth it for the company. Besides, if Plains didn't produce as much as it could, as fast as it could, Hunter and other companies would since everyone was sucking as much gas as they could from the same giant pool.

None of the other producers dared oppose her. Like Plains, they were lining their pockets from Hunter's find, and knew better than to get in the middle of a fight between Susan Scott and John Hess.

Susan felt so great about masterminding the Ladyfern strategy she was about to recommend a daring move to her company's board.

"Is our presentation ready?" she asked her team, gathered in a lobby area, before entering the boardroom.

"Yes, we have the update on Ladyfern," Gordon Wilson said.

"What about our Mission Snared project?" she asked.

"That, too, is ready for the board's review. Our bankers are on standby outside to assist us. Everybody is ready."

Susan entered the still-empty boardroom and took a final look around. She wanted everything to be perfect. As the board's secretary, she was one of those executives who understood the importance of managing up. Paper and pens were arranged in front of every one of the fifteen directors' high-backed leather chairs. A speaker phone sat in the middle of the oval mahogany boardroom table. White orchids rose upright toward the bright ceiling lights. A buffet of warm and cold food was displayed on a table against one of the walls, in anticipation of a long meeting. Most of it, Susan knew, would remain untouched and shipped off to the food bank.

The room occupied the centre of the top floor. It had no windows. Too many secrets in the industry had been spilled because of oil scouts who monitored company board proceedings with binoculars and cameras from nearby buildings. Susan knew this because she'd practically invented the practice.

The directors, all male, greeted each other as they walked in, then sank into their chairs.

"Let's call this meeting to order," George Irving, the chairman, boomed. The rustle of papers stopped, and the room fell silent.

The first hours ticked by slowly. CEO David Anderson reviewed the company's financials – the revenues and expenditures were doing well. He addressed difficulties with environmentalists in Peru and the company's strategy to address them. He distributed the *Journal*'s stories, for which he took full credit.

"Our communications team arranged every aspect of the reporter's visit," he bragged. "We couldn't have said things better ourselves. The coverage was balanced, and several financial analysts have asked us to arrange a similar tour for them so they can see for themselves that we're not shooting Indians. We'll show them a good time by making a side trip to the Galapagos. They'll appreciate the hospitality." The directors laughed.

The chief operating officer, a sleep-deprived, spectacled engineer, provided updates of all operations, except for Ladyfern.

The head of HR, a stylish older woman no one took seriously, announced executive appointments, promotions, and terminations.

There were no questions and no comments.

The second-last item on the agenda, one of the most anticipated, was an update on Ladyfern. George Irving invited Susan, who was sitting beside him, to address the meeting. She rose. With the help of a slick presentation projected on a large screen, she revealed Plains' strategy of syphoning production away from Hunter with minimum investment.

The directors clapped, delighted with the unexpected bonanza, which they knew was the main reason for the stock's recent gain.

The last item on the agenda, Mission Snared, had been billed confidential on the agenda. Susan distributed supporting documents, then left and invited two investment bankers, Wall Street heavyweights, to join her in the boardroom. With their tight-fitting suits, buzz cuts and platinum Rolexes, they looked tough. She introduced them as specialists in hostile takeovers.

"As you know, our stock has strengthened considerably in recent months because of the surge in production from Ladyfern," Susan said.

"At the same time, Hunter's stock has weakened because the market is disappointed that they are having to share Ladyfern with other companies, particularly us, which means it will be depleted a lot faster than Hunter expected and advertised. We are sitting on a cash pile that we can deploy on a strategic acquisition.

"We've had Hunter Exploration on our radar for years. We have a window here to take a run at them and win, increase the size of our company, and add to our portfolio the best new plays – while also demonstrating that John Hess is not the oilman with the Midas touch everyone thinks he is."

The directors gasped. Two eyed each other in disbelief. A hostile takeover? Of Hunter? It was a bold plan and one that could shake up the whole industry, said one. Plains would emerge as the big, undisputed top dog in natural gas in the country, perhaps the continent, commented another. But it could also be uncomfortable, said a third. Hostile takeovers were messy

---

and there was no guarantee of success, since the target could be rescued by a competing bidder.

"Why not do a friendly deal?" George Irving piped up.

"Hess would never agree," Susan said. "We've approached him before, we even spoke to his wife, and it went nowhere."

"What would it cost us?"

"We could offer a twenty-percent premium to start, then increase our offer to a thirty-percent premium to close the deal," Susan said. "We have the cash and access to debt to get this done. The market wants consolidation. There are too many players and too much competition, which increases everybody's costs."

Susan and the investment bankers were asked to leave. The directors discussed the proposal between themselves. Consensus emerged. It would be a risky move, but one that could come with big upside for Plains, which had lost its premium market valuation because it was perceived as an industry laggard. A takeover would send a message to the market that Plains was re-asserting itself as the undisputed leader. The silver lining was that the acquisition would mean absorbing a lot of Hunter's executive and technical talent. The gold lining was that it would shove John Hess off his pedestal.

The chairman asked his CEO if he had the stomach for a long, nasty fight.

"Yes, we have thought about it, and we can get it done," David Anderson said. "Our teams have investigated all aspects of this acquisition, and we believe it's a perfect fit. It's cheaper these days to acquire reserves than to drill for them."

Susan was invited back into the room.

"Do it," George ordered. "Get a news release ready for distribution before the market opens. Congrats on a job well done."

The room erupted into applause. They could hardly believe they were about to knock out John Hess with his own money.

George Irving adjourned the meeting and went to his office to give John Hess a courtesy call. They knew each other. They belonged to the same clubs. Their wives had travelled together regularly.

He felt he owed him a heads up.

"Hey, John, did you enjoy the symphony on Saturday?" he asked, trying to be cordial.

"Yes, that was inspiring," John said, wondering what the late-evening call was about. "I just wish they had more comfortable seats. Three hours on those godawful chairs was a bit much. But this means a lot to Claire. She wants our wonderful art community to grow."

"She's right, as usual. John, I'll cut to the chase," George said, his tone turning frosty. "I am calling you to discuss business. Our company has decided to make an offer for Hunter. We're offering you a twenty percent premium, which will make you even richer than you already are."

"What? Are you serious? You're out of your mind," John said, caught off guard and feeling betrayed. "First you steal my gas, then you launch a hostile takeover with money that you didn't earn. Your bid is inadequate. There is huge value in Hunter, and I won't give it up without a fight."

John didn't wait for George to respond. He slammed the phone down and covered his face with his hands. For the first time in his career, he'd been outmaneuvered.

News of the hostile takeover bid hit the market at 5:00 a.m. It was pitch black outside, a blizzard was pounding the city, and John was already back in his office.

He barely slept after George Irving's call. He'd known him for years and considered him a friend. A hostile takeover bid. Why such a nasty move? Was it jealousy? John asked himself. There was plenty of cash to go around. Shares of all Canadian oil and gas companies were rebounding. Market interest in the industry was off the charts. Foreign investors were flocking in. Calgary was building new towers and paycheques were out of control. His own secretary was demanding to be paid like a lawyer, which he agreed to because she knew too many of his secrets.

He was angry. Plains had robbed him of a big part of the largest discovery he ever made, refused to do the responsible thing and cap production to avoid damaging the reservoir, and now it was using the cash windfall to push him out of his own company.

He read and re-read the Plains news release. It outlined the terms of its offer and explained the reasons why Hunter shareholders should tender their shares, such as the complementarity of the two companies' assets, and why they would be better managed by Plains. Plains offered a sweetener, a dividend. It boasted that while Hunter didn't pay one because it considered itself a growth-oriented exploration company, Plains had rewarded shareholders with growing dividends for years because its business was more stable and sustainable.

When trading started, John noticed Hunter's stock had bounced by nearly twenty percent. Those of other independent producers rose almost as much. The market was smelling the beginning of a consolidation frenzy and was making bets on the next likely targets. He spent the morning reading analyst reports. They seemed excited and anticipated more deals. There had been talk of a big round of takeovers, but no one had the audacity to make the first move. Timing was important in takeovers, and it was easy to get it wrong, the analysts said. Scars of the last commodity price bust were still fresh. There was always a danger of launching an acquisition just before the commodity-price cycle turned, which could be devastating for the purchaser. Big deals required big debt, which would be hard to pay off in a downturn that squeezed revenue, the analysts noted in their reports.

What do they really know about building a company? John asked himself, tossing the reports in his trash bin.

John asked his assistant to organize a call with his directors. He'd known some his entire career. Some were friends, others were former senior politicians, others were representatives of large institutional investors. He needed to talk things through. He hoped for good ideas he hadn't thought of.

"Thank you all for joining me to discuss this unwelcome development," John said, raising his voice toward the high-tech gadget in the middle of his conference table. He sat in his usual seat, with his two most senior executives monitoring the call nearby.

"As you know, Plains has notified us they are launching a hostile takeover bid.

"As of today, I have thirty percent of the stock, and the board and executives own another ten percent, approximately. The rest is publicly traded, which means we don't have control. We have long-term investors who could find a takeover of Hunter appealing. It would be a good time for them to cash out and look elsewhere. However, they probably also know Plains' offer is utterly inadequate.

"We will immediately look for a competing bid at a higher price. We have good assets in Western Canada and there are many American companies looking to expand here. Our dollar is low, which makes a buy here even more enticing."

It wasn't his first corporate fight, he assured them, and he would do everything he could to squeeze every dime out of Plains – or from someone else, a white knight.

"I have to acknowledge that Hunter's days are numbered because companies that become hostile takeover targets are eventually sold," he said, his voice quivering.

He asked for input.

"What price for Hunter would you accept?" asked one.

"Would you consider a foreign takeover?" asked another.

His board seemed more receptive to a sale than he was, he realized. He wondered if they saw an opportunity for a rich exit. He ended the call, feeling let down.

John instructed his senior executives, who said nothing while listening to the call, to hire investment bankers to solicit competing offers. He asked his assistant to cancel holidays for three to four months. He asked Peter Persic to draft a one-paragraph news release to inform the market that Hunter was rejecting Plains' offer and urged shareholders not to tender. By the end of the day, he had talked by phone to all his top investors.

Plains was bureaucratic, technically incompetent, with a long history of destroying value, he told them. Its offer for Hunter was inadequate, he insisted. But he could tell they smelled blood. He also knew his mudslinging would only buy him a bit of time.

Chapter 9

DAWSON CREEK, BRITISH COLUMBIA, JUNE 2001

John knocked on every door he could think of to encourage a competing bid for his company. Elise wrote about the battle between Plains and Hunter, which made news daily as their leaders disparaged each other and their companies publicly. She wrote about other companies, too, that were preparing or fighting similar bids. Consolidation fever was in the air. The Canadian oil industry split in two – the hunters and the hunted.

Energy stocks suddenly were on fire. Calgarians pocketed windfalls from their market bets and bought big new homes, vacation condos, and boats. Restaurants catering to the city's new rich upgraded their steak-and-potatoes menus to satisfy new caviar-and-champagne tastes. Jobs multiplied. Young, hungry job seekers moved to the Western Canadian city from Montreal, Toronto, Vancouver, and Halifax. Alberta government coffers overflowed with money. Politicians announced new spending.

But in northeast British Columbia, Chief Anne Proudfoot watched resentfully from the sidelines. The rich Ladyfern field stretched beneath her squalid reserve, yet the grey-haired chief couldn't explain to her tribe why it got nothing in return. There had been no progress on Hunter's promised community centre in months, and those who had backed her in the past were clamoring for a change in leadership. Her leadership.

Chief Anne was reading all the headlines. She knew Hunter was embroiled in a takeover fight with Plains and had little time for anything else. She resented that the other companies reaping windfalls from the gas find had never even bothered to meet with her to discuss their drilling plans. Promised jobs and business opportunities were not materializing. Less than a year in, Ladyfern was making everyone rich except for her people. Suicide, unemployment, and alcoholism had gotten even worse. Meanwhile, the land and waterways they needed to survive on were under assault, and there were no guarantees – not to her nor to her band – that they would be restored to their original state.

The matriarch called an urgent meeting of First Nations' leaders in her region who were also impacted by the surge in industry activity. She wanted a united front and a plan.

A dozen – seven male, five female, all elderly – responded to her invitation. Some arrived on foot, some in a rusty pickup truck, five in a crammed minivan. They came with bottled-up anger, hopes for a more equitable world, ideas to get the companies' attention.

Chief Anne welcomed them to her ancestral lands and asked them to sit around a table in her modest office. She told them she hoped for a new bond between the tribes, for past differences to be set aside to fight their common enemy, like streams rushing down the mountains to merge into a big, powerful river.

Ideas poured out, some already tried, some new. Some were peaceful, some were aggressive.

"We should start by blockading their main access roads," suggested Chief Louie, who'd earned his stripes organizing rowdy blockades against the forestry industry.

"Some green activists have been calling us about providing funding for legal advice and to organize a resistance," Chief Adam chimed in. "I'd like to meet with them, see what they're prepared to do for us."

"How about a meeting with the companies' executives to work out a deal to get a share of the revenue?" proposed Chief Nellie.

Chief Anne agreed. A revenue deal would be the most beneficial to the bands, she said. She suggested talking to the companies first, and that the hardline should come next.

"You should meet with them on our behalf, then," Chief Nellie proposed.

"Okay," Chief Anne agreed, reluctantly, knowing she would have to fund the trip herself. "I will approach Plains first," she promised. "They are big operators and could be even bigger if they buy Hunter. If they agree to offer us revenue sharing, the others will fall in line."

In case that didn't work, the chiefs agreed to organize a blockade of Plains' access roads to disrupt drilling activity. They all hated Plains. They felt the company was either arrogant or indifferent toward First Nations.

The chiefs also decided to look for public relations help to publicize their grievances. Cooperation with activists would come last. Bad past experiences were still fresh in the chiefs' minds. Environmental organizations from the big cities had campaigned against the fur trade and the seal trade, destroying the livelihoods of Indigenous people across Canada. Decades later, the tribes still didn't trust these fundraising-hungry pressure groups.

It took Chief Anne dozens of phone calls to secure a meeting with Plains. She asked for a chief-to-chief sit-down with the CEO. She eventually got half an hour with Susan Scott.

Chapter 10

CALGARY, ALBERTA, AUGUST 2001

Donning an ill-fitting pant suit bought from a second-hand store, Chief Anne exited an elevator and entered Plains' steel-and-marble executive offices. She felt uneasy. She knew she was ill equipped to be taken seriously in this corporate world.

She had never been inside an oil company's head office. She didn't understand the jargon spoken by many of the oil people. She had never met a female oil executive. She hoped for female camaraderie. Female chief to female chief. She was counting on her role as an Indigenous leader to be respected.

Chief Anne had earned her job as chief of the Bearspaw band after a tough band election against a long-entrenched male adversary. Everyone knew he used government money intended for the tribe to enrich himself and his family. But only she dared to ignore his threats and exposed his wrongdoing, further bolstering her already high standing in her community. She was a university-educated teacher who'd come from a long line of chiefs. Her skin was dark and weathered, her intelligent eyes were sparkling blue. She inherited them from a handsome Finnish sailor who, somehow, travelled to Northern British Columbia to purchase furs. He was then swept off his feet by her lovely great-grandmother. At least, that was her family's lore.

Chief Anne was offered coffee by the receptionist and told to wait in an expensive-looking armchair while Susan Scott wrapped up a meeting.

Twenty minutes after her scheduled appointment time, the female executive, looking elegant in a tight black dress, greeted Chief Anne near the reception desk with a firm handshake and led her to a small, empty room – an area intended for quick-turnaround events.

"Thank you for dropping in. It's a real pleasure to meet you in person. What can I do for your band?" Susan said deftly, as if dealing with a nuisance call.

"I am here to represent the dozen bands impacted by the Ladyfern discovery," Chief Anne said, unsure how to speak to the perfumed woman in front of her, feeling silly that she even thought she was dealing with an equal. "We are not happy that we are not being consulted, that we are not benefitting from the activity, that great damage is being done to the environment in our region, and particularly our burial sites, which are being trampled over," the chief said, summoning all her courage.

"We want to start a regular dialogue to discuss and resolve these issues, particularly since your presence in our areas could increase with the takeover of Hunter. We want to discuss revenue sharing," Chief Anne pressed on.

Susan knew how to tackle an adversary. She had no intention of taking the chief seriously. She'd dealt with her ilk before. Tribes were always asking for something that they hadn't earned. Revenue sharing? They're out of their minds, Susan thought, trying not to look too repelled by the woman's hand-me-down outfit.

"We have the best environmental practices in the world," Susan responded, smiling. "Our lawyers tell me we are doing everything that we are legally required to do. We bought drilling rights from the government, which entitles us to drill. If you don't like that, you should talk to the government. As for our bid to take over Hunter, it's early days. We don't know if it will be successful. We can have further discussions in the future."

Susan's assistant entered the room and told her she was urgently required to join another meeting, which was getting started. Susan thanked the chief for sharing her concerns and promised to give them consideration.

Before Chief Anne could find the words to respond, a photographer walked in and directed the women to stand up and shake hands. He took pictures. Susan smiled for the camera. Chief Anne looked startled. The photographer told Chief Anne that a copy would be delivered to the band as a memento of the meeting.

Susan walked out, satisfied she had done her part for Canada's Indigenous people, wondering if the photo would be a good addition to the annual shareholder report.

Chief Anne realized the meeting was over before, in her mind, it even started. She was escorted down the elevator to the building's lobby by a junior employee, who handed her an expensive-looking package. The young woman asked Chief Anne to open it. She found a paperweight with the company's logo and a dozen fancy pens, also with the logo.

"They're expensive pens," the young woman said, smiling. "Let me know if you need more."

"Thank you," Chief Anne whispered, unable to say more. She walked out of the building and onto the crowded sidewalk. She felt invisible.

On her flight back, Chief Anne sobbed quietly. She'd come in peace and had hoped to make some progress – any crumb that she could offer her people. She left with trinkets she had no use for. She regretted the photo, which she knew would be exploited by the company for its own end. I don't deserve to be in charge, she thought.

What would her late mother have said? she asked herself. The simple woman who had inspired her to be proud of her heritage and to look out for her band would have told her she failed because she had no leverage, not because she wasn't able, Chief Anne realized. Her people had no choice but to fight back, she decided, and it was her duty to lead them.

Chapter 11

CALGARY, ALBERTA, NOVEMBER 2001

The fight for control of Hunter dragged on. John urged his shareholders to be patient while he continued to search for a better bid. An American company eager to expand in Canada jumped in, offering more money and more advantages. Its pitch: Hunter would become a valuable part of its global operation, which had the deep pockets and the expertise to put Hunter's assets and people to optimal use. Plains countered with an even bigger offer. Undaunted, the American company presented a further bid, which it hoped would be impressive enough to close the deal. Shareholders, short sellers, competitors, and politicians watched, spellbound, following every move and every word, and pocketed more windfalls.

The takeover premium swelled by fifty percent by the time John invited Elise for lunch. She'd covered the takeover fight diligently but hadn't heard from the oil boss since the trip to the Ladyfern field. She'd called him several times. The market was hungry for new information. He ignored her. She'd gotten used to his indifference, and she'd stopped trying.

Elise had conditioned herself to expect nothing from others and every-thing from herself. John was no exception. They had a couple of moments, that's all, and she was determined to stay out of his life.

Besides, her focus was elsewhere. She was working on rebuilding her strength, physical and psychological. It was paying off. She felt increasingly at peace with her life as a widow. She had new friends, interesting women who shared her love for the outdoors. The ski season was getting started, the slopes were covered with fresh snow, and her weekend schedule was booked until the spring.

She was happy that her news stories were getting big attention and big play. She was travelling extensively and meeting interesting people in places she'd never been. Now well settled in Calgary, she was developing an appreciation for the oil business, the resilient people who worked in it, their big machinery, the complex market forces behind it. Oil prices, oil stocks, inventories, pipelines, the OPEC cartel – the issues were infinite and complex. It was the most capitalist, most hardnosed industry she'd ever covered. Regulations were few, governments stayed on the sidelines, and consumers barely noticed the market dramas – so long as their gas tanks were full, and prices were still reasonable. Environmental groups were beginning to make themselves heard, but they were fringe players no one took seriously. They were like flies buzzing on top of a bowl of fruit – close enough to annoy, too insignificant to spoil it.

Then, he called her. John said he had some information she might find useful.

"It's about time," Elise said eagerly. "Where would you like to meet?"

"How about I come and pick you up," John offered. "It's best if we drive there."

"I'd rather drive," she responded, worried a ride in his car could be too close for her professional comfort.

"I'd like to take you to a club," he said. "Let me drive this time. It's out of the way and you probably don't know the area. There is more privacy there. The chef knows me well and knows what I like. I can't go anywhere in town without starting rumours. I'm being watched for any hints of next steps in this bloody takeover fight. I'd just like to have a peaceful lunch with a nice person, without having to watch over my shoulder."

She agreed.

The next day, Elise waited for John in the lobby of her office building. She was nervous and curious. He parked in front. She walked briskly toward his new Mercedes and jumped in, hoping no one had noticed. She didn't wear a coat. A warm Chinook wind was blowing in hard from the Pacific, warming up the air.

They drove west toward an exclusive clubhouse just outside the city limits, nestled in a patch of wood that stretched along the rolling foothills between suburbia and the Rockies. The landscape surrounding the edges of the city always took Elise's breath away. Giant homes, built with new oil money, sat on sprawling acreages. Horses and cows grazed on farmlands a bit farther away. Immaculate barns and farmhouses painted blood red completed the vista. Further west, the mountains stood strong against the sky.

John made conversation by telling Elise who owned what house, and other neighbourhood trivia. He parked his car, quickly walked around it, and opened the passenger's door. They strolled together into the near-empty building.

He looked handsome in a black suit, she thought. She felt good about her outfit: a black blazer and matching skirt, with her hair pulled back in a ponytail. A string of grey pearls graced her neck.

The club manager, an older man in a tux, greeted them and took them to a private dining area with panoramic views of the river valley nearby.

"Nice to see you again, Mr. Hess," he said. "All good in the fast lane?"

"Yes, of course. Thanks for saving my favourite table," John responded.

"We're glad to see you," the manager said, acknowledging Elise with a nod and a smile. "Can I interest you in our 1996 Barolo?"

"That sounds interesting. Elise?"

"No, thank you. I have a deadline. But you go ahead."

"I'll take a glass. And the menu," John said.

John behaved like he was a regular. The working lunch at the club was one of many he'd had over the years. If the club manager was surprised to see him with an attractive woman who was not his wife, he didn't show it. They ordered their meals and exchanged more pleasantries, then John looked at Elise and his face hardened.

"Elise, what do you think about Plains?" he asked.

"What do you mean, exactly?" she responded, wondering why the CEO was suddenly interested in her opinion about his competitor.

"How do they seem to you? What is their reputation?"

"They are very professional with the news media," Elise said. "They have been good to me. It seems that they are well liked because they pay high dividends. I don't know their CEO that well – he rarely talks to the media – but I have dealt with Susan Scott. People say she's the one who's really in charge. She's also the leading strategist to take over your company. Other than that, we have an arm's length relationship. They haven't given me any real scoops and I haven't asked. They took me to Peru. I know they think they did me a favour, but I feel we're about even. I paid my way, and it was risky, you know, because of all the kidnappings down there. Also, they're known for their support of the arts and are seen as a generous employer," she added.

"You're a brave woman," John said. "Do you know that they are about to sell their Peru assets for one billion less than they paid barely a couple of years ago?"

"No," Elise said, her eye widening. "How do you know this?"

"I heard it from my banking sources. They are getting beaten up so badly by environmentalists that they feel it's damaging their overall reputation. Plus, they need money to pay for my company."

"Why is this a bad thing? I saw their operations, and they are doing a good job there, but it's a tough place," Elise said. "Maybe they should get out. Plus, they have already made some money back by selling some of their infrastructure."

"Maybe. But it shows they don't know what they are doing. They buy assets at inflated prices and then run them into the ground. That's what they will do with Ladyfern. You heard it here first."

"And just so you know," John continued, "that Peru play made a lot of people rich, including some of the Plains board members. A few had big positions in the company that owned the Peru operation, then Plains purchased it for more than they should have. I looked at it, too. Everyone knew it was a bad investment in an unstable country, the wrong way to go. The board should have stopped it. Instead, they approved the sale and made a killing on the side. Your friend Susan Scott cheered it all the way. It was a conflict of interest, and shareholders are paying the price. If only they knew. We're talking small shareholders. Plains is supposed to be a widows-and-orphans stock."

So, this wasn't a free lunch after all, Elise thought. John was trashing Plains and wanted her to do his dirty work. She liked the story, though, particularly the conflict-of-interest angle. She was in the news business, chased every lead.

"Why are you telling me this?" she asked. "You could alert the authorities if you feel rules were broken. Ask them to investigate."

"It wouldn't look good coming from me," John said. "I would have no credibility, given Plains' interest in taking over my company. This is a tight community, and we don't snitch on each other to the regulators. It would promote more regulation and more oversight, then we all lose. We can take care of ourselves. But you can make this public. And here's a promise to you in return. We're getting close to announcing a deal. I'll make sure you get the scoop before anyone else." Elise's eyes widened again as she pictured frantic market reaction to her story.

"A deal with Plains?" she asked.

"Stay tuned," he responded.

The drive back was cordial. They gave each other personal updates. As Elise prepared to exit the car, John gently took her hand, held it seconds too long, and thanked her for listening.

Is he flirting with me? Elise asked herself again. She decided to ignore John's inappropriate gesture and headed inside to get to work.

She finished a story she had been working on and filed it to her editor but couldn't stop thinking about the Peru tip. She searched all public records online she could get her hands on about Plains' acquisition of the Peru company. There wasn't much. The acquired company was private, based in Lima, and revealed little about itself. She phoned a few of her investment industry sources. One analyst confirmed that rumours had been circulating far and wide about the conflict-of-interest stuff on the board but didn't want to be quoted. He didn't want Plains to cut him off, he told her, but encouraged her to dig deeper and gave her more leads. A lot of large investors knew that Plains' directors had lined their own pockets with the Peru acquisition and instead of reporting the company to the authorities, dumped its stock, the analyst told her. Why bother bad mouthing them? The market had its own ways of dealing with crooks.

Elise made more calls to her banking sources about whether Plains' Peru project was for sale. Two investment bankers confirmed that, too. That meant she had enough sources – John, the analyst, and the bankers – to meet the *Journal*'s requirement for a story based on unnamed sources. Her final task was to phone Plains and get a comment and any other information she could squeeze out of them. It was evening when she reached Gordon Wilson at his home.

"Hi Gordon. This is Elise."

"Hi Elise. What's new and exciting in your world?" he asked cordially.

"I heard you are putting your Peru assets on the block. Is this true?" she asked.

"Maybe. What else have you heard?"

"I heard you're marketing them at a big loss. What's going on?"

"Let me get back to you on this. What's your deadline?" Gordon asked.

"How about tomorrow morning?" Elise said.

"Oh, come on. I need a bit more time. Everyone has left the office. If you hold off a bit, I'll get you an interview with our CEO. Give me a full day," he pleaded.

"Okay. But don't wait too long. I have confirmation, and I will go with the story regardless. I also want to double check something else that is related," Elise said.

"What's that?" the public relations man asked, sounding alarmed.

"I heard that some of your directors made money off the Peru purchase two years ago. I heard they had interests in the company bought by Plains, and that Plains paid too much for those assets."

"I have never heard that," he replied, seeming sincere. "We don't respond to rumours and speculation. The Peru company was private, and the transaction was the right thing to do at the time and received all the required regulatory approvals. I'll get back to you about our Peru plans."

Elise waited in vain for Plains' call the next day. She noticed on her computer terminal that Hunter's stock was rising, and that a large volume of shares was changing hands. Her editor phoned her and asked her to investigate what was going on. She phoned John but he ignored her, as he'd done so many times before.

Something was up. She worked the phones but all she got was speculation. She needed to nail the scoop. She'd done the leg work, the research, and she'd be crushed if another reporter got the goods before she did.

It was evening by the time she left the office for the day. She had filed a story about strong rumours that a Hunter deal was imminent, based on anonymous sources, because that's all she could come up with by deadline.

She was almost asleep when her new mobile phone, a clunky contraption with a tiny keyboard that she was still learning to use, rang. It was John.

"Sorry to call you so late," he said. He was still in his office. "We are making an announcement at six tomorrow morning. I will call you at six-fifteen. I am not talking to other media. Plains is doing a conference call at 10 a.m. It looks like your inquiries about Peru forced Plains to act. Thank you for that. Goodnight." And he hung up.

It was still dark when John arrived at his office the following morning. He'd barely slept. The announcement would hit the news wires shortly. He knew it would be a shocker. Plains had agreed to buy Hunter at a sixty percent premium over its share price before the takeover fight. It was a rich deal that got the market's attention the world over. Its undeveloped oilsands leases would be excluded and become the foundation of John's next company.

John grinned. His game plan had worked. Plains was so concerned about a bad market reaction to the Peru sale, which the company had hoped to keep confidential, it accelerated the takeover announcement and increased its offer price. For John, the cherry on the cake was that Plains overpaid for his company. He was confident Plains would end up in trouble.

John picked up Plains' news release from his fax machine and read it with a mix of satisfaction and nostalgia. It bragged that the takeover of Hunter would make Plains the undisputed natural-gas leader in Canada. The purchase would be funded with cash and the sale of some non-core assets, including its operations in Peru. There was no mention of the major losses that would be incurred from the Peru sale.

He called Elise at the promised time but shared the bare minimum about how the deal came together. Elise pressed him for more, but the oilman remained cautious and stuck to lawyer-approved answers.

Then, he closed his office door and ignored other calls. He wanted to think about the future. He had plenty of cash to start fresh, plus he could tuck some away in safe investments for a rainy day. He thought about using some of his windfall to break free from his wife.

When the markets opened, the stocks of both companies jumped – Hunter's for the huge takeover premium, Plains for the aggressive domestic refocussing and expansion.

In a call with analysts, CEO David Anderson spoke enthusiastically about the Ladyfern discovery and its magnificent performance, which he promised would continue for years to come. He promised new development projects in the region, too, because exploration results in nearby fields looked great, and more Ladyferns were likely to be found, resulting in billions in additional shareholder value. Most of Hunter's staff would be offered jobs at Plains and rejuvenate his company's workforce.

Plains only accepted questions from friendly analysts and friendly media on the call. Elise had questions about Peru, but Plains ignored her. She knew she'd been short-changed by both sides. She also knew Plains had covered up the truth about Peru. She was determined to dig deeper as soon as she had the time.

Her story still had the most depth available and was widely read. She also had the only public statements made by John Hess.

Elise's chief editor called her to convey how pleased he was with her work in Calgary, and with getting John Hess to comment exclusively to her.

"It's a good get," he said, and asked her if there was anything he could do for her.

"Yes," Elise said. "I'd like to come back to New York for a few days, maybe over Christmas. I have been away for a long time. I miss my kids, and I want to see the World Trade Center site with them. We're all in shock. We used to hang out there a lot."

"Done," the editor said. "We'll get you on a flight before the holidays. The city is still on edge over that atrocious attack and working hard to get back to normal. Security is tight. The newsroom wasn't impacted directly – thank goodness – but so many of our sources, readers, advertisers, were. It's a different world. Come see me when you get here."

Chapter 12

CALGARY, ALBERTA, DECEMBER 2001

On the morning of December 23, Elise was sitting in her office and putting the finishing touches on a feature about the outlook for oil stocks – a request from her editor – when her phone rang. It was John. "Hi Elise. I'd like to wish you a Merry Christmas. Your coverage made a big difference to us this year and I wanted to let you know."

"Well, thank you. Merry Christmas to you too. I didn't know I made such a difference, but I'll take the compliment. I just did my job."

"You did, and I feel good about it all, and about the future. The sale of Hunter closes at the end of the year. I plan to get my new company off the ground immediately in the new year."

"A new company?" Elise asked, curious about John's new venture. "That's fast. No time off?"

"Just a few days. We'll be catching up with old friends in London. Claire loves London during the holidays."

"Oh, that sounds lovely," Elise said, noting John's voice seemed downcast. Shouldn't he be happy to enjoy his good fortune with his wife? she thought. "I am off to New York to see my children. I am leaving tomorrow morning. We booked a week at our favourite hotel. They had some great rates, with everyone staying away from the city since 9/11."

"Be safe out there," John said. "Before you go, I'd like to drop something off. I am a couple of blocks away from your office. I'll be there in ten minutes." He hung up without waiting for Elise's reply. If he had, Elise would have told him she was pressed for time, that she wasn't dressed to receive visitors, that the office was messy and everyone else had already left, that she wanted to go home, too.

A few minutes later John walked into the *Journal*'s sparsely furnished suite.

He looked around. He'd never been to a newspaper operation before. He was amused by its informality – the big stacks of old newspapers, framed editorial cartoons, photos taken during assignments. Some were with famous people, some in dangerous-looking places.

Elise was sitting at her desk, tapping quickly on the keyboard, engrossed in her work, when John quietly approached her from behind and put his hand on her shoulder.

She greeted him, even if she wasn't keen to receive him. But it was almost Christmas. She didn't want to spoil her good mood. She decided to let her guard down and enjoy the season.

"So – this is where all those wonderful stories are created," he said, his voice friendly. "This place looks like a lot of fun."

"It's modest, but this is standard décor for editorial bureaus, even for a big newspaper like the *Journal*. We are not in this business to impress with fancy art, like oil companies," Elise said.

"Where is everybody?" he asked.

"They're gone for the holidays. I just need to wrap up a story and then I am done, too."

Elise stood and they were facing each other, he in his fancy suit, she in faded jeans and a cotton button-up shirt. The attraction between them was intense and physically drawing them closer.

He gave her a Hunter golf cap – which he said would become a collector's item – and a Christmas card with the Hunter logo. She opened the card. It had two handwritten lines: "Merry Christmas to the best reporter I know. John Hess."

She tried to look grateful. John had come all the way to her office to hand her a corporate souvenir. She had received more thoughtful gifts from the building's manager.

"Thank you so much. It's very nice of you," she lied. "I think you are the first CEO who has ever walked into this place. I'm so sorry, but I don't have a gift for you. I didn't expect to see you before Christmas. In fact, I didn't expect to see you at all now that you have cashed out and I am no longer useful."

"Oh, you'll see lots of me now," John said. "My new company will be private to start with, so I won't have the handcuffs that I had at Hunter, and

I'll be able to speak more freely. The oilsands are an amazing play, and I intend to ride it all the way to the top."

They were still facing each other awkwardly when he held out his hand, preparing to shake hers. Instead, he pulled her toward him and gave her a hug. Both lingered. He kissed her cheeks. Then his mouth met hers and they kissed passionately in the middle of the suite, surprised at what was happening, unable to stop.

"I am sorry," he said. "I shouldn't have done that. I'd better leave."

"Yes, that was inappropriate," she said, embarrassed, unsure what to do. "I shouldn't have crossed the line either. I'm sorry too."

He left the suite. Seconds passed. Elise was confused. She tried to pull herself together and finish her work.

Minutes later he returned. Elise stood up and they met again in the middle of the room.

"I am so sorry about what I did," he said. "Let's start over. I just meant to wish you a great Christmas. I know how hard these holidays are when you are dealing with a recent loss."

He reached for her hand, pulled her toward him, and then hugged her again. He kissed her once more, forgetting everything he'd just said, and this time he found in Elise a willing partner.

They kissed and embraced for minutes, despite being in a place of business with an open door.

Then they were both at a loss for words. Neither could rationalize what they'd done. John straightened his jacket, walked himself to the elevator, and promised to stay in touch.

Elise didn't know how to process what had become obvious to her – she'd never felt such attraction for anyone, not even for her late husband.

She should have been angry with John. He had invaded her personal space and had used her to further his corporate agenda. Instead, she blamed herself. John was a married man and a high-profile, indispensable source she needed to keep at arm's length. She should have known better. She needed to take a step back and forget what happened.

Yet her mind was racing and considering the possibilities, and she couldn't stop. Was he messing with her – as he'd probably done with a lot of women – or was he was interested in a relationship? She was a widow, after all, and free to do what she wanted, if it didn't interfere with her job. She had been thinking of asking for a transfer back to New York, until then. Suddenly, Calgary, and John Hess, were becoming more interesting.

As if to ensure the moment wouldn't slip away, John phoned her once more from his car before she left for the day. He wanted to let her to know that her perfume was still lingering on his shirt, and that it was driving him insane.

On Christmas day, John was in his grand home on his acreage west of the city, sharing breakfast with his wife. He wished her a Merry Christmas with a diamond necklace and matching earrings. She gave him a painting from Nicholas Bott. She knew he admired his landscapes.

John loved Christmas. Light snow was falling on top of the already thick white blanket. Scattered around the property, evergreens twinkled with colourful lights. Church bells nearby were announcing mass. Neighbourhood children were skating, sledding, or cross-country skiing, making the most of the mild temperatures blown in by another Chinook.

He'd lied to Elise about going to London. He had too many obligations in the city for him to go away. Calls were coming in daily from lawyers working around the clock to close the acquisition of his company by the end of the year. He'd also lied because he didn't want to seem boring, mundane, provincial, which he knew he was.

Elise kept flooding his thoughts. She had made him feel alive for the first time in years. After breakfast, he went to his home office to be alone. He dialed Elise's number. No response. He left her a message: "Merry Christmas, Elise. I just wanted to let you know that I am thinking of you."

John then returned to his wife, hugged her. He was glad she was happy. A pile of money was coming their way. They talked about how to deploy it. She told him she had plans of her own, causes she wanted to support.

John looked at his wife, feeling no guilt. She was as beautiful and as elegant as the first day he met her, in her flattering designer pant suit and her always impeccably made-up face. Claire knew how to look and behave like the privileged person she was, and for all her faults, he had always admired that about her.

They had come a long way together, and it would be madness to change course. He worked too hard to split their wealth, or to start over with someone else. Better the devil you know, he thought. Besides, there was an advantage to having affairs while being married – the other women had no leverage when they knew he was committed to his wife.

John chased away thoughts of Elise. He would not be tempted. She had been another lapse of judgement, he decided, like many he'd had before. Leaving Claire, a thought he'd entertained many times, was out of the question. Their lives were too intertwined and too mutually beneficial.

But he had to string Elise along, he concluded. She was an essential part of his new plans.

He asked his wife when they were expected at her parents'.

"I promised we'd get there late afternoon, that way we have plenty of time to catch up," Claire said. "They are having a few other people over. They hired a choir – isn't that nice? – to sing Christmas songs for us, and caterers to serve dinner. They do such a good job. We are so lucky to have them."

"Yes, we are," John said, overcome by a profound sense of loneliness.

Chapter 13

DAWSON CREEK, BRITISH COLUMBIA, FEBRUARY 2002

It was cold and dark in Dawson Creek. Chief Anne Proudfoot walked awkwardly in knee-high snow to the popular Night Owl, off a road that split the town. Thanks to Ladyfern, it was packed.

A band played country tunes and wood crackled in the fireplace. Rig hands poured in after their shifts through the rusty front door. They greeted each other and acknowledged the well-known chief with a respectful nod. They paid dearly for their beer but needed it to ease the ache of another northern night away from home.

Chief Anne looked around and found Erika Bernstein, the only other woman, in a booth. The environmentalist had asked to meet her. The chief agreed; she needed to consider new strategies after the humiliation by Plains. They greeted each other. The chief sat down.

The activist got down to business immediately. "I organized the fight against Plains in Peru for Amazon Fighters," Erika said, like she was pitching herself to a recruiter. "I have recently moved to Western Canada to start a campaign by a new and related group, Friends of the Boreal Forest. We'll use the same model. We will partner with Indigenous people impacted by oil and gas exploration who agree with our goals and jointly organize a resistance. We'll help you to organize protests, block access roads. We will fund legal challenges. We will ensure we get maximum media exposure. We will get the leverage you deserve."

Chief Anne liked the woman. The more they talked, the more she saw a kindred spirit.

Erika spoke plainly, like her. She was humble, like her. She dressed plainly, like her. She was an underdog, like her. She was a warrior, like her.

"What's in it for you?" the chief asked.

"We want to stop production of fossil fuels to stop climate change," Erika responded passionately.

"That's a lofty goal – we just want more money for our people," the chief said.

"Plains' money is blood money. They are a bad operator that doesn't deserve to get rich by destroying the planet."

Chief Anne had never heard about Plains' activities in Peru and didn't know a lot about climate change. In her world the weather was changing, but her ancestors had seen that before. But she didn't need convincing to work with the activist because her words rang true. Her own opinion of Plains was low after her encounter with Susan Scott. Follow-up exchanges with field staff had left her frustrated and ready for a fight.

She was angry at John Hess, too, for failing to keep promises made to his band. She knew he'd gotten even richer off the resources under her reserve. But unlike Plains, the CEO had the decency to take her calls. They had spoken a few times. He had told her Hunter's future was uncertain because of the takeover fight. He promised to pay her a visit as soon as the company's sale was finalized. She believed him.

But Chief Anne's community wanted action now. They were courting someone to replace her. They were concerned that environmental degradation was threatening their already meagre way of life. They watched as dirty water from operations bled into rivers; forests were cut to make room for drilling sites; garbage was dumped over their once-untouched landscape. They complained about the infernal noises made by the drilling rigs.

They were angry that Ladyfern was running out and they had nothing in return. The displays of wealth by drilling crews made them even angrier. Workers drove fancy new pickup trucks all over town. Drugs had moved into the area, lured by big salaries and too little to do outside of work. Big new homes were built. Two new hotels were under construction, but the dirt road leading to the community remained unpaved. Only the Indigenous people remained poor and out of work, they complained.

"Where are you getting money for this campaign?" the chief asked Erika.

"We have raised a significant amount from American philanthropists. They were thrilled with our results in Peru. We pushed Plains out of the country. They sold their assets at a loss. We can do the same here."

"I'm still concerned there isn't enough in it for us," Chief Anne said. "You are asking us to be the face of your campaign, right?"

"Yes. But we will pay you for every appearance on our behalf. We will sue the companies. We will sue the government for enabling the degradation."

"What about a share of the oil companies' revenue?" Chief Anne asked.

"That's not what we do. We want to shut them down, not let them make their dirty profits so they can give you a share."

"How much would you pay us?" the chief asked.

"We can't afford much, but I promise you it will be several thousand dollars a month. It's good income for your band that you are not getting now."

Chief Anne nodded. "I need to discuss this with our council, and with the other bands," she said.

"Sure," Erika said. "I'll call you back in a week. Let me know if you need me to make a presentation to your people."

The chief said her goodbyes and walked out of the bar. She drove her old pickup truck back to the reserve. She hated it had come to this but couldn't see other options. A deal with the activists was the best she had to work with.

A few days later, the region's chiefs reconvened at her request. Chief Anne updated the group about her encounters with Plains and with Erika Bernstein.

"I know we all have concerns about bringing in activists, but they would give us leverage to fight for our rights and for a share of the money," she said. "These companies are taking our resources, destroying our land, and refusing to show us respect. We can't continue to be on the outside looking in."

"But the environmentalists want to shut down the activity. How would that help us?" Chief Adam asked. "If only we could participate in this new industry, we would raise ourselves out of poverty. It could be our ticket to become part of the economy."

"Let's ask for another meeting with Plains, right here, to let them know we are prepared to sign up with activists, show them we have leverage. Plains is the biggest operator now that they have added Hunter's production. If they continue to ignore us, we'll sign up with the environmentalists and go to war."

The following day Chief Anne drafted a letter on behalf of the group to Plains' CEO and asked for a chief-to-chief meeting. She didn't mince words. First Nations wanted a share of the revenue and were prepared to use all the tools at their disposal to get what they were owed.

Chapter 14

Susan Scott had considered agreeing – for a minute – to attend the meeting with the tribes, and even to bring along her CEO, but then rejected the idea. She asked her assistant to send her regrets.

David Anderson didn't do well in confrontational settings, especially with Indians, Susan knew from experience. He was a finance guy who needed constant protection from himself. He would say or offer too much. He would feel sorry. He would be manipulated. Corporate interests, shareholder value, had to come first. There was no room for bleeding hearts.

Susan felt her own attendance, too, would have sent a message of weakness to Chief Anne Proudfoot. The Indigenous woman needed to be stalled. Revenue sharing? What next? Seats on the board? As if that would ever happen. Plains would become the laughingstock of the market if it ever agreed to such demands.

Susan's plan was simple – string along Chief Anne and the rest of the tribes until the Ladyfern field was depleted. It would happen sooner than they expected. Then her crews would pack up and leave.

Plains would send junior staff to the meeting, with supervision from a couple of lawyers, Susan decided. They would listen and report back. Meanwhile, Plains would use the Ladyfern windfall to pay down debt incurred by taking over Hunter. There would be no free riders. There would be no giveaways to people who did not put up their own capital.

Hunter had cost a bundle, and Plains needed the cash. Concerns that the field was being drilled too fast, too aggressively, were making the rounds, and investors were skittish. They used to be Hunter's problem. Now they were her own. Infighting between producers was escalating. To complicate matters, a small company had just come out of the woodwork to claim from Plains a piece of the find. A statement of claim had been filed, and it was now before the Court of Queen's Bench – and in the news.

Did John Hess win by losing? Susan was already wondering. Plains needed to move on to new plays, less developed, that came with the Hunter purchase. They would be less conflicted and, if Plains got lucky, could even be bigger than Ladyfern. That's how Plains would maximize shareholder value and how she would stay on top, she decided.

The rendezvous took place near the Bearspaw reserve in a hunting lodge, a favourite of big-city game hunters who ventured into the North to blow off steam. The log house had seen better days but was welcoming and clean. On the day of the meeting, deer-meat roast was cooking in the kitchen. Homemade pastries and steaming coffee greeted guests as they made their way in. Chief Anne was mortified that the Plains' CEO and his sidekick, Susan Scott, didn't show up. She kept the feeling to herself. She would give Plains one more chance to achieve an amicable solution to benefit her people.

The two sides sat opposing each other across the lodge's largest table. Both were observed by lawyers. Erika Bernstein was introduced as a partner who had agreed to pay the bands' legal bill. The Plains group was too junior to know she'd led the campaign against their company in Peru.

"Welcome to the traditional territory of the Bearspaw Nation," said Chief Anne, flanked by the region's other chiefs. She looked confident in a new blue suit, with her thick hair caught in a single braid that descended to the middle of her back.

"I'm joined for this important occasion by the chiefs of all bands in our area affected by the increase in oil and gas development. We have been trying for the past couple of years to come to an understanding with the oil companies that would be mutually agreeable. We haven't gotten very far.

"We believe our legal rights are being trampled on. There has been lack of consultation. There has been no discussion about compensation for the environmental damage. There has been no discussion about sharing the benefits, which we deserve because these are our resources, too."

Peggy, the leader of the Plains delegation, stood up to speak. The cheerful young woman dressed in business casual had been seated between two young interns. Two junior lawyers sat further away, in chairs in one corner of the room.

"Plains welcomes this opportunity to get to know First Nations in the region. We have budgeted funds to support several celebrations as well as numerous scholarships for your youth," she said, as the lawyers nodded in approval.

"Sadly, no one has applied," the young woman continued.

"Plains is earmarking a significant portion of our budget for activities in the Ladyfern areas," she said, reading from speaking notes reviewed and authorized by her boss, Susan Scott.

"Plains welcomes ideas about community investment, as long as they fit our criteria and are eligible for matching funds by all levels of government," the young woman concluded.

"How much are you talking about?" Chief Anne asked.

"We are authorized to spend a hundred and twenty thousand dollars a year in this area," Peggy said. "And we can help you apply for the government funds."

"And how much have you earned off the Ladyfern find? Billions? How's that fair?" Chief Anne replied, offended. "We don't want charity. We want to be partners. The gas you produce comes from our lands – lands that we never gave up to Canada. We deserve a share of the revenue to spend as we see fit."

The chiefs then took turns talking about the environmental damage they witnessed firsthand. An elder hereditary chief teared up as he recalled an incident involving a drilling crew that trampled on an area containing an ancient burial ground. Another chief talked about applying, unsuccessfully, for a job that involved monitoring wildlife. It was awarded to a white man half his age who had no experience. An elderly woman complained about industrial waste dumped in the rivers.

The young Plains woman said she was disturbed by the accounts and promised to report the information to her bosses. "I am not authorized to negotiate," she said. "But rest assured that your concerns will be raised at the highest levels of our company and that we will get back to you at the earliest opportunity."

"Very well," Chief Anne responded. "You have two weeks. We are prepared to do what's needed to be taken seriously by your company, and all the others that are drilling on our lands."

The chiefs applauded. The meeting was adjourned. Lunch was served. The mood turned lighter. Erika Bernstein gave her card to the young Plains woman and urged her to deliver it to Susan Scott.

Chief Anne offered blessings and prayed for everyone's safe return.

Before Plains staff walked to two Plains helicopters standing at the ready nearby, the chief warned again: "We want to see progress. We won't stand for more delay. And don't forget to give Erika's card to Susan Scott. She needs to know."

"Message received," Peggy said optimistically, sliding the card in her back pocket.

Chief Anne had one more thing to do before the end of the day. She drove to Dawson Creek for a secret meeting with John Hess. The oilman was in town to shut down Hunter's local office, which he no longer needed, he told her in a short phone conversation earlier in the day. They met in a private room of one of the new hotels.

"How was your meeting with Plains?" John asked after they shook hands.

"What meeting?" Chief Anne responded, startled the oilman had found out.

"Watch your back," he advised her. "Plains love to throw their weight around."

"So do we," Chief Anne responded, smiling. "And we will."

They ordered their meals. He seemed more relaxed now that the takeover fight was over, Chief Anne thought.

"I am sorry I haven't been available," John said. "The past year has been really difficult. I couldn't answer your calls because my lawyers wouldn't let me. We didn't know how things would play out. I was heartbroken to lose Hunter to Plains, but I am glad shareholders came out ahead."

"I am glad for you, too," Chief Anne said. "It doesn't look good for us, though. The new owners are a tough bunch."

"I'm aware. You have more leverage than you think, but you need to act quickly. Ladyfern will run out if they keep producing it at this rate."

"We're working on it," Chief Anne responded. She didn't want to share her plans with the oilman, since he was no longer in the picture.

"I know we have some unfinished business," John said. "I promised you five million to build the Bearspaw Community Centre. I'm here to deliver on that promise."

He pulled out a personal cheque for the full amount. He asked the chief to keep the donation confidential.

Chief Anne was surprised. "This money, it's from your own pocket?" she asked. "No strings attached?"

"Yes, this is my money. And no, there are no obligations. I want to help your community. I don't want publicity. You have been patient and fair to me. I wanted to show how much I appreciate you. I have learned a lot from you about perseverance."

Chief Anne had never seen such a large cheque. It would go a long way to help the elderly in her reserve, and to quiet the hotheads who wanted her gone.

"I could use some help supervising construction. Can I count on you?" she asked, hoping to keep the relationship alive. They'd known each other for a long time – more than a decade, for sure – and she felt comfortable talking to him. He seemed to connect easily with her, too, like a lonely soul who found solace from a stranger.

"I would be honoured," John said. "Now that Hunter is someone else's problem, I could use a new project."

Chief Anne was happy, too, that there would be no publicity. She didn't want the donation to get in the way of her negotiations with Plains.

Chapter 15

CALGARY, ALBERTA, MAY 2002

It was late in the day and Elise was finishing up some background research. She wanted to be ready for Plains' annual shareholder meeting the next day. She expected confrontation. Several Indigenous leaders had told her that they would be in attendance to protest environmental damage from all the Ladyfern drilling and production, and to call out the company's board for not consulting them.

When she left work, the sun was still high in the sky. She walked the long way home through a downtown park to enjoy the warm evening. Crab apple trees were in full bloom, and municipal crews were still working, raking freshly cut grass, fueling the scent of spring.

It was her favourite time in the city.

Yet the depression that had crippled her following Julien's death had come back with a vengeance. This time, the trigger was the strange behaviour of John Hess.

He had avoided her since that unforgettable kiss, making her feel lost and abandoned all over again.

Why is he doing this to me? she asked herself. Why is he leading me on, then vanishing, like I don't exist, like I don't deserve an explanation?

Then she had an epiphany – or what she thought was one. John Hess was all about greed. Oil, money, power, women – he needed it all, whatever it took, no matter what got in the way or what he had to do. What had she hoped for from such a man? she asked herself. A replacement for Julien? Companionship? A relationship?

John Hess offered none of that. She realized she'd allowed herself to be caught in a trap, and she felt like a fool. She wished she'd established clear boundaries right away and defended them firmly.

She thought about her meeting with her editor in chief in New York over the Christmas break, when she'd said she was so happy in Calgary that she wanted to stay for a while longer. Now, she couldn't wait to leave. She was stuck in a dead-end job away from her children and from opportunities. She was in a foreign outpost where meeting new people – men, in particular – was hard. She was a journalist, which meant few dared get too close, unless they had something to gain.

She was annoyed that John had been busy charming everyone else. Thanks largely to her articles, his North American profile had taken off. He spoke at conferences and on TV news shows. He took interviews with anyone who asked. He was building relationships with her media competitors, perhaps because he needed to reach new audiences, perhaps because he now saw her as someone who could ask too much, want too much.

One TV interview caught her attention. He was all smiles while promoting his new company in a new play: Alberta's oilsands. The reporter was a striking black woman wearing a fitted low-cut dress. Elise noticed they were so friendly with each other that it seemed a bit too intimate, like they just had sex.

Then she felt stupid for thinking such thoughts. John Hess owes me nothing, and I owe him nothing. I don't want an explanation. I want him to stay away from me, she decided.

After a troubled sleep, Elise picked out a linen dress and jacket and headed toward a downtown hotel to attend Plains' meeting. She knew she looked great because of the approving looks she received on the street. They helped her move forward.

As expected, dozens of Indigenous people were protesting on the sidewalks in front of the hotel. Some beat drums, some chanted, some danced, some waved signs condemning Plains for refusing to consult with them before drilling in the Ladyfern field, while destroying their lands. Police watched quietly from vans parked nearby. Elise was delighted that Plains – especially Susan Scott – were getting the bad attention they deserved.

Plains was one of many targets. Indigenous protests had become so common during annual-meeting season that the city had taken on a carnival atmosphere. But the protests were mostly ignored by oil and gas executives, who arrived at the meetings from back doors to avoid any direct contact. Profits were reaching new highs, and investors were pleased. In their world, that's all that mattered. Controversy was something to manage.

Before entering the hotel, as the protesters posed for the cameras, Elise saw Chief Anne. She'd first chatted with her in Northern BC, when John Hess announced the Ladyfern discovery. The chief looked happy then. Her intelligent blue eyes seemed to invite another conversation. She approached her and asked her if she was available to answer a few questions. The chief said yes.

"Why are you angry with Plains?" Elise asked.

"Their behaviour against our people is appalling," Chief Anne responded. "We're here to raise awareness. Their activities damage our environment. They are refusing to consult with us. They won't include us in their planning. They won't give us our fair share of the revenue."

Elise didn't know much about Canada's Indigenous people and was curious about growing unrest in regions impacted by new discoveries.

More reporters gathered around Elise and asked the chief their own questions.

"Have you met with the company?"

"We have, but they are stalling us," Chief Anne responded.

"Are you planning to sue them?"

"Yes," Chief Anne said. "Stay tuned."

Then Erika appeared. She had been monitoring the scrum near the hotel's entrance, next to a handful of private security guards. Her hair was shorter and well cut, a second-hand leather backpack was slung on her right shoulder, a tape recorder and notebook were in her hand. Her dishonesty has no bounds, Elise thought. Now she's impersonating a reporter.

"What are you doing here?" Elise asked coolly, recalling how badly Erika had treated her after her trip to Peru.

"I am leading a new team in Western Canada. We are based in Dawson Creek and Vancouver, for now," the activist responded.

"Seriously? Planning to stir the pot here, too?" Elise asked. "I'd appreciate it if you backed off," she continued. "I'm doing an interview with Chief

Anne. She's doing well without your supervision. And frankly, I don't need you looking over my shoulder, either."

Erika stepped back. Elise turned to the chief.

"Are you working with Erika's climate change campaign?" Elise asked.

"Yes. They are supporting us," Chief Anne responded, and walked away, like she was reluctant to say more.

Erika approached Elise again after the interview before she entered the hotel.

"Look, I'm sorry about how I handled Peru. I hope there are no hard feelings," Erika said unconvincingly. "We are working with Chief Anne and many other Indigenous people here to shut down oil and gas exploration in this country. We are starting with Plains because we know them well. But we aren't stopping there. Fossil fuels need to be replaced by clean energy to save our planet before it's too late."

"Just stay out of my way and don't spread lies about me," Elise said. "It doesn't help your cause."

Elise turned on her heel, stepped back and chased Chief Anne, offered her card, and asked her to call if she was interested in giving her a more in-depth interview. She even proposed to visit her reserve to get a first-hand view of conditions in the Ladyfern region. Chief Anne said she'd think about it.

Elise walked up the sandstone hotel's imposing steps, feeling sorry for the chief. She worried Chief Anne had become one of Erika's pawns. But it wasn't her fight. It wasn't her job to warn people – on any side. She was there to report.

As she rushed through the elegant lobby, a red-velvet-and-wood-panelled throwback to Calgary's early days, she found herself face to face with John Hess, who was walking in the opposite direction.

Their eyes locked and he looked embarrassed. She said hello, then walked briskly toward the shareholders' meeting. He followed her.

"Hi Elise, how have you been?" he asked, as if the unreturned calls, the implied promises, their kiss, never happened.

"Wonderful," she said. "But I am in a rush. I am covering the Plains meeting and it's getting started. I need to go."

"We are due for a catch-up," he proposed, putting his hand gently on her arm. "I have a new company. I'd like to talk to you about it. It would make a great story for the *Journal*. Can I call you sometime to set something up?"

"Sure," Elise said, though she had no intention of following up. She just wanted to get to her meeting and away from him.

John Hess needed her more than she needed him now, she realized.

She entered the hotel's large ballroom and took a seat with the rest of the press pack. Two dozen Indigenous people were already seated in the front rows. The directors on the stage looked uneasily at each other. Security guards talked on their hand radios.

The meeting stalled as Indigenous men and women took turns at the microphones and asked why Plains refused to hear their concerns.

"We will give them full consideration in due course," the chairman said from the podium after everyone had their say. "Meanwhile, help yourself to the buffet. The annual meeting is adjourned."

Chapter 16

CALGARY, ALBERTA, AUGUST 2002

The breakthrough in the Peru story landed on Elise's answering machine during one of August's slow news days. She'd just come back from a mid-day walk in the park when she noticed the red light was blinking on her office's answering system, signalling a voicemail had been left.

A former Plains executive in Peru, a man she recalled interviewing during her trip there, was trying to reach her. He said in his message that he was back in Calgary looking for work and that he knew she was interested in the Plains conflict-of-interest story. He wanted to help.

Elise had chased the story for months, talked to as many sources as she could to get to the bottom of it, but had to set it aside because she couldn't make headway. She phoned the man back. They agreed to meet for coffee the following day.

When she saw him, Jim McKinnon looked pale and depressed – not the handsome, confident drilling manager Elise remembered. She knew the look. The oil and gas business was notorious for firing people mercilessly, sometimes over changing market conditions, more often because of silly disagreements, professional jealousies, or even as a warning to other staff that they were employed at the pleasure of their bosses.

But wronged employees could be vicious in return. Companies had dirty laundry that staff knew about – questionable reserve reporting, conflicts of interest with service providers, extramarital affairs, illegal trading by insiders. Elise had received plenty of tips from unemployed workers. Unfortunately, much of what they said was not market-moving news.

Jim arrived on time to the quiet coffee shop on the edge of town which Elise had suggested. It was patronized mostly by seniors living in a nearby long-term housing facility, making their meeting less likely to be noticed.

"Your message intrigued me," Elise said, shaking his hand.

"Yes, I suspected you'd be interested in finding out what really happened in Peru," Jim responded, looking a bit too casual in a golf shirt and shorts, like he didn't want to be recognized. "I liked your reporting. I reached out because I believe I can trust you."

"Of course, you can," Elise said. "Let's talk, and we'll figure out later if we have a story."

Jim teared up as he recalled how he had been unceremoniously fired, without compensation, and escorted out of the Peru project by the same armed guards who used to protect him. It happened on the same day the project's ownership was transferred to a Chinese company, which bought the assets at a bargain price, so Plains could use the cash to pay for Hunter.

"Plains stabbed me in the back," Jim told her. "I moved to Peru with my family to run the project's drilling program for Plains, which was a serious sacrifice. The risk of kidnapping was huge. Once I even came close to being captured. Armed men broke into the project and took some of our Peruvian staff," he said, as Elise thought about how close she had been to danger when she visited.

"They are still missing, as far as I know, but Plains covered it up. Plains didn't want the incident to scuttle their sale," he said. "The Chinese, of course, couldn't care less. They came with their own security staff. They'll pump the oil and let the Peruvians who were taken hostage fend for themselves."

His children hated the country, he continued, and his wife was so sick of being robbed and harassed in the streets of Lima, where they lived, she had threatened to return to Calgary and file for divorce. Before the assignment, he'd been on the fast track at Plains and was groomed to rise to its senior executive ranks. Instead, he was out of a job. Assurances by Plains that the Chinese company would hire all its employees in Peru – a situation that could have given him some time to search for work elsewhere – was just spin, he said.

"The only good thing about this situation is that my family is now back in Calgary and happy to live in safety," he said, looking around nervously.

"Are you suing Plains?" Elise asked, hoping the meeting wasn't about getting publicity for a lawsuit.

"I'm working with a lawyer. He feels I have a strong case for wrongful dismissal," Jim responded.

Then Jim sat up straight, cleared his throat, and became serious as he shared the information that he knew Elise was waiting for. "I heard from my contacts that you are doing research on the purchase and then sale of the Peru assets. In case you don't know, you are a star inside the company, and staff appreciate all you are doing to keep executives in line, especially that Susan Scott. She's vicious and unethical. She'll do anything to get ahead.

"The truth is that Plains overpaid for what we got in Peru, but we – they – sold the assets at a loss, especially after all the drilling success that we had. We should have managed the public relations better. Instead of running away from the environmentalists, we should have confronted them head on. They fabricated facts. They blamed us for environmental damage that was done by others. We had a great project that was on the cusp of doubling production. We completed the pipeline to the coast on time and on budget. We cleaned up old environmental messes and ensured we didn't create new ones. The community was largely supportive – except for the few who were getting kickbacks from Amazon Fighters. I don't want to think about what will happen to the locals, now that the Chinese are in charge."

"Why did Plains pay so much for those assets to begin with?" Elise asked.

"They thought they were getting good assets, which they did, sort of. There was potential, for sure. But they underestimated the corruption, the security risk, the environmental campaign. Plains didn't do their due diligence because the assets were owned, indirectly, by a group that included three people on their board who wanted to cash out. They made the operation look a lot better than it was. Those directors convinced the rest of the board that the project was a better fit for a larger company like Plains because it would be harder to push around.

"They weren't the only ones who made a killing," Jim continued. "The investment banks, senior executives, the analysts, some other influential government people in Peru, all got a piece of that deal."

Plains made a big mistake, he said angrily, when it didn't require him to sign a confidentiality agreement, which meant he could spill the beans about all he knew.

"I was fired by the Chinese company, and they didn't care about Plains' confidential information," he told her.

Elise was trying to take it all in. Corruption was everywhere, but she didn't expect to find it in a long-established Canadian company that was held in retirement portfolios.

"I suspected much of this, and I tried to get to the bottom of it, but I couldn't find a paper trail – or people who could corroborate," Elise said. "Plains said the company they bought was private, and the ownership would remain confidential. I found other sources who knew bits and pieces, but no one would go on the record or was close enough to know for sure."

"Here's what you need," Jim said, handing her a folder he pulled out from his backpack, which he had placed beside him in his chair.

Elise opened it and found the information that had eluded her, in Spanish. There were documents, provided by Plains to authorities in the South American country, that disclosed the names of the private Peruvian company's owners prior to its acquisition by Plains. She recognized the names of three Plains directors.

"Wow. Where did you get this?" Elise asked.

"The information is public, available from the government. But you need to know where to find it," Jim said. "It's bothered me for a long time. These people lined their pockets while we made the personal sacrifices and did the work, and the shareholders put up the money. Then they sold the project when it was no longer beneficial to their bonuses and careers. No wonder they didn't want to get too public with the environmentalists. They needed to keep a low profile. They knew they wouldn't look good if someone dug too deep and found out about their questionable dealings.

"This sale was a disgrace," Jim continued. "We took a damaged project, put blood, sweat and tears into it to make it work, then our executives sold it at a loss when you started making phone calls. They know you are smart. They are afraid of you. They used the money to pay for the Hunter acquisition, which will be another bust. That play will blow up in their faces because they paid too much and are producing too much. Shareholders and authorities need to know the truth about Plains."

"Thank you for all this," Elise said. "I'll take it from here."

They shook hands and parted company. Elise ran back to her office and phoned her editor. She felt bad for Jim McKinnon but was also excited about what he'd told her.

"How do you know the documents are authentic?" the editor asked.

"McKinnon said so. But we need to double check," Elise said. "Do we know anyone in Lima who could search government records and ensure those documents are real?"

"We do. We could use a lawyer who's done work for us in the past. Meanwhile, send me the documents by courier. I'd like to look myself."

Elise copied the papers and sent the originals by overnight courier to her boss.

The information she'd been looking for arrived a couple of days later. The documents were authentic – and had more revelations.

The lawyer hired by the *Journal* told her over the phone that two other directors of the private company were former Peru politicians who had approved the oil leases while in office, and, after they left politics, were appointed to the board of the private company that was taken over by Plains and were compensated generously in stock. When the company was sold to Plains, they pocketed their windfall.

Elise called Peruvian academics to get background on the politicians and information about the government's sale of oil leases, without disclosing why she was interested in the information. She didn't want to give away her scoop.

She wrote her story, a lengthy piece about how senior executives of Plains and leaders of the Peruvian government profited from the sale of the oil project. It was her first real investigative work since moving to Calgary.

Before completing her story, she called Plains for comment, as she was required to do.

"Good morning, Elise. What can I do for you?" Gordon Wilson said cordially.

"Hi Gordon. I hope all is well. Remember the Peru conflict-of-interest story? You blew me off the last time I asked and told me Plains could not disclose details of the purchase. Well, I did more research and I have documents – authentic, we double checked in the country – that show three of your directors at Plains made millions, each, on that transaction," Elise said. "They were clearly in a conflict of interest. We also found that the politicians who helped those directors secure the leases also made millions from the transaction. We know that Plains purchased those assets at inflated prices, benefitting the three directors and the Peruvian politicians, then sold them at a deep discount to the Chinese when things got inconvenient. So, your shareholders lost money twice.

"I have the story," Elise said. "I just need a response from the company."

If Elise could have seen Gordon at the other end of the phone line, she would have noticed that his face had turned gray, and that sweat was pouring from his forehead and his armpits. She doubted he knew the full picture. Gordon was a loyal company man who was told only what his boss, Susan Scott, needed him to know.

"Is it possible to see your documents?" he asked.

"I'll send you a couple of the main pages, just to demonstrate we have them. I'm sure Plains has its own."

"Okay. Please fax them. I'll get back to you with a response. What's your deadline?"

"We are running the story tomorrow. You have until this evening to give us a response. We are publishing it with or without your input."

The company statement came within a couple of hours. In it, Plains said the three directors did not participate in deliberations by the board about the Peru assets and that it stood behind all its decisions regarding Peru, which were taken with the sole purpose of maximizing shareholder value. Elise included the statement in her story and filed it. Then she reviewed it with her editor line by line to ensure she had corroborating evidence – documents, interviews, independent research, background from archives – for everything in it that could possibly be challenged by Plains. When they finished, the story was sent to the *Journal*'s lawyers for a final review.

The next morning, Elise's story made the front page – above the fold – and knocked down Plains' stock by twenty percent, when trading was halted pending a company announcement. While pleased with the outcome, Elise was nervous, as she often was after a big scoop. It usually invited in two types of reactions, and she didn't know which one Plains would pick. The company could deny everything, discredit her and her reporting, and demand a correction. Or it could accept it and announce some form of damage control.

By late afternoon, after trading had closed, Plains issued a terse statement distancing itself from the three directors, who had resigned from its board effective immediately. It said a search for their replacements was underway. It re-enforced that its revenues were on track to beat expectations. The market wasn't convinced and beat down the stock even more in after-market trading.

Newspapers in Peru picked up the story and chased the political-corruption angle. Canadian securities regulators told other reporters trying to match Elise's story that they were starting their own investigation. Elise received a few congratulatory calls, though fewer than she would have expected. It was becoming obvious to her that the Canadian oilpatch was a tight shop that looked after its own.

Before she left for the day, Jim McKinnon called her from a bar.

"Great article," he said, sounding drunk, as voices laughed and shouted in the background. "I have a new respect for the press. Thanks for getting to the bottom of it. I have good news of my own. John Hess offered me a job. I'd been talking to him for a while about running the drilling program in his new oilsands company. He came through today."

"Congratulations," Elise said.

Then she connected the dots. "By the way, just for my own information, was he behind that folder?"

"No comment," Jim said, and hung up.

Chapter 17

By fall, rumours that Ladyfern was dying prematurely were all over the oilpatch. Plains was struggling to justify its expensive acquisition of Hunter and was hounded by the Peru fiasco. First Nations were blockading Ladyfern's drilling sites. Stone Petroleum, a small company that claimed Plains and other companies were syphoning gas from a part of the reservoir that was under its leases, had lawyered up and demanded billions in compensation.

For the first time since she rose to senior management, Susan Scott was worried about being fired. Her conversations with the board – which appointed new, less-friendly directors to replace the newly departed – were strained. David Anderson didn't help himself. He kept a low profile and took time off, claiming he was stressed out. He was mad at her, too, and blamed her for everything.

Susan knew she needed new stock-boosting strategies, fast, to rescue her year-end bonus and to change the conversation about Plains. There was still lots of appetite in the market for gas producers. North American deposits were running out and exploration was moving further afield to tough places like the Canadian Arctic. Plains had Canada's largest portfolio of easily accessible gas deposits, she regularly parroted to investors.

She decided to organize a series of safe meetings between her CEO and top market players, away from the press and uncomfortable questions. He would talk up the company's immense gas potential and multiple new gas opportunities thanks to the Hunter acquisition. Her key messages: Plains had learned its lessons, new directors were in charge, and its stock was a screaming buy.

She envisioned a lavish investor tour. It would be like old times. Toronto, New York, London. The best hotels. Unfettered access to the leadership team.

Planning for big-name guest speakers, special stationery, flower arrangements, corporate gifts, and evening entertainment, would start immediately. Even the fleet of corporate jets would be made available to transport key portfolio managers and investment analysts to Plains' kiss-and-make-up conferences.

"Call all my staff for a meeting," Susan asked her assistant. "We need excitement." Stock promotion had worked in the past and would work again, she convinced herself, and felt optimistic that the worst was behind her.

Her instincts were wrong. Plains' meetings were poorly attended. Investors told the company they were in a wait-and-see mode. They had lost trust in Plains for the time being and the smart money – their money – was going elsewhere. Other Canadian gas producers had less baggage, they said. Some were ripe for a big-premium takeover by a US company, which made them market darlings. They promised to take another look after the bad odour from the Peru scandal had abated.

Besides, there was this intriguing new play getting all the attention: the oilsands, they said.

"Do you have any exposure?" a pension fund manager asked David Anderson.

"No. It's a different industry. We don't have the expertise," he responded, wondering why Plains didn't. He was sure his company had leases in the area. Why didn't he have the right answers? He looked at his briefing materials. Nothing about the oilsands.

Chapter 18

MANHATTAN, NEW YORK, MARCH 2003

Oilsands. Elise was becoming well acquainted with the play. She had visited Alberta's northeast corner several times to size up the first big developments and interview the enthusiastic leaders who operated them. Their potential seemed to her extraordinary. The immense oil deposits mixed with sand sat just below the surface in a safe and friendly country. Advancements in technology made them economic to produce after years of trial and error. They were located next door to the largest oil market in the world. They had existing pipeline connections to refineries eager to turn them into oil products. She imagined what they could do for energy security, how they could change geopolitics, how they could change Canada.

The oilsands was also pulling John Hess back in her life. She hadn't spoken to him for almost a year. But she knew he was working on his startup and that he was one of the speakers at a conference in New York she was assigned to cover. It was one of the first organized by the Canadian industry to tell the world about the Alberta resource's potential and to raise money for development.

Her editor arranged her trip to get re-acquainted with the newsroom, and as a reward for her reporting – her Peru piece was up for a big writing award.

At the conference, Elise avoided John's talk and avoided him. She didn't like how he managed her, and his company was still private and too small to warrant coverage. There were more prominent oilsands leaders in attendance and she wanted to hear their stories.

But near the end of the day, after completing her work from a pressroom, she found him in a hallway, slumped in an armchair, alone, reading the *Journal*. She wondered if he'd parked there to run into her.

"How are you, Elise?" John said cheerfully as she walked by. "I heard you might be here. Do you have a minute?"

"Hi John. I am well. I just have a minute. My children are meeting me in the lobby. We have dinner plans."

"Yes, of course. I forgot this is your hometown. We have lots to talk about. My new company is getting off the ground nicely. We will go public soon. I'd like to give you a scoop."

Elise could tell he was uncomfortable asking for coverage and – almost – felt sorry for him. But she recalled how cleverly he manipulated her the first time they met and decided not to fall for it again.

She suspected his presentation had not received much attention. If it had, he would be cloistered in a room talking to potential investors. It must be tough for someone so used to being the main attraction to be pushed to the sidelines, she thought. But the market was brutal, especially for new companies, in any sector, trying to build a profile and raise money. It wasn't her job to rescue John Hess, she decided.

"What's the scoop?" she asked, hoping to deal with him quickly.

"It's several scoops, actually. Can I buy you lunch tomorrow?" John insisted.

"I have to work," Elise said. "This conference is intense. I need the lunch hour to write."

"How about dinner tomorrow night?" he proposed. "I'm staying here, too. I can meet you after you are done. The conference will be over by then and you won't have to worry about deadlines. I know a wonderful Italian restaurant near Central Park. You will love it."

Elise worried that meeting John for dinner would be a mistake but couldn't think of a good enough reason to say no. She had some down time before catching her flight back to Calgary the following day. She agreed, forgetting all her reservations about John, all her self-imposed boundaries, then rushed to meet her twins in the vast lobby.

Richard looked so much like his dad that Elise's heart stopped for a second. Simone was the female mirror image, except for the red hair, which was a shade lighter than her own.

"Hi Mom," they said in unison, then hugged her like they hadn't seen her for months, which was true. She was proud of them and was eager to get full updates on school.

From a corner where he could watch without being seen, John was moved – and jealous. The scene rekindled the void he often felt because he didn't have children of his own.

On the last day of the conference, Elise wrote a final piece on the key trends to watch. The event had been well organized but drew little interest. She reviewed coverage by competing media organizations. It was slim and cynical. One newspaper wrote off announcements about new Canadian oilsands projects as preposterous hype and unworthy of American cash, based on questionable reserve claims that no credible authority had backed up. America was so used to fighting wars for its oil that the idea of sourcing production from virtually unlimited reserves in neighbouring, law-abiding Canada was too good to be true, Elise heard from organizers, who were disappointed with the turnout.

John asked Elise to meet him at the restaurant. She wondered why he didn't ask her to walk there together, since they were staying at the same hotel. Could it be that John didn't want to be seen with her in public, even in a city like New York where they would both be lost in the crowd? Based on her previous experiences, she knew that was a possibility. The thought made her uncomfortable. Why the secrecy? She was a journalist for a huge news organization who met men and women in all sorts of places, all the time, to gather news.

But she played along and accepted that men like John hadn't figured out how to behave around professional women. Their instinct was to screw them in private and treat them like risky business in public.

She found Amalfi Trattoria – a small place she'd never been to before – and walked in. She was deliberately late. She wanted to let him know that she didn't care. John was waiting in a corner booth. The Neapolitan owner greeted her warmly once she was seated and offered them seafood appetizers.

"Hi Elise. I was beginning to worry that you got lost," John said.

"Apologies. I had a meeting in the newsroom. It took longer than expected. It's quite a hike to get here and traffic was bad."

"Ah. Let's order then," he said.

After the appetizers, they dug into their pastas and the awkwardness between them eased. John told her about his difficulties getting his new company off the ground. His leases were rich in oil and easily accessible with new extraction methods, but he needed more to justify the project he had in mind, so he'd spent a lot of time buying up all the adjacent land he could, he said. His management group was in place but staff in the remote area was hard to find. There was no housing and little infrastructure. The bigger companies were expanding rapidly and hiring everyone in sight. The good news was that Indigenous communities in the region were friendly and building businesses of their own to prepare themselves for the coming boom.

"Boom?" Elise asked. She hadn't heard that word before to describe the future of the oilsands.

"That's right. It's coming. That's what I wanted to talk to you about," John said.

"I have been to the main producing areas, but the industry still seems to be finding its feet," Elise said. "There is little infrastructure, and technology seems in its early days. Lots of claims are being made, but investors don't believe them – at least the ones I have talked to. They think the sector is too promotional and that too much money will be required to make it work. Plus, the environmental damage will be too big."

"The smart money is beginning to flow into the oilsands, but we need more because the investments required will be enormous," John said. "My company will be producing oil from the shallower areas. We will be mobilizing the oil by injecting steam and producing it the same way as conventional wells. It's far better than surface mining, which is how much of the extraction is being done, and which scars the landscape. Steam injection is the future. It's less harmful to the environment."

"I see. Why are there so few players, then? Why is there so much skepticism?" she asked.

"That's about to change. When it does, there will be a stampede. Three of the world's oil majors will announce oilsands projects before the end of year. We are talking dozens of billions in investment. You haven't heard it from me. But if you do your own research, you'll find out who they are.

"Also, the world's authority on oil reserves will recognize the oilsands for the first time, based on advancements in technology that make them economic to produce. This will change everything. They have done their homework and will give the oilsands the expert validation that they need."

"When will they do that?"

"It will happen this year, too. So, I will point you in the right direction to help you find out as much as you can. The next few months will bring the biggest investment rush that Canada has ever seen. And you can be the go-to journalist on the oilsands industry. I'll make sure you're in the know."

"That would be nice," Elise said. "And why are you telling me this?"

"I want to see this industry achieve its full potential, of course. But I also want to build the leading company. We'll have the best startup in a business of giants," the oilman boasted. "I'd love it if you could cover our IPO. I'll let you know when we are ready to go public."

"Fair deal," Elise said. This time, she thought, she would make sure she didn't give John free publicity until he gave her the goods he promised.

They left the restaurant in a good mood and walked on crowded sidewalks back to the hotel. They gossiped about the conference and people they both knew. Before they arrived, they bumped into a group from Elise's late-husband's hospital, including Dr. Jordan Black, a brain surgeon she'd known intimately. They'd travelled together many times, her with Julien, him with his wife, Mary, before Julien passed away.

"Oh my God, look at you!" Jordan said, checking her out with approval.

"Hi Jordan. It's so good to see you. Dr. Black, this is John Hess, an oilman from Calgary I just interviewed," she said. Tall, with curly blond hair, her old friend looked handsome in his business suit. He seemed more confident than the man who often seemed overshadowed by her late husband, she thought.

"Pleased to meet you," Jordan said, shaking John's hand.

But Jordan couldn't resist taking a shot at the expensively groomed executive standing beside Elise. "No offense to you guys in Canada, but I am not a fan of the industry. I just can't understand why we can't use cleaner energy. Oil makes us sick in so many ways. Look at all this pollution." He pointed to the heavy traffic around them puffing exhaust.

"The medical industry couldn't function without fossil fuels," John responded coolly. "Be careful what you wish for."

Elise suddenly recalled that Jordan was an environmental activist who sat on the board of a big foundation and quickly jumped in to change the conversation. "Speaking of traffic, how's life in the big city?" she asked.

"Same old, same old. We just finished a conference."

"How's Mary?" Elise asked.

"You haven't heard? She left me. Took a job in California, teaching at Berkeley. We don't have children, as you know, so it was an easy split. We are good friends. I have been on my own for a year now.

"And how about you?" Jordan continued. "I have always wanted to visit the Canadian Rockies. In fact, I'm going to Banff for a conference this summer, then I'll drive to Jasper, check out that parkway between the glaciers, and maybe do some hiking in the mountains. It'll be nice to breathe clean air for a change."

"Then you have to come and see me," Elise proposed. "You will have to fly to Calgary to get to Banff. I'd be happy to show you around."

"Sure thing," Jordan said. "I'll let you know when I finalize my plans."

John kept to himself as they resumed their walk. The chance encounter shook him. He didn't like the way the doctor put him on the spot. It was obvious he didn't know much about energy, never mind oil and gas, yet felt compelled to lecture him, an oilman, about why oil was bad. It was typical of the moral superiority John was encountering more and more from the anti-fossil-fuel crowd. It got under his skin.

But he was also jealous. The handsome doctor seemed to make a play for Elise. She was a desirable, accomplished, single woman who'd appeal to any successful man, John realized.

They entered the hotel elevator and noticed their rooms – an executive suite for him, a basic room for her – were on the same floor, though in different wings.

"Good night, then," John said after they exited the elevator, looking at her with desire.

"Good night," Elise responded. She saw the look but ignored it. "See you in Calgary. I'll call you." She wanted John to know she was taking charge of the relationship.

Chapter 19

FORT McMURRAY, ALBERTA, MAY 2003

There are two ways to look at the oilsands, Elise thought during a helicopter ride over the deposit-rich region as she took in a panoramic view of gigantic mining-and-oil upgrading operations spread out below. They are a triumph of man over nature for the betterment of humanity. Or they are a terrible example of man's destruction of nature to satisfy his greed. Like two sides of the same coin, both are true, neither is the whole truth.

As the helicopter's blades gripped the air, which was mercifully warm for spring in the North, Elise thought she'd seen both sides of that coin in other aspects of the oil and gas business and felt both views had merit. But the oilsands were so big and so concentrated in Northern Alberta that they magnified both the good and the bad. She wondered if they would become a battleground between two opposing views of the earth's future – one supporting progress, the other preservation.

Elise jumped off the helicopter at the end of the tour and fixed on the task at hand. She was among half a dozen reporters handpicked to write about and photograph the newest plant. The visit was organized by one of the world's largest oil companies to publicize the official start of its oilsands business. It was its first big investment in the new industry, and there were high hopes it would lead to more.

Elise knew that on this celebratory day only one side of that coin, the good one, would be on display. She agreed to participate because she wanted to witness and report what she saw, without judgement, and create a record for all to know.

She couldn't help being impressed by the resourcefulness of so many people – thousands – to make the project come alive, with all those moving parts, huffing and puffing in the wild, so barrels of oil could be squeezed from bituminous sands in one of the most remote regions on earth to produce energy from the new resource.

Workers had come from all over the world to make it happen, lured by high salaries, for sure, but also by the challenge. It took decades, all hands on deck and technology leaps to build the engineering marvel that stood before her, and to make it all work at a profit.

That was the real turning point – that the oilsands could finally be produced at a profit. Profitable oil was no longer a monopoly of the OPEC cartel. Canada could do it in big volumes, too. Nothing wrong with that, Elise thought. The investments came from private companies that figured out how to do it and deserved a return for taking the risk.

The plant-opening celebration was held in a vast dining area where workers ordinarily took their meals or entertained themselves at the end of their shifts, far away from their loved ones, and often, their countries.

In addition to the media, there were proud politicians with dollar signs in their eyes who wanted a quick ramp-up of the industry, before other oil deposits, perhaps cheaper and more accessible, were discovered elsewhere in the world.

Speeches started during lunch. Brass from the International Oil Company had come all the way from European headquarters to make sure their cash and expertise were well spent, to take credit for the work, and to thank all those who played a role.

With their foreign accents, they praised Indigenous leaders for the many services they provided, including catering and land removal. They applauded some friendly environmentalists for improving operations with their ideas, which, they said, demonstrated that the business was open to all points of view.

Then the project manager, a Canadian, took the podium. He said his company's operation was a big improvement over the facilities built by industry pioneers. The first was funded with American money and started in the 1960s. Then a second and a third were built. But it was tough slugging, and there were expensive accidents that almost shut the oilsands down. Technologies were developed to cut costs so the oilsands could compete with other oil sources, particularly those from the Middle East, where oil could be pumped from the ground with little effort and little cost. Advancements would continue, the executive promised, as more new technologies were integrated.

He explained that in his project, big shovels scooped oil-soaked ore from an open-pit mine, loaded it on giant trucks that transported it through a maze of muddy pathways, and deposited it near a processing plant, where bitumen was separated from the sand using hot water, then upgraded so it could be moved on pipelines. Liquid waste was piped into tailings ponds. Everything was synchronized to work around the clock so the plant could reach its daily production quota and the company could meet its quarterly expectations.

A press briefing with the foreign CEO, a celebrity in his home country, was next. Elise was rounded up with the rest of the press. She had always disliked the media handling that came with such events, but it was part of the job and a condition of gaining access to corporate leaders.

"How long will it take to ramp up to full capacity?" she asked the CEO.

"It will take about six months to a year. We are taking our time to ensure everything works as it should," the well-briefed leader responded as photographers snapped photos. He was sporting company-sanctioned attire: khakis, a windbreaker, steel-toed boots, a hardhat with the company logo, and safety glasses in his pocket.

"Are you planning to expand further?" another reporter asked.

"Yes, but we will do it through debottlenecking first – it means we will increase production by making our facility work harder. Next, we will build a new mine. We have big plans for Canada. We can increase our production five-fold over the next decade. It's a safe place to do business and we like the government's stability."

"That's a lot of oil for just one company," Elise argued. "Only very large fields can produce that much."

"The oilsands are so large they can support that and more," the CEO bragged. "There's so much oil buried beneath the surface in the region surrounding Fort McMurray that it could end US dependency on Middle Eastern regimes for dozens of years," he said.

Then, from a table in the dining hall, Elise wrote a straight-up story, capturing the highlights of the day, with a large aerial photograph of the new plant and of the celebrity oil leader. Both ran on the *Journal*'s front page, and jolted the skeptics, and the world.

Chapter 20

WASHINGTON, DC, JUNE 2003

The Save the Climate campaign called an urgent meeting to be held at its DC headquarters to discuss the oilsands. It summoned the few environmental activists it funded in Canada, including Erika Bernstein, to attend.

"Why did we not know about this?" Barb Heinz asked. She was the coalition's executive director, a Yale Law graduate with political aspirations. She pointed to multiple copies of Elise's story strewn on the boardroom table, as well as other news and financial analyst reports, all exalting the resource's extraordinary potential to meet rising global oil demand – and rescue the world from peak oil.

Tall and attractive, with round, gold-rimmed glasses, she had the resumé to build a powerful career in one of the blue-chip law firms or policy think tanks surrounding the Capitol. Instead, she chose to make her mark as an activist in the green movement. She was all about following the money, and the greens were flush with cash from high-profile, deep-pocketed donors. Some were big polluters with guilty consciences who were looking for ways to clear their names. Some were impatient to get their green-energy investments to pay off. Others were oil people who wanted to knock down competitors to improve their profits in any way they could.

Barb was convinced that activism was the new fast track to political leadership. Activism and politics were similar in many ways: building war chests, mobilizing the masses, collecting data on opponents, making connections, developing public policy. Unlike politics, activism didn't require compromise. It was about finding the right pressure points to move the powerful to act.

Besides, Barb was hardly roughing it at Save the Climate. The headquarters where she worked were modern, well equipped, airy, teeming with ambitious young bodies eager to remake the world to fit their own image of justice. From their cubicles, they raised funds, organized protests, and supported campaigns of like-minded political candidates at all levels, so they were forever beholden to her organization. Meanwhile, salaries were competitive, and large bonuses were paid for successful fundraising.

Until now, Save the Climate had regarded the oilsands the same way as most people in DC regarded Canada – inconsequential. Most couldn't name Canada's prime minister or capital city, never mind understand its oil and gas sector. It was news to many Americans that Canada was quickly replacing the Saudis as America's top source of oil.

"The oilsands, if they are indeed as big as advertised, will undermine our efforts to curb fossil fuels," the activist leader said, addressing the group from the head of a boardroom table.

"These deposits could set us back decades in our quest to transition to renewable energy. We can't allow this new oil to be produced right in our backyard if we want our presidential campaign to be taken seriously and our donors to keep funding us."

Erika was disappointed that Barb, her boss, was out of touch with her work, but smelled an opportunity to get the recognition she'd always wanted. She'd campaigned for years on shoestring budgets. She knew she'd done a heck of a job pushing Plains out of Peru. She could do it again on a much larger scale north of the border.

"We developed a very successful model," Erika said, "first in Peru and then in Western Canada, to fight oil and gas development by aligning our movement with local people, particularly Indigenous people, who are concerned about losing their way of life. In Western Canada, we already have solid and effective alliances to frustrate oil and gas activity, mostly in the natural gas side of the business, and to push for new environmental regulation. We have made some progress.

"We have not focused on the oilsands – yet – because they are in another league. We don't have the money, nor the staff, to take them on. The green movement in Canada is small, fractured, and willing to cooperate with the oil companies. Big Oil is moving in. They are spending billions. They have armies of lawyers. They're tight with governments and are not as easily obstructed."

"What would it take to derail the oilsands?" Barb asked, impressed by her foot soldier's knowledge.

"What we have been doing, times ten. Putting our own people in positions of influence. Hiring lawyers to fight regulatory approvals. Causing reputational damage so investors pull out. We need to disrupt their plans and increase their costs. It's a high-cost resource already, and it won't be hard to make it uneconomic. But we are talking big efforts and big money," Erika suggested, her voice rising.

Ed Wolf, one of the Canadian activists, was alarmed by what he was hearing. He said he had advised oilsands companies for years to improve environmental performance, not to shut them down. He considered them partners. He knew the business inside out and saw the benefits of the industry for his country. He knew the environmental impacts could be reduced as the industry matured. As far as he was concerned, Erika, an American, was advocating a style of activism that Canadians would find offensive.

"What you are talking about goes too far," Ed argued. "Canada is a sovereign country and a US ally and top trading partner. You are talking about meddling in Canadian politics and regulation. Canadians are already fed up with American interference. This campaign could backfire – badly – if it's seen as American intrusion into a Canadian industry."

Erika was unconvinced. "The fight against fossil fuels transcends borders and national governments. It's the fight of our generation, just like the civil rights movement was the fight of our parents' generation. Sure, Canada is a sovereign country, but so was South Africa. It took international pressure to force South Africa to stop apartheid. This is no different. Canada can be on the right side of history and shut down this dirty oil, and do its part for the climate, or it will become a pariah state. We could make it a pariah state."

"Yes, this is different," Ed said, resenting the lecturing. "Oilsands development is not apartheid. It's an industry that benefits many in the North, including Indigenous people. Canada has the best energy regulation in the world. Canadian companies are responsible operators and are receptive to ideas to improve. If you want to curb fossil fuels, you need to go after the big producers, the ones who don't care about pollution, like Saudi Arabia,

Russia, even China. Venezuela has similar deposits of heavy oil and shows no respect for the environment."

"True," Erika said. "But we can't get into those countries. We have tried. Our activists are languishing in their jails. We can get into Canada. Canadian companies can be pressured because they need market support to fund their programs and they fear bad publicity. Campaigns against the Saudis, or the Russian, or the Venezuelans aren't as effective because their oil companies are state controlled, and there could be messy political repercussions for the US. We can target the Canadian oil industry instead and hold them out as an example of what happens when fossil-fuel polluters go too far. Look at how Plains handled their assets in Peru. They caved in no time. They sold at a loss and left with their tails between their legs. The Canadians are a soft target.

"There is another advantage," Erika added. "The oilsands are ugly to look at and can be easily photographed. We can't do that in other places. Besides, the Canadian oil industry exports exclusively to the United States and has large American ownership. It's a legitimate target for our movement. There wouldn't be a Canadian oilsands industry without American customers and investors."

The more she heard, the more Barb Heinz imagined a fundraising juggernaut. A campaign against the oilsands could resonate around the world. The oilsands could be made the poster child for all that was wrong with fossil fuels. The industry could be flooded with controversy and held up as a cautionary tale for anyone planning to increase oil production.

"Let's put together as much information as we can," Barb said to the group. "We need first-rate intelligence about the oilsands, how they are produced, how the Canadian regulatory system works, how the oil is transported to the United States, whether we can build political alliances. Give me a strategy. I'll take care of the funding. We'll call this new campaign The Canada Project."

Ed said he could not support the campaign and walked out.

Barb asked Erika to take charge. The other activists were told to report to her if they wanted funding from Save the Climate to continue.

The meeting adjourned with a promise to regroup in six months. Barb offered some preliminary cash to bolster staff and research.

Barb returned to her office and dialed Dr. Jordan Black, an influential member of her board of directors.

"Hi Jordan, I need a favour," she said.

"Sure. Anything for the cause," he said.

"You mentioned in the past that you know Elise Chamonter, the *Journal* reporter."

"She's an old friend. Her late husband and I worked together."

"She's one of the key reporters in Western Canada covering the oil and gas sector," Barb said. "We need her on our side."

"Elise has a mind of her own," Jordan replied. "She is a very good writer for the world's top business newspaper. She knows about my views on the environment, so we avoid the subject altogether. She's important to me, and I don't want to spoil our friendship."

"How about you arrange an introduction? We need to know what she knows and make sure she is exposed to the full range of views on the oil-sands," Barb proposed.

The doctor agreed to try. He'd already made plans to meet Elise in Calgary in August. He told Barb he would ask her then.

Chapter 21

CALGARY, ALBERTA, JULY 2003

By mid-summer, oilsands-related announcements were coming fast and furious, and Elise and her growing team of reporters were covering every angle. As John had predicted, more of the oil majors announced multi-billion oilsands plans, while international energy experts recognized the oilsands for the first time in their influential accounting of remaining world oil reserves, crediting advancements in technology that, at long last, made the deposits economic to produce. It meant that Canada surged in their rankings to second top oil reserve holder in the world, just behind the kingdom of Saudi Arabia, which has immense deposits of conventional oil, and followed by the Bolivarian Republic of Venezuela, which has similarly abundant deposits of heavy oil. In fourth place was the Islamic Republic of Iran, which also had big reserves of heavy oil. Saudi Arabia, Venezuela, and Iran, all members of OPEC, had used oil as a weapon against the West. Financial analysts gushed that Canada alone in that elite oil group stood for democracy, rule of law, political stability, and respect for the environment.

Canada's meteoric rise as an oil power was so sudden most Canadians didn't know what hit them, Elise summed up to her editors in their daily phone calls to discuss news leads. Because the country's oil bounty was far away from the centres of power in Toronto, Montreal, Ottawa, and Vancouver, many outside Alberta shrugged off the whole thing as unacceptable. They saw the oilsands as a gift they had no use for, a wealth creator out of step with Canadian values, a smoke-stack industry that would stain Canada's international image as a clean and progressive country.

So, what if Canada made it to the big leagues of oil producing nations? In the minds of many Canadians, Elise explained, oil was a dirty word, the Alberta-based oilsands industry was a backward step, and Albertans were the embarrassing cousins of the Canadian confederation for embracing such a dirty business.

Calgary was so accustomed to being diminished by Canada's big thinkers the city couldn't care less, Elise said to her bosses. It was busier and richer than ever. Money was flowing in from abroad to pay for corporate takeovers, new partnerships, drilling projects, pipelines. Armies of oil executives, from Norway to China, the US to France, were flying in to get a piece of the new oil bounty, knocking on all the right doors and dangling billions in cash, hoping it would save them – and their careers – from the end of oil.

The oil-hungry visitors gladly traded their stuffy suits for jeans and cowboy hats and boozed up at the Calgary Stampede, like teenagers getting their first taste of freedom. Indeed, the foreigners confided to Elise, the oilsands freed them from the tyranny of oil exploration and expensive dry holes because the deposits were so bountiful and ready to be produced. Meanwhile, the more they looked around, the more they were attracted by the city's high standard of living, the free health care, the high-quality public education, the safe and clean neighborhoods, the restaurants serving Alberta beef, the unspoiled mountain playgrounds a short drive away. They told her that next to the backwaters where their oil companies usually operated, in partnership with regimes they abhorred, Calgary felt safe. They did their deals, signed leases for office space in new glass towers, bought expensive homes, and moved their families to the Western Canadian city. They supported the arts, joined golf courses, took up skiing, and sent their kids to summer camps in the mountains.

In all its history, Calgary – and Alberta – had never seen so much wealth, so many plans to create more. Over the years, the city had experienced more than its share of booms and busts, but this time everyone was convinced it was different.

The world was running out of oil, Alberta had billions of barrels in its basement, and everyone – including the Easterners who looked down on Alberta and its questionable oil – was invited to move west and get rich.

A year and a half after selling Hunter, splitting off its oilsands leases and placing them in Aurora Oil Sands, John Hess was back where he wanted to be.

His piece of the oilsands had a big new advantage, he said to investors who supported him in the past. The deposits were located deeper below the surface than the mining projects to the north. He would use more advanced technology than the trucks and shovels used in mining operations, which meant less land disturbance, less energy use, and lower costs.

He told them he was more motivated than ever to build another successful company. He expected it would be his last. Aurora would be his legacy. They opened their wallets; confident John Hess would deliver again.

He didn't tell them he planned to cash out at the right time and enjoy life, travel a bit, perhaps, maybe seek higher office in politics or near political power. Nor that he was finally the majority owner of his company – without his wife's money. He paid back every cent he owed her and her parents after selling Hunter, making them richer than they had ever been – and freeing him from family obligations.

None of this had anything to do with the state of his marriage. He was content with his relationship with Claire, for now, even if it meant continuing to complement it with flings on the side. He started an affair with another woman, a married banker he knew, after his encounters with Elise. Claire seemed pleased, too, to have a rich and handsome husband who was the envy of her social circle, even one as unfaithful as John. She liked her lifestyle and looked forward to an even better one. Now that she was independently rich, she funded ventures of her own. She started planning the luxurious hotel in Calgary's downtown she always wanted, where the city's expanding class of super rich could party in style.

John's vision for his final act was ambitious. It required some of his own capital – and much more from investors. He'd seen too many of his peers lose everything by putting on the line their entire fortunes rather than invite partners to share both upside and downside. One of his mantras was that really big wealth was built with other people's money. He was living proof.

John had found enough private capital to help him buy oilsands leases and rent new offices in downtown Calgary. They were more spacious and more expensive than his old ones and had the feel of a hip technology startup, which it was, because so much of his oilsands business relied on new technology. The light wood furniture was imported from Sweden. The peasant-inspired art was from Central America. Potted plants were arranged on top of each other to create a wall of cascading leaves and exotic flowers. Espresso machines dripped coffees with rich aromas.

But he needed much more money. He wanted his new company to compete with the best. He considered some options: go public, sell a piece to a major investor, partner with another company.

Other options, perhaps some he hadn't thought about, were open, too. That was another of John's mantras, in business and in life: keep all options open. Many of his Calgary peers felt the same way. It had become part of the corporate culture. What it really meant was that John never stood for something or committed to anything or anybody that could keep him from pursuing a better option. Some would have called him an opportunist, untrustworthy, unreliable, because he was always looking for the next shiny thing. John didn't see it that way. He believed flexibility was necessary for survival, in business as in life. He'd seen too many changes – political, financial, technological – to risk too much by hitching his wagon to the wrong horse with no escape plan.

A major American oil refiner got his attention. The company was planning to pull out of Venezuela's heavy oil business – the thug who led the country was changing too many terms, the refiner complained to him. The Canadian oilsands looked like a picnic in comparison because of its stable politics and reasonable regulations, the American told him. John suggested they meet.

As John thought about his next steps, he thought about Elise. He missed her. He knew he was getting older. He felt his life was incomplete. That scene in New York, when he saw Elise happy with her children, had stuck with him. I will never experience that, he thought. He regretted not returning her calls in the past. He wondered why she hadn't contacted him lately. He worried she was no longer available to him if he wanted her.

He secretly read all her stories as soon as they were published. He worried that she had replaced him with others – analysts, other corporate leaders, politicians. He saw it in her work. He longed for her attention and even her approval. He'd heard somewhere that the benefit of marriage was that spouses were witnesses to each other's lives. He'd never had that kind of connection with Claire. He had felt it with Elise.

But he had to be realistic, under the circumstances. A relationship was out of the question. He knew there was gossip about him and the *Journal* reporter. It puzzled him. No one in his circles was concerned about his extramarital affairs, but his relationship with Elise, or whatever it was, was seen as inappropriate.

"She's press, be careful," one of his lawyers had warned him. "She'll do anything for a scoop. Besides, she's not one of us."

But he needed her to succeed so he could succeed. His corporate growth strategy counted on Elise's supportive stories about the oilsands. Her coverage was widely read and copied. She was the leader in her space. "The trend is your friend," he liked to say, and he believed that increasing awareness about the oilsands among *Journal* readers would promote market interest and result in the highest possible value for his company.

He would create an opportunity to reconnect with her, he decided, perhaps a tour of his new operations to showcase his new and revolutionary oilsands technology to investors. He envisioned a big reveal, with lots of hype and the right people.

He knew he could charm Elise to achieve the most favourable coverage. He'd done it before with Ladyfern, he'd done it to increase her interest in the oilsands, and he could do it again to promote his new company. Yes, that was the way to go. The road to Aurora's success involved Elise, and he would take it.

Chapter 22

CALGARY, ALBERTA, AUGUST 2003

Elise asked for permission to take a few days off work. Jordan was flying to Calgary, and she wanted to keep her promise to show him around. They agreed to meet in the arrivals area of the city's international airport. He had told her he had a business commitment for a day in Banff, where he was the keynote speaker at a medical conference on brain injuries. But he was free after that and planned to spend a couple of weeks hiking in the Canadian Rockies.

He invited Elise to join him for a drive to Jasper, an experience he'd looked forward to for years. He'd even booked a suite in a famous lodge near Jasper, on the shore of an idyllic lake, where decades ago his parents had celebrated their honeymoon.

Elise agreed to go for the drive but wasn't sure about the rest. She'd always liked Jordan. He was crazy smart and, like so many New Yorkers, adaptable to any environment, urban and otherwise. Julien had introduced Jordan to the mountains. The two had often disappeared for days meandering in the Swiss Alps, sleeping in rustic chalets. Elise had never thought of Jordan in a romantic way. Julien had been her superstar. But Julien was long gone, and she missed having a life partner.

She suspected Jordan, now that he was single, was ready for a relationship, but also that he would take his time to find the right person. She sensed that he knew that she was still coming to terms with Julien's death. At best, her and Jordan could rekindle their friendship.

Then he appeared on the other side of a glass wall. After clearing customs and picking up his bags, Jordan walked through a pair of heavy sliding doors, spotted her in the waiting crowd, and rushed toward her. Elise felt a jolt for the first time since that moment with John Hess. She realized she was reconnecting with a man who, more than anyone, had shared a big part of her past and, she was sure, would never take advantage of her. Dressed in frayed jeans and a light-blue cotton sweater, he was handsome. She embraced him and kissed him on both cheeks as the waiting crowd looked approvingly at them.

"I am so glad we made this happen," Jordan said, admiring Elise, who was still wearing her work clothes – a breezy linen suit. "This place has been on my to-do list for a long time. I heard so much about it from my parents. They loved the wide-open spaces, the fresh air, and those beautiful, unspoiled mountains."

"Yes, this place grows on you," Elise said, blushing as he grabbed her hand, feeling his energy run through her. "I wasn't sure what to expect when I moved here. Then I discovered its beauty and fell in love with it. In some ways it's the opposite of New York – sparsely populated, natural, clean. In others it's the same – industrious, high achieving, wealthy."

"You sound like someone who is here to stay," Jordan said.

"I like it so far," Elise said. "I don't have a long-term life plan for now. The *Journal* is fully committed to expanding our presence in this area. In fact, my editors are talking about hiring even more people in Calgary, perhaps establishing a world oil desk here. Our readership is expanding, and it's been very interesting."

"I was hoping to convince you to move back to New York," Jordan said. "We miss you there. You've been away too long. I meet with your children once in a while. They have their own lives, but they'd like you to be closer."

"Yes, I know. I miss them too. But we see each other during school breaks and talk on the phone a lot. They'll come for a visit later this month. They love the mountains, too. Besides, they are both hoping to move to Boston soon – if they get into Harvard for their graduate studies."

"Elise, I miss you too," Jordan revealed, shyly, as they walked, still hand in hand, through the parking lot. The words, and his sincerity, surprised her. She didn't know what to say. She didn't expect it. Jordan seemed to want to make the transition from friendship to romance. She didn't know if she was ready.

Elise took the wheel of her new Subaru, an SUV crowned by a well-loved ski rack, and reset the conversation. "The weather forecast for the next two weeks is glorious. At least 30 Celsius and not a cloud in the sky," she said. "You'll be experiencing Alberta at its best, promise. You are staying at the Grand downtown, right?"

"Yes, I'm booked there for the night. I'm going to Banff tomorrow afternoon," Jordan said.

"When would you like me to meet you in Banff?" Elise asked.

"How about Saturday morning? That will give us time to drive to Jasper, take breaks along the way, and check in by dinnertime."

"I'm looking forward to it," Elise said. "I have never been to Jasper. It's a bit out of the way for Calgarians, who tend to go to the mountains near Banff, which are so much closer, or south to Waterton, across from Montana. But I've heard lots about Jasper. There are many glaciers along the parkway, and they are receding quickly. They say it's because of climate change, but many people here dispute that. There are people in Calgary who work in oil and gas and will tell you everything you ever wanted to know about rocks and ice ages. They say glaciers have come and gone many times through history, and this is no different."

"Well, I disagree," Jordan said. "There's overwhelming evidence that the climate is changing because of greenhouse gases from growing fossil fuel use. The retreat of glaciers is a wakeup call that we've gone too far. We are destroying our planet."

"I'm open to all views," Elise said as they arrived at the hotel, preferring not to get into an argument with her friend about something that was already so divisive.

"Thanks so much for coming to pick me up. Do you have dinner plans?" Jordan asked. "I would be honoured if you could join me for dinner."

"Yes, I would love that. In fact, I was going to ask you, too. How about I drop you off and we meet in the lobby of your hotel in an hour? I'd like to change my clothes. I came directly from work."

"Great. That will give me time to unpack and make some calls. See you in a bit," Jordan said.

Elise went back to her place, took a quick shower, and put on a silky summer dress, a reminder of a trip to Italy. A turquoise broach she purchased in Camogli was still pinned on it and took her back to the Ligurian coast, where only a decade ago she celebrated Julien's fortieth birthday on the terrace of an old villa they had rented for a few days. Life was perfect then. So perfect she kept wondering why she'd been so blessed. Then it changed without warning.

Elise's thoughts returned to Calgary, where the sun was still shining brightly in the warm evening sky. Jordan's *I miss you* lingered like an unsent message. She still didn't know what to say. She was afraid of being hurt again. She no longer knew how to respond to a man courting her. Her experience with John had been such a failure that she had shut off that part of herself.

Jordan changed into khakis and a light, soft-leather blazer. His handcrafted glasses and a vintage watch, a gift from Julien, completed the look.

They found each other in the elegant hotel lobby and, once again, Elise liked what she saw. There was a bit of Julien in him – good-looking and accomplished, yet unaware of his attractiveness. They embraced again and headed toward a steakhouse nearby, which was highly recommended by the hotel.

After they were seated, Elise noticed the watch.

"We're both wearing reminders of Julien," Elise said. "I bought this broach with him. You're wearing the watch he gave you. I feel like he's sitting here between us."

"Elise, I know you miss Julien," Jordan said. "I miss him too. He was my best friend and the best colleague I ever had. But I haven't stopped thinking about you since we ran into each other in New York. When Mary left me, she accused me of being in love with you. I thought it was an absurd statement, but when I was back on my own, and had lots of time to think, I realized she was right. I have been in love with you for a long time. I know this is a lot to take in, so I don't expect you to respond. Just give me a chance in the next few days. I need to know if there could be a future for us."

Elise looked at Jordan in a new light. She had no idea he'd had feelings for her. What a cliché, she thought. Man falls in love with his best friend's wife. She'd hung around enough doctors to know they tended to pair up with others in the medical profession or related fields. Journalists were not first choices. Julien had stepped way out of his comfort zone when he courted and then married her. Dear Julien. He liked medicine, but was just as keenly interested in everything else, too, from politics to the arts, travel to science. He had told Elise he loved her because he felt she truly completed him.

"I appreciate your candour," Elise said. "Julien was my universe. His loss left me devastated and empty. I'm still coming to terms with it. When he died, I didn't think I could ever love again. But being single is hard. I am a strong person, yet I feel so unmoored. I am very fond of you, and I am glad to see you. Let's have a great few days and see where it takes us."

Jordan smiled. He felt encouraged.

They feasted on Alberta beef and a full-bodied Syrah. They talked about their New York friends, life at the hospital, and life at the *Journal*; the good and the bad of their careers.

"Julien left a huge hole at the hospital," Jordan said. "The staff was distraught for weeks. We recruited two top people to replace him, but they will never measure up. I was promoted last year," he added, proudly. "I am the new head of my department. I like being a doctor, but I enjoy leading a team, too."

Elise spoke about her new job, why she enjoyed her new beat, why she accepted the move to Calgary, and her career prospects.

After the meal, Jordan walked Elise to her apartment building and hugged her affectionately again. "See you in Banff?" he asked.

"It's a date," she said, feeling drawn to the caring man who held her hand.

The next day at the office a phone message was waiting for Elise. John had left a voicemail the evening before when she was dining with Jordan. What a coincidence, she thought. John and Jordan crossing paths, and her path, again.

"Hi Elise. We haven't spoken for a while. I was wondering if you have time to meet. I have news for you. I promise it'll be worth your time. Please call me back."

Curious, she dialed John's number and got his assistant, who told her the boss was in the office but unavailable. Elise left a message. She knew she wouldn't hear from him for days and didn't care. She'd done her part.

His patterns were now familiar to her: he reached out, waited for her to respond, then went silent. It was some kind of power play, she realized. She didn't understand it, and it irritated her. In the past, she took offense. She thought he was manipulative, like he loved to bait her, then string her along to re-enforce he was in control. Now she refused to let it bother her.

She turned her attention to a big political event she needed to cover at the other end of downtown. To avoid hearing from John, she drove there, then completed her work from home, away from her business phone and from his games. It was her way of winning her power back. Power that was not given could not be taken away.

Chapter 23

BANFF AND JASPER, ALBERTA, AUGUST 2003

The next day, Elise left bright and early. She looked and felt young in her favourite black jeans, tight t-shirt, and a high ponytail that tidied her thick ginger mane. She stuffed casual outfits, hiking gear, and pajamas in an overnight bag.

As early as it was when she hit the road, traffic on the TransCanada Highway was already building up. Vehicles loaded with canoes, mountain bikes, and children were rushing west toward the mountain peaks. Driving into Banff an hour and a half later, she noticed groups of tourists walking up and down Banff Avenue, taking in the fresh air and the rising sun, or watching people from busy outdoor cafes. Souvenir shops were already overflowing with Asian tourists purchasing expensive furs, mountain gear, and big sweaters they would never wear.

Elise parked her car on the street near Jordan's hotel, a landmark modelled after a Scottish castle, where she had agreed to meet him. She found him in the imposing stone-walled lobby, holding court with a group of attractive women, and felt a bit jealous. But she wanted to be happy for him. His talk had obviously been well received and he deserved the attention.

Jordan saw her, hugged her, and introduced her to one of the women.

"Elise, this is Barb Heinz, who heads the Save the Climate campaign. I am on the board of her group," Jordan said. "Barb, this is Elise, my dear friend and the *Journal*'s correspondent in Western Canada, based in Calgary."

Elise shook the woman's hand and immediately wondered what was going on. She knew Barb Heinz by reputation. Barb was connected somehow to Erika Bernstein, the activist Elise had clashed with in the past. What was Barb Heinz doing in Alberta, currently, with Jordan? Elise wondered.

Barb took charge of the conversation and asked Elise about her job, whether she liked the area, and her beat.

"I like it a lot. There's lots to report on and we have a growing readership," Elise said. "Canadian oil and gas are a big deal these days in the market. All the global oil players are moving here, so investors are tuned in."

"You should hear the other side of the story, then," Barb proposed.

"Is there one?" Elise asked.

"Of course. All this new development will set us back decades in our goals to reduce global greenhouse gas emissions. We need to stop it."

"Canada is still a small producer. The oilsands industry is in its infancy," Elise argued, a bit put off by the woman's forwardness. She hated being accosted by interest groups outside of work.

"Canada can become a big problem if all these oilsands projects go ahead," Barb continued, ignoring that Elise looked uncomfortable. "We need more green energy, not more of this dirty oil. I'd be happy to discuss this further with you. Are you available to chat?"

"Yes, of course," Elise said politely, wanting to disengage. "After my holiday?" The women exchanged phone numbers and agreed to reconnect.

Elise then turned her attention to Jordan and reminded him it was time to go. Her reporter's instincts suggested she'd been set up. Did Jordan have a hand in it? She walked with him to her car, which they agreed to take for the drive to Jasper.

"What was that all about?" she asked him.

"Sorry to ambush you like that," Jordan said, coming clean. "Barb happened to be in Banff too, and we agreed to meet for coffee this morning before my talk. She is a fan of your work and asked to be introduced. I hope it's okay. She's a terrific lady and has done a lot for the cause. She's here for a strategy session about coordinating her campaign with local groups. I don't know much about it. We don't get that close to day-to-day operations on the board. We mostly raise funds and open doors. But I think you should follow up with her. She's a real powerhouse in Washington, and she will be a great resource for you."

"I see. Of course. I haven't had good experiences with environmentalists – they don't like writers like me, since I don't buy their exaggerations about looming climate catastrophe – but I am always happy to listen. I agree, however, they are a big part of the story and that they could do a lot of damage. Investors need to know the risks of these types of campaigns."

"Let's talk about what's really important," Jordan said. "Are you excited about Jasper?"

"Yes," Elise said. "How long are you planning to be there?"

"A week, then I'll see. Banff looks spectacular, too. I might come back here for a while. I plan to do as many hiking trails as I can. You should come with me."

"I can hang out for a few days. I must go back to work!"

"I'll take whatever time you can give me," Jordan said, taking her hand as they walked back to her car.

They drove slowly through Banff and returned to the highway, then aimed west. They passed Lake Louise, another mountain paradise, then took the turnoff to the Icefields Parkway and headed north.

Soon they were encountering emerald-tinted lakes, thick evergreen forests, rugged mountain peaks, wide river valleys and, soaring above them, the glaciers. White, with hints of green and blue, the walls of ice sparkled like crystals against the clear sky. Elise and Jordan were so excited that they stopped in a rest area to take it all in. They saw a grizzly bear barreling down a slope with a cub in tow. The bears stopped in a grassy clearing and laid down on their backs, scratching themselves on the grass and ignoring the visitors and their cameras.

"This is the most beautiful place I have ever seen," Elise said, pleased with the bear sighting.

"Yes, it takes your breath away," Jordan said, then took Elise's face in his hands and kissed her. "And this is the most beautiful woman I have ever seen."

Elise realized she liked the man. She felt ready for more.

Jordan took the wheel of her car, and they continued the drive north, arriving at the Columbia Icefield. They parked at the toe of the receding glacier and stepped outside, then walked uphill on a rocky trail that took them close to the heap of ice straddling the Continental Divide. Markers of the glacier's retreat over the last century were displayed prominently. Jordan was disturbed by the extent of the glacier's shrinkage.

"This is a frightening example of what we are doing to the planet," he said. "How can Albertans be so blind to the damage they are causing by supporting so much unwanted oil industry growth?"

"That's one way of looking at it," Elise said with an edge to her voice. "Here's a different view: the glacier was shrinking long before fossil fuels were widely used, and no one with so much oil would leave it in the ground. Besides, the oilsands are just now becoming a profitable industry. Companies know the world is watching and are very focussed on improvements to reduce their impact on the environment."

"I just think we need to switch to cleaner energy sources as soon as we can, not create new fossil fuel sources," Jordan said. "Why waste so much capital and technology on an industry that will need to be phased out soon?"

"It's easy for you to say," Elise said. "People who live elsewhere love to tell Alberta what to do. Meanwhile, they keep driving, flying, and powering up their electronic devices with energy from fossil fuels. Albertans see the urban elites as hypocrites who blame everyone else for emitting carbon, while feeling entitled to their own use of energy. You flew here, right? We drove here, right? We are visiting this national park that would be a lot better off without us here. We are all damaging the planet. If you really believe fossil fuels are the culprit, then you should stop using them and accept to have a lesser life."

"You are right, and I struggle with that too," Jordan conceded. "But making more oil is not the answer."

"No, it isn't. But saving the planet must be a shared responsibility, one where everyone pitches in to transition to cleaner energy. We are all responsible for the damage, and we all need to come up with real solutions – not smear campaigns that single out one industry in one region or push new energy sources that do only part of the job."

Elise regretted her sharp tone and took his hand. Together they walked back to the car through the ancient glacier's debris. She took a final look at the unspoiled scenery.

The sun was beginning to slide behind the mountains when they entered the manicured property of the lodge where Jordan was booked for the week. Elk grazed on the grounds, barely interrupting the silence. Loons waded on the emerald lake. Signs warned that there had been sightings of bears in the forest. With his senses filled up by the area's beauty, Jordan finally understood why his parents had fallen in love with the place, and more deeply with each other.

"Dr. Black?" a young woman asked him at the lodge's reception.

"Yes. That's me. I have a booking for a week."

"Of course. Welcome to Jasper, Dr. Black. We upgraded you to a larger suite. Let us know what we can do to make your stay more comfortable."

Jordan and Elise took the trail that led them to a log chalet with a view of the lake. When they walked in, they found champagne cooling in an ice bucket, chocolates arranged on a tray, and a log crackling in the fireplace.

"We each have a bedroom," Jordan told Elise. "Take the big one."

Elise flung her arms around Jordan's neck and kissed him like she meant it. "I don't think we need to mess up two beds, do you?" she asked, feeling joy. "I think this one will be just fine for the both of us."

Early the next day, Elise and Jordan were jolted awake by a family of geese squabbling outside their bedroom. From the picture windows in front of their bed, they could see the sun's rays shining on the lake and a convoy of moose grazing on a spit of land shooting out from its banks.

They'd slept soundly in each other's arms, with Julien's memory binding them closer together instead of pulling them apart. They felt as serene as the nature that surrounded them.

"Good morning, Elise," Jordan said.

"Good morning, Jordan," she responded, pulling her hair away from her face and hugging him again.

They showered, dressed, headed to the main cabin for breakfast, and discussed plans for the day. They decided to take an easier trail where Jordan could get warmed up for harder hikes later in the week, and Elise could get re-acquainted with hiking.

While marching forward on a narrow path, they discussed American politics, wars, the oil industry, the benefits and problems of fossil fuels, both eager to hear and challenge each other's views.

"You know what I love about you?" Jordan said as they moved through a patch with dense forest on one side and cold deep water on the other.

"What?"

"I like how you get to the bottom of things. You have informed views. You are open-minded. The people I deal with just seem to join tribes that re-enforce what they know. They don't challenge what they are told."

"Thank you, Jordan," Elise said. "There are always many sides to a story, and there are many sources, too. Some of them are credible and some of them are not. I love that I get to talk to so many people with so many backgrounds and so many views. Views are based on what you know."

The next day they canoed on the lake to give their legs a break, and on Elise's final day they picked a tough, six-hour trail that took them above the tree line to a summit with views of the park's peaks and valleys.

Exhausted but happy, they kissed as they took in the scenery.

"This place is as close to heaven as you can get," Jordan said. "I have been looking for a long time for a second home in the mountains to escape New York. I was searching in all the wrong places – Colorado, the Swiss Alps. They are too congested, or it takes too long to get there. I'll look at real estate around Banff when I get there next week. What do you think?"

"It's a perfect fit for a mountain man like you," Elise said. "But don't kid yourself, it will be a lot colder in January."

"I'll manage. And until I lure you back to the big city, we could spend more time together here – on long weekends and during holidays," he suggested.

"I could get used to that," Elise said, delighted by the prospect, but also scared that things with Jordan were moving too fast.

The next day she drove back to Calgary alone and replayed in her mind the special moments they shared. She was happy. She tried to envision a future with Jordan. Was she ready for a serious relationship? Would she miss her freedom? Would Jordan pressure her to move back to New York before she was ready? Was she in love with him?

In truth, she was afraid to think too far ahead, or make new plans. She'd made so many with Julien. Then they were shattered, painfully, unfairly, unexpectedly. She decided to let life take care of itself.

Meanwhile, she realized she was finally at peace with herself and with the world, and that Jordan – and Alberta's mountains – had helped her get there.

Chapter 24

The Banff strategy session, held in a secluded hotel in the forest hovering above the town, brought together a dozen green-movement leaders from the United States and Canada. They signed an agreement to start organizing a legal and public-relations campaign against the Canadian oilsands. The oil play was so accessible, so visible, so loved by international oil companies, they agreed it was the ideal target to stick it to Big Oil.

The agreement involved creating a cross-border organization to raise funds, build a network of activists, and form alliances with current and aspiring politicians, communities, and Indigenous leaders.

The American delegates took charge of the fundraising, of stalling access of Canadian oil to US markets, and of building partnerships with those who regarded the Canadian oilsands as a threat to their businesses.

The Canadian delegates were responsible for collecting industry intelligence, building alliances with Indigenous people, targeting media, identifying opportunities to disrupt industry activities, and monitoring and sharing public information.

Nothing was off limits. Everyone agreed the mitigation of global climate change justified an aggressive campaign.

Erika and Rob Cortez, a former community organizer from Chicago who built his reputation on political campaigns, were named co-leaders. Both reported to Barb Heinz, who had been appointed chair of the environmental committee of the progressive candidate for US President.

"We need to know as much as we can about which companies are entering the business, the investors who are backing them, and the customers who are buying their products," Barb said as they wrapped up the session. "We can target all of them and make their lives very uncomfortable.

"We need Indian friends, the more the better," Barb added, turning to Erika. "Your work in Peru was ground breaking and showed us that Indians make effective anti-oil advocates."

"I'm on it – but please don't call them Indians," Erika said. "They don't like that in Canada. They want to be called Indigenous. Meanwhile, I already have some great allies, and I am working on more. I'll need to hire more people. Indigenous communities live in remote areas and are hard to meet with. It will take time."

"Whatever. Do what you must," Barb said. "We're in this to win."

On the road back to Calgary, Erika was deep in thought about the opportunity in front of her: scuttling the oilsands could be the beginning of the end of the fossil-fuel era. She knew it would be her most challenging work yet, that she would be disliked. It was a burden she was prepared to shoulder, she decided, to save humanity from its destructive ways.

Chapter 25

FORT McMURRAY, ALBERTA, NOVEMBER 2003

By the time Anthony Littlechild, a high-school dropout from the Buffalo Head reserve, agreed to meet Erika Bernstein, he'd had enough. He took her to a bluff overlooking the busy highway that led to growing oilsands operations and together they stood and watched big machinery thrash the forest.

"I will do whatever it takes to put an end to this," the young man said to the activist. "That forest was my refuge."

The oilsands were a big part of his story, he told her. His ancestors had lived on top of them for time immemorial and used the bitumen-soaked sand to waterproof their canoes. The oil they held was so abundant it naturally seeped from riverbanks, like syrup from a chocolate cake. Now the wilderness he knew and cherished was under assault.

The oil companies, he explained to Erika, had schedules to meet and investors to please, so they were in a hurry to build their projects. Trees were cut, soil was trucked away to expose the ore, which was scooped up and processed in infernal-looking plants. Meanwhile, wildlife was running away, and water was drawn from the river – his river.

Communities were filled up with newcomers. Thousands from all over the world were answering the call of the oilsands, he said. They were recruited in job fairs, responded to job ads, were encouraged by family and friends already in the region to come to the North so they could earn big money together.

Anthony met a few, he said to Erika, and occasionally even enjoyed their company. They were farther away from comfort than they had ever been. They endured Arctic temperatures, endless winter nights, expensive housing. They were rewarded with unbelievable salaries and work experience. In time, they learned to love the wilderness and took up hiking and canoeing. There was so much work for so many that labourers quickly rose to managers, managers to executives, executives to leaders.

"The young ones are on a three-year plan," Anthony shared. "They want to save enough money to set them up for life. Some dream of purchasing new houses in their home countries, some of helping their families, some see the work as the first step to permanently settle in Canada. The bold are investing in oilsands' stocks and buying real estate and businesses in the area, to earn even more money."

Erika nodded. "There is certainly lots of money to be made. But they're being lured here under false pretenses. This business is unsustainable, as are their jobs and their investments. It will be painful when it all comes crashing down."

"I think they genuinely believe the money train will never stop," Anthony said.

There were plenty of opportunities for Anthony's band to make money too, he acknowledged to Erika. Members could start businesses – catering, cleaning, emergency response, land clearing – or take jobs in the oilsands plants and in the workers' camp.

Some did, especially the chief and his family, he said. They had businesses that provided services to the oilsands, which made them even richer and more powerful. There were rumours the chief demanded bribes and expensive gifts from the oil companies, such as vacations to Las Vegas, where he liked to gamble, and that he prevented other members from getting contracts of their own. He wanted a monopoly. The oil companies obliged him, Anthony said.

But the oil jobs and the get-rich-quick schemes didn't appeal to him, he said. Pleased that Erika seemed to understand, he told her he wanted more for himself and for his people.

"These companies are offering us crumbs while they take our lands and profit from our oil, all with the help of the government. Meanwhile, we cannot hunt, fish, or even live our lives in peace," Anthony said.

"You're right. You are being screwed," Erika responded.

But she had her own ideas. She pictured a world tour for the tall, long-haired, handsome youth. There would be interviews with international media, appearances with celebrities, a leading role in protests.

"We can help you a lot," she said. "In fact, I am prepared to hire you as a consultant. We will pay you well for every appearance on behalf of the cause and we will provide you with a coach to help you be as effective as you can. We will pay for all your travel expenses."

"How much are we talking about?" Anthony asked, his curiosity piqued.

"How about twenty thousand in consulting fees, plus expenses?" Erika proposed.

"I'm in," Anthony said. "Let me know what I need to do."

"We will need to get to work right away," Erika said, impatient to get her recruit to the front lines. "I will send you a contract that will spell out the terms. Do you own more traditional garb – you know, beads and feathers?"

"I do. I have outfits for my performances. Why?" the young man asked.

"You perform?" Erika asked.

"Yes. I am a hoop dancer – junior champion this year. But if you want me to dance, you'll have to pay me extra."

"Sure. How about an extra two hundred an hour for dancing? We will need you in full costume, to dance for audiences and for photo ops."

Anthony couldn't believe his luck. He'd never envisioned earning that much money. He thought about what it would be like to have a fuller life, with open doors, opportunities, and respect.

He didn't tell Erika he was the child of a broken family – his dad was an alcoholic, his mother made ends meet working as a waitress. His parents divorced when he was young. He lived with his mom and six brothers and sisters. He was sexually abused by people who were supposed to take care of him.

He knew he was smart, but school was not for him. He dropped out because he didn't relate to the white man's education – and even less to white students. Determined to stay away from substance abuse, he had few Indigenous friends, too.

Hoop dancing became his salvation, a way to heal. Soon, he became good at it. Often, it made him happy. He loved to share that happiness with his audience. His performances were electrifying. In time, he was hired for big events. He loved it when important people walked up to him after the show and asked him for autographs, took his picture. They were kind to him. He felt valued.

But he had bigger dreams. Maybe this new gig with Erika would help him find bigger audiences and even see the world. Maybe it would help him right the wrongs among his people, perhaps even put him on track to become chief someday.

Anthony and Erika moved their conversation to one of Fort McMurray's newest hotels, where the activist had become a regular. She'd even rented an apartment in town, which doubled as an operations centre for the campaign, she told him. She ordered steaks and beer. Anthony abstained.

Do you have a passport?" Erika asked.

"No," Anthony responded.

"You'll need to get one. We'll be on the road soon," Erika said. "Also, if you can give us names of others who'd be interested in joining our campaign, we'd be very grateful. You'd be the leader, of course, but they can support us in many ways."

It was getting dark as the two parted company. Anthony hitched a ride from a friend to return to his reserve. She flew back to Vancouver, encouraged that her plan was making good progress.

Chapter 26

A warm Chinook wind was blowing in from the Pacific while John waited outside the main doors of Calgary's conference centre. He had planned another chance encounter with Elise. A major industry announcement was in progress, and she was one of the invited guests. He was aware that he looked out of place, which made him anxious. Oil barons didn't stand on street corners without a good reason and a proper entourage to shield them from the media, disgruntled investors, and resentful competitors. Oil barons belonged in the exclusive orbit of executive office suites, private clubs, private jets, private events, and high-end travel destinations, often with other oil barons and their wives. Anything less was beneath them.

But business was business, meeting with Elise was a priority, so he stuck to his spot of sidewalk while trying to look busy by catching up on work messages from his mobile phone.

John needed the debut of his new company to be successful. He was working hard to establish it as the first oilsands pure play that produced oil entirely using new steam-assisted technology. He wanted the world to know that he was back and ready to reclaim his crown as the king of Canada's oil business. He wanted the markets to value his company at a premium.

He had picked mid-March for a tour of his operations. He expected the temperature to be milder, but still biting enough to show how cleverly his company was overcoming the North's challenges. He would spare no expense. A private jet would transport two dozen industry analysts, institutional investors, the provincial premier, even his new minority partners – the large American refiner with big thirst for Canadian oil – to his operation in a new part of the oilsands region. He even negotiated a generous agreement with the nearest First Nation, which he planned to announce during the tour. He wanted to show that his new company, in addition to its profit potential, had a heart.

But he needed to fix the Elise problem. She was the gatekeeper to the platform he needed to be on to spread his good news far and wide. He hadn't talked to her for a while. He didn't know how to reconnect after miscalculating her response to his last phone call. He had delayed getting back to her for a few days on purpose, as he had done many times before. He wanted to have power over her by calling her back when *he* decided the time was appropriate. But when he finally did, she didn't answer. He left messages, but she ignored him. She was doing to him what he'd done to her, he realized. She was onto him.

After much thought, he decided to orchestrate the chance encounter, which in his mind was a face-saving way to reconnect. He was confident he could get her attention by offering – in person – an exclusive. He had a backup plan, too, though it would be inferior. If he couldn't lure Elise, he would round up one or more of her rivals to send her the message that messing with John Hess came at a cost.

Elise bolted out of the building with a photographer, bumping into the door and then into John, who was standing – strangely, she thought – in her way.

"Oh, I am so sorry," she said, looking frazzled.

"Hi Elise. How is it going? That must have been some announcement!" John said with a big smile, looking authoritative in his black coat. I couldn't have made a better plan, he thought.

"Well, yes, and I need to file something right away," she said.

"Let me help you," John said. He picked up her notebook, which had fallen on the snowy sidewalk, and put his arm under hers to ensure she was steady on her feet.

"Are you okay?" he asked.

"Sure. You startled me. Why are you here?" Elise asked.

"I was on my way to the office. Let me walk you to yours," John said, ignoring the photographer who was trailing behind them. "How have you been? I haven't heard from you in ages!"

"Life is good," Elise responded. She wanted to avoid talking about the silence between them during the last few months. "It's been busy at work, and I have been making a few trips back to New York."

"You're not leaving us, are you?" John asked, alarmed that Elise could be gone before he got a chance to really know her – and get his new venture off the ground the way he wanted.

"No. I'm here for a while. We are expanding our office and I need to see that through," she said.

"A *Journal* expansion? That's great news," John said. "I have been reading your stories with interest. You are doing a great job and raising awareness about our industry. I look forward to bigger and better things. Meanwhile, I have another big scoop for you if you are interested."

"What's the story?" she asked, worried about her approaching deadline, not keen to get ensnared in John's schemes again. His tricks are getting old, she thought.

"We have lots to catch up on," he said. "I am organizing a big announcement at our new oilsands operation in mid-March. We will do our IPO right after. Big names will be there. You must come. I'm offering you an exclusive. I need to know if you can make it as soon as possible," John added. "If you can't come, we will issue a news release and invite media who can join us."

"Who else will be there?" she asked.

"The provincial premier, industry analysts, our new partner, and several top investors. We will have a surprise announcement involving the local First Nation. It'll be a first in the industry."

"I'll think about it. Send me the details," Elise said.

John wanted a firm commitment. He sweetened the deal by offering a background briefing, exclusive to Elise, so she'd have all the information she needed before the event.

Elise asked if she could give him an answer after consulting with her editor. John agreed.

She rushed back to her office and wrote her story, then talked to her editor about the oilman's offer. She downplayed its newsworthiness.

Her editor suggested that she go and insist on an exclusive. He wanted the story. Access to John Hess was a benefit to *Journal* readers and would increase the paper's following in Canada and elsewhere, he reminded her.

"He's a good source," he told her. "You should feel flattered."

She agreed but didn't tell him what was troubling her. She didn't like the oilman's power over her. She was aware John was pulling her strings – personal and professional. She didn't want him to get in the way of the closeness she felt for Jordan. They were moving forward cautiously, rediscovering each other in their new circumstances. They spoke on the phone often. He travelled to Calgary when he could. He looked at several properties near Banff. She travelled to New York. They spent Christmas together, with her children, in his new home, a big spread near Columbia University he said he had inherited from his father. He'd moved in after splitting from his wife and updating it to reflect his taste – sterile white walls, dark wood floors, a large built-in library to display his extensive collection of vintage books and vinyl records. The long-distance relationship wasn't ideal, but a good compromise. Elise enjoyed her independence and her work, and Jordan was happy to get as much of her as he could.

It was evening by the time Elise phoned John's office, expecting to leave a message on his voicemail. Instead, he answered his phone.

"Hi Elise," he said, sounding friendly.

"Hi," she said, determined to keep her distance. "I spoke to my editor and I'm good to go. But we want your assurance that this is an exclusive to us."

"Of course," John said. "When can you meet me to go over the background? I want your assurance, too, that you will not use the information until the day of the tour."

"Sure. How about next week? That will give me time to understand it and start writing the back end of the story," Elise said. John checked his calendar and proposed lunch on Friday. "How about my office? I can have lunch catered here. We have the best coffee in town, too," he added.

"Okay," Elise said, dreading the encounter.

A week later, Elise showed up at Aurora's executive offices at the appointed time and was asked to wait at reception, which gave her time to size up the new décor. She liked the modern furniture, and the new art. John Hess's previous workspace was a trip down memory lane. This one had a futuristic look, she thought, as if to show that the oilsands were about looking forward, toward a new era of advanced energy technology, not backward, to oil derricks and rusty pipes.

John greeted her. His smile was eager. Elise noticed he was wearing a white shirt and black suit, just like she was.

His executive assistant asked to be excused for the day. Elise realized they were alone.

He escorted her to his executive suite. The main room was large, bright, quiet, with little furniture besides a modern metal desk. In an adjacent boardroom, lunch was displayed on an oval table.

Folders containing reports on the new operation were displayed neatly on a console. They sat at the boardroom table across from each other.

"Our new company will produce from the oilsands, but we will be using a new technology that will be less harmful to the environment," he explained.

"We can do that because the deposits are located deep underground, instead of near the surface, which requires strip mining," he said. "In our projects, all the hard work will be done underground. It will look like a conventional oil operation. It means less impact on the land.

"It will also be cheaper to produce the oil because we use natural gas to warm up the bitumen. Natural gas is abundant and inexpensive. We will be building four projects, one after the other. They will be carbon copies of each other, which will reduce engineering costs. We expect to produce a comfortable rate of a hundred thousand barrels a day, once all phases are up and running in seven to ten years – depending on how fast we can build them – for the next half century."

Elise, surprised by the project's advantageous features, took notes furiously and asked more questions to nail down all the details.

"When are you planning your IPO?" she asked.

"Right after the tour, so, by the end of March. We want the market to digest all this new information. We will list in New York and in Toronto," he said.

"How big an equity stake will you keep?" she asked.

"I will own forty-one percent," John responded. "Our American partner will own twenty percent. My management group will have ten percent. The remaining twenty-nine percent will be publicly traded. My management group and I will retain full control, for now. I have the right of first refusal to purchase shares from our partner."

"Do you have pipeline space to transport the bitumen?" Elise asked.

"Yes, for the first phase. Most of it will go to our partner's refineries in the US Midwest – though we have the option to sell it to other buyers, if needed. But there are lots of plans for new pipelines, so I am not worried."

Elise barely touched her food and hung on every word. No other business leader she'd met matched John Hess's charisma, she acknowledged. His pitches were more like a seduction. He was aware of – and fully used – all his advantages.

Two hours came and went as he spoke about the great future of the industry and its potential to grow into Canada's economic engine, while ensuring oil security for both Canada and the United States for decades to come.

Elise checked her watch. It was time to get back to the office.

They ended the meeting and stood up. Elise tucked her tape recorder and her notebook in her purse.

"Thank you for the briefing," Elise said, shaking his hand, relieved he'd been all business. "It looks like an impressive operation. I look forward to the tour."

John looked into her eyes and thanked her for her interest in his new company.

"What's really impressive is your understanding of our industry," he said, then caressed her cheek.

Elise froze. He was doing it again. She felt used. Why did he do that? She asked herself.

John didn't apologize, and Elise didn't complain. Instead, they stood silently for a few seconds staring at each other and then awkwardly shook hands again.

Quivering, Elise left the office suite. She analyzed her feelings as she walked back to her office, braving what she hoped was a final winter storm.

She felt diminished and valued at the same time. Why? Because she, a middle-aged widow, was getting attention from John Hess – a billionaire industry titan who could have any woman he wanted. And yet, she also felt disrespected. What did he want from her? And what was the upside for her, if any? Was he aware that he sabotaged himself in her eyes by acting the way he did?

She didn't have answers. But she was worried that she was right back under his spell. She considered ditching the tour, talking to her boss about the unwanted advances. She suspected her editor wouldn't understand, that he would tell her to buck up and do her job.

Chapter 27

FORT MCMURRAY, ALBERTA, MARCH 2004

Elise took her assigned seat at the back of the private jet leased by Aurora Oil Sands, next to an official from the office of the provincial premier. The politician had made separate transportation arrangements from Edmonton, the site of the provincial legislature, and would join the group at the plant, John had told her.

"Hi. I'm Elise Chamonter from the *Journal*," she said cordially as they buckled their belts.

"Pleased to meet you. I am the premier's official photographer. I have read many of your stories. But I didn't know there was media on board. Should I be careful about what I say?"

"Of course not. John Hess invited me for a look. Most of my story is written and ready to go. I just needed to check the project firsthand – so I can put a Fort McMurray place line on my story – and pick up a few more fresh quotes when we get there. Is the premier coming?" Elise asked.

"Yes, he is. He's looking forward to finding out as much as he can about this new technology. Plus, it's a photo op. We'll be taking our own photos for posterity. We are planning our own news release tomorrow morning. This new technology is a big deal for the future of the oilsands," the photographer said.

"I'd love to chat with him if he's available for a few questions. And if you have photos, do you mind sharing them with us?" she asked, handing him her business card.

"Of course. I'll tell him about your interview request after we land."

Elise had donated to a charity to offset the cost of her seat on the plane. The gesture didn't always work, as she found out after her trip to Peru, but it was a potential defense in case someone accused her and her newspaper of taking free rides to shill for the oil industry.

She didn't want to take sponsored trips. But she often had to rely on company-arranged transportation to visit places that could not be reached efficiently or safely with a commercial airline or by car, especially operations in the North. Companies usually didn't ask journalists to pay. Their airplanes travelled to field operations all the time, often with empty seats, so there was no additional cost for the companies to take guests.

Elise was glad, in the end, she decided to participate in the tour, for reasons neither John nor her editor would appreciate. She felt there was value in seeing operations with her own eyes, interviewing those who knew things firsthand, rather than being on the outside looking in. There was no substitute for being on the ground, talking to real people. The *Journal* wrote for investors, and investors wanted the highest-quality information to make the best investment decisions. They wanted witnesses who saw and heard things they couldn't see or hear themselves, especially in the aftermath of the recent scandal involving a large mining company that lied about discovering massive gold deposits in a remote part of Asia.

The airplane took off from Calgary airport with a full load. Those on board seemed delighted to be part of the billionaire's chosen few. All would see the project for the first time.

Elise was curious about the people on the plane. She knew the oilsands owed a lot to those who contributed their capital when projects were just an idea. John had told her that some early investors would cash out after the IPO. It would be a big payday for them. They bankrolled the company in its startup phase for pennies a share. Now they expected to sell their stock at a big profit so they could do it all over again with another startup.

John, dressed in a heavy parka and black corduroy pants, sat at the front with them. They looked like an exclusive, tight group. She suspected they socialized with each other, too, and shunned the limelight. They were not different from the big money people she knew on Wall Street, who lived large, with big beach homes, yachts in the Mediterranean and private jets at the ready.

Elise also knew they had no time – or respect – for the press, unless it suited their vanity, and they could control the outcome. The seating arrangement seemed deliberate, just like everything else John did. He wanted to keep her as far as possible from the front of the aircraft to protect his inner circle from her questions.

After takeoff, Elise noticed that John moved to another row of seats in the middle of the plane, where he turned his attention to a trio of big-time analysts, including an attractive woman employed by a major bank. She wore expensive-looking outdoor chic and was seated beside him, acting like a familiar old friend. He was probably making his pitch that Aurora Oil Sands had the best potential for stock appreciation – whether as a standalone or as a takeover target.

She was disappointed that John behaved like he didn't know her. She decided not to care. She took out her notebook and reviewed the areas she still needed to address so she could finish her story, file it to her editor by the end of the day and be done with John. She thought about how much she missed Jordan and her kids. She took a mental note to call them at the end of the day.

Jordan. She replayed the happy times they had together. The memories gave her comfort. He was in her inner circle.

The plane landed on a frozen runway built by the company, located a few miles from the plant. A bus was waiting to bring the group on the tour. It was a cold and sunny day, with air so pure it hurt to breathe. Other than noise from the jet's engines, it was a place of silence – undisturbed through the ages, like the oil deposits sleeping underground.

A trailer at the end of the runway doubled as the arrival terminal. Inside, Jim McKinnon, the plant's manager, whom Elise recognized as her source on her investigation about Plains in Peru, was waiting to receive the group with a welcoming handshake and warm coffee in his free hand. Elise nodded at Jim McKinnon. He smiled back. Neither spoke. Both had secrets to protect.

Safety gear for all in attendance – hard hats, steel-toed boots, goggles, coveralls – was lined up neatly on and under a table for everyone to pick up and wear.

Elise suited up and climbed onto the waiting bus. She noticed John was engrossed in conversations with his new American partner.

They drove on snow-covered dirt roads between thick, evergreen forests, then arrived at a clearing the size of a football field, where rows of pump jacks moved diligently up and down. Nearby, a few trailers housed the field's operations crew.

"Is this it?" one analyst asked. "It sure doesn't look like a scene of environmental devastation, as some would have us believe."

"This is it," John replied. "This technology is doing its job and will get better over time. We are recycling most of our water, so we withdraw as little as possible from the river. We are required to restore the land to its original state when the reservoir is depleted, but we are doing it continuously. We are relying on natural gas to fuel our operation, which is cheap and low in emissions.

"This is the future of the oilsands," John continued, opening his arms wide to show off the site. "The mining operations are giving the industry a bad name. We're not all the same, and we believe we, at Aurora, have a competitive advantage. We also don't need as much capital, or as much labour, to build our project because we do it in small steps."

"How long will it take for your project to get to full capacity?" one analyst asked, wondering about the near-term upside of the stock post-IPO, and how to value John Hess's talent for generating buzz.

"It will take us about a year to ramp up our first phase of twenty-five thousand barrels a day," John said. "We are about mid-way now. We took our time to do it right because we wanted to ensure the technology worked. The next phases will be faster because we already know what to do."

"Is the reservoir the same throughout?" another analyst asked.

"Yes, it is, as far as we can tell from the data we have," John said.

"When will it be depleted?" the analyst asked.

"It will take decades for each phase, and we have plenty of expansion room," John said.

Like the rest of the group, Elise was caught up in the enthusiasm. She'd seen first-hand the open pit mines north of Fort McMurray, and Aurora's plant seemed to cause less land disturbance in comparison. Yet the production projections were significant.

She solicited views from the analysts, spoke to the plant's staff, and interviewed the premier. He was an affable man-of-the-people, pro-oil, in a hurry to secure windfall revenues for his government so he could boost his own budget – and his grip on power.

"If you look at projects that have received regulatory approvals, we, Alberta, are the fastest-growing oil producer in the world," the politician told her proudly, as if the province's oil wealth was all his doing.

"But can this area handle all this development?" Elise asked. "Some argue that we don't need all this new oil, that it's too hard to produce it and that it will keep us dependent on fossil fuels."

"We disagree. We have the top environmental standards in the world," the premier responded. "We need to produce it while there's demand. American refineries want it, and we want to sell it to them. This is a great story for Alberta and for Canada. We are creating a new industry that will pay for our social programs, our education, our health care. We will save money, too, for future generations."

It was getting unbearably cold. The group returned to the bus for the short drive to the Deer Lake Nation's lodge, a new log house where a meal would be served. The First Nation was the plant's closest neighbour.

The chief and members of his council were waiting inside, eager to announce their own good news.

"Welcome to the territory of the Deer Lake," said Chief Chris Laboucaine, a hefty middle-aged man.

When everyone was seated at a handful of tables in the main hall, Laboucaine took the podium and started his speech, reading from a prepared script.

"We are proud to share this meal today with such an important group," he said. "We are particularly proud to announce our partnership with John Hess and his company, Aurora Oil Sands. It's a first for the Indigenous people of Alberta and it will set us on a new, prosperous path for generations to come. It's already resulted in major benefits.

"First, the lodge where you are enjoying lunch today was funded by Aurora and by a government grant. So, thank you, Mr. Hess and thank you, Mr. Premier, for making this possible," he said. The audience erupted in applause.

"Second, Aurora has agreed to fund a dozen scholarships for our youth so they can attend university – and possibly more scholarships if there is demand. This is a big step forward for us and it means we can develop the expertise to become full partners in this project.

"Third, Aurora has agreed to offer us contracts so we can start businesses to provide services and to share our Indigenous knowledge on the environment.

"Fourth – and this is what I am most proud about – Aurora has agreed to give us a share of the revenue from the oil production. It's a small share to start, but it will increase over time if certain milestones are met. It's the first revenue-sharing agreement that we know of in the oil industry. We hope this becomes a model for future oilsands development so that our Indigenous communities become full participants in this promising new industry."

There was more enthusiastic applause, and then John walked up to the podium.

"I want to thank you all for taking time out of your schedules to join us today. When we started thinking about this project and how to improve it for the future, we decided to make our relationship with First Nations our number-one priority. As you see, we are in a remote area of Northern Alberta, where skilled labour is scarce, but where there is a large and motivated population of Indigenous people. We are prepared to help them build their skills so they can work in our project. We also wanted to ensure they benefit from the oil under their lands." More applause.

"I am thankful to the chief and council for their leadership, the time they put into many meetings, and their efforts to arrive at a mutually advantageous agreement," John said. Visitors and hosts stood up and applauded more vigorously.

Lunch was served. The mood was upbeat. Elise was pleased that John's company was breaking new ground by including Indigenous people as partners.

She started a conversation with one of the chiefs, an elderly woman with a beaded wool jacket, who took a seat beside her.

"I am curious about your partnership with Aurora," Elise said. "All I hear is that Indigenous people are organizing to oppose the oilsands."

"I'm aware," the older woman replied. "But we don't share their views. We believe we must be pragmatic and use this opportunity to improve our lives. Progress is coming, with or without our approval, and we might as well get something out of it. We have high unemployment in our community, and young people are restless. They need a hand up. Besides, we are not going back to live in teepees and to eat what we kill. It's unrealistic. We enjoy our new cars, our new homes, our central heating, just like everyone else. But we need to get something from all this development. We can't be left behind. If we are involved, we will ensure the environment is treated with respect and we will use the funds to improve our community.

"Someday," she added, smiling, "we will have our own oilsands project. That's our goal. But we need to learn how it's done."

After the meal, Elise retreated to a quiet corner of the lodge to complete writing her report. It was fair and balanced – but she suspected it would make waves. Her lead was that Aurora was proposing an oilsands project that addressed the big concerns of those opposed to development of the resource. She dialed her editor from a phone in the lodge and dictated her final piece. Her editor was pleased. She also arranged to have photographs transmitted. By the time her group got back on the waiting buses, it was mid-afternoon. She was exhausted but relieved that her work was done.

John, after ignoring her during the tour, took the empty seat next to her on the back of the plane for the flight back to Calgary. Elsewhere in the cabin, conversations were loud, and people were laughing. A flight attendant was taking drink orders. "A penny for your thoughts," he said as the engines revved up.

"Are you asking me as a reporter, or off the record, as a person?" Elise asked.

"Off the record, of course. I assume you did your reporting thing. I'm interested in your views as an industry expert."

"I am flattered," Elise responded. "But I must be off the record, too, so you cannot quote me on this. I have a reputation to protect, too, as an honest broker. Is that clear?"

"Sure," the oilman responded.

"You did a great job announcing the project. You had the right people there. Everyone was very impressed. The technology will get a lot of attention because it deals with a lot of the oilsands' shortcomings. I assume you will publicize the operation's launch first thing tomorrow, after my report is printed, which is smart. My reporting will get a lot of attention and will give your announcement credibility.

"I particularly liked your deal with the First Nation. That's very generous. It's the right thing to do, particularly if you want to avoid Indigenous discontent, which is brewing. I saw firsthand in Peru and in northeast BC how eco-activists form alliances with Indigenous people to bolster their own off-oil agenda. It's brilliant on their part. Their game plan involves scaring Indigenous people into thinking the environment will be destroyed by magnifying the risks and painting all private oil and gas companies as greedy capitalists who will abandon them after resources are extracted, which has been true in some cases.

"By partnering with Indigenous people first, by offering them an opportunity to make money and help plan your projects, you are making allies instead of enemies. And this is very off the record," she said.

"You are perceptive," John said. He was not surprised Elise had read him so well. "You got the strategy right. I wish my board was similarly supportive of the partnership. If I didn't have control of my company with my team, the revenue-sharing agreement would never have been approved."

"Why not?" Elise asked.

"The rest of the board felt the First Nation should not be allowed to get a share of the revenue because it didn't put up the bucks to build the project. That share means a lower return for all the other investors," John explained. "And that wasn't all. There are big concerns that we are raising expectations and that we are creating a dangerous precedent that will be exploited by other Indigenous communities.

"Also, it will be a rude awakening for the Deer Lake when oil prices tank – which they always do – and they end up with no revenue at all. They will count on that money to pay for things important to them. They could end up in financial trouble if they're not careful."

"Couldn't you explain this to them, so they don't spend the money before they have it?" Elise asked.

"We did. But they are like everyone else. They don't see the business risks because they haven't been exposed to them – yet. They just see dollar bills. These high expectations are a problem, and we'll have to be cautious," the oilman continued.

"The bands in this area all talk to each other. We insisted on confidentiality with the Deer Lake, but it won't be long before word gets around about this agreement. The next band will ask for more, so demands will escalate. We are prepared at Aurora to do our part, but other oil companies won't be as open minded. That alone could cause a rift in the industry."

"I hadn't thought of that," Elise said. "Regardless, you can show leadership, and I am glad you did. Investors will need to step up. They may complain about your deal with the band because it erodes their returns, but they aren't in it for the long term. They'll sell your stock at the first opportunity. You are in it for the long term. Plus, this is great PR for your company, and you can turn it into a competitive advantage."

"I like how you think," John said.

"Thank you," Elise responded.

John returned to his seat at the front of the plane to answer any remaining questions from the rest of the group. The tour had been a success, even better than he envisioned, and, in his mind, started planning the next one.

The aircraft landed in Calgary by early evening, when the sky was dark, and heavy wet snow was covering the frozen ground.

John waited for Elise, who was the last to leave the aircraft, before walking to his car.

"Do you need a ride?" he asked her.

"I was going to get a taxi," she said.

"Let me give you a ride," he insisted. "It's cold and slippery and it will take a long time to get a taxi here. You are going downtown, right?"

"Yes, I need to go back to the office and unload this equipment," she said, lifting a large shoulder bag containing her portable computer, camera, and tape recorder.

"Come with me," he told to her, putting his hand on her waist. "I could use the company."

Despite her reluctance, Elise got into the oilman's car as the falling snow got thicker. Visibility diminished and traffic slowed to a crawl. As they drove downtown, they resumed the conversation they had on the plane. He offered more details of the project, the land reclamation plan, and how the agreement with the First Nation came about. They had a few laughs about some of the people on the tour, particularly the analysts who wore fancy clothes and inadequate shoes that were covered in mud by the end of the day.

"How did you pick them?" Elise asked.

"They are largely people who followed us for a long time," the oilman said.

By the time they arrived at Elise's office building, any tension between them had dissipated.

Elise thanked John for the ride and opened the car door.

He held her left hand and looked her intensely in the eyes. "Elise, thank you for coming today," he said. "I suspect you felt awkward as the only media person there. But you made a huge difference to me. I haven't seen the story, but I am sure it will be excellent, as usual."

"Thank you for inviting me," Elise said, reclaiming her hand. "But I need to know something," she added, nervous at first, then feeling more confident. She needed to clear the air between them.

"You confuse me," she said. "You are constantly crossing the line from professional to personal. I don't understand what you expect from me. I don't know how to behave around you. I don't do affairs. You are not the first corporate leader who's tried to get close to gain an advantage. It comes with my job. I am flattered that you are interested in someone like me. I'm not exactly the type of young hot number who would appeal to someone like you. So, thank you for your interest, but I'd rather keep this professional."

"I'm sorry," the oilman said, surprised by Elise's directness, not knowing how to react because in the past he always got what he wanted. "I didn't mean to make you uncomfortable. Truth is, I really like you. You understand me. All of me. I just want to get to know you more. It's never happened to me before, feeling so close to a woman who's such a super achiever and who understands my business. I wish I met you a long time ago. I apologize for being so clumsy."

"I don't know what to say," Elise said. "I am in a relationship right now, anyway, and you are married. What's the point of getting to know each other on a personal level?"

"I didn't know you were seeing someone," John said. "Is he you doctor friend?"

"Yes. How did you figure that out?"

"The way he looked at you when we bumped into him in New York last year. And the way you looked at him. I understand why he would appeal to you," he continued. "I also know I am married – for now – which makes me very complicated, and any relationship with you very difficult. I shudder when I think about the gossip, the hit to my reputation. Yet here I am. I can't help it, although I have tried."

"Please, don't shut me out," he pleaded. "I need you, and I am prepared to wait. Let's let life take care of itself."

Elise was aghast. Those were the same words she'd repeated to herself lately. John had a scary ability to read her mind.

She was also stuck on two words: *for now*. When she arrived at her home later that evening, she did not call Jordan as she had planned. Instead, she sat down with a glass of wine in hand and thought about John, his hint that his marriage could end, and how to make him an acceptable part of her life.

Chapter 28

MANHATTAN, NEW YORK, MAY 2004

Barb Heinz worked the room like a practiced politician. She was the keynote speaker at the annual meeting of the Save the Climate campaign. The main event, a social highlight of the spring season, was a glamorous gala where major donors had their photos taken with Hollywood celebrities, Wall Street bankers, and Washington notables. The campaign's goal was to put the spotlight on the cause. The oil-supporting crowd – oil and gas executives, oil investors, and their right-wing friends – was not invited.

Midway through the evening, Barb walked to the stage and grabbed a microphone. Looking elegant in her long black dress, she thanked her guests for answering the campaign's urgent call. She bragged about the big successes. She urged them to do more.

"We need a solution to climate change before it's too late," Barb said. "At Save the Climate, we have successfully blocked fossil fuel projects, developed policies that have been embraced across Europe and at the UN, and formed strategic alliances with groups that share our concerns.

"But much more needs to happen to deal with the climate crisis and save the planet. Too much investment is still pouring into oil production around the world, too many governments are subsidizing the oil industry, too many lands are being destroyed, too much carbon is being dumped into the atmosphere. With your help, we will target every company, every big investor, every government, every regulatory process, and put this dirty business behind us, and we can accelerate the transition to clean, renewable energy. We can't do it without you, so please give generously. Thank you for supporting us."

The crowd applauded, then quickly resumed the networking and photo-taking with the stars. At the end of the evening, most of the invited guests walked to their waiting limos, and a few jumped into their helicopters, impatient to get to their sprawling homes, with their bank accounts just barely lighter, happy to be seen to be doing their part for such a worthwhile cause.

The next day, Save the Climate held a closed-door session with its board to discuss strategies for the coming year. A dozen directors, hosted by a like-minded hedge-fund billionaire, listened intensively. Among them were renewable-energy entrepreneurs, aging actors motivated to revive their careers, lawyers looking for billable hours from climate-change litigation, young community activists restless to kickstart their political careers.

And then there was Dr. Jordan Black, the renowned brain surgeon, the charity's longest-serving director and a top financial contributor, who wanted to pressure the oil business to do the right things.

Seated at the head of the table, Barb rose to speak. "The work we have done so far has been effective in the courts and in some policy areas but doesn't have the broad support we need in the United States," she said. "Not enough people see the consequences on the environment of their own oil use. We would like to change that by focussing our efforts on a number of visible projects, the Canadian oilsands. We couldn't ask for a better target to serve as a wakeup call. Those oilsands projects are quickly becoming the most destructive projects on earth and transforming Northern Alberta's landscape. Some of the world's major companies are making large investments there, financed by some of the world's major banks. There is the added advantage, for us, that the oilsands are very accessible and that many Indigenous people in the region are opposed to so much development, so fast, and are eager for our financial support.

"Let me show you," she said, dimming the lights and starting a slide show on a large screen. The audience gasped as they saw supersized open-pit mines, monster trucks carrying loads of tarry sand, and plants used to upgrade the oil emitting thick plumes of steam.

"This is just the beginning," Barb warned. "The projects will multiply if we let them. This oil has only one market – us, the United States. If we allow it to continue, the oilsands will keep us hooked on oil for decades. We don't have decades. We need to reduce oil consumption and deal with climate change now, before temperatures rise too much and there is no turning back."

As the room digested the information, Jordan stood up. "If we go ahead with your proposal, would we be meddling with the policies of a foreign country?" he asked.

"That's one way of looking at it," Barb responded. "But climate change has no borders. Still, that's a good point, and we plan to ensure we don't stoke anti-American sentiment up there. We will work closely with our Canadian partners. We are building a network of Canadian environmental organizations that share our views and our goals. We plan to fund those organizations so they will be seen as managing this campaign, while we stay in the background."

"Isn't it unfair to target the Canadian oilsands while we produce oil in the United States that is just as dirty?" Jordan asked.

"Our oil production is not increasing. The Canadian oilsands will increase production of dirty oil more than any other source in the world, according to their projections. Besides, we wouldn't have much success in the United States because our oil lobby is too influential. The advantage of targeting a Canadian industry is that we get to send a loud message to the entire world that increasing oil supply from these dirty sources is not okay," Barb continued. "Meanwhile, Canadians don't vote in our elections, so we don't have to worry about their industry interfering in our politics. From what we've heard, some of our oil people are even pleased we're targeting Canadian supplies because it reduces Canadian oil prices, and they make a killing on refining those supplies."

Impressed by Barb's strategy, another director, the CEO of a solar startup, asked how much the oilsands campaign would cost.

"Our goal is one hundred million a year to start, more as we build up," Barb responded.

"Who are you targeting for funds?" the director asked.

"Renewable energy companies like yours – we do hope you're on board – philanthropists, major foundations, and finally, if we must, foreign oil producers who don't want the new Canadian competition, either. They are not at the top of our list, but some have approached us and offered us lots of money. This is all on background, not for public consumption. We don't want to take foreign money unless we have to."

"Which foreign oil producers?" another director asked.

"Russia, Iran, Venezuela, Saudi Arabia are motivated. They are Canada's top competitors and don't want to lose their share of the US market to new Canadian oil."

"Why would we take the money of such undemocratic regimes that also produce oil? Isn't this an anti-oil campaign?" the director asked.

"It is, but we believe the end justifies the means. They don't want global oil production to grow, and we don't either. So, our goals are aligned. They want to keep their market share and get the highest possible price for their oil until it's depleted. They want to build their state funds so they can diversify their economies. They see the oilsands as new competition that will eat into their revenue."

Jordan asked whether the evolution of oilsands technologies to reduce carbon emissions would make the industry more acceptable. "They will be producing more oil using steam, rather than through strip mining," he argued. "That's not nearly as damaging or as energy intensive."

"I see you are reading your friend at the *Journal*," Barb snapped back. "Look, the *Journal* is a capitalist rag. These new technologies don't change our views of the oilsands. The new projects will be powered by big quantities of natural gas, another fossil fuel. If we want to save the planet, that oil and gas needs to stay in the ground."

The board approved the strategy, with only one opposing vote – Dr. Jordan Black.

The meeting adjourned and Barb approached the doctor, who looked like he was in a hurry to get out of the room.

"I'm sorry if I was too aggressive in my response. I didn't mean to. We looked at other targets and none offered the bang of this Canadian play. It has everything we are looking for: the visuals, the scale, the market profile. They will be our cautionary tale for the whole industry."

"I understand," Jordan responded. "But I am uncomfortable with the way this is going. I don't like the focus on the oilsands. We're messing with a different country, our trading partner. I understand that you are trying to hold them up as an example, but it seems very dishonest and inconsistent to me.

"I wish you spoke to Elise before going ahead with your campaign," he continued. "I am sure she would be glad to fill you in about that industry and how it's improving."

"I considered that, but I didn't see the point," Barb responded. "We don't need people like her to publicize – and criticize – our campaigns. We are aligning ourselves with new media that allow us to communicate what we want directly to the people, particularly young people who get their information online and are concerned about what is happening to the planet. No more filters. We're done trying to convince big media organizations that we are worthy of their attention."

Jordan picked up his briefcase and departed alone, feeling like he no longer belonged. He was concerned about the confrontational tone of the campaign. He was dismayed that it could take funds from foreign regimes.

It was a warm spring evening, and he decided to take a long walk to improve his mood. He had much to look forward to. Soon, Elise would meet him in New York. They would both attend her children's university graduation ceremonies. He wanted her to move back to New York – and to be his wife. He decided to surprise her in August with a marriage proposal when he was due to go back to Calgary. Indeed, he couldn't wait to unwrap two surprises for Elise: the proposal, and a new vacation home in the Canadian Rocky Mountains, which he was beginning to build, and where they could all spend time together as a family.

Chapter 29

BANFF, ALBERTA, JULY 2004

At an executive management meeting to set strategy for the coming year, Susan Scott, looking smart in her designer pant suit, outlined a plan to her executive team to fast-track Plains' entry into the oilsands. She had been elevated to president after David Anderson took the fall for the Hunter fiasco, despite her complicity, and was determined to demonstrate she deserved the job. She would share power with a new CEO who was many years her junior. She knew the company inside out, so she was instructed to mentor him and help him get up to speed. Susan suspected the board had an undisclosed plan for her: to get her to train her own replacement, since CEOs were also usually presidents, and then show her the door.

But Susan knew how to land on her feet. She was confident the oilsands strategy could be her ticket to job security.

Plains Exploration had rebounded modestly thanks to higher commodity prices, a fire sale of marginal assets, and a big bet on new technology. But it remained out of favour with investors. The Ladyfern field, the main reason for the Hunter purchase, never lived up to its promise and remained embroiled in conflict. Relations with nearby First Nations were strained. The field's partners were bitter with each other for producing too much, too fast, depressing gas prices. Some were even losing money. Key technical staff had left and joined smaller companies with better opportunities, better pay, and most importantly, more generous stock option grants. On the upside, a billion-dollar lawsuit with the small company that had claimed that larger partners had syphoned reserves from under its leases was settled out of court.

For all the progress, Plains' board, especially its new directors, was unimpressed. Big investors complained that the company remained a follower, a bloated Canadian giant with no exciting growth opportunities.

Activist funds were circling like vultures, accumulating positions, pushing for change.

Meanwhile, the Aurora IPO had been so successful that shares had doubled in mere months, making John Hess and his backers even richer than they already were. More IPOs by other oilsands startups followed.

"We have three options in the oilsands," Susan said to the dozen men assembled in the conference room of an exclusive resort near Banff, away from their staff and from prying eyes.

"Option one, we have lands in the southern Athabasca region with reserves that could be richer than anything else out there, including those of companies like Aurora," she said, using a presentation developed by her team.

"We could start our own oilsands unit. We would be in the SAGD business, which is not as controversial as mining. We have received interesting offers for those lands, which shows that others agree we're sitting on very good resources. We won't know for sure until we do some drilling and take a serious look. We are late in the game, but we could get up to speed quickly by stealing technical talent from companies already in operation and learn from their mistakes. This is my preferred option," she said, noticing she was impressing the new CEO with her knowledge.

"Or, option two, we could take over one of the small operators that are already established. There are a few that are on the verge of going public. We could make a good offer. We can study this approach, but it's not first on my list. We would be paying a very high price in a heated market. We would have to take on a lot of debt and could end up with a lemon, and there are quite a few out there," she warned.

"Or option three, we could join the big consortium that is already in the business. A couple of the partners want to sell their shares and build their own oilsands projects. We could purchase their interests and build a sizeable position, become a consolidator. We would be in the mining business. But we would get cash flow immediately to pay for the purchase, and we would learn how it's done. This option is attractive, affordable, and would be the easiest. Any questions?"

"What's the driver here?" the head of the gas group asked. "The oilsands are a different beast. We are a conventional gas producer. We just refocussed our business in Western Canada. It would make more sense for us to grow in conventional oil. In the oilsands, we would have to start from scratch again. We don't have much to bring to the table."

"The board has directed us to do it. The oilsands are hot and we need to be in it," Susan responded. "The market wants the exposure."

"Would this involve layoffs in our other plays?" asked the head of human resources.

"Yes, we may end up with redundancies in some areas because we need to re-allocate capital to this new business," Susan responded.

"How would we staff the oilsands division?" the human resources head continued.

"We would have to hire from established companies because we don't have inhouse expertise," Susan said. "For example, we have been approached by a head hunter about some senior people at Aurora who are disgruntled and who are ready to jump ship. They seem to know our oilsands reserves better than we do, since the Aurora play is near ours and has similar geology.

"They believe they have not been appropriately rewarded, nor recognized, for their technical leadership, while John Hess and his team got rich on the IPO. Hess can do no wrong, according to the market, but he's not easy to work for. He hoards the spotlight and doesn't let other people shine. There is no second-in-command in his company. If he were to get hit by a truck, the company would collapse.

"Besides," she continued, trying to lighten the mood, "there is a bonus for us. Hess stiffed us on Hunter. It's time to return the favour. Let's raid his technical group and burst his bubble. We can offer his people big titles and top compensation. We can offer the excitement of an oilsands startup without the risk of being in one, and the biggest pay package on the street."

Discussion about the pros and cons dragged into late afternoon. By the time the group broke for dinner, it decided to develop its own lands and to start a search for a technical leadership team. Susan would lead the charge. The other two options would be studied, but only to show the board that all opportunities were investigated. If approved at the next board meeting, the new oilsands unit would be formed by early fall and could start producing oil within three years.

Susan knew the late entry would be costly and finding skilled labour would be hard. But she was excited about getting a new business off the ground. World oil supplies were tightening even more, and oil prices were climbing to new records. There was endless money to be made in the oilsands, right in Alberta, where Plains had its roots.

After dinner, while walking to her room, a day-old newspaper displayed on a coffee table caught her eye: "Oil billionaire criticized for bribing hand-picked analysts and the media to boost his stock," the headline screamed. Photos of John Hess during Aurora's pre-IPO tour, and of John Hess and Elise in his car, accompanied the piece. She grinned, satisfied she'd done it again.

Chapter 30

Overnight, Elise became a minor celebrity for all the wrong reasons. A media competitor wrote a vicious article calling her out for getting too cozy with John Hess and his Aurora project. The article was paired with photos showing her and the oilman in his car, and photos of her attending his oilsands tour.

"Newspapers like the *Journal* are bought and paid for by the oilsands industry," Barb Heinz, leader of the Save the Climate campaign, was quoted as saying.

"It's unbecoming for a journalist like Elise Chamonter to take free rides from the people she's supposed to cover at arm's length. Why were there no other reporters on that trip – reporters who could have asked more critical questions about the environmental damage done by Aurora's oilsands operation? Was the *Journal*'s positive spin part of John Hess's strategy to boost his IPO price? It's obvious Elise Chamonter is shilling for oil billionaires."

The next day, Elise was told by her editor to address the controversy. She wrote an article that explained to *Journal* readers why exclusive access to industry leaders was good journalism, not favouritism.

Then she phoned her boss to explain what really happened in John Hess's car. She had planned to order a taxi to get back to the *Journal* office, she told him, but the oilman offered her a ride, which she accepted because it was cold, snowing heavily, and she was exhausted after the long oilsands tour. There was nothing to it, she insisted, other than a professional relationship. She reminded her boss that she hadn't wanted to participate in the tour in the first place, and that he'd wanted her to go. She told him she'd saved the receipt for her generous donation to a charity on behalf of the *Journal* to offset the cost of the ride, to demonstrate the newspaper paid its way. She urged the *Journal* to publish it along with her story. After reading her piece and hearing her out, her editor told her he was satisfied that she had met the paper's ethical and professional standards.

Elise didn't tell her boss that she was disheartened by what was happening to her profession. She had always been the writer of the story. She'd never been the story – except for the Peru blowback piece, which got little attention and was quickly forgotten. She recalled it was organized by Erika Bernstein, the environmentalist who was now working for the Save the Climate campaign. She suspected Erika had a hand in the latest takedown, too. Elise worried that journalists – until now trusted for their accurate, fair, and balanced accounting of events – were becoming targets of campaigns to suppress facts that didn't support their goals or were even used to bolster those campaigns.

Despite her effort to control the damage, she worried the critical article would live online forever and become a stain on her reputation that would be used against her – perhaps by the green lobby, perhaps even by her own employer. She worried for her safety. The photo that was secretly taken of her sitting beside John Hess in his car implied someone had followed him or her with the intent to do harm.

After her rebuttal story was edited and reviewed by the *Journal*'s lawyers, Elise walked back to her apartment for one more humiliating task. She called Jordan. He'd left her a long, angry phone message earlier in the day. He demanded to know what was going on between her and John Hess. He told her he was disappointed by her lack of personal and professional integrity. Clearly, Jordan had believed everything the offending story had said.

"Hi Jordan, it's Elise. Sorry I'm calling so late," she said to his voicemail, feeling tired and depressed, hoping for his understanding. "That story is a fabrication. Let me explain. Please call me back."

But he didn't.

Elise feared that her relationship with Jordan was damaged, probably beyond repair. Julien would have supported her, unconditionally, because he understood her and the risks of her job. He wouldn't have judged her. Jordan didn't want to listen to her, give her the benefit of the doubt. Jordan would always be an activist first, she concluded. A part of her, the one that was unsure about whether her relationship with Jordan had a future, felt relief that she saw him in full before it was too late.

John spent the day huddled in the offices of his lawyers, cursing the leftist media, and preparing a defamation lawsuit against the newspaper that published the offending article. The firm's managing partner, a friend, phoned its editor and threatened an expensive court fight unless a retraction, approved by John, was published in a prominent spot. The editor promised to take the feedback into consideration in discussions with the paper's own lawyers but stuck to his guns.

When he returned to his office in the early evening, John found a stack of messages from investors, partners, and friends, mostly sympathetic.

"I'm cancelling my subscription," one said. "I'll back you up if you sue them. I was on that tour, and I have a completely different recollection," said another.

Another pile was from various media, no doubt eager to amplify the controversy and boost their readership. He tossed the messages in the trash. None were from his wife, who was somewhere in Europe with one of her friends, purchasing art for her hotel.

He checked his company's stock price. It had moved higher. It re-enforced to him that investors cared about one thing: making money from the development of the oilsands. He even wondered if they were they rewarding him for having such an influential inside track at the *Journal*.

He asked himself if he crossed the line in seeking attention for his company. Did he go too far with *managing* Elise? Was the tour a bad idea? Were the oilsands a bad idea? He was simply doing what he'd always done before.

He was shaken, too. It was the first time that his character had been so viciously attacked in a newspaper, and he didn't know why or what to do.

He felt bad for Elise, too. He wanted to talk to her but opted to wait until he knew more about what went on: Who followed him and why? Who orchestrated the article? Were his office, his oilsands leases, his house, secure? And most importantly, was his reputation – his biggest asset – damaged?

Early the next day, John took a phone call from Jim McKinnon from the Aurora oilsands site.

"Good morning, John," Jim said. "I read that nonsense story about the oilsands tour, and I want to let you know we all feel bad about it. We worked hard to make it a success, and we were very pleased with the initial *Journal* story because it accurately reflected what really went on and what we are all about.

"But those unauthorized pictures of the oilsands tour, the ones used with the story, those are alarming because it looks like they were taken by someone nearby. I wanted to let you know that we surveyed the area and found a big hole in a chain-link fence, and many footprints in the snow near Plains' oilsands leases. Someone broke into our property," he said, as John listened intently.

"Our friends at the Deer Lake Nation said something else that I found interesting. There has been a lot of activity on the Plains' side of the fence. Maybe they are doing some prep work to start their own oilsands project. I doubt that anyone at Plains would have broken into our site. They know better. But since I worked there and I know how they operate, it wouldn't surprise me if they assisted some of those activists to break in, just to cause us some grief."

"Seriously?" John responded. "Thank you for the info. It explains a lot. What you say worries me on so many levels." He was angry. He thought about the ways Susan Scott had hounded him in the past and did not look forward to having her as a direct competitor once again.

"And it's not all," Jim said. "Word here is that the Save the Climate people are all over the region, offering money to anyone prepared to oppose oilsands development, particularly Indigenous people."

"I doubt they'll find too many takers," John said. "Is there any way of telling who broke into our project from our security cameras?"

"Our security contractor is reviewing the footage right now. It could cost us money to get to the bottom of this," Jim said.

"Do what you have to do. Did you report this to the police? John asked.

"Not yet. I wanted to discuss it with you before getting them involved. Do we really want the publicity?" Jim asked.

"No – for now," John answered. "But we need to increase our security and keep a closer eye on the activists, and on Plains. They're up to no good, I'm sure, and we need to be prepared. I'll use my own sources to find out if Plains are really getting into the oilsands business. And by the way, great job on getting the info. When are you due to come to Calgary?"

"I'll be there next week," Jim said.

"Please come and see me. I'd like to discuss a few things, including staff retention. It's been on my mind for a while. I'd like to get your input."

At the end of the day, John walked through the downtown to Elise's office and found her engrossed in a discussion with other *Journal* staff about the nasty article.

"Hi Elise," he said, surprising the group, which knew him by reputation and was unaccustomed to seeing high-profile oilmen make office calls.

"Hi John," Elise responded, then introduced him to everyone.

"Elise, can we talk privately for a minute?" John asked, noticing Elise's eyes were swollen and red. "Let's go for coffee."

They walked to a coffee shop where they didn't expect to be recognized, ordered large lattes, and settled in comfortable leather chairs facing each other. It was a warm, mid-summer afternoon and the place was deserted. A few people were bicycling near the riverbanks. The rest of the downtown crowd were either on holidays or working overtime, in a hurry to finish their work so everyone could take off for the August long weekend.

"I feel bad about the way you were portrayed in that story," John told her. "It was all my fault. In my eagerness to get Aurora's story out there, in the best possible light, I picked you because I trust your reporting and your understanding of the industry. But I failed to see how it could affect you and your reputation.

"But it's nothing I haven't done before. It's important in my business to be transparent – and media coverage is an important part of doing that. My goal was to show what we are doing and how, and I am proud of it. I believe something has changed, though – and you need to know this because it might explain what went on."

He told her about the break-in in Aurora's property, what he knew about the recruitment drive by the Save the Climate Campaign, and his suspicion about Plains' nasty tactics to undermine him so it could make its own entrance in the oilsands business.

Elise asked the oilman if she could write about the revelations.

"Not yet," John said. "We need to get to the bottom of all this ourselves. We are looking at our own security footage to see if we can recognize anyone. If we get something that is usable, you will get it. Meanwhile, we are doing our own research about the activists."

"Alright," Elise said. "But you can help me in other ways. Since it's obvious the same campaign wants to intimidate me and my newspaper, we're going to double down and cover the oilsands even more. So, to strengthen my standing as a credible source of energy news, to crush my media competitors, and to give the Save the Climate activists a proper response, I need to produce the most compelling reporting on the sector. The oilsands are becoming big news and will be the big battleground, I believe, against the global fossil fuel industry. I can't do it alone. I know that from experience. You, on the other hand, have access to information that I don't get, until it's already in the public domain. I need you to help me get it. Mergers, IPOs, government policies, industry gossip – keep me in the loop. I need you to answer my calls.

"By helping me provide the most reliable and highest-quality information about the oilsands, you'd be helping your company, too. The trend is your friend, right? And you would finally get to treat me as the professional that I am, rather than as someone to manipulate, emotionally and professionally, for your own advantage. It's a growth opportunity for you.

"I will never reveal you as the source," Elise promised. "If I get it first, and if it's relevant to the markets, I'm happy. Will you help me?"

John thought about Elise's strange ask and quickly wondered about the risks of getting into such an unorthodox pact with a reporter, with no guarantee of results. His instinct was to do the opposite and keep a low profile for a while.

"Would you protect me, have my back, so to speak?" he asked.

"Yes. I never reveal sources," Elise repeated, adding that for the agreement to work they had to be careful about being seen together in public places.

"What about the activists? Don't you have to cover them fairly, too?" he asked.

"I do. But I no longer regard the Save the Climate people as trustworthy sources. They hung me out to dry. They made it personal. They lied about me. I want nothing to do with them. I will not seek them out in the future. There are other environmental organizations I can go to for views on environmental issues," Elise said. She didn't share with him that she had another reason to avoid Save the Climate – Jordan was no longer in her life.

Once again, the oilman was struck by Elise. No other woman had seen through him so clearly or challenged him the way she did. He was looking forward to a reset of their relationship, too. If Elise was right, he wanted to be on the front lines of the coming fight on behalf of the industry that he loved, which he felt was also the right fight for his country's future.

"OK. I'm in," he said. "Let me be your partner in truth telling. But let me be my old self just once more."

He picked up the white paper napkin Elise had used to wipe her mouth, which had a perfect, rose-coloured imprint of her lips, and put it in his jacket pocket.

Chapter 31

BOSTON, MASSACHUSETTS, AUGUST 2004

With her summer plans with Jordan cancelled, Elise pushed back her holidays until the end of August. She flew to New York, rented a minivan, picked up her children at the apartment they shared with friends while studying at Columbia, and together they drove to Boston, where the twins would start their graduate studies at Harvard in September.

Elise hadn't seen her children since their graduation in the spring when Jordan had come along. They almost looked like a happy family then. She had asked herself many times whether she missed him at all. Maybe a bit, she concluded, or, more precisely, she missed the thought of them together.

She was proud of her children and grateful the three of them had remained so close, despite having lost so much and living so far apart. Simone and Richard had turned twenty-three in June and were inseparable, yet they had different interests. Simone would do a graduate degree in public policy and Richard would take medicine.

"Have you seen your new digs?" Elise asked while driving on the crowded highway.

"Yes, we saw the apartment a month ago. We took over the lease of a friend. It's a pretty good spot and we are in walking distance to our classes," said Simone, who sat in the back with her cat.

"How much is it?"

"It's pretty expensive, but don't worry, we're both going to work part time to help pay for it," Richard said from the front seat, beside Elise, ravaging a burger. "Jordan even offered to help us with tuition, but we turned him down," he added, aware of the frayed relationship between Jordan and his mom, though not of the details.

"You stayed in touch?" Elise asked.

"Yes. But it's awkward," Richard said. "We saw pictures in a society column of Jordan in a tux with that activist, what's her name, Barb Heinz, who badmouthed you in the newspaper, and asked him if they're together. He said they're dating. How can he do that to you? I don't get him."

"He's probably offering to give you money for school because he feels guilty," Elise said. "He has avoided me since that awful article. He never called me back to hear my side of the story. I don't think he understands I have a job to do, and that I am not someone's lap dog. I suspect Barb Heinz got the better of him. I only met her once, but I know her by reputation. She is manipulative and has big political ambitions. Jordan is a pretty good catch for someone like her who wants to climb the political ladder."

Elise was digesting the news of Jordan's new relationship, trying not to seem too bitter in front of her children, but feeling even more betrayed. Barb Heinz was younger, attractive, and in the right location. She was disappointed that Jordan hooked up with her so quickly after turning his back on her.

"I worry that he's in over his head," Simone said. "Jordan is a smart guy, but he seems naïve about women. Anyway, moving to Boston will make things easier for us because he won't be so close. I think he feels the need to be a replacement for dad, but frankly he's so uncool."

"It's hard for people who don't have children to figure them out," Elise said, eager to change the subject. "Anyway, I wish him well. Our family has bigger and better things to worry about, right?

"Speaking of big things," Elise continued, growing restless by the growing traffic, heat, and pollution, which she had forgotten about in Calgary. "You're old enough now to know that your father left you a large fund to pay for your education and to get you started in life. There is some money, in addition, from your grandparents' estate. I managed the funds on your behalf until now. But it's time you make more of your financial decisions. The funds generate plenty of income to pay for all your school expenses. You don't need to work while you're in school, or to take anyone's help – particularly not Jordan's. Work hard to get good grades. That's what your father would have wanted."

Elise's children had suspected they were well off but didn't know their late father, and their grandparents, had provided so generously for them.

They spent the rest of the drive talking about the many ways they missed them. When they arrived in Boston, the twins asked Elise if she was ready to move back to New York so they could be closer.

"I have been thinking about it, but I am not sure there is a job for me in the newsroom," Elise said.

"But you just told us we don't need the money. Why not come back and retire?" Simone pleaded.

"I'm too young to retire," Elise said. "I need to do something that makes a difference. And I have too much unfinished business in Calgary. Besides, I am pretty sure you don't want your old mom hovering over you. I promise, I will talk to my editor about new opportunities closer to you. Let's see what comes up."

They spent a glorious week together, re-discovering Boston, cleaning the new apartment, buying new beds and other furniture, and reconnecting with members of their extended family. She left feeling rejuvenated and ready to sink her teeth into something big.

Chapter 32

Life on the road to advocate for the Save the Climate campaign was not what Anthony Littlechild had envisioned. Erika Bernstein had kept her promise and paid him promptly to don his traditional attire and dance for audiences of politicians and donors in faraway places. But the young Indigenous man didn't like what he'd become. He was told what to say, how to act, how to think by people who barely knew him or his band.

Elise had seen his picture on the Save the Climate's new website. She thought he was the ideal poster boy – handsome, with a strong jaw and piercing black eyes.

She contacted him and asked if he would agree to an interview for a feature profile.

A few days later, Anthony responded with a nervous phone call, after wondering why such a prominent newspaper was interested in talking to someone like him. He warned her that he was no longer working for the group. Elise responded she was even more curious about him and his experience with the campaign.

When they finally met in Fort McMurray, Elise saw a young man, dressed in jeans and a hoodie, about the same age as her children. She wondered if the sadness etched in his face was the mark of a rough past. She asked him why he quit the campaign.

"They treated me like a circus act," Anthony complained over coffee in a Fort McMurray community hall crowded with oil service workers enjoying drinks after their shifts. "All I wanted was to improve things for my band and make a bit of money for myself. These activists just want to create controversy and raise money. They don't want things to get better for us."

"Let's start from the beginning," she said gently, pulling her notebook and tape recorder from her purse. "Tell me why you agreed to participate in the first place."

"I don't like what the oilsands companies do to our lands," Anthony responded. "By scarring the land, they scar each one of us. The land, the water, the sky – they're part of who we are, our history, our livelihood, and our health. I can't separate myself from the land that made me."

Struck by the depth of his words, Elise asked him about his life.

Anthony talked about the financial hardship faced by his broken family, his difficulties in school, his years of sexual abuse. "You're not including all that bad stuff in your article, are you?" he asked.

"I'd like to. It's a big part of your story. I will do it in a way that you feel comfortable with, okay?"

"Okay," he responded, wanting to trust her.

"Tell me more about the campaign," Elise pressed on.

"Look. I know they mean well, but the campaign failed to achieve real improvements for my people," Anthony said. "I was disappointed by the activists' tactics. They hire Indigenous people to front their war against fossil fuels. Meanwhile, they are fundraising machines in the background. I guess they do what they need to do. Anyway, they won't miss me. They have found someone else to replace me."

"Why didn't you look for solutions to the oilsands within your community?" Elise asked.

"They don't listen to me," Anthony said. "Our chief and his family make too much money from the oilsands. It's like they're hooked on a drug."

"What's next for you?" Elise asked.

"I want to go back to school, maybe study to be a lawyer. The money I made from Save the Climate will help pay for some of my expenses. I feel that I need more education, put my past behind, and then provide better leadership for my people. I believe that oilsands development can be a good thing for us if it's done properly. What else do we have up here? There are no other opportunities. We need to be full participants and we need to ensure our lands go back to their original state when industry moves out."

"That's a great plan for you," Elise said. "I hope my story helps."

To complete her research, Elise spoke to Indigenous leaders who acknowledged not everyone was happy but highlighted the benefits of their growing participation in the business. She spoke to the oilsands companies about their programs to train Indigenous people for jobs on their projects, and to politicians and historians. Her last call was to the Save the Climate campaign. Despite her intention to avoid contact she was obligated to offer it an opportunity to respond. Several messages to Erika went unanswered.

Elise's profile of Anthony Littlechild was so touching it went on to win her writing prizes in both Canada and the United States. Anthony was awarded a full scholarship to study at the University of Toronto – subject to finishing high school. An anonymous benefactor pledged to pay for his tuition in a law school anywhere in the world.

Chapter 33

MANHATTAN, NEW YORK, JANUARY 2005

Elise landed at JFK, was picked up by a *Journal* car, and she then checked into one of the suites owned by her newspaper for visiting executives. The modern condo with concierge service was a short walk from the New York Stock Exchange. She wondered why she was asked to stay there. Returning correspondents were usually put up in a modest hotel adjacent to the *Journal*'s newsroom.

She'd been summoned to a meeting in the newsroom by the new editor in chief. She hoped – dreamed – it was about discussing a new assignment, perhaps a new beat in a new location. She'd expressed interest in moving back to New York to write a column, or to Washington to follow politics, or to San Francisco to report on technology.

Elise felt good about the job she'd done in Calgary. She'd helped grow readership for her newspaper. The Save the Climate campaign against her was fading into the background. She felt she deserved a new opportunity. After five years in a foreign outpost, away from her family, she demonstrated her loyalty to her employer, she thought. She was ready to start a new chapter and return to the familiar world she'd left behind. But she was nervous. Many of her colleagues had been laid off after the 9/11 terrorist attacks and it was common knowledge that new competitors were eroding her employer's advertising revenue.

The next day, she woke up late. Her meeting was at noon. Elise ordered breakfast and enjoyed the suite, then put on a coat and took the long way to her workplace. She wanted to savour every second of her return to her newsroom, which was in many ways her first home.

She inhaled the smoggy humidity. Calgary was so dry that New York's mugginess felt good.

When she arrived at the Depression-era building that housed her newspaper, she saw that major renovations had been completed. The newsroom had been expanded to accommodate new workstations arranged in pods, each specializing in a beat, many of them new. Quiet computers replaced older models. Editors' crowded offices were clustered near the windows. Executives took up another floor. Advertising, the conference division, and the giant IT army toiled in the basement.

Elise found her new boss's office on a higher floor with dozens of empty workstations, equipped to accommodate new staff. She knocked on his door.

"Come in," Mark Wimhurst said with a warm smile, standing up and offering his hand. "It's a pleasure to meet you, Elise."

"Glad to meet you, too. Welcome to the *Journal*," Elise said, and smiled back. She reckoned he was a decade older than her, with red hair sprinkled with silver and a well-groomed beard. She'd read he was a Brit with top Fleet Street experience who'd joined the paper to implement an aggressive growth plan.

"I heard lots about you and your excellent work up in Canada," he said, seated casually on the corner of his desk, his white shirtsleeves rolled up, a cheap pen resting behind his right ear. "I spent a few years in Montreal when I was starting my career. Great place. I hope it was as good to you as it was me. I also overcame some very difficult times there."

Elise realized he had looked her up. Good, she thought. He does his homework. She liked his energy.

"It's exciting to hear the *Journal* is growing again," she said.

"I asked you to come back to the mothership because I'd like to discuss a growth opportunity and get your input," he said. "I came to the *Journal* because I love newspapers, but I also believe this industry will be fighting for its life and needs to embrace new technologies and new growth strategies. New entrants are disrupting our business, using the internet to distribute information, and capturing advertising dollars. I'm sure you've noticed that they are stealing our content, rewriting it, and posting it on their platforms like it's their own."

"I have, and it's frustrating," Elise said.

"News will be increasingly commoditized, consumed digitally, and hard copies of newspapers will be phased out," he continued. "The *Journal* will be the leader in digital delivery. We have a worldwide, sophisticated audience that already works on computers and that is hungry for everything we write. Delivering newspapers to them is very costly. We can make our news available in digital editions as it develops and at lower cost than shipping our newspapers to their offices once a day. As we move to this new delivery method, we will build our own trading platform. Time is money, so quick access to market-moving information will give our readers an advantage."

Then Mark leaned in, trying to gauge Elise's interest. "Here's where you come in," he said. "Thanks to you and your team, we have been the leader in energy information. We would like the Calgary office to be one of the test sites for a new venture. It will be the only one outside the United States. There is a large trading community there. Global investors are already tuned in to what's going on in Canada. Its oil business is hot.

"We'd like to expand your team to increase coverage of energy news – not just Canadian, but global – and start a digital *Journal* energy report to deliver to all the subscribers who want it. We will deploy marketing and technical support to assist you. We would like you to co-lead this effort. You would ensure that our editorial content is second to none. John Daly – you'll meet him later today – will move to Calgary to build the rest of the operation."

Elise absorbed every word. She had never envisioned herself as a leader. She hadn't sought those positions in the past because she knew they weren't open to her. Journalism was a man's world, and the best that female journalists could hope for was to work hard and get a high-profile beat until they got a better-paying job in public relations.

"Look, I know this is a lot to take in," Mark said. "I am offering you a pathway to senior management. You have an impressive background – Columbia and Harvard, right? – and a great reputation. We need you in our leadership team."

The opportunity was so different from what Elise had expected that she had to digest it, think about the upside and the downside.

"This is very exciting," she said. "I'm up for a new challenge, as you know. I literally grew up at the *Journal*, and I would do anything to help it thrive. If I look a bit surprised, it's because this is the first time that I have been offered an opportunity to move into management. I love the idea of embracing technology to deliver the news. I agree with everything you said about our readers. They are already way ahead of us in consuming information from online sources.

"I need to sort out one thing first – would I be able to be here in New York at least part time?" Elise asked, explaining she wanted to spend more time closer to her children.

"Absolutely," Mark said. "This pilot requires a high level of coordination. In fact, we will need you to come back to head office every month, say for a week?"

"That works," Elise said. "Will I be able to continue to write?"

"You must. We want you to be as visible as possible. Our journalists are our greatest asset. Readers trust you. At the same time, we'll need you to bring on board the next generation of journalists, show them the ropes," the editor said. "We need to expand coverage of energy commodities, mergers and acquisitions, oil politics. Anything that moves markets. The beauty of a digital edition is that it amplifies your readership, and you'll be even better known. We need you be more high-viz – speak at conferences, do commercials, whatever it takes to promote you and the *Journal*."

"Then I am in," Elise said, pleased with the unexpected turn of events.

They discussed compensation, a new title – associate editor – to reflect her senior role, and next steps.

Elise met other members of the new digital team and participated in planning sessions over the rest of the week. On Friday evening, after signing off on the newspaper's next edition, Mark and three other senior editors took her out for dinner to celebrate. Elise's insights on the energy industry had been so valuable that they unanimously felt they were in good hands. Life was taking care of itself, Elise thought, and felt Julien's presence.

Chapter 34

MANHATTAN, NEW YORK, JANUARY 2005

Elise was feeling good when she entered the crowded eatery. She spotted her children quickly. They had driven in from Boston, after they made plans to meet before she returned to Calgary. Then her heart skipped a beat. Jordan was sitting with them in a booth. They looked comfortable with each other.

"Hi Mom," Richard said, hugging her tightly. "Canada becomes you. I hope you don't mind that we invited Jordan to come along." Elise didn't know what to say. She hadn't heard from Jordan in what seemed like a lifetime.

"Look, you two need to patch things up," Richard pleaded. "Jordan has been really helpful. I need his guidance. Medical school is tough, and he's helping me stay sane."

Elise straightened herself and buried down the hard feelings that were suddenly resurfacing. She knew she had to let things go for her children.

"Hi Jordan. It's so great to see you. And Simone, I'm going to steal that outfit," Elise said, hugging her daughter.

They ordered food and caught up on school, life in Boston, life in Calgary. But it was superficial talk. Elise didn't feel comfortable sharing news about her new job. Jordan was close to Barb Heinz. The last thing she wanted was to undermine her employer's strategy by disclosing details to someone she felt no longer wanted the best for her.

"How are things in Calgary?" Jordan said, trying to break the ice.

"They're very busy," Elise said. "There's lots to write about, and I am travelling a lot."

"Are you planning to move back?"

"Not for a while. But I will spend more time in New York in the future," she said, without offering details. "In fact, I decided to take back my apartment. My tenants are leaving in a couple of months. I will renovate it and use it when we are all here, just like old times."

"Mom, that's great," Simone said, excited by the news. "We miss our home. We come to New York all the time. It'll be nice to have our place back."

Jordan gave his own update about the hospital. His department was expanding, and he'd taken a side gig as a medical contributor on a TV network.

A sense of intimacy resurfaced. They drank red wine and ordered dessert – tiramisu for everyone. They all needed the pick-me-up.

Elise noticed he looked more polished. He was wearing a cologne. A part of her hoped for a reconciliation. We have too much history together to not be in each other's lives, she thought.

"I have news of my own," Jordan said nervously. "I'm getting married this summer." Elise felt faint. She did not expect Jordan to take such an important step so quickly.

"Who's the lucky lady?" Simone asked, looking disappointed.

"Barb Heinz," Jordan revealed. "We have known each other for a long time through our work on climate change. We see the world in the same way. We're tying the knot in Barbados in May. I wanted you to hear it from me first."

Elise wanted to warn him to be careful, to see Barb for the political operative that she knew her to be. She wanted to tell him he should get to know her better. But she didn't. She was hardly in a position to offer him advice.

"I wish you all the best," Elise said, forcing a smile. "You'll be great together."

After their uneasy reunion came to an end, they all hugged each other outside the restaurant. Elise wished her kids good night. They made plans to meet the next day.

Jordan asked Elise if he could accompany her to wherever she was staying. Elise hesitated. She didn't want him to know how hurt she felt that he chose someone else. Then she realized she had no right to feel that way. Jordan needed someone who shared and supported his values.

"Sure, let's walk," Elise said, wanting to break the impasse between them. She had much to feel good about, she thought, such as the almost warm mid-winter evening, the boisterous crowd that surrounded her, the job promotion that would recharge her career.

"I'm so pleased with my children's progress," she said. "Richard is so much like his dad – always working, pushing himself to the limit. And Simone is a knockout. One year to go and she'll have to decide what to do. She's thinking journalism, which would make me very happy, but who knows."

Jordan nodded, looking like he had weightier things on his mind.

"Elise, I wanted to apologize for the way I behaved," he said. "I know you had a rough go when you got caught up in the campaign. Some of our people can be irresponsible. They mean well. They're young and impatient. They don't appreciate how much damage they can do."

"I have asked Barb to leave you alone," he continued. "Let's go back to the way we were. We have a lot of history. Your children mean a lot to me. I'd like to be helpful, in any way you are comfortable with."

Elise agreed and felt more relaxed. Then they spoke about old times, about her apartment – he offered names of tradespeople he used to renovate his – and her plans to return to New York more regularly.

"Will you come back for good?" he asked.

"Not yet," she said. "I have lots on my plate."

"Can you talk about it?" he asked.

"No," Elise said. "Unfortunately, this climate change campaign has pushed us into opposing camps. I did not choose this. They did. I must watch my back, now more than ever. The only way this, you and me, is going to work is if we don't talk about my job."

"I understand," Jordan said. "I agree."

By the time they arrived at Elise's destination, they were on better terms. They hugged on the sidewalk. Then Jordan held Elise's face in his hands and kissed her lips. They held each other more. They both knew they were moving in different directions, far away from what they once had. Elise stepped away and opened the door of her building, hiding her face. She didn't want Jordan to see the tears.

Chapter 35

CALGARY, ALBERTA, OCTOBER 2006

Paul Chen looked tired as he took the executive elevator to his penthouse office, where a steaming breakfast prepared by his Chinese chef was waiting on his desk.

"The bankers are here to see you," Lorna, his plain looking assistant, said, poking her face through his office door.

"Let them in," he said, flicking away a piece of food that had landed on his red silk tie, an attempt to liven an ill-fitting suit he'd purchased off the rack in Hong Kong.

The Chinese executive had firm orders from his bosses: Build a large position in the oilsands and install China's flag. He knew next to nothing about how to produce the deposits, and he was just getting acquainted with the strange, cold place where they were located.

But he knew oil and he knew money. Born in Beijing and educated in the United States on a university scholarship, Chen was an accountant with good understanding of Western business practices and taxation. He spoke respectable American English. He was unusually tall and handsome, which in China gave him an edge.

He used those strengths to rise to the highest levels of one of China's state-owned oil companies, one of the first in the country to be allocated vast sums of state money to make strategic acquisitions abroad. But his Canadian mission had proven difficult. After three years in Calgary, Chen had moved hundreds of staff from China to evaluate opportunities, leased a large office tower to house them, enrolled his children in Canadian schools and made them apply for Canadian citizenship, hired lawyers and bankers to advise him, joined the board of six charities to make new friends – and was still empty handed.

He'd made several offers to purchase companies or assets. But he'd been too cheap or too slow. Prices of oilsands companies were rising to silly levels. Sellers avoided him. Nothing personal, his new friends told him discreetly. Canadians were nervous about partnering with the Chinese. They saw them as too bureaucratic and too Communist, and too much in the crosshairs of the United States.

Beijing had become so impatient with Paul Chen's lack of progress that his superiors phoned him regularly in the middle of the night, accusing him of incompetence and of squandering the Chinese people's money. They ordered him to make a move so they could load Canadian oil onto tankers headed for China as soon as possible.

The bankers arrived at Paul's office bearing promising news. They'd heard through their contacts that one of the oil industry's best-known companies, Wilson Exploration, was considering selling a large part of its oilsands business to concentrate on other parts that were a better fit for their expertise. Duke Wilson, the founder and CEO, was in his late seventies and ready to reduce company debt so he could hand off a better capitalized company to his heirs, the bankers explained.

They were top-drawer assets, they assured Paul, and the price tag would be large. The unit came with its own workforce and new extraction and processing technologies that could be useful to Beijing.

"How quickly can we get into their data room?" Paul asked, inviting the men to share his ample meal, an offer they politely declined.

Donning immaculate white shirts, expensive-looking suits and buffed black leather shoes, they smiled but kept their distance, just like the other Canadians he met, Paul thought. He envied and despised them at the same time. The bankers were all the same – trust-fund kids who owed their big jobs and elite education to family connections. They were warm on the surface but ice-cold just below, like the ground in Alberta in late spring. And yet they were kissing his ass, a poor farmer's son who earned his way up by studying and working hard.

"We suggest that you make a move before they open a data room and start marketing the unit," one of them said.

"How do I know I am making the right move for the right price?" Paul asked. "If I have to rely on public information, I wouldn't be doing the due diligence that I am required to do."

"We could help with that," one of them said, already counting in his head the exorbitant commission he'd be entitled to if the purchase went ahead. "The company is private but well known. We can talk to their executives on background. The key is to keep this tight and come up with a number they will like." The bankers agreed to return the next day with all the information they could assemble in a hurry to prepare a bid.

Paul Chen convened his executive team. He wanted them to start doing research on their own.

"What do you know about the company?" he asked his second-in-command, an engineer who knew the oilsands well. Paul had lured him over to his company from a competitor by doubling his pay.

"Wilson Exploration is well regarded, but they have lots of debt and more opportunities than they need. Duke Wilson is a pioneer," the engineer said.

"Are the assets good enough to build on?"

"Yes, they're a good start. They have probably three thousand employees, a producing operation with lots of growth potential, and advanced plans for upgrading and refining. We could work with that."

"That's a lot of people – and a lot of obligations," Paul said. "But I am interested," he added. "Beijing has been on my back. They're concerned we have been missing opportunities and want us to make a move. This may be bigger than we planned, but it would certainly give us a big footprint to expand our oil business in the West."

A few blocks away, Susan Scott's career was on life support. Plains Exploration was limping along. Its stock was battered by hedge funds. Major investors were demanding her dismissal. Plains' mediocre performance contrasted with virtually all its major competitors, which had grown their oilsands business significantly and were taking advantage of their strong stock prices to take more debt and expand.

She knew Plains needed to re-invent itself. Its years of focus on natural gas was a drag. Gas prices had collapsed because new technology caused an explosion of new production from shale formations in North America. But opportunities in the oilsands had been expensive, and her company's balance sheet already stretched. Plains' oilsands leases were under development but building a project from the ground up was taking much longer than expected. Finding staff was a problem. Few wanted to work for a market loser.

Then one of her banking sources told her that Wilson Exploration, a big private producer, was quietly floating the idea of selling a part of its oilsands business. They'd decided to grow in a different area of the basin and monetize some of their assets.

"I'm listening," she told him.

"This would be a big piece of business," the banker said. "It would significantly increase Plains' size if you're successful and diversify your operations. I heard they'd rather deal with a Canadian buyer because it would be a better fit for their staff. But money talks, so be prepared for a fight with the Chinese. This is likely one they'll go after."

Susan perked up. She already knew Wilson Exploration's assets. The ones in question were located next to Plains' own properties in the oilsands. She was excited about acquiring its staff, too, to accelerate her plan.

"I am surprised this unit is coming up for sale," she said to her team during a briefing on the new opportunity.

"I thought these guys were here to stay. These assets could be expensive. We would require more debt and new equity, which the market won't like – at least until they see good results. But it's worth a look," she said.

"We need to find out everything there is to know – reserves, production, marketing arrangements, etc., and get ready for a bid. I'll do some research of my own. We need an inside track."

After the meeting, she returned to her office to make a call.

"Find out about Duke Wilson and his family," Susan said to the private investigator at the other end of the line. "Extramarital affairs, insider trading, tax issues, litigation. There have been rumours. I want to know what is true."

At the private dining club of the most exclusive golf course in the city, Duke Wilson was greeted like a legend. He hugged the staff – especially the young waitresses – who adored him because of his big booze orders and large cash tips. In return he expected them to be discreet.

John was sipping sparkling water in the club's most secluded room. Duke had asked John to join him for lunch and get his input on his plan. Despite their age difference, they'd been good friends. Over time, they'd looked out for each other.

"How are you, Duke?" John said, standing up to greet him, shaking his hand firmly.

"Life's good," Duke said. "And how's that lovely wife of yours?" he added.

"Claire is as busy as ever, running construction of the new downtown hotel and looking for more opportunities to build her empire. She's having the time of her life," John responded.

"Thank you for making time for me. I'm not getting any younger and I'd like to talk to you about my next chapter," the elder oilman said. "As you know, I have been in this business for more than fifty years. I have never seen a frenzy like this. We have more opportunities than we can handle, and more plays than we can fund.

"But I know this is a cyclical industry, and I am thinking of raising some cash, pay down debt, before hanging up my boots. I'm glad the oil industry is finally getting the recognition it deserves, but I have been around the block too many times. I want to act before it's too late."

"Seriously? I thought you'd never quit," John said, his thoughts racing, wondering if the older man's thinking was a sign that he, too, should have a Plan B. "What do you have in mind?"

"I'm thinking of putting part of the oilsands business on the block – near your properties in the Lower Athabasca basin, and those of Plains. I'm putting out feelers to see what price I could get." They stopped talking as two waitresses in black uniforms walked in to take their food orders.

"They're good properties," John said after the waitresses left. "Tell me more."

"We think they will be top producers, but we don't have all the data yet. We're building an upgrader, which has been labour intensive and will require more investment soon. New technology. Between you and I, we don't think the deposit is as good as our stuff up north. We'd rather focus on our best plays."

"I'm not surprised," John said. "I have evaluated many of the properties in that area – thought I don't know yours as well as I should. I think my company sits in the sweet spot. The rest could be more challenging to produce because the deposits have gaps between them, which could be a problem if you drill in the wrong spot."

"True. But they're better than anything that is still available, and there's lots of them," Duke said.

They discussed the growth potential and the infrastructure that would be required.

Then Duke asked John if he was interested in making a deal. He explained that he cared about his people and wanted them to be led by someone like John.

John hesitated. He liked his company the way it was. He had plenty of internal growth opportunities. His stock was trading at a premium in part because of the high quality of his reserves. He had little debt. Going down market and leveraging his balance sheet could drag down his stock price.

"I tell you what," John suggested. "I'll take a look. Regardless, I'll help you get the highest price you can get."

Duke seemed satisfied. He knew better than to ask how. They talked about the hockey season – both oilmen were top sponsors – as they finished their meals. Before they departed, Duke put his arm around John's shoulder.

"John, there have been rumours – about you and that reporter, you know, the one from the *Journal*."

"What rumours?" the younger man asked, feeling embarrassed.

"Rumours that you are romantically involved. People talk. She's not good for you, John. Look, your private life is your business – but a reporter? You can't trust her to keep her mouth shut. You don't have leverage over her."

"For the record, I am not involved with Elise – she has been useful, that's all," John said. "I wish we had more like her. She's influential, and she understands our business. But thanks for letting me know."

"What are friends for?" the older man said, satisfied the message was delivered.

They walked out of the club separately – John from a garden entrance, Duke through the front door. Outside, a driver was waiting at the wheel of Duke's golden Rolls.

They'd not been careful enough. A banker dining with his partners at the club caught a glimpse of the titans' exclusive meet, and by evening, rumours were circulating that something big was up.

John took a long drive through the foothills to carve out time to think. The rumours about Elise concerned him. That story on the two of them in his car had done a lot of damage. He would be even more careful, he decided. But he needed her more than ever. In fact, he was increasingly counting on her and their secret pact.

As for Duke, he wanted to help him – he owed it to him – but he also wanted to help himself. What he really needed were Plains' underdeveloped oilsands reserves.

He suspected Plains didn't fully understand them – yet. He'd heard about their struggles to find staff and money. But he knew their oilsands. He'd looked at the geology and concluded they were at least as oil rich as his own and sitting conveniently on the other side of his fence. There was no better expansion opportunity for his company. He also wanted to buy them for as cheap as possible.

Yet Susan Scott would never sell the leases to him. He knew that, too. There was too much bad blood. It was time to push Plains over the edge, he concluded, and Duke had just handed him the keys.

Elise was working her sources when John rang her from his car.

"Hi Elise. Long time, no talk," he said. "I'm glad you're still at work."

"Yes, it's been very busy," Elise said. "I have a lot on my plate these days. We expanded our operation here. Plus, big news is breaking every day."

They'd settled into a mutually beneficial professional relationship, a sort of low boil that suited both well. She was enjoying her broader work responsibilities, her children's fast-moving lives, and the scoops John sent her way through back channels. John was grateful for Elise's in-depth coverage, which brought more investor interest and better understanding of the oilsands, particularly producers' plans to reduce impacts on the environment.

"Well, then. You'll have to bring me up to speed someday. Meanwhile, I have a bit of a scoop if you want it, but it must be off the record, okay?"

"Of course. Just give me the goods. I'll take care of the rest," Elise said.

"Are you familiar with Wilson Exploration?"

"Yes. Big player in the oilsands. Run by Duke Wilson. Private. Often talked about as a takeover target. Interviewed him a couple of times. What a character!"

"They are looking at spinning off a part of their oilsands business. Big bite. We're talking ten billion or more. Call our banker friend. He'll give you all the details about the assets and who might bid. I've asked him to talk to you on background.

"Again, on very deep background, we're interested," John said. "I'm sure many will be as well. I wouldn't rule out a bidding war. That's all." He hung up. He didn't want to answer questions. He had a game plan he didn't want to share.

Elise knew she was being used. Hedge funds, large investors, promoters, and executives fed her regularly tips about potential market-moving events. Everyone had an angle. All wanted a fast buck. Elise was no longer naïve, idealistic. She'd become a user, too. Readers wanted to know. Rumours moved markets. Informed speculation made her look plugged in. She served them what they wanted to read. Journalism was evolving because of competition from upstarts on the internet. She had to pick a lane. Her employer needed to stay in business.

Most tips were farfetched, so she did her best to check them out. She knew from experience that John Hess was the biggest user of all. But she was benefitting from his knowledge now. He was the ultimate insider and always a step ahead. She wondered what his angle was this time.

She phoned their mutual banker friend and got the goods she needed to put together a detailed report on Wilson Exploration, such as quality of the assets, value, potential bidders, and company history, especially Duke Wilson's backstory.

The next day, she made another round of calls. She filed her story by noon, moving markets for oilsands companies. She was excited. Nothing compared to the rush of revealing to readers something she knew they wanted to trade on.

Early in her career, when newspapers were still printed in giant printing plants late at night, she often watched with delight the fast-moving presses spit out copies by the thousands, thick and neatly folded to display the big headline on page one. Now she watched the headlines flash across her computer screen and then quickly ripple around the world.

Duke Wilson was a Canadian icon. Elise knew a deal involving a big chunk of his oilsands business would get plenty of attention. Prices for oilsands properties were setting new highs. A part of her worried that deal-making was becoming irrational, like a poker game gone too far.

In Plains' downtown office tower, the board of directors was meeting to finalize its bid for the Wilson assets when the *Journal* story broke. Susan shared a photocopy with the group. She looked concerned.

"It looks like we could get scooped," she said. "The article suggests Aurora could be one of the bidders. The good news is that if they are interested, it means these are quality assets. The bad news is that the price has just gone up."

"We can still back out," one of the directors said. "I'm not keen to bet the farm on this deal. And I don't want another fight with John Hess. It didn't work out that well for us the last time, right, Susan?"

"You are right. But this may be our last entry point for a significant presence in the oilsands," Susan insisted. "These assets give us an excellent and mature platform. They are a good fit with what we already have, so we are able to build a material business."

They reviewed the pros and cons. By evening, they decided to raise their bid to $12 billion from $10 billion, funded with new equity and debt, and hope for the best.

Paul Chen received approval from Beijing to bid $13 billion. He knew he could not let another opportunity pass him by. He would make the purchase, then resign and let someone else take care of the business, perhaps start a new company of his own in Canada. He was sick of being a puppet of Beijing. He knew the price he was bidding for Wilson was too high, which would make it difficult to make money, but it was all about geopolitics. He phoned Duke Wilson to break the news himself.

"Hi, Mr. Wilson. Paul Chen here," he said.

Duke was in his cattle ranch south of the city, up to his ankles in mud, impatient to move his animals and equipment indoors before the first snow.

"Hey, my friend," the older man said. "How's the oilsands hunt?"

They had spoken before. Duke had been to China many times and respected the country and its people. He knew they'd be interested in his properties. But the Chinese weren't his first choice. No offense. No political statement. Duke was a Canadian first, and an American friend second. He worried that selling so much Canadian oil to China, and all his technology, would be seen as handing over a strategic asset to the enemy. He cared about his reputation and about his legacy.

"Duke, I wanted to tell you personally that we are bidding for your oilsands holdings. We haven't had the opportunity to do full due diligence. Subject to everything checking out, we'd like to offer you thirteen billion in cash for the lot. We would keep all your employees and hire new ones. For a couple of years, we'd want you to be on our board. You'll get our official bid within forty-eight hours."

Duke was pleased. "I like that number," he said. "I look forward to receiving your written offer."

"Are you soliciting other bids?" Paul asked.

"We don't plan to for now, but news is spreading fast," Duke said. They exchanged pleasantries and simultaneously hung up.

Within minutes, Susan Scott was on the line. She told Duke she'd been authorized to put forward a bid: $12 billion, in a combination of debt and new stock, plus a sweetener: Plains would allow Wilson Exploration to share its infrastructure, including pipelines and storage tanks, at very competitive prices. Plains was committed to keeping the oilsands under Canadian control, Susan emphasized, and ensuring the smoothest possible transition for the unit's employees. Unlike other foreign bidders, which she didn't name, Plains' bid would not be stalled by regulators worried about foreign purchases of strategic Canadian resources.

"It's an interesting offer, Susan," Duke said, feeling a bit uncomfortable talking business to a female executive. "But I should let you know that other bidders have already approached us, and I expect at least one more." He was still hopeful that John Hess would step up. He wondered why Susan talked about foreign bidders.

John didn't make an offer but did the next best thing: he fanned speculation that he was considering a bid. Betting in the market on which company would scoop Wilson Exploration's oilsands leases was widespread. The company, hoping to stir even more interest, issued a news release that confirmed it was in talks with several parties to dispose of some of its top oilsands properties, but that there was no assurance a deal would be made.

Elise was astonished that the boom in the oilsands picked up the pace. Plains' stock rose on the potential of an overdue entry, which would be a good fit for its existing lands, and which could revive its flagging stock and get the Canadian company back on track. Aurora's stock rose to reflect the higher quality of its existing properties. Other producers' stocks soared because values were going up, therefore their assets were worth more. Oil prices surged because the oilsands frenzy showed that the market was supporting high-cost oil because cheap oil supplies were scarce. Pipeline stocks rose because more oil transportation would be needed. The stocks of drillers rose because more drilling would be required.

Albertans, who knew their oil stocks better than anyone else, grabbed everything they could.

Less-knowledgeable investors jumped in because they were fearful of missing out on the easiest money they expected to make.

Governments took credit for the manna and spent their new oil revenues faster than it came in the door.

Loans and mortgages were taken out.

New housing was built in anticipation of more people moving to Alberta.

More office towers were planned so the executives plotting the next growth phases of Alberta's oilsands boom would get the large headquarters they felt they deserved.

More vacation properties were built on the British Columbia coast, Mexico, and Hawaii to accommodate the oil rich looking for a break from all the money-making stress.

More oil analysts expected oil prices to rise even more. More economists predicted record economic growth.

Competition for everyone and everything escalated. Geoscientists were at a premium. Pipefitters, plumbers, electricians, and cleaning staff were billing like lawyers. Parking spots were so scarce they were harder to find than jobs.

No one expected the boom to end. No one dared to call it a bubble. This time, everyone told Elise, was different.

Chapter 36

A dozen more bidders emerged for Wilson's oilsands properties. There were big wheels from the Arabian gulf, several large American companies, a few European concerns.

The rush into the oilsands was so widespread that Duke Wilson started questioning his own judgement. Had he put his oilsands properties on the market too soon? Would he get more money if he waited? Was this time different? Would this be a never-ending boom, unlike any he had never seen? Duke selected a short list of bids whose leaders he felt had the corporate culture, the financial capacity, and the vision to take over from him. Plains, the Chinese, and a European company were invited to meet his team. Discussions took weeks. Promises were made. Plans were explained.

Duke liked them all. He asked the companies to start background talks with governments to ensure regulatory approvals would be granted. Then he asked them for their final bids. Plains upped its offer to $13.5 billion, plus a partnership on infrastructure, which it said would be worth another $1 billion in savings to Wilson Exploration. The European company bid $14 billion. The Chinese took the biggest leap: $16 billion, all cash, and agreed to all demands that Duke made.

Since John Hess took a pass, the senior oilman had wanted Plains to succeed, just to keep his oilsands in Canadian hands. He invited Susan Scott for a meeting. He didn't know her well, other than casual encounters at the Petroleum Club. He'd heard she ruled Plains with an iron fist. It was not his style, but it wasn't a deal-breaker. He admired survivors, and Susan appeared to be an exceptional one.

He chose his office for the rendezvous and asked the Plains' president to take his private elevator. She walked past the empty desk of Duke's assistant and into his large corner suite.

"Thank you for joining me," Duke said, offering his hand to the confident-looking woman in front of him.

"It's a real pleasure, Duke. I have been looking forward to this chat," Susan said.

She sized up Duke's décor – dark wood panels, old carpets, too many cheaply framed photos revealing milestones of his family and career. Her eyes widened when he wasn't watching her. He should know better than to put himself on display, she thought.

"I wanted to have a frank discussion with you because I want to make the right choice," he said. "I am inclined to favour a Canadian company, everything else being equal, because I feel it would be a better cultural fit. Integrity means a lot to me – and to all of us at Wilson Exploration. I need your assurance that you will keep all your promises, and specifically that you will retain all our employees."

"Of course," Susan responded. "As you know, this purchase would become our platform to grow our oilsands business. We would need all the expertise that your people bring. We would honour most employment contracts and offer any redundant employees job opportunities elsewhere in the business. Plains is a big, diversified company with lots of employment options. There will be new areas for growth."

"Given what happened in the past with your Peru acquisition, I also need your assurance that there are no conflicts of interest at the board level or anywhere else," the senior oilman said.

"Our board has changed completely since those times," Susan assured him. "We learned our lesson. We have tightened our governance, so no one gains improperly from this acquisition."

She asked Duke if he might be interested in joining Plains' board to ensure the integration of the two companies would be seamless. He said yes.

"Have you secured the funding you need to pay us?" Duke probed.

"Yes. Our balance sheet will be stretched for a while, but we plan to reduce our debt aggressively after the deal is concluded by selling gas properties," Susan said.

They spoke about potential synergies, building upgrading and refining, and pipeline space. Duke felt confident that a sale to Plains would transfer the assets he built – and loved – over to a good pair of hands.

Susan was barely out of the building when John returned his call.

"Hey, Duke, how's the battle?" John asked.

"I'm getting close to making a decision. Our board is meeting tomorrow to evaluate the final bids. I have to say, I'm disappointed that you didn't put in a bid, but I understand."

"Look, there are reasons I didn't," he said. "I'll explain my thinking in a bit. But it seems to me you did very well on your own. I hear you received multiple bids."

"Yes, we did. We have some interesting offers, for more money than I expected."

John asked his friend if he was alone. Duke said yes. John proposed to meet in his office because he had something important to discuss. He needed to do it in person.

John took Duke's private elevator and arrived with a thick leather briefcase. The older oilman closed his door.

"I suspect that Plains is on your short list, if not at the top of your list, so before you make a decision, there are some things you need to know," John said, pulling several professional-looking reports and a stack of large photos out of his briefcase.

"A friend of mine who runs a hedge fund in New York did some research on Plains. They've been following the company since they took over my Ladyfern properties – remember that deal? – and then ran that beautiful play into the ground," he said. Duke became more curious.

"Plains is probably telling you they have the financial backing to pay for your assets. The reality is they are hanging on by their fingernails. They have too much debt, and even if they manage to pay you, they won't have the money to invest in your oilsands business and grow it. Some short sellers think they're crazy to make this move. They're shorting the stock because they believe it's just a matter of time before Plains trips up.

"Susan Scott is driving this deal hard because she knows she will be fired if she doesn't come up with a new strategy to revive the company.

But you probably already know some of that. Here's what you probably do not know. Plains' administration costs are so high they are off the charts. They own five corporate jets. They give corporate money away like it's their own – charity balls, political bribes. We're talking dozens of millions a year. They even use Plains' resources for their own use. For example, there's a rumour Susan Scott used Plains' office decorators to redo her own home, and then charged the company.

"And here's a good one: Susan Scott is a part owner of several service suppliers that Plains hires to do work in its oilfield. So, she's lining her own pockets through her employment at Plains and through ownership of these outfits. It may not be illegal, but it sure seems unethical to me," John said. Duke's face hardened.

John saved the best for last. He picked up a stack of colour photographs and displayed them on Duke's desk. There were photos of the older oilman meeting privately with his board, of meetings with his bidders, and then close-ups of their presentations, revealing details of each offer. Susan Scott knew how much her competitors were offering, John said.

Then he turned to a stack of older black-and-white photos. One showed a younger Duke Wilson in his underwear in his office, with a nearly naked young woman sitting on his lap. In another, a different young woman was parked on his desk, smoking a cigar. He was nearby, looking dishevelled, drinking from a liquor bottle.

The older oilman's jaw dropped. "How did you get these?" he asked, his face turning red.

"Susan Scott has been on your tail for a while. In fact, she might be watching us right now," John said, as they turned their gazes toward the office's large glass windows. Duke had previously noticed that two window cleaners seemed forever stuck on the same floor in the tower next door.

"I got these photos from my hedge-fund friend," John said. "He paid big bucks to get them from the consultant Susan Scott hires to dig up dirt on her competitors – and even people she works with, like her former boss or members of her board. How do you think she keeps getting promoted while everyone else gets fired? It's a safe assumption she has these photos.

"She pulled a similar trick on me a while ago, when I was getting my oilsands company off the ground. She had pictures taken of me and of the *Journal* reporter you asked me to be careful about.

"Now I make it my business to keep track of her, too," John continued. "I hired a detective of my own and found out a great deal about Susan Scott. Here's a prediction: If you take her offer, and you sit on Plains' board – has she asked you, yet? – she will use these photos to pressure you to do what she wants."

Duke Wilson was aghast, fearful for his reputation, ashamed about his past behaviour, disappointed by what he saw and heard. "How do I make sure that these photos never see the light of day?" he asked John, his legs failing him.

"You can keep the ones I gave you. I suggest that you get your lawyers involved. Susan Scott has crossed the line too many times. That's how she operates. You may want to address this quietly with her company's board."

Duke collapsed in his chair, feeling more exhausted than he'd ever been. It was time to move on, he thought. The business had gotten too nasty. He'd been a builder, a proud employer. Sure, he'd made mistakes. He'd not been faithful to his wife. They'd gone through rough patches. But all that was in the past.

John wished his old friend good luck and walked out. He regretted hurting him. But he also believed Duke needed tough love. He didn't deserve to get caught in Susan Scott's evil web.

Back in his office, he called his hedge-fund friend and asked him to place a short bet on Plains' stock from his personal account.

The next morning, Susan arrived in her office early. She anticipated a celebratory day, so she dressed in one of her favourite outfits – a winter-white pant suit with beige pumps and a large matching purse. Her executive assistant placed a birds-of-paradise flower arrangement on her desk, a gift from her group for what they thought was a done deal with Duke Wilson.

She expected a final decision from the oilman early in the day and rated her company's chances of taking over his oilsands properties at more than 70 percent. Her gut told her the stars were aligned. Her meeting with Duke

Wilson had been good. The old man wanted to place his beloved assets in Canadian hands. Plains was the only Canadian company on his short list.

Of course, she had no intention of keeping all Wilson's staff, despite her promises to him. After the deal closed, she knew she'd have to lay off at least half, especially administrative people with big salaries she could not afford.

Sure, she'd asked Duke to join Plains' board, but she had what she needed to keep him in line and ensure she'd keep her job.

Susan rang her board chair, curious about whether he'd received any news. His assistant told her he'd be busy in meetings outside the office for the rest of the day. She tried other members of the board and received the same response.

Strange, she thought, and wondered what was going on. By mid-morning, she became restless. She'd never been excluded from important meetings before. She was the president, the keeper of all corporate information – past, present, and regarding the future. And she'd led negotiations on the Wilson deal. She was the corporate secretary, too, which required her to be present at board meetings. She was indispensable, she thought.

She took a walk of the executive floors. All her colleague's doors were shut. Their assistants told her they were at off-site meetings, too.

At noon, she ordered a salad and ate alone at her desk. Something bad was underway, she realized. Exclusion from important meetings was a tell-tale sign of career doom. She'd practiced it many times herself. She'd taken pleasure in it. It had made her feel feared, in control of her own destiny – and of the lives of others. She kept watching Plains' stock price. It was plummeting, another bad sign.

In late afternoon, the chairman of the board walked into her office, accompanied by company lawyers, Plains' head of human resources, IT support, and four security guards. They found her at her desk, sending personal files to her computer at home.

The chairman's face was red and tense. "The board has decided to terminate your employment, with cause. The details of your termination package are in this envelope," he said, handing it to Susan, who looked at him like a thief caught in the act.

"It's come to our attention that we lost the oilsands deal because of your deplorable practices, which we fear are, at the very least, unethical, at worst, illegal. We are seizing all your computer files – including the ones you are trying to send to your home," he said, pointing to Susan's computer screen.

"We reserve the right to turn everything over to the authorities. Susan Scott, we're done with you," the chairman said, and walked out.

The four security guards waited for her to get her handbag and put on her coat. They warned her to not pick up other personal belongings, which would be packed and sent to her home after they were reviewed. Susan knew the rules – she'd made them herself – yet they still stung like a pitchfork in her back.

She was marched out of her executive floor, as her stunned and now former colleagues and staff watched her endure what she'd done to so many in the past: the walk of shame.

Next morning, Elise attended a no-expenses-spared press conference. As champagne with orange juice and hors d'oeuvres were served on silver trays to hundreds of invited guests, many of them employees, the CEOs of Wilson Exploration and the Chinese oil state giant announced their $16-billion transaction. By many measures, it was the richest the sector had ever made.

The man of the hour, Paul Chen, was the first to take the podium. Dressed in a sharp black suit couriered by his Beijing bosses for the occasion, he expressed appreciation on behalf of the People's Republic of China for its inclusion in the oilsands family. Applause. He said he looked forward to his company expanding its presence in Canada – and producing its first oil in a Western democratic country. More applause.

He promised that all Wilson Exploration's workers would keep their jobs and committed to creating new ones as his company expanded vertically, horizontally, and geographically. Applause. He said he was assured by the Canadian government that there would be no regulatory hurdles. Enthusiastic applause.

He expressed excitement about learning the oilsands business and finding applications for its technologies in China and beyond, where the

Chinese were buying up reserves to meet their growing oil needs. Applause and standing ovation by his staff.

Duke Wilson got emotional as he recalled his early days in the Alberta oil industry. Applause. He said he was grateful he was able to build such a major company with so many great people. Applause. The oilsands, if properly developed, had the potential to lift the standard of living of all Canadians for decades to come. Applause and standing ovation by his staff.

He welcomed the Chinese to Alberta and expressed hope China and Canada could learn from each other and be stronger together. Duke shook Paul's hand and photos were taken of the two smiling oil leaders.

With that, oilsands' share prices rose again, because the market interpreted China's long-waited arrival as a harbinger of more Chinese acquisitions in the months and years to come.

Elise was so captivated by the celebration that she had to look twice at the news headline flashing on her laptop.

The board of Plains Exploration, which included several new directors, had just announced it was looking at strategic alternatives to enhance shareholder value, which meant it was putting Plains up for sale. Some of the executive team had resigned, including Susan Scott, due to a disagreement over strategy and other matters.

"What the heck," Elise whispered. She recalled that Plains was one of the bidders for the Wilson assets.

She walked out of the event and rushed back to her office.

Gordon Wilson, Plains' public relations man, had left an urgent message for her to call.

"Hi Gordon, I just saw your news release. What's happening?" Elise asked, out of breath.

"Our board has decided we need to look at our options," he said.

"What changed?" Elise asked. "Just weeks ago, you were planning a major acquisition to pivot to the oilsands."

"Several hedge funds have acquired a large position in our company. They have asked for new leadership and a change in direction. I can tell you more, but we need to go off the record because there could be legal implications."

"Sure," Elise said, dumbfounded by the turn of events.

"Susan Scott was fired last night. It was ugly. Her files were seized, and she was marched out of the building. The new board has appointed a law firm to investigate whether she was stealing from the company."

"Stealing? How was she stealing?" Elise asked, not entirely surprised about the bad behaviour, given her own experiences with Susan Scott.

"We'll have more to say in the future – or at least someone will. I have resigned. I've had enough of this. Tomorrow's my last day."

"I'm sorry to hear that," Elise said, feeling sorry for the man, who'd been decent to her over the years. "But change is good. There are lots of good jobs in good companies out there. Let me know if I can help." She was trying to cheer him up.

"Thanks, Elise. I may have to take you up on that – I could use a good reference."

"Meanwhile, you'll need to tell me more about this alleged stealing," Elise said. "I can't use this information unless I get it confirmed by other sources."

"A couple of the new directors have agreed to talk to you, but it has to be on background," Gordon said.

Elise followed up and got all the information she needed, then talked to her editor about the allegations.

Plains had appointed a law firm to conduct an independent investigation. She learned the company found evidence of theft of corporate services for personal use, abuse of the company's corporate jets, kickbacks from service providers, the awarding of contracts at inflated prices to other service providers in which Susan Scott was a major shareholder. Her editor told her to start writing and file as soon as she could.

The exclusive story appeared before the markets opened the next day. It was so scandalous it overshadowed the big Chinese deal and pushed oilsands stocks sharply down.

Chapter 37

CALGARY, ALBERTA, NOVEMBER 2006

After her Plains reporting appeared, Elise left work early, feeling exhausted. She took a long walk through a downtown park. It was chilly outside. A few snowflakes filled the air. When she arrived home, she heard from the two men who'd lately been in and out of her life.

Jordan phoned first. He'd read her coverage of the China deal and of the execution, as he called it, of Susan Scott. He asked her how she felt, since he knew about Elise's unpleasant past experiences with the Wicked Queen, as he called her, of the oilpatch. He complimented Elise on her fair handling of the story.

"I'm surprised by what happened," Elise responded, pleased to hear from her old friend, but making sure not to offer any information she had received from off-the-record sources that could end up with Barb Heinz.

Jordan persisted, asking her if she knew any more about the background leading to the event. Were more Chinese companies lining up to buy assets? he asked. Elise clammed up. Was he just curious, or was he looking for news he could use at Save the Climate? She changed the subject to other things, including Elise's imminent trip to New York to see her children, and promised to stay in touch.

Then, there was John Hess. He complimented her on her coverage, too. He said he loved the story about Susan Scott.

"She got what she deserved," he said, seeming a bit too pleased. "The closer to the top, the closer to the door – especially when you rise by using unethical or even illegal means."

"But wasn't she doing what a lot of other oilmen do all the time?" Elise asked, naïvely. "We all know they use shareholders' money as their own."

"Maybe. Off the record, Susan burned a lot of bridges over the years. She was despised both inside and outside her company. She blackmailed people – something you probably didn't hear from the directors you spoke to. She was planning to blackmail Duke Wilson to back out of commitments made in the deal, and who knows what else. That kind of stuff catches up to you. Plus, behaviour like that reflects badly on all of us."

"How do you know these things?" Elise asked, wondering how John found out about her off-the-record interviews with Plains' directors, and realizing she was right to suspect there was more to Susan Scott's termination. Maybe he was involved, she thought.

"I have my sources. It's a small town," he responded.

"What do you think will happen to Plains?" Elise asked.

"I suspect the company will stumble for a while, then it could be broken up into pieces. They have good assets, but they are too big and poorly run."

Industry taking care of its own, Elise thought.

John asked her out for lunch. He told her he wanted to show her his appreciation for a job well done.

"Sure," Elise replied. Neither set a date.

Elise felt the change was in the air. There were too many excesses, too much money changing hands, too many big plans and expectations, too much attention, too much greed, too much dishonesty. People were getting hurt.

As a journalist, she shouldn't care. Her job was to write about it and move on. *Journal* readership of the energy beat had exploded. She felt she'd delivered on the *Journal*'s transition to a digital platform. She was an authority on the oil industry. She was making more money than she ever had.

Except she did care. She worried that she'd bought into the story and helped to shape it by covering it. The medium was the message, and the message – including hers – had helped the industry become what it was. Perhaps she'd gotten too close, lost herself in the hype, was moving away from the truthful journalism she grew up with and loved. Was it too late to change course? She didn't have answers, just a bad feeling that she was standing on quicksand.

Chapter 38

WASHINGTON, DC, NOVEMBER 2007

Presidential election fever was in the air as Barb Heinz called another meeting of the leaders of the environmental movement. She needed new ideas on ways to re-invigorate the anti-oilsands campaign. After big efforts to shut down the Canadian industry, the Save the Climate leader was dissatisfied with her progress – which would stand in the way of her aspirations to lead the climate-change strategy for the man she hoped would be the next President of the United States.

The campaign's framing of the oilsands as a looming environmental disaster and as a cautionary tale for the US fossil fuel industry garnered decent headlines, but business in the Alberta oilpatch was growing more than ever. When asked in opinion polls, Americans said they favoured friendly Canadian oil over unethical Middle East oil, which didn't help her cause.

What they did care about were soaring gasoline prices, the result of soaring oil prices. Fears of supply shortages were driving ever-growing oilsands investments, with a lot of the money pouring in from Americans. Despite her lobbying efforts, there was reluctance by international policy-makers to shun Canadian oil. Her calls for climate change mitigation got frosty responses from Canadian governments. There was no appetite by regulators to tighten the screws – they were rubber-stamping approvals as fast as project proposals were landing on their desks.

"We need to change our campaign, be more effective," she said to the two-dozen people gathered in the windowless basement of a second-rate Washington hotel, one the campaign's favourite places to hold secret meetings. "The industry is getting a free pass because everyone is so concerned about energy security," she continued, hoping to spark the urgency she felt was required.

"If we allow this Canadian oil growth to continue, they will lock us into a high-carbon future," she said. "That's how big the oilsands are. They will derail all our efforts to avoid climate catastrophe. They'll suck capital away from renewable energy. We need the oilsands to be framed as the climate's top threat."

Erika Bernstein, disappointed that her efforts in Alberta were not getting the recognition she felt they deserved, looked around the table and stood up to speak.

"We are doing our best with the resources we have and the tactics we are allowed to use," Erika said. "To take this to the next level, we need to become more disruptive, stop playing by the rules."

"What do you mean?" Barb asked, her curiosity stoked by the confident woman, who had proven herself as her best asset by far.

"First, we need more people on the payroll – campaigners, Indigenous people, lawyers, communicators – which means we need more money. Second, we need to do a full review of the oilsands' weak points and go after them, which means we need to do more research of our own. We can't just rely on newspapers for our data. We need intelligence we can use to our own advantage. We need to get inside this industry and get first-hand information.

"Third, we need to increase our communication through sympathetic media, discredit those who are hostile to our goals, and bolster our own information channels. Let's reach people directly. Fourth – and this would be the biggest leap – we need to play a bigger role in decision making that relates to the environment – the courts, the regulators, the politicians."

"Those are the institutions that hold the country together," Barb said. "It sounds like we need to take over Canada." She was half joking, and half intrigued by the possibilities of such an escalation.

"In some ways, yes," Erika responded. "Not officially, of course. This would not be like a military invasion or a political coup. We don't need to do that. We can infiltrate and influence Canadian institutions that enable their fossil-fuel industry by using as proxies Canadians sympathetic to our cause. Canada is our largest foreign supplier of fossil fuels now and will become even larger in the future if all that production growth goes ahead. The oilsands are funded by a lot of US money. They are holding back our green energy producers by taking up a lot of the available capital, as you noted, and by increasing their share of the energy market. They are polluting our air. We need to take control of what is ours."

Barb was impressed. It was the type of big idea, the unconventional thinking, she needed to make the leap forward. It wasn't even unprecedented. The United States exercised leadership and influence in a lot of countries. Climate change was global and needed a global approach.

It would be risky, she acknowledged to the group. Canada could be hard to manage, with its superior attitude and insistence on charting its own course on the environment. And if such strategy leaked, it could stoke anti-Americanism and undermine the climate cause, she said.

"Any Canadians here?" Barb asked, looking around the room.

None.

"I went to summer camp in Canada," said a young man. "They have beautiful forests and lots of wildlife."

"My grandmother is Canadian," said another. "From Quebec."

"I snowboard in Whistler almost every year," said another.

Erika Bernstein put her hand up. "I spent the last four years in Western Canada, running this campaign. I believe there are ways to make this work. The oilsands are in Alberta. The province is not well liked in the rest of the country. They're too rich and too arrogant because of their oil. They're like Texas, just colder. We need to align ourselves with like-minded people on the West Coast, the East Coast, and in Central Canada, where anti-oil views are rising because the oilsands boom is giving Alberta too much political leverage and luring all their young people with their Big Oil salaries.

"Also, we should work with left-of-centre parties," Erika continued. "They need campaign money to make it to government. They can't wait to kick the oil-corrupted parties out of power. They would be useful allies. And let's not forget Indigenous communities. They're restless and motivated. They can be helpful because under Canadian law they have unique rights to block energy projects."

Barb Heinz was sold. She proposed that the group come up with an in-depth strategy looking at further ways to re-invigorate The Canada Project. It would be presented to more potential funders.

One of the participants offered to put together a comprehensive strategy document. Another signed up to work his contacts at wealthy foundations. Another promised to reach out to famous people to find out if they were available to speak for the campaign. Another offered to look for more partners – in both the United States and Canada.

The group ended the meeting feeling optimistic about the future. Half measures hadn't worked. Change was hard and they needed to meet the challenge with greater force than the pushback they faced. They agreed to reconvene in two months, and to stay in touch in the meanwhile.

Barb asked Erika to stay behind for a one-on-one chat. "I have been very impressed with your work and your thoughts," Barb said. "I wanted to tell you that I appreciate what you are doing up in Canada. I wanted to apologize for not giving you more credit because I really wanted to shake things up with the rest of the group. You're doing all the heavy lifting already.

"I'd like you to think harder about what we need to do to increase the effectiveness of the Canadian campaign. We need a stronger Canadian network to make this work. We can't let the Canadians think that we are pulling the strings from here. We need them to think that this campaign is their idea."

"I agree," Erika said. "We need allies. We need to build capacity. It's been challenging because the oilsands industry has so much money. Everyone is on their payroll. We need to do the same, offer people incentives to come to our side. Work with local environmental organizations. They have a few but they are not well coordinated."

"Come up with a plan and let me know what you need," Barb said. "I have complete faith in you."

The two women slipped out of the hotel from different exits, aware that Washington had eyes and ears everywhere, especially on Save the Climate, which was expected to be influential if a new government was elected.

On her drive back to Manhattan, where she spent weekends with Jordan, Barb thought about the enormity of the task at hand.

Canada would be the first foreign country targeted so forcefully by Save the Climate. If it worked, if she gained unprecedented influence over Canada's decision-makers, other fossil fuel holdouts would follow. It would be the most efficient way to get the whole world to embrace carbon reduction before it was too late.

"What do you think?" Barb asked Jordan after arriving home and explaining the highlights of the DC discussion. He still sat on her campaign's board, and she often relied on him for sober second thought.

"Susan, I don't like it," Jordan said, sipping a glass of Chianti that reminded him of Elise.

"I have said this before, and I will say it again: You're talking about interfering with a country's decisions. A campaign against fossil fuels should be done above board, have a message that gets people's support because it's the right thing to do."

"We've tried that, and we are going nowhere," Barb responded. "Industry has too much money and is too powerful."

"There's got to be a better way than organizing a scorched-earth campaign. We're talking about Canada, not a banana republic. They're a sovereign country. You can't go in there and disrupt their institutions and tell them how to run their economy. How would you feel if Canadians came here and did the same thing?"

"They're sort of doing that by selling so much of their oil to us, and by building pipelines that will keep us hooked on their dirty oil," she argued.

"That's true. But they are playing by our rules," Jordan said. "You are planning to disrupt their power structure and impose your own rules."

They were arguing again, Barb realized. They'd been married for less than two years, and they couldn't see eye to eye on anything. What happened to the handsome doctor who shared her goals and aspirations? Why did he not see that the campaign had no choice?

There was so much tension between them she'd put off telling him that she was becoming more involved in the presidential campaign. If her candidate won, as polls suggested, she'd have to spend even more time in Washington – perhaps all her time in Washington. It was the career move she'd prepared for all her life, and she needed Jordan to be on her side.

Chapter 39

Dramatic music jolted the room as a presentation lit up on a large screen, displaying a hazy photo from space of Alberta's Athabasca oilsands region. The Athabasca River, the Athabasca Lake, a tailings pond, and the Indigenous community of Fort Chipewyan were clearly marked to help viewers understand the area's northern geography.

The attendees – representatives of potential donors, environmental organizations, and the campaign's growing cross-border team – gasped when the next slide lit up.

It showed a large, blackish, bitumen-soaked oilsands mine where trucks the size of three-storey houses seemed to lumber back and forth on tarry paths. Barb couldn't have picked a more provocative battleground – mother earth in the wild, wounded by monstrous machines built for Big Oil in the pursuit of profit.

"We are gathered here today to announce our plans for The Canada Project 2.0 – our re-energized campaign to shut down the Canadian oilsands – the most destructive fossil fuel project on earth," Barb said from the stage of a mid-sized conference room in a Midtown hotel, as the music faded and another slide lit up, showing a big tank farm and a bitumen-upgrading complex.

"The tar sands will accelerate global warming," she said, emphasizing the word *tar*. More slides flashed on the screen, one after the other, each re-enforcing her message.

"They will perpetuate our oil addiction. They will mean the expansion of refineries and the construction of new refineries. They will mean construction of more pipelines to the United States.

"If growth goes ahead as planned, we will see a large increase in tanker traffic along our shores – tankers that could spill their dirty oil on our beaches and kill the fish in our oceans.

"The tar sands need to be stopped, and we believe we have the strategy to make it happen. It's more ambitious than anything we have done. Excess begets excess, extreme begets extreme. It's time we stop this for our children and grandchildren. Thank you for joining us to fight this important cause. We are excited to lead this project for the benefit of humanity."

A 50-page report on the new approach was handed out to participants to explain the campaign in detail. The Canada Project 2.0 would be louder and more far-reaching than anything done in the past, by Save the Climate or any other group.

It would flood multiple platforms – TV and print news, social media, talk shows, shareholder meetings, etc., with the message that good, represented by the environment, would triumph over evil, the fossil fuel industry, particularly the tar sands, a villain so harmful it had to be eliminated before it got too big. It would build alliances with other environmental organizations on both sides of the Canada/US border. It would capitalize on the increasing transfer of public attention and information to the internet. It would recruit real actors with large fan bases to promote awareness. It would make the most of the oilsands' ideal location, only a plane ride away, in a free and civilized place with good hotels and internet access, where Save the Climate operatives could perform, publicize, and post online their courageous acts of oilsands disruption. The oilsands would be branded 'dirty oil' or 'tar sands oil'– names vetted by the campaign's new marketing agency.

Barb introduced the campaign's leader based in Canada – Erika Bernstein – and asked her to the podium to expand on the campaign.

"A network of leading American and Canadian environmental organizations has come together under a coordinated structure to fight the tar sands industry," Erika explained.

"We will raise the negatives, raise the costs, slow down and stop infrastructure, and enroll and fund key decision-makers to bolster our cause. More specifically, we will target pipelines and refinery expansions, force environmental reforms, and put pressure where we can, to significantly reduce future demand for tar sands oil.

"We will leverage the tar sands debate to push for progressive environmental policies in the United States and Canada," she continued, surveying the audience. "We will push decision makers to unite in a global movement of movements to fight climate change."

In Canada, campaign funds would be used to bankroll lawsuits, organize protests, establish new communication activities, and lobby for new legislation, Erika explained. In the US, the campaign would pressure investors to stay out of the oilsands by raising their risk profile and getting the support of political leaders.

Donors in attendance were so impressed they pledged millions, with more to come if the approach proved successful and could be exported elsewhere as needed – maybe to fight development of liquefied natural gas, big hydro, coal.

Some big donors demanded, and got, seats on the board. Barb Heinz was re-confirmed as chair.

However, the donors unanimously demanded that their cash contributions and the campaign's US leadership and coordination remain confidential so they wouldn't be seen as meddling in the politics of a foreign country.

To that end, Barb proposed that their funds be deposited in accounts in Caribbean banks and channeled to carefully vetted organizations in the US and Canada to avoid scrutiny of authorities and the media – for example, through charitable donations, consulting fees, research grants.

Barb was delighted with the response. Among her backers were more big foundations that cared about environmental issues and were frustrated by the lack of progress on climate change, especially in the United States; philanthropists looking to ease their guilt after making fortunes in polluting industries; political contenders looking to draw the youth vote; hedge funds that got rich on fossil fuels that switched their bets to renewable energy; even some oilsands producers that agreed to support the Save the Climate campaign to avoid becoming their target, so they could have a strategic advantage over their competitors.

She wasn't too concerned about the donors' motivation. Cash was cash. She needed it to make her growing payroll. Quickly. The global financial meltdown was beginning to convulse markets. But Barb assured her supporters the uncertainty was good for the campaign because times of crisis were the most ideal for disruption.

A cocktail hour capped the event, and everyone mixed and matched. Barb kept checking the room's entrance. She'd hoped to see Jordan, who had promised to support her in her day of triumph. She was disappointed he didn't show up.

Chapter 40

Although widely expected, the end of Plains still came as a shock. Plains filed for bankruptcy after failing to raise enough cash from asset sales to reduce its debt. The next sales would be run by bankruptcy trustees at whatever prices they could get to pay off creditors.

Elise found out about the Canadian giant's fall from a news release that was obviously written by lawyers. No one at the company was available to provide anything more.

But she already knew the financial context was dire. Markets around the world were melting down so fast from the tightening of credit that no sector of the economy was spared. For the Canadian oilpatch, the party was over, or at least on an extended hiatus. Oil prices had plunged, and investment had evaporated. Highly leveraged companies like Plains were the most vulnerable.

Duke Wilson felt lucky he sold at the top of the market and left town. The Chinese oil company, on the other hand, was stuck. Communist party brass was so disappointed that it had bought Canadian oil resources at an inflated price that Paul Chen was ordered to return to China for 're-education,' which he knew meant punishment. According to Chinese press reports, he was arrested after landing in Beijing and disappeared.

Elise had never experienced – or covered – such a market shock. Calgary's streets were empty, shopping malls looked abandoned, many company shares were worthless. No one knew what the next new normal would be like. For the first time in her career, the unravelling of the financial system affected both the sector she covered and the industry she worked in. *Journal* revenue cratered and many of her colleagues in New York were laid off. Her bosses assured her that her job was safe – but plans for her full-time return to New York were now on hold.

"Elise, you are better off staying put for now," Mark Wimhurst told her over the phone. "But come and see me when you are back, and we'll chat more about your future."

Elise was disheartened but didn't complain. She still had a job and a career, which meant a lot to her. Canada's meltdown was mild relative to the United States, thanks to its stronger banking system. Elise would still travel extensively and return to New York at least once a month. The *Journal's* energy information and trading platform remained a key profit centre, her editor told her. She was needed in Calgary to preserve that revenue stream. Readers were still interested in the Canadian oilsands story, even during bad times. The oilsands were seen as one of the safe places to store cash.

Minutes after Plains' bankruptcy announcement, another news release from Aurora Oil Sands crossed the wire. The company had acquired Plains' undeveloped oilsands leases, which were adjacent to its own projects, for an undisclosed sum. All cash.

Elise realized John Hess got what he wanted. That's why he helped push Susan Scott off the cliff, out of his way. He eliminated any barrier to the purchase of Plains' oilsands lands and settled an old score.

Elise phoned the oilman, hoping to collect more details, expecting to reach his assistant or his voicemail. Instead, John answered her call.

"Hi Elise, it's been too long," he said, sounding pleased with himself. "It's nice to hear your voice."

"Hi. Yes, it's been a long time," Elise said, uncomfortable with his familiarity. "I just noticed your announcement. Can you say more about your acquisition?"

"Not a lot. We negotiated this deal before Plains filed for bankruptcy. It's not large enough to be material, so we don't have to disclose details."

"I'm surprised. Plains was really excited about these leases. They were going to build on them to ramp up their new oilsands business. Can you say how much you paid?" she asked.

"No. Sorry. We are not disclosing terms," he said.

"They're next to your own properties, right?" Elise asked.

"Yes, they are, and they will be a nice addition to our portfolio," he said. "They're the same leases from where activists broke into our property a while back, remember? Those break-ins have continued, and we had to do something. Now we will have more control over who comes into our property. It had to be done. I can fill you in if you are interested, off the record. You promised me lunch the last time we spoke. Do you have time tomorrow?"

"Yes, of course," Elise said after checking her schedule.

She had other pressing things to ask him, too, and wanted to see the reaction on his face when she raised them.

A few days earlier, Elise had received a package. It was dropped off in her office after she'd left for the day. It contained a photocopied colour presentation by what appeared to be a network of environmental organizations and was entitled "The Canada Project 2.0." There were no other details – no address, no contact information.

Elise suspected someone wanted the document to be made public. She didn't know who was behind it – or why it was sent to her. She didn't even know if it was authentic.

It looked amateurish, with ominous photos of the oilsands and inflammatory headlines. Canadian politicians' photographs were smeared with black and red ink, and there were cutlines like: "Canada keep your dirty oil."

It appeared to be a step-by-step manual for activists on how to shut down Canada's oilsands industry, she thought as she flipped through a few pages. A section about how to handle the media to raise awareness of the negatives caught her attention. She wondered if she had a target on her back.

The logos of several environmental organizations, most of them based in the United States, were printed on the cover page. She decided to call a few to find out what the document was about. She started with a major foundation in New York she was familiar with. Jordan had mentioned it as a wealthy environmental philanthropy with global connections.

"Hi, this is Elise Chamonter from the *Journal*," she said. "I have received a document that seems to show you are involved in a campaign against Canada's oilsands called The Canada Project 2.0. Are you one of the backers?"

"Oh, that one. Yes, we are," the woman said. "It's one of many initiatives we are funding to fight climate change."

"Do you support their tactics?" Elise asked.

"We don't get involved in tactics. We support climate change initiatives. We can't really say much more because we are just funders."

Elise tried another environmental group she recognized that was based in California.

"Hi, this is Elise Chamonter from the *Journal*," she said. "I have a document that shows you are one of the backers of a campaign against Canada's oilsands called The Canada Project 2.0. I need to verify that this document is real. Is it?"

"Yes – but I am surprised you got a copy," said the male voice at the other end of the line, seeming concerned. "It was meant to be a confidential document. Who gave it to you?"

"I don't know," Elise answered. "It landed on my desk the other day. Someone obviously wanted me to have it. I found it intriguing, and I wanted to know more about this campaign."

"This campaign has been underway for some time," the man said. "It's no secret that many environmental organizations are opposed to the tar sands. We will do everything we can to stop them."

"Who is funding it?" Elise asked.

"We get funding from many sources, but particularly small donations from individuals who are worried about the impact of fossil fuels on the climate."

"The tactics look aggressive," Elise pressed on. "Are you really looking at funding lawsuits, co-opting decision makers?"

"We don't get that involved in the tactics," the activist said. "We'll keep you posted if you'd like. Would you like to talk to Barb Heinz, our campaign chair? She's our designated spokesperson. She can talk to you more specifically about why we believe the tar sands are bad for the planet and for investors. I can arrange that for you."

"Thank you," Elise responded – and realized what she was dealing with another, more ambitious version of the Save the Climate campaign against the oilsands.

She was concerned. Barb Heinz's involvement was bad for her because of Jordan, the man between them, and because Elise had recently read the activist was rumoured to be in line for an appointment to the White House to lead the new administration's climate-change strategy, which meant the new effort had legs.

"I know Barb Heinz," Elise said. "I can reach her directly on my own."

Elise decided to fax a copy of the document to her editor, be up front about her connection to Barb Heinz, and get him to decide whether she should report on the leaked document.

"These people are crazies," her editor said after reviewing it. "We are targeted by anti-business activists daily who want to remake the world into a haven for the proletariat. If we write about them, we give them credibility and a platform. Frankly, you should ignore them."

"If this campaign unfolds as planned, it could do a lot of damage to the oilsands business," Elise argued. "We need to let people know this is a risk. Barb Heinz is not an amateur. She could be very powerful if she's appointed climate czar for the new President. Investors need to know. Industry needs to know."

"Okay. How about you ask a few industry leaders what they think," the editor suggested. "Talk to investors. Talk to politicians. See if they care. If they do, we'll cover it. If they don't, forget about it. It's just noise."

Elise agreed to join John Hess in a private room at his club.

Meeting in a public venue was out of the question, he told her, since he knew people recognized him and would start rumours. Elise joked she wasn't keen to be seen with him either, given the scandal that ensued the last time she took a ride with him after his oilsands tour.

They drove separately – John in his new red Porsche SUV, Elise in her aging Subaru. Both vehicles were equipped with tires for winter driving. It was snowing lightly. The roads were icy and the weathermen on the radio interrupted regularly with updates.

Elise still took care to dress up for the meeting, picking a new shirt and a skirt. Christmas was just around the corner. She wanted the outing to be special.

The club, with its sparkling Christmas trees and nicely arranged nativity scenes, was as welcoming as the first time she had lunch there with John.

"It's nice to see you, Elise," John said when she entered a private room, where a table for two was set near a window. "You are more beautiful than ever," he added, and complimented her on her elaborate gold necklace.

She told him it was a cherished gift from her late husband. "You're looking well, too," Elise said. He was years older than she was, yet he seemed ageless, she thought.

"So, tell me about your big job," he said. "I noticed the *Journal* is becoming a powerhouse on energy information."

"We are. The *Journal* has been transitioning to a digital platform to reach more readers around the world, while also building a trading platform," she explained, using her elevator pitch. "I'm one of the editors responsible. The energy industry was picked to lead the way, but other industries are making the transition too – tech, mining, finance. It's been a very good plan so far, which has enabled us to expand our workforce here in Calgary and elsewhere around the world while cutting the cost of producing and distributing an actual newspaper."

"Sounds impressive," John said. "Are you affected by the financial crisis?"

"Yes – but not as much as my colleagues in New York. We've had lots of layoffs. The biggest impact on me is that I will not be moving back to the newsroom full time any time soon."

"I didn't know you were planning to move back," John said.

"Yes. I was due to move back in January. My editors feel I can do more for the *Journal* here, for now."

"I am glad you are staying," John said. "You've been doing a great job covering the industry. We need you here." He stared at her. She felt flattered and smiled. The undercurrent between them resurfaced.

"I am sure other able people will fill my shoes when I am gone. Meanwhile, I'm still on the beat, plus working on the digital strategy," she said.

They ordered their food – steak for him, halibut for her – and made small talk with the club's manager, who opened a bottle of Beaujolais.

When they were alone again, they resumed their conversation about the state of the industry and the impact of the financial crunch.

"I'm actually looking at this downturn as an opportunity," John said. Always the optimist, she thought.

"We don't have a debt problem at Aurora. With so many companies laying off good people, we'll have lots to choose from to staff our own expansion projects."

"What about the properties you acquired from Plains? How soon will you develop them?" Elise asked.

"As soon as possible. They're like ours. They'll enable our next expansion. They are oil rich and right next door to our projects."

"How did that deal come about?" Elise asked, hoping he would share useful insights now that the deal was in the past.

"I can't tell you much, other than we put in a stink bid for the assets – which means an offer for a low price – and won because no one else showed interest. But this is off the record," he said.

A waiter delivered their food order as Christmas music played in the background.

"You mentioned that there were more break-ins?" Elise asked.

"Yes. We are seeing more activists sneak onto our sites – or people paid by these activists. They were cutting our fences and moving freely across our lands."

"Have they done any damage?"

"Not too much so far. They are taking pictures, checking out our operations. What they are doing is very dangerous. They could get killed or kill others. These are sites that produce oil and that are powered by natural gas. All our workers wear safety gear and have extensive training. These people sneak in and behave like they're in a playground. Now that we own the Plains properties, we'll be able to increase security and keep them out," John added.

Elise became more attentive. She wondered if the activity was related to the anti-oilsands campaign. "Speaking of activists, I'd like to show you a document," she said, pulling The Canada Project 2.0 presentation out of her purse.

The oilman read a few pages and returned it to Elise.

"This is pretty typical of the stuff these organizations produce, but it doesn't worry me," he said. "They're just trying to scare us. They use big words they don't understand. We are the ones fighting the good fight. We are The Canada Project – not them. We are building an industry that is creating wealth for our country and pays for programs like health care and education. Our environmental impacts are improving and will get better over time as our industry matures. We are developing technology that will be useful all over the world."

"You are not worried the environmentalists will disrupt the industry?" Elise asked. "Look at the damage they are already doing to your properties."

"No," John said. "These activists are a nuisance, and frankly, not very smart. How long has this Save the Climate campaign been going on? Years. They're going nowhere. These deposits are too big and too valuable for the world to ignore or to keep in the ground. They are the engine of Canada's economy and will get more productive over time. They will replace other sources of oil from unreliable places. They will ensure energy security in the West. There's no way we will let a bunch of American hoodlums tell us how to run a Canadian industry. I'd bet on us any day, not them."

Elise asked the oilman if she could quote him. He refused, reminding her the meeting was off the record. He suggested she contact the industry association for an approved quote she could use.

Elise was speechless. John didn't want to see past his own immediate interests – or was too arrogant to acknowledge that his carefully laid plans could be scuttled by industry outsiders, she thought. John Hess, the visionary king of the oilpatch, was underestimating the environmental movement and overestimating the importance of his industry. Money did strange things to people – it made them feel invincible, she realized.

"Activists destroyed Plains in Peru," she argued. "They infiltrated Western Canada's natural gas fields and built connections with Indigenous people. Barb Heinz is no dilettante and could do a lot of damage – especially if she becomes a Washington power broker.

"These smear campaigns are becoming more effective, more sophisticated, and more targeted," Elise continued. "Organizers use new internet platforms to reach the public directly – platforms my newspaper is increasingly competing against."

"Look, I wouldn't give this campaign too much airtime," John said dismissively. "We're not the poorly funded newspaper industry, with all due respect. We're the oil industry. We can take care of ourselves. They're coming after the wrong people."

John's words stung. It was not her job to warn smug CEOs, and she would say no more.

Sensing the tension, John asked Elise if she had plans for Christmas.

"I'll be in New York with my children," she said. "It'll be nice to enjoy our apartment. It has been renovated beautifully, and I can't wait to move some of the things I put in storage when I came here."

"How about that doctor friend of yours – is he still in the picture?" he asked her. Elise didn't know how to answer. It was none of his business, she thought. But she decided to play along to avoid parting on a sour note, which was how the lunch had evolved.

"No. Jordan got remarried a couple of years ago. I'm very happy for him. He's still very close to my children, especially my son."

"Will you see him in New York?" he asked.

"I don't know. He may have other plans," she said.

Elise asked John about his plans. He said he would be working over the holidays.

"No festivities with the family?" she asked.

"I don't really have any," he said, looking gloomy.

"What about your wife?" she asked.

"We're going through a rough patch," he admitted, his voice faltering. He stood up from the dining table, looking uneasy. "I have to get back to work," he said.

He helped her put on her coat.

They shook hands in the parking lot and wished each other Merry Christmas, then went their separate ways.

Back in the office, Elise called a couple of high-ranking politicians and financial industry types to get their views on The Canada Project 2.0. She even sent them copies of the document.

Their responses were like those of John Hess and of her boss. Both felt the campaign was ridiculous. Even during tough economic times, the oil-sands looked solid as a rock, they told her.

Elise still wrote about the leaked campaign document. She wanted it on the record under her byline. It was published on an inside page, had little readership, and was temporarily forgotten.

Chapter 41

DAWSON CREEK, BRITISH COLUMBIA, JANUARY 2009

A whiff of fresh paint lingered at the Bearspaw Community Centre when Chief Anne Proudfoot welcomed Erika Bernstein at the front door. The imposing teepee-shaped log house, with large windows showing off the forest, was newly completed after years of construction. The main hall, decorated with comfortable leather couches and artifacts made over generations by her band, was already hosting a lively meeting of the nation's elders. Steaming food prepared in the large kitchen was displayed on a table against a wall. Smaller meeting rooms and bedrooms were available for guests.

"There are a few things we need to finish up, but the centre is up and running and already fully booked," Chief Anne said, looking pleased with herself.

"You're moving up in the world," the activist said, hiding her sorrow over the poor conditions she saw on the reserve, with its dilapidated housing and muddy, unpaved streets. "This will be a nice oasis for your community."

"We're very proud of it – even if it's all we got from all that activity in the Ladyfern field," Chief Anne said. "And the funding didn't come from industry, it came from a donor."

"A donor?" Erika asked skeptically, convinced oil money was involved. "Are there any strings attached?"

"No," the chief replied. "I wouldn't have accepted the funds if there were."

"There's no such thing as a free lunch," the activist warned.

"I'm aware that nothing is free – not even your support," the chief shot back.

Chief Anne knew the activist well by now, though she didn't consider Erika a friend. She didn't trust her to have her community's best interests at heart – nor her own. The activist had bigger goals, not always aligned with hers.

Indeed, Chief Anne's first-hand experience with Erika was lingering like a bad taste. The activist had helped the Bearspaw Nation organize and publicize blockades to put pressure on companies producing natural gas from Ladyfern to provide greater benefits, but nothing came of it. It got messy, dangerous, counterproductive.

Indigenous unrest escalated and industry facilities were bombed as some misguided people took things into their own hands. Chief Anne had wondered who they were, why they did such terrible things. The bombings received national news coverage and stoked bad views of her people.

Fearful for their security, companies had accelerated their drilling programs, produced all they could, then moved on to less controversial oil and gas projects. First Nations never got their cut of the revenue because industry packed up and left, refusing to engage with radicals. At least that was their spin.

Only the environmentalists won, Chief Anne concluded. She knew Erika had boasted widely that Ladyfern's early death was a victory for her campaign.

But Erika said she had something new and exciting to discuss, and Chief Anne was desperate for help. Forestry and tourism had dried up because of the recession. Most people on the reserve were unemployed. Incomes were so low they couldn't feed their families. Plains' bankruptcy had left a trail of environmental damage – abandoned wells, shuttered facilities, roads to nowhere that disfigured the landscape. "I'm listening," Chief Anne said as they sat across from each other in a small meeting room. "We can't be picky these days. We need money."

Erika nodded. She noticed the chief's hair, neatly weaved in a braid, had turned completely white since their last encounter. Her face looked more weathered. Erika admired her outfit – a beaded leather jacket with matching slippers.

Chief Anne's recruitment would be a coup for the re-invigorated Save the Climate campaign, the activist thought. She was articulate, educated, wise – a role model. Now that Anthony Littlechild was gone, she imagined the chief leading rallies, testifying at hearings, speaking to the media.

"We are expanding our cause against fossil fuels, focussing on the tar sands," Erika said. "We have a lot more funding and some big plans. We'd like you to be one of the Indigenous leaders at the front of this campaign."

"Really? But we're not even close to the tar sands here. Why aren't you talking to First Nations closer to Fort McMurray?" the chief asked.

"You're closer than you think," the activist explained. "Industry is planning big new pipelines to transport all the new tar sands oil they will produce. You may have heard about the West Pipeline. It's a massive project that will cross Northern British Columbia. Some of it will cross your traditional territory."

"That project again? I thought we buried it a long time ago," Chief Anne said, surprised.

"It's coming back – much bigger than before," Erika warned. "Industry representatives will be calling in months. They need your support to get regulatory approval. They will offer you stuff, maybe some community investment like this centre, maybe some opportunities for business. Don't fall for it. You have much to lose if this project goes ahead. The pipeline will cross hundreds of waterways. If there is a spill – and it's a question of when, not if – it will contaminate your water and kill your salmon. It will mean losing control over your land."

"I know about the potential for environmental damage," the chief said, recalling the devastation wrought to the West Coast by an oil tanker that ran aground in Alaska, spilling its black cargo on land, wildlife, and water, terrifying Indigenous people across Western Canada.

"I value my fish and my water more than I value money. We can count on our fish, our animals in the bush to feed us. If my grandchild must buy water and have it shipped in, it's no good. We will not allow that pipeline to be built. That door was closed a long time ago. It will not be re-opened."

Oil from Alberta's tar sands, Erika explained, would be even worse for the environment than oil from Alaska because it was thicker and harder to clean up in case of a spill. But the biggest damage would be done to the climate, she said.

"Then we can't let them come through here," the chief said, setting aside her concerns about Erika. "We never signed treaties with Canada. We're still owners of this lands and we will decide what's best for us. What do you need from me?"

Erika was surprised that the chief was an easy sell. She was aware the matriarch had been critical of their previous dealings over Ladyfern.

She explained her campaign was organizing an Indigenous coalition to oppose all proposed tar sands pipelines – West, South, and East – as part of a big international effort to reduce climate change caused by the fossil fuel industry. The campaign could pay large fees – much larger than during the Ladyfern campaign – to her band and to her personally, Erika proposed.

Save the Climate would do all the support work required to assemble the Indigenous opposition front, fund all legal and regulatory challenges against new pipelines and represent Indigenous interests in those lawsuits, organize protests, organize media coverage and other communication, and arrange travel for appearances at important events, Erika promised.

All Chief Anne Proudfoot needed to do was show up – in full regalia.

"Where is all this money coming from?" Chief Anne asked.

"We have many funders in the United States, Canada and elsewhere who want to shut down the tar sands," the activist said. "We believe the tar sands would make us dependent on fossil fuels for too long. The campaign is called, unofficially, The Canada Project."

Chief Anne paused to think. She was worried about US funding. "I have bad memories of foreign environmentalists campaigning against the fur trade and destroying the livelihoods of Indigenous communities across Northern Canada," she said to Erika. "Hunting and trapping sustained my people for generations. Once the anti-fur movement took hold in foreign lands, and furs became unwearable because of public harassment, the environmentalists declared victory and moved to other causes. They didn't care that First Nations became impoverished and dependent on government money. This cannot happen to us again."

"That campaign was misguided, and I apologize for the harm it caused," Erika said. "We want First Nations to be friends and allies in our fight against the oilsands."

"Very well," the chief said to Erika. "I will join the fight against the West Pipeline. I fought hard in the past, when a similar pipeline from the tar sands was first proposed and we defeated it, and I will fight this one too. However, I don't want to get caught up in your big climate-change campaign. The way I see it, it's your fight, not ours. These are my views, but I will have to convene our council to get their input."

Erika said she understood and offered to address the council at the earliest convenience.

"One more thing," Chief Anne said. "If we agree to participate in this effort, how will we get paid?"

"We will open a bank account for your band, and a separate one for you, and deposit funds directly – no paper trail," Erika explained. "They could be charitable anonymous donations, like the one made for this centre," she said, smiling.

A month later, Erika returned to the reserve to address Chief Anne and her council. She put two options on the table: support for a campaign against the West Pipeline, or support for all actions against tar sands pipelines. In both cases, Chief Anne would represent the Bearspaw First Nation and help recruit other Indigenous communities for a new Indigenous coalition against the tar sands. The broader campaign would bring three times the money, with bonuses for achieving successful milestones.

Chief Anne expressed reservations about taking on such a large role, but her council overruled her. It picked the richest offer. It was finally raining money for the Bearspaw people, and they wanted their share. Industry had betrayed them, they told her, while environmentalists were prepared to pay.

Sensing Chief Anne's hesitation, Erika had a final private word with her before returning to her growing office in Vancouver.

"Chief, I know you have concerns about past environmental campaigns. This is different. We are well funded and well managed this time. Think about what you can do for your people. We're talking millions, plus all expenses related to the campaign. In addition, we will pay you extra for all your work. We need an Indigenous leader that people will respect. A leader of your standing to stop these destructive projects."

Chapter 42

Damage from the global financial meltdown had ruined many industries, but the oilsands quickly bounced back as oil prices recovered. Weak companies merged with strong ones and others were talked about as consolidation candidates. New production growth plans were announced. New pipelines were discussed to transport all the planned new Canadian oil to customers.

But Elise felt the Save the Climate campaign was finally gaining ground. Greed was turning into fear, pride into shame, certainty into doubt. She sensed it for the first time when she attended the oil industry's most prestigious annual conference, a big event in Houston where she was scheduled to moderate a panel discussion sponsored by the *Journal*, file stories, and pick up leads for future coverage – the usual grind of journalists on tight budgets.

On her way to the conference's hotel, she walked through the city's downtown core, between glass castles named after the world's most powerful oil companies, then barricades and armed security to provide protection from demonstrators.

There were thousands of them. Some were waving placards calling for the end of fossil fuels, or for Canada to keep its dirty oil, or for oil executives to be arrested for crimes against humanity. In the sky, small airplanes hauled signs demanding the shutdown of the tar sands. Effigies of Canadian politicians, some of them in attendance at the conference, were burned.

Some of the slurs were directed at Elise's own industry. "Boycott dirty oil, boycott dirty money, boycott capitalist media," the demonstrators shouted, beating their drums, blowing their horns, chanting Indigenous songs.

They were young and old, long-haired, and white-haired. They wore jeans and T-shirts. They came on foot and on buses. They danced and marched on the street. They talked to the media and posted their own stories on the internet about their just revolution against the elites and the coming doom of their enabler, the fossil fuel industry. They were digital natives who knew how to spin a yarn with fanatic zeal and reach large audiences directly, without interference from the media gatekeepers.

Conference participants seemed unmoved. A sea of men in well-cut blue and black suits and white shirts glided through the opulent hotel hallways. A few wore flowing white robes. The big shots – CEOs, oil ministers, celebrity investors – arrived in chauffeured limousines with big entourages of inhouse experts, advisors, and media handlers, like monarchs with their courtiers.

Elise found Chief Anne on the frontline of the protest. Donning regalia and beating a drum, the elder leader was surrounded by other Indigenous people from many tribes.

Elise approached her. "Hello, Chief Anne. You're a long way from home," she said.

"Hi Elise. Yes, I'm here to represent Canada's new Indigenous coalition against the tar sands," Chief Anne responded, halting her drumming.

"But you don't live in Alberta," Elise said.

"The tar sands affect all of us. We are fighting against pipelines and against the destruction of our planet by the fossil fuel industry," Chief Anne responded.

Elise took note of the comment. She thought the chief sounded robotic. She asked her if she could do a more in-depth interview.

"You need to talk to Erika," Chief Anne said politely, pointing to the activist in the crowd of demonstrators.

"Seriously? She's running the show?" Elise asked.

Chief Anne did not respond and went back to her drum. A camera was filming her. She looked impressive in her costume, Elise thought, but also sad, like she felt out of place. Elise took a picture of her own to file with her story. Nice performance, she thought, as Chief Anne picked up her beat.

Inside the hotel, the conference unfolded as advertised. Organizers assured participants that security and Houston police would keep everyone safe. To compensate for the situation, they offered more free food, more free drinks, and more free tours of the area.

Discussions revolved around the industry's next big moves. None dealt with climate change. TV reporters chased the big names, especially those in white robes from the Middle East. They asked them questions about gasoline prices – the only thing they really understood or cared about.

Elise was surprised to see John Hess engrossed in an interview with an attractive female TV reporter. He'd just spoken enthusiastically at the conference about his own industry, offering his optimistic take on the coming growth of the oilsands and the environmental improvements. Elise had just found out he was at conference. He must have been a last-minute addition, she thought, feeling a bit offended that he agreed to do an interview with someone else.

"Our extraction technologies are world leading and our costs are coming down," John said confidently, smiling for the camera, thankful for the media-training refresher he'd just received. "Our goal is to make oil projects competitive with other oil sources around the world, including Middle Eastern oil.

"We believe we have other advantages. Our industry is the world's most regulated. We have the highest environmental standards. We offer secure oil to replace oil from regions where production is declining because of lack of investment and political strife, like Mexico and Venezuela. We have high ethical standards, unlike places in the Middle East, where they don't care about human rights."

"Are you concerned about growing opposition to the tar sands?" the TV reporter asked.

"We respect demonstrators' right to have a point of view, but we don't agree with it. We care just as deeply about the environment. Oil from Canada offers US consumers the energy security that they need and reduces greenhouse gas emissions because it's transported on pipelines, which are more efficient than tankers coming from far away. The oilsands is a young industry. We are committed to further reducing our environmental footprint."

"The demonstrators say your oil is the dirtiest on the planet," the TV reporter pressed on, baiting the oilman to say something more provocative.

"Our oil is not as dirty as it's made out to be. Canadian oil has high emissions, but we're committed as an industry to innovate and to reduce our impact on the environment," John responded, looking frustrated.

Back in her hotel room, where she retreated to file her story, Elise watched the TV reporting. Most of it focussed on the demonstrators disparaging Canada's dirty oil. Chief Anne and her grievances dominated the coverage. John Hess got in four words: "Canadian oil has high emissions." They were used over and over by the network to promote the story. Next to the sage, sad Indigenous woman beating her drum in traditional garb, the confident oilman looked out of touch, which was not untrue, Elise thought.

Minutes after her own reporting on the oilsands' growth plans was published on the *Journal*'s website, her inbox was flooded with hundreds of messages from the Save the Climate campaign.

Some were press releases about the dangers of the oilsands, some were nasty comments that accused her of shilling for Big Oil, or of being a climate denier, or of being incompetent.

She felt nauseous.

Her phone rang. It was John Hess.

"Did you see that TV report? It's a disgrace," he complained. "I gave the reporter plenty to work with. They used one line and took it out of context. It's going to be a long time before I do another TV interview.

"And I couldn't believe Chief Anne, what she is doing to us," he continued angrily. "I supported her and her nation personally, more than anyone ever did. And that's how she thanks me?"

John asked Elise if she was busy and offered to buy her dinner. Both were attending the conference for another two nights. Elise was tired from the intense day and demoralized by the nasty comments directed at her. She needed a supportive shoulder, and maybe a lead or two she could chase, and accepted.

John proposed to meet at a steak house close to the conference hotel.

Elise took a taxi to get there and noticed the demonstrators were gone. They left behind piles of trash – fast-food leftovers, broken signs, liquor bottles, weed butts. A crew of street cleaners who looked like Mexican immigrants were cleaning up.

John was already at the restaurant when she arrived. She could tell he admired her fitted black dress as she walked in. She sat down across from him in a private booth. He apologized for his need to be careful about being seen with her, even in a foreign city, then continued venting against the TV reporter and the protesters.

"I tried to warn you," Elise said. "This is a big campaign. The people behind it are dangerous. The end game is to shut down the oilsands. Even if they don't succeed, they'll leave a trail of reputational damage. The person who used to lead it – Barb Heinz – is speaking at the conference tomorrow. I'm not sure about her involvement now, but she was just appointed by the new President of the United States to lead America's climate-change program. It seems to me that her fingerprints are all over this."

"Do you know her?"

"Yes, by reputation, mostly. She's the one who is married to Jordan, who criticized me in that awful article. She's not one of my fans, nor one of yours," she said.

"It's unfortunate she feels that way," he said. "We are pioneers, explorers, employers, risk takers who built an industry by developing our resources. We should be supported, not tarred and feathered. People like her don't understand how tough it is to create wealth that supports our standard of living, and that will pay to transition to greener energy.

"We cannot meet Canada's growing expectations without money from our oil. Canada happens to have world-class fossil fuel deposits. It's out strategic advantage. We cannot let some foreign activists force us to shut down our biggest export and value creator. That's insane. It will cripple our economy and set us back for generations. Barb Heinz is out of her depth."

What he said made sense to Elise, and yet she wished he could see that his industry could no longer ignore the movement against it, that it needed to fight its critics head on, not just complain in private.

Then John sat upright and inhaled. His face softened.

"Let's talk about something more pleasant," he continued. "I have been looking for an opportunity to tell you that my personal situation has changed. My wife has filed for divorce. She met someone she cares about a lot. She's motivated to get this done quickly. It's amicable so far. She has plenty of money of her own – more than she will ever be able to spend."

"I'm sorry to hear that – I mean, about the divorce," Elise said, finding herself eager to hear more.

"It's not unexpected," John said. "I'm telling you now because I sense you are finally free, and I want to get to know you better. I have always liked you. You must know that." He looked into her eyes, hoping to see a favourable reaction.

"I held back in the past because you deserve better than an affair. Also, I wanted to give you time to grieve your husband's loss, and process anything else that was still lingering, such as your doctor friend. To be honest, I am much older than you, which means I am not the confident man I used to be."

Elise didn't know what to say. It was a lot to take in. John had said everything she had hoped to hear long ago when they first met. Their relationship had been such a slow burn, so complicated by their situations, she no longer knew how she felt about him and his advances, whether she could ever truly trust him.

"I'd like to get to know you, too," she said, surprising herself. "I think you know this, too. I have felt the energy between us since the first day we met, during that interview in your office. But my life is complicated now. I am single, but I have found happiness in my work and in my children, after much struggle and much grief. I like where I am. Also, I must be careful because of my job. I don't want to be accused of having conflicting interests and I don't want to be disappointed again."

"Elise, I promise I won't let you down," John responded. "You won't be working forever, and neither will I. Aurora is my last company. I want it to succeed, of course, but I don't enjoy the work as much as I used to. These knocks on our industry are tough to take, and I am getting too old to defend what I helped build."

The oilman looked tired. They left the restaurant and walked together in the warm evening to their respective hotels. Elise found the courage to share her plans with him.

"I'm not ready to retire," she said. "I expect to return to the *Journal* in New York as a senior editor. I was integral to our transition to digital. My bosses know I am well positioned to apply that experience to new areas. That's where I want to go next."

"That sounds very interesting," John said, deflated. "I hope you get there. You worked hard for it, and you deserve the promotion."

"That doesn't mean there is no future for us," Elise continued, wanting to keep the door open. "It will just require some patience – and your divorce."

They arrived at Elise's destination feeling more connected. They'd talked frankly to each other for the first time. They parted with just a smile. Both were aware that they were on public display and that their future depended on keeping their relationship – if that's what was next for them – a secret.

The next day, Barb Heinz entered the main conference room surrounded by former senior leaders of the environmental movement. Like her, they were recruited by the new administration to speed up the transition to renewable energy. They looked confident in their new dark suits and important titles. Many had already worked together at the Save the Climate campaign.

"I want to thank the organizers for inviting me today to speak about our new plans to reduce our addiction to fossil fuels," Barb said to the standing-room-only crowd that had invited her to speak. Organizers had hoped to make nice with the new political leadership, perhaps temper some sharp edges, after all the anti-fossil-fuel rhetoric that was bandied about during the election campaign.

"We believe much needs to be done to save our planet," Barb continued. "The demonstrations you saw outside are a preview of what's to come if we don't change our ways. Young people will no longer stand by and watch the continuing degradation of our earth by your generation. They want to save what they can, while they can.

"The oil sector has an important role to play by switching to clean energy. We will offer financial incentives to support that and increase regulation on pollution. We plan to prohibit drilling in many areas. We urge you to do your part and start with divesting from the dirtiest sources of oil, the Canadian tar sands."

The crowd clapped politely and dispersed in the hallways. Everyone wondered how to best protect themselves.

Barb hosted a news conference immediately following her speech, repeating the same points more succinctly for the TV cameras.

The media found members of the Canadian delegation in a hospitality suite and asked for a response.

"Activism against the oilsands had become commonplace and has failed to gain traction," a spokesman said. "The public is more concerned about affordable energy, a clear and present danger, than climate change, a threat that is decades in the future. Canada produces oil responsibly, following the highest environmental standards."

"What do you think?" Elise asked John, who was standing with her in a corner of the suite.

"It's bluster by the new administration," he said. "Americans are invested up to their eyeballs in the oilsands. There is no way oilsands developers will allow a bunch of activists to tell them how to run their businesses. There is too much money at stake. Besides, the US needs the oil. Gasoline prices would skyrocket without Canadian supplies."

"Will you ignore the threat, then?" Elise asked.

"These attacks hurt, for sure, but it's just PR. They'll get tired of picking on us. This is all off the record."

Elise was about to exit the room when Barb Heinz tapped her shoulder from behind.

"Hi Elise, I was hoping to see you here," she said. "Nice to see you again. Richard has been a regular guest at our place. I hope you come to see us the next time you are in New York."

"Hi Barb. I enjoyed your speech. It sure caused a stir," Elise said, not sure how to feel about the woman's apparent familiarity with her son. "I go back to the newsroom at least once a month. I'll get in touch and look for a spot in your schedule."

Barb produced her new calling card and wrote down on it her personal mobile number. "I'd love to get your perspective," she said. "I read all your stories and I really admire what you do." She left the conference from a back door and was whisked away by a limo.

Elise walked back to her hotel alone, wondering why Barb Heinz was trying to be her friend.

Her speech had made national news on all the TV networks, on emerging social media platforms, and on mainstream and financial news outlets, including the *Journal*, which led with the headline "New Climate Czar Pushes Green Energy, Knocks Canada's Dirty Oil."

The next day, just as delegates were preparing to leave, New Era Energy, a Canadian pipeline company, held a press conference confirming that it was seeking approval from US regulatory authorities for a large oilsands pipeline linking Alberta's oilsands projects to Houston's refinery complex, the largest in the world. It was confident that its application exceeded all US regulatory requirements for environmental protection and that the project was aligned with the new administration's goal to reduce climate-change impacts.

Elise was one of the few journalists still around to cover the announcement. She filed a story in a rush from the conference's media room before leaving for the airport. Her story noted that the South pipeline would be the first of a series of planned oilsands pipelines from Alberta to the south, west, and east coasts of the continent.

Barb Heinz read the story on her new smart phone while waiting for a flight back to DC. She interpreted the announcement, so soon after her speech, as an act of defiance. Canada's oilsands industry was telling her it was not backing down.

The climate change leader was delighted. She was just given an excuse to push back even harder against the Canadian tar sands, without losing a single American vote. Her spin would be that a foreign company was bullying her country into buying its dirty oil and polluting its land, water, air for decades to come, and the new administration had an obligation to fight back.

Elise was lost in thought in a tight seat at the back of her Calgary-bound plane. She was re-energized by the pipeline announcement. She had always rooted for people who didn't give up. Her thoughts drifted to John. She tried to imagine a closer relationship with the man. Now that he was in his early sixties, she believed he was more comfortable with himself and with life generally, perhaps ready to address the void in his personal life.

A decade younger, Elise knew she was in a different place. She cared about her career and still felt the need to grow professionally. She was proud of her children, who pushed themselves hard to measure up to their beloved late father. Her life was full. She craved companionship at times – but not at any cost.

He'd offered her a seat on his private jet back to Calgary, which she politely declined. She had to explain to him she could be fired for accepting such favours. He responded that any other journalist would have jumped at the opportunity to fly back in comfort. He quickly filled that seat with a female industry lobbyist, and then made sure she knew. She wondered whether John was just looking for someone to fill the new vacancy in his household, just like he quickly filled that empty seat.

More importantly, Elise wondered if he was truthful about wanting to get to know her, after he strung her along so many times. She thought about whether Julien would have approved. Probably not. Her late husband would have been dismayed by the oilman's deviousness. He certainly wouldn't have been impressed by the way he got rich. She could hear him say: "Be careful, Elise. Just because he's rich, it doesn't mean he deserves you."

Chapter 43

Elise was overjoyed when Anthony Littlechild showed up at her door with her children. She hadn't spoken with the Indigenous young man since their interview years ago in Alberta, before he went back to school. She'd read somewhere he was accepted at Harvard Law on a full scholarship – the first Indigenous Canadian to be admitted.

Simone and Richard had met him at a house party near the university's campus, where Anthony had become a celebrity because of his glamorous looks, agile hoop dancing, and original thinking. He was a regular at the twins' place, where they discussed the big issues of the day and played their guitars.

One day he shared with them a recent article he particularly liked, and they revealed the writer was their mother. He told them he read her religiously since she wrote a feature on him. He credited their mom for changing his life. Delighted with the coincidence, they invited him for dinner with her in New York.

"Life is full of surprises," Elise said, hugging the man like a long-lost son. "I can't believe you've been hanging out with my children. I always knew you'd do well for yourself. But this is a miracle! Harvard Law and meeting my kids at Harvard."

"I owe you a great deal," Anthony said. He looked sophisticated with his pitch-black hair cut short and a well-cut blazer jacket that hugged his tall frame, Elise thought.

"That story you wrote about me – it led to opportunities that I didn't know were possible. It helped me get into Harvard. Going to school allowed me to put the past behind, and to discover I had a lot more control over my life than I knew. I had some great mentors and made amazing friends – such as your children."

They caught up over dinner, served in the formal dining room of the large flat, which was once again buzzing with interesting conversation with eclectic guests, a lot of them now introduced to Elise by her children.

"When do you graduate?" Elise asked.

"Next month. I've asked Richard and Simone to come for the festivities. You are invited, too," he said.

"I'll be there if I can," she said. "I'm on the road a lot these days. Let's see if I can make it happen. If I can't, I'll make it up to you in some other way."

Simone had moved back to New York after finishing her graduate studies and doing an internship in Switzerland, where she reconnected with her paternal grandparents. She was working in a survival job while looking for work in the media. She hoped for something in broadcasting. Richard had a year to go at Harvard and was optimistic about landing a residency in his dad's hospital, where Jordan was doing his best to get him in the door.

"What are your plans?" Elise asked Anthony.

"I will be articling in one of the law firms here in New York. But I want to return to Alberta, one way or the other, to help my community," he said.

"What do you have in mind?" Richard asked.

"The past few years have shown me that Canada's Indigenous people need to do more to overcome their past, but someone needs to show them the way," he said. "I want to be that person. I want to help them participate fully in the economy by shaping their own future, making more of their own choices.

"What they are doing now is all wrong," he continued. "They're either dependent on resource companies for work – which is usually temporary and not a good cultural fit, or live off government money, or are hired by these environmental groups to oppose progress. They should be starting their own companies and reaping the full benefits of the resources on their traditional lands – from oilsands to natural gas, diamonds to forestry."

"I thought Indigenous people were opposed to resource exploitation," Simone said, fascinated as always by her friend's views, which were often different from those of the young urbanites she knew.

"Some of them are, but the majority just want to get a fair share of the work and the wealth," Anthony responded. "Our First Nation, for example,

is so poor that some members are going hungry – I was one of them –
unless they work for the chief and his family. Yet under our reserve are
some of the richest oil deposits in the world. I believe they need the leadership to benefit from them. Expertise can be hired. We have a motivated
workforce. I was fortunate to get a hand up and learn how to make things
happen for myself. I want to help others do that as well."

"What's the situation with the activists?" Elise asked.

"It's not good," he said. "They have deals with bands all over Alberta and
British Columbia. They offer cash to anyone who'll join their campaign to
shut down the oilsands industry. I heard the going price is fifty thousand
per head. They walk into band offices and shove that money in their faces,
like drug lords pushing cocaine.

"The bands all talk to each other and squeeze them as much as they
can. They're seeing more money than ever – real money, not the empty
promises they're used to getting. However, our people are missing the big
picture. They're selling themselves and their rights to the highest bidder.
They are selling their future, because once the activists are done with their
campaigns, and succeed in shutting down industry, they will move to the
next cause and leave our people with the same poverty and dependence
on handouts."

"What are the activists paying for, exactly?" Elise asked.

"As far as I know, the campaign wants to file lawsuits on behalf of
Indigenous people against the fossil fuel companies, claiming they were
not properly consulted. Or they want them to show up at demonstrations
or to disrupt shareholder meetings. Our people are props. They have no
say over the campaign.

"If they refuse the overtures, the activists just go to the next Indigenous
band. There's always someone who will take the free money. I did, at first.
They made me feel special for the first time in my life, provided I did
what they wanted me to do. When I started questioning them, they cut
me off and smeared my reputation in my community. I was lucky I was
able to return to school, thanks to people like you and those who paid for
my education."

Elise had suspected much of what Anthony shared but didn't know the
extent of the campaign's activities and had never heard it directly. She knew

the oil companies were throwing a lot of money around to win Indigenous support – but obviously not enough and not without strings.

Elise asked him about Chief Anne. She was fond of the chief, she told Anthony, and couldn't understand why she got lured into a campaign that wasn't even relevant to her tribe, since its reserve was in Northern British Columbia, too far to be impacted by the oilsands.

"They offered her and her band a lot of money because she's great on camera. She's a strong woman and a good leader. She wasn't fully on board with the campaign. But her council made her do it – for the good of the band. They're getting paid millions. Besides, she knows her position as chief is precarious. They'll replace her if she doesn't do what she is told by her band council."

Elise wanted to ask the Indigenous man to share his story with *Journal* readers. But she held back. She didn't want to spoil their renewed friendship or put him at risk of creating new enemies just as he was beginning his career.

Simone was fascinated. She wanted to meet more like him – people with real stories and different perspectives. She couldn't wait to follow in her mother's footsteps in journalism and get her own front row seat to the world, instead of the fabricated one playing out on social media, which all her friends relied on for information.

"Why don't we hear more about this?" Simone asked Anthony. "Why are Indigenous people always portrayed as victims of development who need to be rescued by the green movement? No offense to you, Mom, but we need more truth."

"Good question," Anthony said. "That picture is not wrong. Some of our people had bad experiences with private-sector companies, including oil companies that left a lot of damage behind. But our salvation won't come from handouts – from activists, resource companies, or the government. It will come from taking charge of our destinies. My people are capable. Throughout our ten-thousand-plus-year history on this continent, we were entrepreneurs – hunters, gatherers, and then traders with the first settlers. We need to re-learn how to care for ourselves, build our own sustainable businesses, stop the cycle of dependency."

Elise couldn't resist doing a reality check. "Not everyone is a super achiever like you, Anthony. You overcame incredible odds. You're the exception rather than the rule. It would be unrealistic to expect others in your community to replicate what you did – go from an unsupportive environment, to put it kindly, to one of the world's elite schools."

"True. But we need to start somewhere," Anthony said. "I was surprised by how much support is available to people like me. You just need the courage to ask for it – and work like mad to demonstrate you deserve it."

Since they were in a sharing mood, Elise confided that Barb Heinz, whom they all knew, had invited her for dinner with Jordan. Barb had been nasty to her, Elise said. She had been critical of her reporting and likely instigated the flood of hate mail she was getting from the Save the Climate campaign.

"Should I bury the hatchet and try to get to know her, perhaps find a way to work more closely with her?" she asked her children and their friend. "She is in an influential position and her perspective would be useful to our readers. Besides, even if I don't buy the hyperbole, I believe her campaign is having an impact on industry, whether they like it or not."

Richard, who knew Barb best, could not believe mother's naiveté. He complained Barb tried to act like an adoptive parent when he spent time with Jordan in New York.

"She's only a few years older than I am and thinks I need a new mother with the right values, just because Jordan has taken me under his wing," Richard said. "Barb Heinz is the most manipulative person I have ever met.

"Mom, she sees you as a rival and she is trying to replace you," Richard continued, shaking his head. "I think she's jealous of you on a personal level and on a professional level. You are the thought leader she wants to be – just on the opposing team. If she wants to get close to you, it's because she wants to find out where you are vulnerable so she can shove you out of the way."

Elise was troubled by her son's dark thoughts. She'd never suspected Barb saw her that way. She wondered if she'd been away for too long, too focussed on her own grief and career, and neglected to be the parent her children needed. They'd been so mature about their dad's loss, so eager to please and to accomplish to make him proud.

"There's got to be something good about her – otherwise Jordan wouldn't have married her," Elise argued.

"Mom, Jordan is very unhappy right now," Richard revealed, glad to get the truth off his chest. "He doesn't say much because he doesn't want to admit he made a mistake marrying Barb. I am spending as much time as I can with him because he's so lost. I think he really misses Dad. I think he clings to me because I look so much like his old friend."

Elise looked at her son and was struck once again by how much he resembled her late husband – his physical appearance, his voice, his intelligence, his compassion. The similarities were increasing with time, like Richard was moving into Julien's vacant space.

"I had no idea," Elise said. "Jordan and I don't talk much these days. I thought it was best for me to stay out of his way. I honestly thought he was happy, and I wanted to be happy for him."

"Well, he isn't, and I am really worried about him," Richard said. "He's been talking about quitting his job and doing a tour in a war zone, maybe Afghanistan. I believe he feels manipulated, used by dishonest people. I think he's looking for an honourable way out."

Well then, Elise concluded, a meeting with Barb Heinz would have to wait.

It was midnight, and Anthony Littlechild hugged everyone before leaving and promised to stay in touch. Elise told him she was happy they reconnected.

But she couldn't fall asleep. She thought about Jordan and decided to call him before returning to Calgary. He'd always been so pure, cared so much. He didn't seem to understand that activism was more about power than about saving the world. Perhaps it took an activist, Barb, to show its true colours.

"Hi Jordan. It's Elise. I'm in New York for a few more hours. Give me a call if you get a chance," Elise said in a voice message on Jordan's personal cell on her way to the airport.

She was waiting in a lounge when he called her back. Her flight was late, held up in Toronto by a spring snowstorm.

"Hi Elise," he said, his voice weak. "It's so good to hear from you. Are you still in the city?"

"No. I'm at the airport. But we can talk. My flight has been delayed."

"When are you coming back – I mean, permanently?" he asked.

"I'm not sure. We've had a lot of layoffs at the *Journal*, so I was asked to stay in Canada a while longer because our business there is still growing. But I do come back here regularly – usually at least once a month. It's a good arrangement. I get to see the children, but not so much that I am in their way. I'm still travelling a lot on assignment, so I am a citizen of the world these days."

"I sure miss you," Jordan said, tentatively. "Richard has been a real help. I can't wait for him to start at the hospital. He's brilliant, just like Julien – maybe even better with the right mentoring."

They caught up about mutual friends, their recent holidays. She waited for him to talk about his marriage. He didn't. She was about to hang up when Jordan asked her something unexpected.

"Did you get that document – the one about The Canada Project?"

"I did – did that come from you?"

"Yes. I wanted you to have it."

"How did you get your hands on it?"

"It was discussed at a meeting of the board of Save the Climate. I am – was – a director. What you got was a partial version. There is more to it, but I thought that would give you a flavour."

Intrigued by the revelation, Elise wondered why Jordan had taken such a big risk. "What do you mean that you were a director? Have you quit?"

"Yes. I left on principle."

"You weren't comfortable with the strategy? I have to say, when I saw it, I was sickened by it. They seem to be organizing an uprising in a foreign country – Canada has been our loyal ally. It's shameful, really. Regardless, I worry about you. These people are vicious. I know from experience," Elise said.

"I know, and there will be consequences, for me," Jordan said. "But I feel the campaign is going too far, has lost its way."

"You probably saw that I did a story on that report," Elise said. "I was disappointed that it got little traction. Even the Canadians kind of brushed it off, like they didn't believe it, or don't want to believe it. They feel that nothing can get in the way of their biggest export industry."

"They shouldn't ignore it," Jordan said. "As you know, Barb is in the White House, but is also unofficially running the oilsands campaign. One of the key planks of their climate strategy is to shut down the oilsands. It's clever and stupid at the same time. Clever because they are targeting a foreign oil source, so they don't have to worry about losing jobs and votes in the United States to show they are making progress. Stupid because they are not doing what needs to be done here to reduce our emissions. It's all political theatre that won't result in us – the largest polluter on the planet – changing our ways."

"I agree," Elise said. "I can't believe it's come to this."

Elise's flight was beginning to board. She urged Jordan to stay in touch. She told him she was glad that he was so close to her son.

"Elise, before you go, I urge you to be careful. The campaign has a big media component. Their goal is to discredit people who challenge them. I know how much your job depends on your reputation."

"Thanks, Jordan. I'll raise it with my editor. He needs to know. But you need to be careful, too," Elise said.

They hung up. She hoped Jordan had finally realized the article that broke up their relationship was a fabrication. Perhaps his leaking of the campaign document to her was his way to make amends.

Chapter 44

CALGARY, ALBERTA, MARCH 2010

Elise bumped into Paul Chen at a social event following an investment conference. The former oil executive from China looked more relaxed but thinner than the last time she saw him. She had heard from *Journal* staff in his country that he was jailed for mishandling government funds. Elise suspected he was punished for overpaying for Canadian oilsands assets, which made his government look bad.

"Hi Paul, what brings you back to Calgary?" she asked him in the lobby of the new hotel owned by John Hess's ex-wife.

"Hi Elise. I live here now – permanently," he said, looking more Canadian than Chinese with his longer hair and corduroy slacks. "I quit my job and immigrated with my family. I'm building my own business. I work for private Chinese investors who are buying oilsands leases and anything else they can – real estate, hotels, restaurants. They love Canadian oil."

"Seriously? It's a tough resource to produce," she said.

"Yes, it is. But I have some expertise, and we will hire technical people from Canada to help us. My clients want to get their money out of China, establish a base in Canada to diversify their investments and send their children to Canadian schools. They don't trust their government, and neither do I."

He didn't supply more details and Elise didn't ask. She knew he couldn't answer truthfully.

"How many investors do you represent?" Elise asked.

"Hundreds. I had to hire six tour buses to show them opportunities. We're going to Fort McMurray tomorrow."

"Investment tourism?" Elise asked, amused.

"I suppose you can call it that."

"Aren't they concerned about the campaign against the oilsands?"

"No. They just want to make money. They take the long view and don't see oil demand declining for decades."

The Chinese were in good company. A couple of years after the global financial downturn shook the world, those global oil companies that had doubted the potential of the oilsands were rushing to Calgary. They were looking for purchases, partnerships, supply arrangements – any remaining crumbs that got them a foothold in the industry. Oil prices were resuming their climb because supplies were, once again, tight. Some paired up with large refiners to build seamless supply chains from the oilfields to the gasoline pumps. The matches involved big deals, which boosted stock prices all along the value chain.

Calgary was bursting at the seams. Downtown streets, sidewalks, restaurants, malls, and industry trade events were teeming with people coming from elsewhere. Entire condo towers were bought to house the growing multinational workforce. Luxury brand retailers opened shops or expanded their presence. New restaurants were launched, and new golf courses were built. Unemployment was so low that Help Wanted signs were displayed on scores of shop windows.

The increased economic activity in Alberta meant increased influence for the *Journal* in the world of energy, but for Elise, it came with new challenges. She was becoming a victim of her own success – the better job she did, the more she was needed in the city, while her long-promised return to New York, where layoffs were continuing, kept being pushed back. She loved Alberta but missed the newsroom, was tiring of travel, and was worried that she'd been in the same beat for too long.

Meanwhile, the relentless attacks from the anti-oilsands movement were taking a toll.

Environmentalists saw her news coverage as a promotion of the industry, which ran counter to their goal of shutting it down by elevating the negatives. Because of her dual role as a journalist and editor, they discredited her and her employer relentlessly.

Old photos of her sharing a ride with John Hess and new photos of her speaking at oil conferences resurfaced on the internet, with unflattering captions such as: "*Journal* mouthpiece gets cozy with dirty oil billionaires."

People with strange names and poor writing skills wrote repulsive comments about her stories.

She was included in extensive lists of climate deniers, alongside academics who dared to question the anti-oilsands lobby, or analysts who covered oil and gas stocks. It was obvious to her that the Save the Climate campaign was monitoring all information and information sources relevant to its crusade, kept score of its enemies and slandered their reputations.

She noticed new websites were launched to promote parallel narratives that demonized all forms of fossil fuel development. They claimed to do real and independent journalism. Their offerings included sensational attacks of industry, regulatory, and government representatives. Several had printed profiles of Elise, accusing her of taking bribes, of being 'captured' by the oil lobby, of representing foreign media interests, of being elitist, of being a Republican.

Emails from campaigners sent directly to her *Journal* account and copied to her editors questioned her news judgement and accused her of profiting from the expansion of dirty oil. Some threatened to demonstrate in front of her office or home. The feedback had become so frequent and so vile that she felt abused.

Elise went the extra mile to be fair and balanced in her reporting. But that didn't stop the campaign against her. Activists used the *Journal* to reach its audience, while continuing to discredit her on online platforms they controlled to reach their own followers. They felt so righteous about their cause they didn't care who got hurt.

Many readers encouraged Elise to keep covering the oil business with the journalism standards they knew she was capable of, but others were so influenced by the new media sources they demanded corrections and, increasingly, called for her firing.

The disparaging view of the oilsands presented by the Save the Climate campaign was so pervasive it was making it difficult – even to her – to separate truth from fiction.

A strange new dynamic was taking place – established media was matching stories that appeared first on social media without verifying the facts, instead of doing its own reporting based on its own research. The new narrative about the oilsands as the source of all climate evil spilled into Canadian and world politics, feeding bigotry against Alberta and its oilsands-dependent economy.

Elise was so exasperated that she called Mark Wimhurst to give him an update on what was happening.

"Hi Mark. Thanks for taking the time to chat," she said.

"Anytime. I am glad you called. I'm getting a lot of emails about you," he said.

"I'm getting a lot of emails about me. I don't know how to handle them. I need guidance." She described the situation, trying to present the facts as dispassionately as possible.

Her chief editor said other industries covered by the *Journal* were dealing with similar campaigns, which he attributed to the rising power of new media looking to replace legacy media as sources of information.

"They don't do journalism," he said. "They think it's okay to put stuff out there and let the public figure out what is true. It's unsettling. And yet they're money-making machines that are syphoning advertising dollars away from us and killing our profession. We are better off than most at the *Journal*, thanks to our global brand and the digital transition you are involved in. We'd be in trouble if we didn't have a solid trading operation and a worldwide digital audience hungry for tradeable information."

"But these people are deliberately discrediting what we do – what I do," Elise complained. "They are destroying my reputation. People who know me continue to be loyal, but I have come across many who are refusing to talk to me after reading all this bad stuff on the internet."

"Yes, they are going too far on energy and on journalists like you. The climate-change debate appeals to young audiences, who never read newspapers. But there is a silver lining," Mark said.

"What is it?" Elise asked.

"The clash between these worldviews is promoting readership on our platform. The energy beat is the most widely read at the *Journal*, and so is your reporting. We are a trusted source by investors worldwide and they are paying us to report all the news. No one in social media will replace us. My suggestion is that you keep doing what you are doing. Don't let them intimidate you."

"What about my reputation – our reputation? What about safety?" Elise asked, worried her boss wasn't taking her situation seriously enough.

"Just let me know every time these people cross the line," Mark said. "I'll ask our lawyers to get involved. I will also make sure we tighten security of our offices in Calgary. Meanwhile, is there an opportunity to increase coverage of renewable energy? That may appease the green lobby."

"There is – and we should. A lot of government money is going into it. Maybe we should start regular features," Elise said. "But don't expect them to do us any favours. That's not how they operate."

"I'll look into it," the editor said. "We need more information about whether our readers care. So far, green energy only works because of government subsidies. Who's in charge of the Save the Climate campaign?"

"I heard Barb Heinz is continuing to pull the strings from the White House," Elise said.

"*The* Barb Heinz?" he asked.

"Yes. She used to run the campaign against the oilsands, then was appointed climate czar. Officially she is on leave from Save the Climate. She asked me a while ago to meet. But I haven't followed up because I'm in an awkward position – I have a personal connection," Elise said, and told him about Jordan.

"Of course. Makes sense. How would you feel if I met with her?" the editor suggested. "I'll be in Washington next week on other business. It might be worthwhile to have a chat with her."

"Great plan," Elise said. "Let me know what you think."

She felt better after the call – until the next day.

Elise went to work earlier than usual and was greeted at the door by a young courier in shorts and a bicycle helmet who'd been waiting for her. He handed her an envelope and asked for her signature.

She was being sued. An environmental law firm had filed a multi-million-dollar claim against her personally, as well as the *Journal*, various industry associations and the largest oilsands companies – including John Hess's Aurora – for reporting false information about the true climate impacts of oilsands operations.

She read the extensive allegations – dozens of pages of alarming climate-change projections based on planned oilsands expansions, mixed with research from climate-change experts. *Journal* stories were included as evidence the industry was promoting investment while downplaying risks.

Elise felt her inclusion in the claim was absurd. It was based on her straightforward reporting about an industry growth forecast. In her view, it was a classic case of libel chill to scare her from doing her job. She phoned Mark Wimhurst to let him know about the lawsuit.

"Hi again," she said. "I am being sued, unfortunately, as well as the *Journal* and other industry people. You'll probably be served shortly."

"Damn!" the editor said. "We don't need this."

Elise explained the essence of the lawsuit and her boss breathed more easily.

"Did we get anything wrong?" he asked.

"No. We're included based on a straightforward report. I'll fax you the document right away."

Then she added: "Perhaps I could have asked the Save the Climate activists to provide their point of view on the growth projections and included that in my reporting. But they would have contributed their usual anti-fossil-fuel hyperbole. We would have just given them more space they didn't deserve. They are not credible sources. I think they're coming after us because they are looking for maximum publicity. We're a capitalist bastion. They want to bring us down a notch."

The editor wasn't concerned. If the reporting was accurate, he agreed the *Journal*'s inclusion in the lawsuit was a publicity stunt.

"I'll raise it with Barb Heinz," Mark said. "She has agreed to meet me in DC. This stuff goes too far, and if she doesn't back off, we'll fight fire with fire. If the campaign is as misleading as you say it is, we need to take an in-depth look at who these guys are and what they are doing. They seem to have oversized influence, yet they lurk in the shadows, saying little about themselves and who funds them, while pulling strings in the corridors of power."

After everyone named in the lawsuit was served, the Save the Climate campaign held a news conference in a downtown Vancouver hotel to tell the world about its legal fight against the oilsands industry and its enablers.

Erika Bernstein – with a cast of lawyers, environmental activists, Indigenous leaders, and academic experts standing behind her – accused industry groups, oil producers, the *Journal,* and its senior energy reporter Elise Chamonter, of making false claims about the climate-change impacts of the oilsands.

The announcement was televised on national networks and amplified on social media platforms. The *Journal*'s main competitors covered it thoroughly, using photos of Elise speaking at industry conferences.

Elise felt betrayed by her peers. Why had no one questioned the validity of the lawsuit? Why had no one asked why Erika Bernstein, an American, was singling out the Canadian oilsands industry? Why had no one asked the names and credentials of the people standing behind her? Instead, everyone was fixated on the conflict. Journalists are supposed to cover news, not make news, she thought. They used to stick together and protect each other from threats to press freedom. They used to question and verify what they were told by the powerful, which the Save the Climate campaign had certainly become.

The *Journal* issued a statement denying the allegations and ran a brief story about it. The pro-oil camp made available its spokespeople, who re-assured the markets that industry would defend itself vigorously and growth plans would continue as planned. Behind the scenes, a few oilsands companies decided to increase their funding of the Save the Climate campaign to get the activists off their backs.

Elise worried she was getting caught up in a battle she could not win, that she risked losing everything she'd worked for, and that she was powerless to defend herself. She tried to shift her attention to her work but lost her drive. She wondered if her portrayal by the Save the Climate campaign – that she was undeserving of her job, that she had become biased – had merit. She considered quitting for the good of the *Journal* so she could be replaced by someone who better understood the priorities of younger generations and their obsession with disrupting things they didn't build. She knew she was falling back into her dark hole. She thought about Julien and their life together. She reached out to her children, who urged her to soldier on.

Elise thought about John Hess, too. She had barely spoken to him since their meeting in Houston the previous year. Once again, he'd gone missing, after auditioning her to replace his ex-wife. The flow of useful information had also dried up. Hot and cold. Hot and cold. The same pattern since the day they met. She'd been right to doubt him.

She knew he had finalized his divorce because she'd read about it in a local paper, and she knew he'd been spending a lot of time in the field. But he never bothered to follow up with her.

She decided to take the initiative. She dialed his number, hoping for a sympathetic ear, a word of support from someone she thought was on her side.

It was late. "Hi Elise, how are you?" he asked, like not a minute had passed since that distant evening when he asked her to be in his future.

"I'm okay. Things could be better."

"Is this about the lawsuit?" he asked.

"Yes, a bit. Life in journalism is tough these days – almost as tough as in the oilsands industry, without the pay," she said.

"I wouldn't worry about it too much," he said. "They have no case."

"I do worry about it. My reputation is on the line. I could lose my job over this. Reputation is a big deal in journalism."

"You have nothing to fear. We're putting together a legal team to give them a run for their money. Look at the bright side. There's no such thing as bad publicity. They think they are putting us on trial, but we will show the world they don't know what they are talking about."

They caught up about their jobs – he'd been busy, he said, with more projects to grow his company's oil production and more plans to secure transportation and refining space. A team from Houston was flying in to see his operation, including several investment analysts and politicians looking for reassurances that the oilsands were not the horrible place they were made out to be. His company was beating expectations and deploying many new technologies, which were the talk of the industry.

The oilman didn't talk about his personal life and didn't ask about Elise's. Then he told her he had to go and hung up. Elise felt she'd been dismissed.

A few days later, one of Elise's top competitors filed a flattering report from Aurora's oilsands operation about a large delegation invited for a visit by John Hess, the billionaire oil entrepreneur. Another report was filed by a TV station.

Both featured lengthy interviews with John, politicians, analysts, and Indigenous leaders, all on hand to reassure the public that countless environmental improvements were under way to produce the cleanest possible oilsands oil.

Elise's heart sank. John had gone on the offensive and orchestrated his own campaign against the activists, while ignoring her.

It hurt her that he never offered her the opportunity to cover it. Perhaps the snub meant John regarded her now as damaged goods – even if he'd contributed enormously to the damage. She resented him for not having her back after she stood up for him and his industry without reservation, because she thought it was the right thing to do.

Her thoughts were interrupted by a call from Mark Wimhurst, who wanted to vent after meeting with Barb Heinz.

"You are right. She's a zealot, a power-hungry crusader," he told Elise. "She demanded the moon and agreed to give nothing in return. Let's ignore the lawsuit and keep up the good reporting. If you have any ideas about putting the spotlight on this campaign, let's do it."

Chapter 45

Two awful oil spills – one in the Gulf of Mexico, the other involving a pipe-line rupture in Michigan – were welcomed by Barb Heinz as lucky breaks. While the oil companies responsible struggled under the glare of live TV to contain the disasters, Barb saw them as an opportunity to recharge her campaign.

"Good morning, everyone," she said at a progress update meeting of Save the Climate's Canada Project 2.0 campaign in its growing headquarters, where she was saluted like a returning hero.

Officially, Barb was the President's climate-change advisor. Unofficially, she remained in charge of Save the Climate, though part of her old job was handed off to new hires. She convinced her boss that the two roles were complementary. The more the campaign against the oilsands was successful, the more the new President could brag that there was deep and broad support for tough climate-change action.

From her seat at the head of the group's conference table, surrounded by old colleagues, a few new ones, and a pair of potential wealthy donors eager to take a closer look at the campaign's program before opening their wallets, Barb said she was excited about how the group was changing environmental activism.

Before the campaign, she said, the oil spills would have been regarded as costly accidents by two companies whose penny-wise, pound-foolish bosses deserved to be fired. Investors would have dumped their stock because of lawsuits that were sure to come. Creditors would have pushed them into bankruptcy. Governments would have pulled licenses and imposed fines. Environmentalists would have rolled up their sleeves and helped mop up the mess.

"No more," she said. "Save the Climate is rewriting the playbook on how we deal with polluters. You should be very proud. Our people are on the ground, taking pictures, creating videos, and posting them on social media for the world to see. We are framing the cleanup as a cautionary tale about the dangers of oil to the planet's air, water, and land. We're warning America that if such horror can happen in Michigan and in the Gulf, then everyone's backyard, rivers, and coastlines are at risk from Canada's dirty oil, the biggest new oil source. It's not a matter of if, but when, the oilsands monster will rear its ugly head. We are creating a powerful narrative.

"Response to the new approach is exceeding all our expectations," Barb said, feeling the room's excitement. "Kayakers in Vancouver are alarmed that Alberta's oil could foul their coastal playgrounds, housewives in New York are blaming Canada's dirty oil for their basements' flooding, actors in California are railing against Canada's oilsands for causing forest fires that are threatening their mansions, farmers in middle America are raising their fists against Canada's foreign oil for causing bad weather that damages their crops, Quebecers are rejecting the imposition of oil pro-duced by Alberta's Anglos on its French-speaking population, residents of Vancouver Island are refusing to allow any more oil tankers near their shores to protect the whales, West Coast tourism operators are refusing to let the oilsands threaten their salmon and their bears.

"We've never reached so many people," Barb said. "We've never raised so much money because people who matter see a path to success. I'd like to welcome our two visitors and hope they will support us generously, too." She smiled in their direction, her eyes locking on the celebrity billionaire hedge-fund manager who helped put her President in the White House.

Then Barb got to the main reason for calling the meeting. She paused and looked around the room again. She needed her team's undivided attention.

"We have momentum," she said. "Let's up the pressure.

"We believe that the proposed tar sands pipelines are their biggest weakness, their Achilles heel," she said. "We need to shut them down. Our first target will be the South Pipeline that just started construction. It will need presidential approval to cross the Canada/US border, which presents a golden opportunity for the White House to get involved. We need Save the Climate to organize an uprising against this project. Let's make sure it never gets built.

"Any ideas, feedback?" she asked the room.

"How about more protests? They'll give us the publicity we need," said one of the campaign's top organizers, a student who put his political-science studies on hold to learn how to mobilize people for maximum impact.

"Our legal team can work on ways to stall progress in the legal and regulatory arenas," said the campaign's senior lawyer.

"We need to work Congress. There's got to be ways to build a political coalition to oppose this foreign dirty oil project," said the campaign's lobbyist.

"We need to strengthen our network of supporters – work with and fund local organizations of landowners," said the coordinator of grassroots networking.

"What about targeting investors? We need to make it painful for investors to support tar sands extraction and infrastructure," said the financial markets strategist.

Debate continued about the pros and cons.

"Would such a high-profile attack on a Canadian project affect bilateral relations?" the market strategist wondered.

"Probably, but that could be managed by supporting Canadian political candidates who prioritize climate change over oilsands production, or by working with Canadian politicians already opposed to tar sands expansions," the lobbyist proposed.

"Will the US oil industry defend its Canadian counterparts?" the lawyer asked.

"Some will, but some will look at it as an opportunity to knock out a competitor, or to earn bigger profits by depressing the price of Canadian oil because of lack of pipeline capacity," the lobbyist responded.

"Will the Canadian company that proposed the pipeline give up?" asked another campaigner.

"Possibly, if the campaign causes delays that make the project too expensive," the lawyer said.

"Will international goodwill for Canada make Americans look like bullies?" asked an intern.

"Few will care that Canada isn't producing its dirty oil," Barb responded.

"Will the Canadian industry go on the offensive?" the lawyer asked.

"I doubt it. The Canadians will keep a low profile, play by the rules, make money for as long as they can, and hope demand for their product continues," Barb responded.

"Will investors get upset about losing money?" another intern asked.

"For sure, and that is a good thing, because it will force them to migrate to renewable energy," the market strategist responded.

"Will the media defend tar sands pipelines?" the grassroots organizer asked.

"Journalism attracts liberals. Most journalists are sympathetic to climate action," the media strategist responded.

"Will the campaign drive up oil prices?" the lawyer asked.

"Maybe – but that's also a good thing, because it would lead to a quicker transition to renewable energy," the market strategist responded.

One final question froze the room.

"Is the campaign going too far?" one of the potential donors asked.

Barb, sensing the discomfort, took a deep breath and stood up. She felt it was important to re-enforce to all in attendance the righteousness of the cause.

"We're organizing a revolution to accelerate the adoption of a new energy system. Revolutions are not fought with half measures. They're not reasonable and they are not fair. They're not about compromise. They're meant to shock, to make the leap forward, to make the comfortable uncomfortable, to change the world's order, which is now bound together by fossil fuels. There are too many vested interests, too many entrenched politicians, too many livelihoods, too much influence, too many institutions, too much money, too much legal precedent, too many norms that are woven together to keep us from breaking in and establishing a new, better order that values the preservation of our climate in all our choices. Without extraordinary pressure, the system will not break.

"Change does happen through evolution, but it takes time. We don't have enough time to save ourselves from the devastating impacts of climate change. We have a decade, two at most. We need to act now. We cannot wait for the majority to come around and support what we do. We need to start from the margins and pull the rest with us.

"There will be blood, unfortunately. There will be collateral damage. That damage will be concentrated in the Alberta region of Canada – for now. Many people will lose their jobs. I don't like that. I wish we could do this differently. It's a sacrifice that is necessary so we can breathe and continue to live. Our revolution has no borders because the climate has no borders. The tar sands are our first target for a reason – they're visual, accessible, and are becoming the largest source of imported oil consumed in the United States.

"If we defeat the oilsands, we take down fossil fuel's last great hope. We won't stop there. We are creating a template for fossil fuel disruption that we will apply to other fossil fuel sources in the future. Are we going too far? You bet. We're going as far as we need to protect our climate."

Barb sat down. The room was mesmerized. There were no more doubts that the campaign was doing the right thing and was ready to do what was needed.

Before concluding the meeting, Barb thanked everyone and made a final request. "I need you to regard what was said here as highly confidential. I'm not happy that our strategy document was leaked," she said, making eye contact with all those present.

"It put us in a difficult position. It could have derailed our efforts. My current role within the administration makes my presence in these offices very sensitive. Our new administration is ambitious. It's fully on board with our Save the Climate goals and strategy. We have a historic chance to transition away from fossil fuels and persuade the world to come with us. But we need to manage this carefully and avoid situations we can't control."

The meeting was adjourned. As was customary, the group moved to the nearby bar for some socializing. Both donors were invited to join. One declined.

Barb walked over with the hedge-fund billionaire.

Tom Young was a handsome man in his early forties eager to deploy his fortune on good political causes, which complemented his heavy bets on renewable energy. A resident of Silicon Valley with roots in Singapore, he was increasingly visible in the White House because of his knowledge of the tech sector. It was rumoured he fancied a political run of his own.

"That was a stirring speech," he told her, noticing she wasn't wearing a wedding ring. "I was certainly concerned about the direction of the campaign, that it was a bit too heavy handed against Canada, but you convinced me that it's for their own good. It's tough love. I agree with you that we can't wait for most of the electorate to come on board after all the angles and all the interests have been addressed. That's how you miss opportunity. Fortune favours the brave, in the investment world as in politics."

"Thank you. I'm glad we see eye to eye," Barb said. "We need your support at Save the Climate – not just your money, but your leadership and your knowledge. We need to show that clean energy is our best option, that governments need to invest in it to encourage adoption."

"I'm in," Tom said. "This energy transition won't happen without government pressure, and I like what you are doing. So much innovation that we take for granted today started as a government project. Green energy won't be embraced unless political leaders show the way – through investment, regulation, taxation."

The conversation drifted to the President's agenda on climate-change policy, pending tax changes, international agreements, Washington gossip.

Barb was excited – intellectually and sexually. Tom Young understood her for the ambitious political operative she was. She contrasted him to her husband. Jordan was too honest to accept her in full, she accepted.

Things had not been well with Jordan. She knew he'd become disinterested in her and in her new career, just as she was soaring to new heights. He'd resigned from Save the Climate over The Canada Project 2.0, which she suspected had much to do with Elise.

He felt the campaign had strayed from his original goal – to create greater awareness of climate change – into a revolution with questionable funding that had no business remaking Canada, he told her. The tension got so bad that she spent most of her time in Washington while he worked long hours at his hospital in New York.

Drinks with Tom Young led to dinner. Then, both a bit drunk from too much Veuve Clicquot, they retired in his downtown penthouse suite, a pied-a-terre he bought to gain a view of Washington from the inside.

Two weeks after the update meeting, fossil-fueled busloads of protesters stormed the trenches dug up in Oklahoma by the Canadian pipeline company to lay the South pipe, forcing workers to put down their tools and their equipment to sit idle. Elise sent reporters to the scene. They wrote stories about protesters setting up camps, harassing workers, damaging equipment, starting fights, littering, beating drums, and chanting slogans:

"Canada Keep Your Dirty Oil!"

"Tar Sands Kill!"

"No More Fossil Fuels!"

"Fight for Climate Justice!"

"Save the Climate for the People!"

"Blood Oil!"

Social media exploded with posts about the offensive project. Actors flew in to condemn it to their fans. Politicians embraced the just cause. More activists from more organizations showed up in solidarity.

Eventually, New Era Energy, the Canadian pipeline company, obtained a court injunction to stop the illegal protest, and construction resumed under heavy private security. Costs soared and the pipeline was behind schedule.

More demonstrations against the South Pipeline erupted elsewhere – in the streets of DC, on Indigenous reserves, in farmers' fields. Lawsuits were filed to cancel permits already obtained; landowners were refusing to allow pipeline construction on their lands. Foreign oil competitors watched the Canadian takedown with glee and fomented online rage.

The campaign was creating the impression of an unstoppable and widely supported revolt against the dirtiest source of fossil fuels, one that was forced on Americans by a foreign country, one that was instigated by a reckless foreign operator that put profit ahead of their health and right to clean air, Elise noticed.

Yet she was torn by a question that the campaign refused to answer: How did a single oil pipeline – one of thousands in operation or under construction that was following all the rules and regulations, that was providing secure oil to meet American needs as Canadian oil had done for decades, that was built with the best available technologies to prevent spills and reduce carbon emissions, that was creating jobs for thousands of Americans, that would replace oil from unstable regimes like Iran, Venezuela, and Russia – become the culprit of the world's changing climate?

Chapter 46

Erika Bernstein took the early-morning ferry to the pastoral island near Vancouver where she established the secret Canadian headquarters of the Save the Climate campaign. Her team was spread out over the entire second floor of a large log building. The wide-open office space was located atop an art gallery, a big attraction for visiting tourists along with locally produced ice cream, homegrown vegetable stands, and quaint restaurants renowned for their fresh crab.

Her new staff complained about the remoteness of the offices and the high cost of living, particularly during the summer tourist season. But the activist leader loved it. One reason was that islanders – a laid-back bunch that lived off tourism dollars and organic farming, especially marijuana and coffee – had no idea that a sophisticated campaign to remake Canada's economy was being organized right under their noses.

Besides, the ferry ride through unspoiled islets, rock-strewn beaches, and clear ocean water inspired her to do whatever she could to protect the earth and the air that kept it alive.

Before boarding the ferry, Erika drove her new electric car to the airport to collect Chief Anne Proudfoot. The leader of her legal team, and several new recruits from across British Columbia and the Seattle area, followed her in their own vehicles.

Encouraged by the early success against the South Pipeline in the United States, Erika was allocated more funding to organize a more ambitious resistance in Canada. DC headquarters had decided that the West Pipeline, which was ready to seek regulatory approval, would be next in line for a full-blown attack.

In addition to the tactics used in the United States against the South Pipeline, the leader was instructed to lobby all Canadian levels of government with jurisdiction over pipeline construction and energy policy to oppose the project, and to encourage reforms of Canada's regulatory system so that all future decisions would consider impacts on the climate.

"Welcome to our headquarters," Erika said, entering the new offices with her group. She was proud of her war room – similar but much bigger than those she ran in the past.

Her immediate priority was to ensure the chief remained a committed ally. Chief Anne had proven to be a good asset for the campaign, yet Erika sensed a lack of conviction. The chief had worked hard to satisfy her tribal council but had refused to use her influence to recruit Indigenous bands along the pipeline route. The activist hoped that a first-hand view of the campaign's operation would address the chief's doubts, so she would use her network for the campaign's benefit.

The activist introduced her guests to a dozen staff already hard at work, including two young Indigenous university graduates excited to play a role in the campaign, and to collect their first steady paycheques.

Powerful computers with double screens blinked on top of modern workstations. Several TVs hung on a wall. Phones rang incessantly. Several members of the team had experience working on political campaigns on both sides of the border. Others had technology or social media back-grounds. All were young, urban, and casually dressed in ripped jeans and T-shirts, with large lattes on their desks delivered by the organic/fair trade coffee bar across the street.

Erika explained that the office organized protests against the West Pipeline across Canada, including running a multitude of social media accounts to fan fear of a pipeline spill; distributed funds to a growing web of Canadian grassroots environmental organizations and political candidates; and provided funding to academics interested in researching topics that supported the campaign. She did not disclose that much of the funding was coming from the US, nor that none of the Americans had work permits.

"We have identified several key objectives," Erika explained. "We are organizing a group to push for reform of Canada's regulatory system because it's too influenced by industry. We are working with our legal team to challenge all regulatory decisions already made and those that we expect in the future so that climate change impacts are considered. These actions have the additional benefit of raising the cost of producing and transporting oil from the tar sands.

"We are building a network of Canadian environmental groups, following a hub and spoke model – we're the hub – to expand our climate-change movement and to support the election of a new political class that prioritizes climate change action across North America.

"We are upgrading our social media campaign to publicly shame and expose supporters of the tar sands industry."

Erika then turned to Chief Anne. She needed to re-enforce that she valued her and that she was important to the campaign.

"Our most important goal is to partner with more Indigenous people across Canada, but particularly along the West Pipeline route. Our campaign will have greater success if we align ourselves with Canada's oppressed First Nations. Their rights are being trampled on by settlers, and they are not being adequately compensated for projects and impacts on their lands of so much oil and gas activity. They're offered trinkets like community centres – while companies earn billions from extracting resources on their traditional lands. Meanwhile, Indigenous people will pay the price of the environmental damage that is left behind."

The elderly Indigenous woman was only half listening. She barely related to what the activist said. Settlers? She hadn't heard that word in a long time. Are those the people who immigrated to Canada? she wondered. She felt out of place. She was the oldest person in the room, a grandmother who had little experience with social media, a chief with a long and proud record of fighting her own battles for her own people.

Her gaze and mind were struck by a series of posters on the walls, all showing her in various poses wearing one of her traditional costumes and, on her wrinkled face, despair. She noticed the same photos of herself on computer screens, full of anti-oilsands, anti-Alberta, anti-Canadian government slogans, accompanied by instructions to donate to the Save the Climate campaign.

Chief Anne vaguely recalled that the photos were taken at a demonstration in the United States where she felt sad – not because of the oilsands but because she was ashamed of being a prop in a movement over which she had no say. Instead, young people she didn't know, and who didn't know her, told her what to do and how to do it. It was Ladyfern and the fur trade all over again, but on a bigger scale.

Sure, she was getting compensated, as did her people. She was earning more money than she ever had. But she wasn't fighting for what she thought was right. She felt like she sold out to someone else's fight involving politics she did not relate to and that would not lead to permanent improvements for her people like jobs, education, and a higher standard of living. As she performed for the cameras, she recalled feeling colonized all over again.

"I see you made me famous," Chief Anne said to the activist boss, her voice reflecting her anger. "I didn't know the campaign would use my image this way. I don't recall giving you permission."

Erika was shaken. She thought the chief understood that her image would be used for the good of the campaign.

The rest of the group watched the two strong-headed women. They were not sure how to handle the tension between them. They were used to getting their way in the virtual world but were unequipped to deal with conflict involving real people in the real world.

"Chief, it was part of our overall agreement with your band," Erika said, turning for guidance to her lawyer, who remained silent. "You look great in those photos. They capture so much about your struggle to preserve the environment. We got a lot of compliments. We tested them with our focus groups. They were moved by your sadness. Your image is a major part of our fundraising efforts."

"I was never told you would use these photos – and my name," the chief responded. "I never consented. I don't like how you attack our governments – I don't need to aggravate Canadian politicians. I need their cooperation on many issues. Please take those pictures down," she demanded.

Embarrassed, Erika tried to convince Chief Anne that she was integral to saving the planet from fossil fuels, that she was fighting the good fight for all her people.

"You know, life becomes clearer in old age, and I don't like what I see," Chief Anne responded. "I came here to convince myself that supporting this campaign was worth the sacrifice of letting someone else lead us to a better place. But what I see is a fundraising machine. Why are you not using your image? Why are my name and picture front and centre, while yours is nowhere? It seems to me that your group is hiding behind us to achieve your goals, without giving us a say. We have no input. I have no input. You treat us like puppets. You are lining your pockets at our expense, while staying in the shadows because you know that without us you don't have a chance to advance your cause.

"You are worse than the oil companies," Chief Anne continued. "At least they are offering us partnerships now, which will result in benefits for decades to come. It's not enough, but it's a start. What are you offering us? What are you leaving behind for us after we are no longer useful to you? What happens to us when you win your fight? Your campaign is about shutting down fossil fuels. Our survival depends on improving our livelihoods. The past is gone. We want to benefit from our land, so our people have jobs, and our children get a shot at success. You and I – we don't want the same things."

The activist did not offer a counterpoint. She didn't see room for common ground. The chief's beliefs were too firm. Clearly, she'd misjudged her. Right there and then, Erika decided she would replace Chief Anne with someone else more malleable to the cause. Other Indigenous people were lining up to cash in on the Save the Climate bounty.

Erika led the chief to a private room so she could have a confidential conversation about ending the contract with a small severance in exchange for a non-disclosure agreement. The chief had anticipated the request and flatly told her to keep her money and walked out of the campaign office. She found a taxi near an outdoor restaurant patio and asked to be driven to the ferry terminal, feeling empowered to face the consequences.

After the chief's departure, Erika turned to her team. "There is no question that this is a setback. We'll have to replace the chief and re-do our marketing materials. The lesson is that we need to be more careful about our recruits. If anyone else has doubts, please leave now. We have a big job to do and little time."

No one did – though several of them asked for, and were granted, higher pay.

Then the team's leadership group got to work on the first item on the agenda – legal challenges.

Erika said the lawsuit about the oilsands' false claims provided confirmation that Canadians were interested in and open to climate-change action, particularly if the burden was piled onto a single province, Alberta, whose oil wealth was widely resented. Whether or not it had merit, the lawsuit generated great publicity with every move and countermove, she said. Donations were pouring in. Erika updated everyone about pleas by the *Journal* on behalf of itself and its star journalist, Elise Chamonter, to be excluded from the lawsuit. She said she decided against it. She believed influential journalists in capitalist media like the *Journal* were fair targets because of the role they played in building value for fossil fuels by providing information to investors. In addition, the lawsuit had the secondary benefit of acting as a cautionary tale to other media that they could be next unless they supported the campaign, she said.

One team member proposed a more focused legal challenge on whether the national regulator was ignoring climate change and marine impacts in its review of the West Pipeline. Another suggested challenging its municipal permits. Yet another suggested suing the company proposing to build the pipeline on behalf of First Nations along the pipeline route over insufficient consultation. All were legal longshots designed to delay the West Pipeline project, generate publicity, and discourage investors. The lawyer promised to investigate all ideas and come back with a game plan to expand court action, as well as an estimate of legal costs.

The next item was an update on planned demonstrations. Hearings on the West Pipeline were starting in the first BC community along the proposed route and arrangements were made to bus in as many activists as possible.

"We have about one hundred activists on our payroll from all over North America," one of the organizers said. "They are on standby and very motivated."

"What about locals?" Erika asked.

"We are working on it."

"Make sure there is a large Indigenous presence," she said. "And work the university campuses. Pay higher fees if necessary. We can also hire actors."

There were more updates on longer-term issues – recruitment of anti-oilsands candidates for several upcoming elections in all Canadian jurisdictions, strategies to discredit regulators, and funding of new social media websites to bolster impressions of a widespread and growing anti-oilsands, anti-pipeline movement.

It was almost evening when Erika's cell phone rang. She was surprised to see Elise Chamonter's name flash on the screen. She picked up the call, assuming the journalist wanted to discuss the lawsuit.

"Thanks for taking my call," Elise said. "I'm working on a story about the Save the Climate campaign. Just so you know, I am recording this interview to ensure I am quoting you accurately."

"Okay," Erika said, putting the call on speaker so the rest of the team could hear.

"I just spoke to Chief Anne. She called me – in case you are wondering. She said she quit your team because of your unethical fundraising practices."

"What practices?" the activist said, shocked that the chief had betrayed her so quickly. "We have nothing to hide."

"She said you are raising funds by using her picture without her consent."

"I didn't know she felt that way. Chief Anne has been a valued member of our team and she will be missed," Erika said, trying to stay cool, being careful with her words.

"How much money have you raised by giving the impression that Chief Anne Proudfoot was one of your campaign leaders?" Elise asked.

"I don't have that information," Erika said, feeling trapped.

"I have spoken to several other Indigenous people approached by your group," Elise pressed on. "They said that they are being harassed and offered bribes to participate in your campaign. Is that true?"

"We are talking to numerous Indigenous people, but there is no pressure. Many are already part of our team. We want to help them fight the fossil fuel companies and ensure they won't be stuck with the environmental damage."

"How much money are you offering them?"

"I am not at liberty to disclose that information," Erika responded.

"I'm told the going price is a sign-up bonus of fifty thousand for each recruit, plus fees for each appearance on behalf of the campaign. Does this sound about right?" Elise asked.

"This is a private arrangement. We cannot disclose the details," the activist responded, worried the information had become public, which could mean the escalation of compensation demands.

"Is it true that you discredit Indigenous people who are critical of your campaign?"

"I don't know what you are talking about," Erika responded.

"Is it true that you are recruiting Indigenous people who have no standing in their community – people who have not been elected, who speak for no one but themselves?" Elise asked.

"We value all Indigenous people who believe in what we do," the activist said, feeling under attack, resenting Elise.

"Is it true that you are recruiting Indigenous people from all over North America who are not at all impacted by the West Pipeline project?"

"Indigenous people are greatly impacted by climate change, which has no borders," Erika said.

"Some of the Indigenous people I spoke to said that your practices are dividing their communities and creating animosity between members. Are you aware of that?" Elise asked.

"Our intent is to unite Indigenous people against exploitation by the fossil fuel companies."

"Thank you for answering my questions," Elise said.

"When will your story appear?" the activist asked, exhausted by the questioning, fearful about how it would play out.

"After we finish our research."

"Is there more to it?"

"We don't share the content of our stories before publication, nor timing of publication," Elise said, and hung up.

Erika Bernstein felt the story would be damaging. She decided to give a heads up to DC headquarters to ensure the leadership would not be caught off guard.

Before she reached anyone, the *Journal* story appeared online.

It was an extensive investigation about the Save the Climate campaign by a team of *Journal* reporters, with surprising details about its strategy and tactics to derail the Canadian oilsands, recruitment practices of Indigenous people, funding and leadership from the United States, the precise location of its Canadian headquarters on the island just off the West Coast with photos, and names of its affiliated organizations across Canada.

A sidebar on Erika Bernstein summed up her career as a professional agitator in South and then North America. It had background on her early years in New Jersey, criminal record for illegal protests and drug use, questions about her legal status in Canada.

The articles were based on interviews with numerous Indigenous people, Canadian law enforcement, political sources, some of her former co-workers, and leaked documents.

Erika was astonished that so much her campaign's strategy had been uncovered and decided to tighten her inner circle. She realized her job had become more difficult.

Early the next day, she participated in a conference call with her DC counterparts to assess the damage.

"It's a harmful article, extensively researched, with multiple bylines and lots of sources," the head of the legal unit said. "It's accurate, which makes it harder for us to rebut."

"We could discredit the piece on our social media channels and platforms – or ignore it, which is what I prefer. Let's keep feeding our own narrative directly to our own audiences," Erika proposed.

"How about getting our side of the story through other legacy media?" one of the Washington leaders suggested.

"We can. But we won't be able to control the outcome. It's risky," Erika said.

"Have we created an enemy by going after the *Journal* in our lawsuit?" the legal unit head asked. "They're very influential, and we risk damaging our plan to increase their coverage of green energy."

"We didn't anticipate them coming after us like this," Erika said.

"We could appease them by dropping them from the lawsuit," the lawyer suggested.

"That will make us look weak," Erika said. "Let's wait a few days, then go on the offensive. We will attack their credibility and their brand. Confrontation is good for us. We need to show there is a cost to shilling for the oil industry, as they do."

Erika's game plan was endorsed by the team, but she could tell there was discomfort. She was shaken by the stories, too, though she kept her feelings to herself. In all the campaigns she'd worked on, she'd been on the offensive – destabilizing, surprising adversaries by pushing boundaries. She would have to escalate even more, she decided.

Later in the day, another *Journal* piece landed like a bombshell at the Save the Climate headquarters – this one with a Washington place line and a photo of Barb Heinz with her arms around Tom Young.

The article alleged the administration's married climate-change czar was having an affair with the hedge-fund billionaire, one of the campaign's top funders. It raised questions about whether Tom Young was receiving insider information that could benefit his green energy ventures, before the government announced programs involving generous financial support.

Elise's heart sank when she read the story. She was not aware it was being worked on and had not contributed to it. She phoned Mark Wimhurst to ask why she was kept out of the loop. Her main concern was for Jordan. She knew he would be devastated and embarrassed by such broad public disclosure of his failing marriage.

"Sorry, Elise, but I knew you had a personal interest and didn't want you be involved, just in case it becomes an issue in the Save the Climate lawsuit," the editor said. "It's an awesome story and it needed to be told. We didn't want you to hold us back. They play dirty, and we are responding in kind."

Chapter 47

Elise was driving through a snowstorm on her way to Vancouver along the TransCanada Highway, past the Continental Divide, through mountain peaks and evergreen forests on the western edge of British Columbia, when thoughts of Julien resurfaced. They were so vivid she could hear his voice.

"Stay the course and make yourself stronger," he had told her in the past when she was anxious because of attacks from readers. "If you retreat, they succeed. Your job is to tell the truth, as you see it, not to cave to vested interests. Don't give them oxygen they haven't earned."

Yet in those days critics were still respectful, she wanted to tell him, as k.d. lang's love songs on the car radio brought her back to their times together.

Now, the discourse had become so obscene, hurtful, vengeful, humiliating, it felt primitive, she wanted to tell him, feeling his presence in the empty seat beside her. Few had the courage to confront it to avoid being targeted themselves, or, as in her case, become even bigger targets.

"What do I say to readers who tell me I am a mouthpiece for industry, or that I am a stupid woman, or that I am incompetent, or that I am unfit to call myself a journalist, or that I am contributing to the destruction of the environment, or that I profit from my stories, or that I am part of a conspiracy to enrich the white and privileged?

"It's like I am being baited to get into a fight I can't win, down in the gutter, where they make their own rules, while I am strictly bound by the old ones," she said aloud, hoping he was listening.

She had decided to drive through the Canadian Rockies, instead of flying, to process her feelings and come up with answers. Being close to the wilderness was her most cherished job perk since moving to Western

Canada, and she took advantage of it as often as an opportunity presented itself.

As she drove, unsure what to do, she thought about past times of great upheaval, when much good was destroyed with the bad, lynch mobs tore down old norms and introduced new ones, crushed old powers and installed new ones, promised utopia and delivered dystopia.

Is this what is ahead of us? she wondered. Old but reliable energy systems forcefully dismantled to make room for new ones? What happens if the world is not ready? What happens if new ones don't work? What happens if the activists' view of the future is wrong? What happens if the alternative to fossil fuel energy is, for most people, no energy at all?

Elise's thoughts were sparked by reaction to her team's stories exposing the inner workings of the Save the Climate campaign. They had been widely read and energized a counter insurgency from supporters of Canadian oil and gas. But they had come at a high cost: more nasty takedowns of her, of people quoted in her articles, of the *Journal* and its editors. Even Mark Wimhurst got his dose of character assassination.

The attacks came from people she'd never heard of, on new websites sympathetic to the campaign. She'd seen evidence they were amplified by pariah states eager to sow discord in the West, or to shut down competing oil production. Meanwhile, the article about Barb Heinz's extramarital affair had barely made a ripple outside Washington. If the affair had been between an oilman and a female in an influential government job, it would have sparked outrage, Elise thought.

She wondered if the answer she had been searching for would have to be the same one that had guided her in the past: She would not get invested in someone else's fight. She would cover the fight. Oil prices were breaching US$100 per barrel for the first time in history and were expected to rise even more because of supply constraints.

Encouraged by Wimhurst, Elise would follow the money, and expand oil and gas reporting in Houston, where new technology to unlock oil production from shale was re-invigorating the oil industry and beginning to compete for capital with Alberta.

After spending the night in a small mountain hotel off the busy tracks of one of Canada's historic railways, Elise resumed her drive through cottage-lined lakes and the last of the snowstorm. She arrived in Vancouver by the late afternoon, in the middle of rush-hour traffic, as heavy rain fell.

Elise was to be one of the guest speakers at a conference about the West Pipeline – an invitation she accepted because her newspaper saw Vancouver as a growth market. She was asked to provide a general update on the big stories in Alberta's oilsands industry.

When she arrived at the conference centre, she was met by hundreds of protesters, most of them standing outside the conference venue waving signs condemning Alberta's dirty oil, oilsands pipeline plans, the killing of whales, the fouling of rivers, the corporate elites, the oil elites, the media elites, Canada's irresponsible energy policy, Canada's deplorable environmental record, Canada's lagging climate-change plan.

Indigenous protesters she didn't recognize danced and sang for the cameras in colourful garb and called for climate justice. They were backed up by students, seniors, even homeless people – all demanding something, all accusing someone, but particularly Alberta's shameful oil industry.

Elise picked up a handout from one of the protesters. It was a Save the Climate campaign news release about another planned lawsuit against the West Pipeline, launched by a dozen Indigenous bands on its proposed route and a coalition of environmental organizations.

She walked into the hall, where she was cordially greeted by the young organizers. She noticed that Erika Bernstein, dressed in green fatigues and a red toque, was holding court with a group of reporters, taking questions about the legal challenge.

There were no oilsands industry representatives on the panel, Elise was told, but there would be four leaders of environmental and Indigenous groups opposed to the West Pipeline. Her heart sank. She knew she'd be put on the spot and that she would be asked to answer questions for the sector, which she didn't want to do. She asked one of the organizers, a young woman with purple hair, why no one from the industry was invited.

"We invited several, but no one accepted," the young woman told her. "Even the West Pipeline people wouldn't come. We are very pleased you came and thankful that the *Journal* agreed to be a sponsor."

When it was her turn to speak, Elise walked to the podium and started talking about a new technology that reduced carbon in the oilsands by capturing it and storing it underground. A group of protesters broke into the hall and heckled her, interrupting her train of thought.

"We don't need Alberta's dirty oil," one screamed.

"You're a discredited journalist. Stop feeding us fake news," said another.

"Why doesn't Alberta learn how to manage its budget instead of producing dirty oil? All it wants is to squander more money," said the first.

"We will not allow your murder of our wildlife," said another.

"Climate change is real. Keep your dirty oil in the ground," said another.

TV cameras filmed the drama. Elise expected it to make national news, paired with the announcement about the new legal challenge. She wrapped up her presentation and quietly sat on the stage as the rest of the panel knocked Alberta's oilsands industry, pipeline plans, and the corporate media.

She was embarrassed. She waited for a break before the question-and-answer period to get out of the room. She'd had enough.

Elise spent the rest of the day doing interviews on the West Pipeline controversy. She found that the anti-oilsands and anti-Alberta messaging spun by Save the Climate had penetrated the area deeply. If a campaign against the oilsands could so easily drive a deep wedge between Canadians, what was next? Who was next? she asked herself.

Before the campaign, British Columbia and Alberta were joined at the hip, she had heard over and over from people in both places. Canada's adjacent Western provinces had different histories and cultures yet compensated for each other's strengths and weaknesses. Alberta was the hard-driving value creator, its survival instincts shaped by harsh weather, independent cowboy culture, and boom-bust oil cycles. British Columbia was laid back and fun. Its forests, sublime lakes, and stunning coastline filled the senses and inspired respect for mother nature. Their residents moved back and forth – British Columbians worked in the oilsands, Albertans enjoyed spending on vacation properties and wineries in BC. Both were steeped in American history. Vietnam draft dodgers moved to the BC coast, contributing to its rebellious nature. Texans got rich on Alberta oil and taught the province how to be entrepreneurial.

But the anti-oilsands campaign had influenced British Columbians to reject everything that Alberta did and stood for, Elise heard in her interviews. British Columbians thought Albertans were making dirty money, spent it poorly, earned it at the expense of the environment, including British Columbia's. They didn't give Alberta credit for making all of Canada richer with its oil revenue, or for employing British Columbians. They didn't acknowledge that only one oil pipeline from Alberta had ever been built in British Columbia and had never had a major oil spill, or that Albertans were big spenders in British Columbia's economy.

The divide between the two neighbours had become so deep that Albertans were refusing to visit British Columbia or to buy any of its products. British Columbians were making greedy monetary and regulatory demands to keep the new West Pipeline from moving forward.

"We'll use all the tools in our toolbox," a BC politician told her. "Our environment will not be threatened by Alberta's greed."

Elise left Vancouver early the next day. On the road again, her cell phone interrupted her thoughts. It was John Hess, calling her after months of silence.

"We missed you at the press conference today," John said cheerfully, like not a minute had passed since they last spoke.

"Hi John. Nice to hear from you," she said as unenthusiastically as she could, trying to hide the bitter feelings she felt toward him. "What conference?"

"We announced a takeover today that will double the size of our company," he said, proudly. "We would have loved to get *Journal* coverage. Is there any way you could follow up with an interview with me?"

"I'm sorry, John, but I am driving through British Columbia," she said, regretting answering her phone. "I can't write an article right now. I won't be back in Calgary until tomorrow evening. But I am sure my deputy in Calgary is on it and has already covered your announcement. In fact, I can call and make sure he's filed something."

"Yes, he's filed a story, but it's very basic – not what you would have done," John said. "He has no context, no background on our company nor on me, no depth on the oilsands. Plus, he doesn't have your following. He didn't even show up for the announcement. He watched it on his computer. We had lots of executives there and others. He would have gotten all the right background."

"Well, I'm sorry about that," Elise said. "But I cannot re-do a colleague's work. He's a competent reporter. This beat has become very controversial, and some reporters just don't want to get dragged into the mud the way I have been. I respect that. They want to play it straight and stick to the facts."

For a few seconds John didn't know what to say, and Elise didn't help him fill the dead air.

She thought about the way he had played her against competing journalists when it suited him. She resented that he was missing in action while she was targeted by the Save the Climate campaign. She deplored that he refused to address the campaign's lies while continuing to enrich himself from the oilsands. She resented the way he expected her to fight his battles, while he stayed in his ivory tower and counted his billions.

She was offended that he'd dangled the carrot of a relationship when his intent was to use her for as long as possible to achieve more wealth and more power. But she said nothing because she had moved past John Hess. She knew she had misread him and that she had allowed herself to be manipulated. She accepted she made a mistake.

"It's been too long," John said, his voice becoming smoother. "Are you available to catch up when you are back in Calgary – say in the next couple of days? I'd love to hear more about the Save the Climate campaign. To be honest, I haven't given it too much thought since that conference in Houston. It hasn't affected our stock price; it's up again today on our takeover news. But something is changing, and investors generally are getting nervous, for sure. They say they don't like the controversy. Too much noise. They don't want to get dragged into it."

Elise said she needed to check her calendar for her next opening.

"Come on, Elise, what happened to the scoop-loving journalist I used to know?" he asked. "My company just announced the deal of the century. We've acquired the best remaining oilsands assets at a fantastic price. It should be front and centre in the *Journal*, above the fold," he bragged. "Investors need to know. There's still lots of money to be made in the oil-sands, despite what the climate warriors say. Look at oil prices!"

"I still love scoops, but I have lots on the go these days. This campaign, the lawsuit, the attacks – they've made my job more complicated, my life busier," Elise explained, hoping he'd understand.

"Why don't you stop covering all that conflict?" he snapped back. "It's spooking the markets. You are giving the environmentalists a platform they don't deserve."

Elise didn't see that coming. John Hess, of all people, should have appreciated the *Journal*'s effort to shine a light on the Save the Climate campaign and its meddling in Canada's economy and particularly his industry – a job he and his fellow oilmen should have done themselves if they really believed the oilsands were produced responsibly and deserved a future. She was surprised that he didn't see what she saw and that his judgement was so narrowly focussed on his own interests. Was he blaming her, now?

"My job is to cover the industry – the good and the bad – not to be a cheerleader for the oilsands, or your company," she responded patiently. "Investors need to be aware of all the risks, and in my opinion, this campaign is a major risk to your business. It may not be immediate, but it's coming. Instead of ignoring it and carrying on as nothing is happening, or expanding as you just did, or blaming me, you should mitigate it and defend what you do. The market is already pivoting to oil shale. I follow the market.

"And speaking of doubling down," Elise couldn't resist saying, "I thought you were ready to phase yourself out, not double the size of your business."

"Touché. I suspected you'd notice," John said. "Yes, I wanted to phase myself out. But I concluded that I still enjoy this business. I wouldn't know what to do with myself if I didn't have my company. As you know, I don't have family. Aurora Oil Sands is my family."

Elise wanted to tell him that not too long ago he – almost – asked her to be his family.

Elise realized she understood him more than he knew. John Hess would never be truly devoted to anything but his oil money – and the power and stature that came with it. She had been a means to that end.

Confirming Elise's thoughts, John Hess dangled a carrot he knew Elise couldn't refuse. He told her his company was co-sponsoring a conference in New York on the oilsands' environmental improvements. The keynote speaker was the US energy secretary. Could Elise chair a panel discussion with investors? he asked.

"It would be good publicity for you and for the *Journal*," he told her.

Elise agreed, provided her editors were on board, too.

She felt trapped but had no choice. She had a job to do and knew that if she declined, the oilman would turn to one of her competitors, as he'd done before.

"How about that lunch?" John asked, knowing that Elise was right back where he wanted her, under his thumb.

Tears streamed down her face as she drove from the coast toward the first mountains. She realized that insulating herself from people who didn't like what she did would be easier than from those, like John, who were supposed to be on the same side.

Chapter 48

Dr. Jordan Black avoided all sympathy calls after the story about his wife's affair broke in the *Journal*. He felt the scandal tarnished his professional standing, which shattered his self-esteem. To escape his co-worker's concerned looks, and with the support of his hospital's board of directors, he took a leave of absence from his job and signed up for a one-year assignment in Afghanistan.

A news release from the hospital's charitable foundation, forwarded to Elise by her editor, announced Dr. Jordan Black was appointed executive director of a new children's clinic in Kabul, starting immediately.

Jordan knew the pay would be lousy and the mission big: He would teach and practice surgery in a dangerous country where medical facilities affiliated with Western organizations were choice targets of terrorists. Yet he felt he needed a fresh start, and the people of Afghanistan needed his help.

Jordan was running away from the Save the Climate campaign, too. It had once satisfied his need to rescue the earth from unfettered fossil fuel development but had degenerated, in his view, into a corrupt organization influenced by bad actors with goals he didn't agree with.

He blamed Barb Heinz's hunger for power for the campaign's misguided change in direction, and himself for falling to stop it. He felt bad for Canada's oilsands industry and for all those caught in the campaign's crosshairs. He felt awful for the way Elise was treated, and for the way he let her down.

Afghanistan would be a good place to reset his life, he decided, and to get back to saving lives and giving people hope.

He enjoyed having more time to think, too – between his shifts, between his episodes of depression, between his young patients – especially of Elise. Sometimes he called her office just to hear her recorded voice. "Hi. You have reached Elise's answering service. Sorry I missed you. Leave a message at the beep." Her voice calmed him, brought him back to the some of the happiest days of his life.

One day, Elise happened to be in her office late, getting ready for her trip to the New York conference, and answered her phone when he called.

"Elise?" Jordan said, shyly, like a child caught stealing forbidden sweets.

"Jordan – is that you?" she said, surprised to hear his voice.

"Yes. I didn't expect to find you in the office this late – it's morning in Kabul. I just wanted to leave you a message."

"Oh my God. Is that where you are? How are you?" she said, excited to hear from him after such a long silence.

"I'm okay, doing good again – for a change."

"Are you safe?"

"Yes, so far. Our clinic is heavily guarded. I live in a military compound. I am in good hands."

"Do you get time off?"

"Yes. I'm allowed to return to New York every two months. I will be back in a couple of weeks to sign my divorce papers."

"Ah – the divorce. I'm so sorry about what happened. I tried to reach you. I want you to know that I wasn't involved in the *Journal* story about Barb, that I had nothing to do with it."

"I know. The *Journal* reporters told me. They were very professional about it. And just so you know, I helped them out. They gave me time to inform the hospital before publication, to do some damage control."

"I'm sorry. I had my run-ins with Barb, too, you know. It's been tough lately. We are paying dearly for some recent stories on Save the Climate. They are doing their best to ruin my reputation," Elise said.

"I'm not surprised. When Barb is committed, she's a pit bull. Stay away from her. Listen, I am on the job right now. I didn't expect you to pick up. How about we chat again in a few days?"

"I have a better idea," Elise said. "I need to be in New York for a few days in a couple of weeks. How about we coordinate our trips? I'm buying you dinner."

Jordan hesitated. He told her he wasn't ready.

Elise insisted. Jordan agreed. They picked a date and a place – a restaurant in Little Italy where they had met in the past, when they were young and ambitious, and married to others.

They were farther apart geographically than they had ever been, yet Elise felt closer to Jordan than she had in years.

They said goodbye and hung up.

It was late. Elise wrapped up her research in preparation for the panel discussion in New York, then walked out of her office tower into the freezing air. Calgary's winters retreated slowly, reluctantly, between blasts of warmth from the Pacific. There was still snow on the ground and the sky was dark. As she walked toward her condo complex, she took care not to slip on the ice.

The next day, Elise took the lunch hour off to meet with John. She was dreading it now. The way he pulled her strings upset her.

He had picked a restaurant away from prying eyes, a hole in the wall on the edge of downtown known for its fresh Newfoundland catch, flown into Calgary twice a week due to high demand from the oil-rich crowd.

"How are you, Elise?" he asked cheerfully as she hung her heavy coat on a hook, taking a seat across from him. They were near a large bay window with a view of the snowbanks piled high on the street.

"We picked a good day. It's quieter on the news front for a change," she said, noticing the restaurant was strangely half empty. "Perhaps the bitter cold is dulling appetites."

"Quiet isn't good," the oilman replied. "We need to keep up the excitement, give the market lots to talk about."

"There is lots of excitement – just not here," Elise said. "A lot of capital is flowing into shale plays in the United States, as you know. Our office in Houston is hopping. I'm transferring some of our Calgary staff to work there."

Elise noticed John looked older. He was still an attractive man, elegantly dressed, patrician in his bearing. But there were deep wrinkles around his eyes and his hairline was receding. Reading glasses were tucked in his breast pocket.

"Calgary becomes you," the oilman said, feeling the weight of her gaze. "You look more beautiful than ever. And you are doing a great job of staying slender. You must work out a lot."

Elise smiled but was hurt by his comments. They were out of line. They diminished her. He should have known better. A younger woman would have put him in his place, even walked out, she thought. But she was used to John and other powerful men saying inappropriate things. He was from a different generation when such comments meant to flatter. The best defense was to ignore them, she thought.

"Have you closed your big merger deal?" Elise asked, changing the subject.

"Off the record, we're almost done – but selling this deal to the market has been harder than I expected," the oilman said. "Some investors are divesting from the oilsands altogether. They're being harassed by environmental activists who are threatening to sue them if they invest in our company. There is no legal case here, just theatre. But it makes them uncomfortable. They don't like bad press."

"What's the implication for your company?" Elise asked.

"It's hard to say at this point," John replied. "The deal is not threatened. It's well financed, and the assets will spin off cash flow immediately. But I am worried that people are seeing lots of problems they didn't pay attention to before, or didn't care about, like future environmental liabilities and potential lack of market access if pipelines are delayed. Many are taking their money to the US because shale plays are not as controversial, and they are profitable faster. They don't need to build big projects like in the oilsands that require a lot of money up front.

"What do you think about this campaign?" John asked.

Elise updated him on her latest reporting and added a few impressions of her own.

"I think the oilsands' brand has been irreparably damaged," she said. "You have been massively outplayed. The activists are relentless and well organized. They won't stop until they have shut you down – or at least landlocked you so you can't export your oil. But there is more to it, and I can't put my finger on it. It's hard to get people to talk. Everyone is scared. There are big names behind this campaign, big groups pushing money up here and disguising it as charity.

"I think the campaign is so aggressive it's over the top, even by American standards," Elise continued. "Everyone is piling on, like shutting down the oilsands is the answer to fix global warming, which of course is untrue. They've turned these deposits into a caricature, and they seem to be delighted that there is so little reaction from the Canadian side, which makes your industry look guilty. You certainly don't see the same disdain for oil shale, and yet it's wrecking big parts of the US. They are literally drilling in people's backyards. How's that okay, while the oilsands aren't?"

"Come on, Elise," John responded. "I agree that they are having an impact, but you are giving these radicals too much credit. There's no way they have that much power. There's lots of money at stake here – a lot of American money. The environmentalists will get tired eventually and move on to the next target. We're not going anywhere. Money talks, money is being made in the oilsands, and money and self-interest always win the day."

Elise shared with him what she knew about Barb Heinz, Erika Bernstein, the foreign funding, how the campaign was recruiting Indigenous people, and how it was preparing to bankroll Canadian political candidates who supported off-oil views.

Elise knew it wasn't her job to educate the oilman. She did it anyway because she was concerned about the growing power of activism and the exaggerations it was based on. It was new competition for her own industry, too, she told him.

John listened but wasn't convinced. It was all too much, too bold, too perverse, too clandestine, perhaps even illegal, he responded. Besides, there wasn't much the oilsands industry could do, other than to keep promoting its story to people who wanted to hear it.

"We are not going to stoop to their level," he said. "We are highly regulated. We produce a product that people want. I don't see the point of arguing with them. We'd give them attention they don't deserve."

"Speaking of attention," he continued, "we reached out to your editor, what's his name, Wimhurst? Jovial British guy, right? We are working on a major advertising deal with the *Journal*, one that will showcase all the good things about the oilsands that will target investors. The ads will coincide with the conference in New York. But here's the thing. We need you to back off reporting on the controversy about Save the Climate – it's spooking the market."

"Who's *we*?" Elise asked, concerned he was going over her head to pull her strings even more, or worse, that he'd totally misunderstood her profession.

"The whole industry. I speak for them. I'm on the board of our industry association."

Elise felt humiliated. He seemed to be more concerned about suppressing her reporting than addressing the real threat. She regretted that she'd shared so freely with John Hess what she knew, and that she strayed from her resolve to stay above the fray. She felt put her in her place, like hired help. John Hess was hopeless.

Elise blamed herself and stopped talking. She decided to disengage, distance herself from John once and for all. She would follow through this time, she told herself. She dug into her salad and looked out the window, noticing a car that was still illegally parked nearby. John kept speaking. She barely heard him.

She needed to speak to her editor to find out what was really going on. Did he sell her out? Did he do an advertising deal at the expense of journalism? How could the *Journal* continue to fight the Save the Climate lawsuit on the same side as the oilsands industry while being manipulated by it so brazenly?

John, confident Elise got the message, bragged that he had high hopes for the New York conference. High-level politicians from both sides of the border agreed to participate and discuss the energy sector's future. Wimhurst, of course, was invited to all events, he told her. He couldn't wait to meet him.

John also hinted – off the record – that a meeting had been organized between the biggest names in oilsands, including himself, and the US administration, to discuss pipeline plans and find out if there was room for compromise between good neighbours with common interests.

He smiled like someone who had an ace up his sleeve. Barb would be there too, he revealed. He promised to let Elise know, still off the record, if anything came out of it, so the *Journal* could get all the right scoops, the ones that were worth writing about.

Elise nodded. She'd underestimated the oilman, she realized. He had covered all his bases, just like he had done in the past.

But he had lost *her*.

Lobster was served and they made small talk about safe topics – real estate prices, the latest smart phones, an art show that he was invited to attend. She didn't ask him about gossip that she had heard about his new bachelor lifestyle – a yacht in the French Riviera, his new ranch in California, photographs suggesting liaisons with women half his age. She didn't offer more about herself, either.

She saw him more clearly now, she thought as she watched him enjoy his meal, like he had lifted a veil.

John Hess loved living on the edge. He pushed everything to the limit. He gambled big and expected big results. He did what it took. Risk was always about upside, never about downside, because he knew how to re-arrange stumbling blocks to his advantage.

His self-esteem was linked to stature. His company had to be the biggest, the most profitable, the best valued. He had to be the top dog. He had to be admired – like a diva who drew her energy from her adoring fans.

He was used to power and would never allow others to have power over him, which explained his dismissal of the environment movement, his backroom dealings with politicians, his manipulation of those he needed to preserve what he had.

His relationships were transactional, including the one he had with his ex-wife, or the one he had cultivated with her and probably countless other women, all based on vague promises that were never kept. He was about acquiring, keeping, and dangling – just enough to ensure his options were open. John Hess was the same as the oil he produced: slippery, tempting, corrupt, controlling.

But he also seemed more out of touch with reality, Elise thought. Perhaps the pressure got to him, perhaps his big merger was in peril, perhaps he met a threat he couldn't easily crush.

Elise felt ashamed that once upon a time, when her judgement was clouded by personal loss, by loneliness, she was captivated by him, even imagined a life with him, saw him as an exceptional man who could be in her life.

"I read about your doctor friend's divorce," John said, referring to Jordan, hoping Elise would tell him more.

"I haven't spoken to him in a while," Elise lied, becoming protective.

"Any news on the job front?" he asked. "Are you still planning to move back to New York? I hope we get the benefit of your journalism for a while longer here."

"Yes, I'll move back full time eventually. But nothing firm at this point," she said.

Elise surprised him by picking up the bill – a gesture she hoped conveyed that she wasn't for sale. Then she stood up and shook the oilman's hand.

"Got to go," she said

"See you in New York," he said, not sure why Elise had become so distant, even disagreeable.

"I look forward to helping out on that panel," she said, looking impatient to walk out.

"Will you be there for the whole conference?" he asked, wondering if his charm had stopped working.

"I'm not sure. We have a whole newsroom in New York. We'll find a way to cover it – especially if we expect big news." She left John at the table to finish his meal alone.

Elise phoned Mark Wimhurst the minute she walked back in her office. She was tired and demoralized. He was away, so she left a message.

But her day was not over.

Within minutes, dozens of emails, texts, and voice messages were flooding her computer and cell phone. Photos of her having lunch with John Hess appeared on multiple social media platforms.

"Old Habits Die Hard – *Journal* Reporter and Oil Billionaire Trade Oilsands Secrets," said one headline.

"Corporate Media Colludes with Big Oil," said another.

"Oil Shill Gets Marching Orders from Oil Billionaire Hess."

The latest serving of harassment was interrupted by Mark Wimhurst's call.

"Hi Elise. Are you calling about these new attacks? They're disgraceful," he said. "I haven't seen anything like it. They're jamming all our inboxes."

"Yes, I had a bad day," she responded, trying to compose herself. "I had lunch with John Hess," she continued. "He asked for it. I accepted because he's been a good source over the years. He wanted to talk about the New York conference."

"Of course. That's what good journalism is about," Mark said. "Our readers like you because of your high-level connections."

"Someone must have followed one of us. I wonder who … why," she said, thinking about the illegally parked car. "This is disturbing."

"Look, we're playing hardball on the lawsuit," her editor said. "Maybe the activists are trying to prove that we're not just bystanders conveying information to our readers. They claim we're one of the oil industry's major instruments. They don't understand what we do. They believe we're a propaganda machine and trying to make an example of us. They don't understand the difference between journalism and activism. We collect information, they push an agenda. We're not backing down because they are putting journalism on trial, too. We need to stand our ground."

"I'm happy to hear that," Elise said. "Speaking about being a propaganda machine, John Hess told me during lunch to back off covering the oilsands controversy because it's spooking the market. In exchange, he said the industry association is negotiating a big advertising deal with the *Journal*. Is that for real? Are we selling out?"

"That's false," her boss said unequivocally. "We are working on an advertising deal to publicize the conference, but our journalism is – and will always be – off limits. We need to stay independent, stand for the truth. So, don't worry about advertising. Keep digging. But given what John Hess said to you, I suggest that you stay away from him. We need to be above reproach."

"I have figured that out already, but it's going to be hard," Elise said. "He's everywhere, has his fingers in everything. I'm chairing that panel discussion in New York, remember? He'll be at the conference."

"Of course," the editor said. "I'll be there too. Barb Heinz has confirmed she'll be there as well."

"How do you feel about me going ahead with the panel – but letting others do the reporting?" Elise proposed. "And you can represent the newspaper. I don't have to be there for the whole thing."

"Sure. But Elise, you should consider staying in New York a little longer before returning to Calgary. Take a break. We miss you in the newsroom."

"You are right. I could use a break," she said, then hung up.

She read more emails. She looked at social media posts. With each new wave of outrage about her lunch with John Hess, from people with obviously made-up identities, she felt more humiliated and more disempowered.

Elise knew that the intent was to ruin her reputation – and that of her employer – and lower her standing her as a source of news. Perhaps the secondary goal was submission.

She thought about Erika Bernstein's early efforts to disparage her reporting after her Peru assignment a decade earlier. She realized the activist was just dabbling then and testing the potential of public shaming.

The campaign had refined it into a weapon to wipe out the achievements of its opponents. Elise got no credit for working at one of the world's storied news organizations, for her decades of experience, for her formal education, for her advancement in a male-dominated field, for her vast network of sources, for knowledge of her beat. All the campaign saw in her was a threat to its worldview that the oilsands had to be shut down.

Elise thought about the barbaric practices of zealots in ancient times aimed against those who didn't play by their rules. While the new iteration didn't involve such physical violence, it too was meant to knock out those who posed a threat.

Elise wondered if there was any way to repair the damage that was being done to her. Perhaps she'd been unfair to the campaign. Perhaps she hadn't tried hard enough to understand the people behind it. Perhaps there was too much complacency over the degradation of the environment.

But if saving the climate was such a just and noble cause, a common good, why such malicious approach? she asked herself.

Elise erased thousands of offensive emails, shut down her presence on social media, and decided it was time to get a new job.

Chapter 49

MANHATTAN, NEW YORK, APRIL 2011

The Canadian oil posse's meeting with the US energy secretary was scheduled for early in the morning, at the request of the CEOs, to ensure confidentiality ahead of the public energy conference located across the street. A dozen of the sector's top CEOs from Calgary sat around a large table in a windowless room of one of Manhattan's prestigious law firms. Jetlagged and anxious, armed with detailed presentations and a cadre of aides, they gulped coffee to stay awake.

Nearly an hour after the scheduled start time, the prominent energy secretary, a long-haired, pint-sized former Harvard professor, and his entourage – including climate leader Barb Heinz and two young assistants knowledgeable about Canadian oilsands – arrived.

John welcomed him with a cordial, expectant smile. Then he sized up Barb. It was the first time he had met her in person. Attractive, he thought, but too sure of herself. A hard ass.

He knew she was his real adversary and wondered what it would take to break her – or at least get her to a truce so his industry could get on with building its South Pipeline, finalize oilsands expansions, and get the returns on investment it felt it deserved.

He knew the energy secretary and his entourage had showed up late on purpose, having used that trick himself many times. Once even on Elise. The first time he was at the receiving end of such mind games he was in Siberia, when he was trying to extricate himself from a bad deal, he recalled, and the counterparty showed up four hours late.

Message received, he thought. The Americans wanted the Canadians to know they held all the leverage, and that the Canadians were supplicants. John didn't care.

The oil industry – of which he was a proud and successful leader – accepted that it needed to work under governments of all stripes, from dictatorships to democracies, thugs to sheiks, and negotiate the best possible terms. It was part of the business's 'above ground' risk, as opposed to 'below ground,' the drilling in the earth's bowels. The groveling for terms gave those in power the illusion that they were in charge.

But John knew better. His industry stayed on top by playing the long game, over many decades, in contrast to government cycles, which could change in years. Heads of state came and went. If their terms for development were unreasonable, the oil industry backed out – often all at once – and found other jurisdictions hungrier for their investments.

John compared Barb to the assessment offered by Elise. Elise had been pretty accurate, he thought, and was now thankful for her insights. Barb, stone faced and domineering, looked like a true believer. She was an ideologue who fought to win, who never gave an inch, who ruled by fear, he concluded.

He also knew about her sex scandal with the tech billionaire, which made her vulnerable. He'd dug up some of his own dirt after reading the *Journal* story. Flaws could be exploited, especially in high-stakes games, especially since she had not hesitated to exploit his flaws. He thought of his photos with Elise, which kept appearing on social media.

He stared at Barb across the table and got the impression that she knew that he knew about her. They were two of a kind.

"Without further ado, we'd like to get started. Mr. Secretary, Ms. Heinz, thank you for agreeing to meet with us," John said, his icy blue eyes and striking good looks electrifying the room. "If it's okay with you, I'd like to ask support staff to leave the room." Everyone nodded.

Almost smitten, Barb caught herself thinking that it was too bad the handsome oilman was batting for the other team. She felt another pinch of jealously over Elise. She wished her campaign could attract people of his caliber.

"As you know, we're here to look for a middle ground. The United States needs Canada's oil for its energy security. Canada needs the US market," John said.

"We believe our positions on the environment are not far apart. We are spending more than any other industry in Canada to reduce our greenhouse gas emissions. We believe in being the best possible stewards of the environment. We're developing technologies to make our oil cleaner that will be useful all over the world, including in the United States.

"The Save the Climate campaign's messages are based on outdated information," he continued. "We are not the same industry we were ten years ago. We are improving every day and we are spending heavily on research to ensure we leave the environment better than when we found it, while offering good-paying jobs to thousands of people, including many Indigenous people.

"Shouldn't the campaign – which you led, Ms. Heinz, and which, according to public reporting, you continue to oversee – focus on our efforts to do the right things, show the world that Canadian oil is responsibly produced and that other sources, including American sources, should match our environmental record? Shouldn't you welcome more Canadian oil to replace the oil you import from unsavoury regimes, which are not transparent about their emissions and their other environmental impacts? Shouldn't you approve the South Pipeline, which has met all your regulatory requirements, which is supported by most Americans, and which will be a lot safer and emit fewer emissions than any of the pipelines in operation in the US today?"

Barb Heinz stood up, stretching her tall frame, making eye contact with everyone in the room, then fixing on John Hess.

"I commend you for the improvements, which I would like to review more closely," she responded as the energy secretary watched silently nearby. "I sure hope they continue, because without them the campaign to shut down your oilsands would be even more aggressive.

"You are wasting your time with your planned production expansions and with your pipeline plans. There is no room for middle ground on the climate. It's changing as we speak. Fossil fuels needed to go yesterday, especially dirty sources like the tar sands in Canada. You should join our cause and put your money in clean energy and get out of fossil fuels while you can – I predict that by the end of this decade, the oilsands will be worthless," she said.

"Look, you cannot afford to shut down fossil fuels," John snapped back, irritated by her aggressiveness, as the other CEOs watched, fearful the meeting was going off the rails. "The US is still the world's largest oil consumer, and Canada is your largest foreign supplier. How will you energize your economy? How will Americans get to work, take holidays, warm and cool their homes, their hospitals, their schools? Your goals are unattainable. Green energy will not replace fossil fuels for decades. You are peddling false information and false hope."

"No. You are selling people false hope," the climate czar countered. "The fossil fuel industry is on its last legs, and we will do what it takes to put it out of its misery. We will not build more oil pipelines that make us dependent on the oilsands for the next century."

"The South Pipeline has met all your requirements," John replied. "We've spent a billion to get it through your regulatory process. You cannot kill a pipeline that is lawful under your laws and under your trade agreement with Canada."

"We can – and we will deny its permit if it doesn't fit our new priorities. Sue us if you want. We'll turn it into a show trial. The dirty oilsands versus a cleaner environment. Who do you think will win?" Barb asked. "We were elected by the American people to implement our climate-change agenda and that's what we are doing."

John was so dismayed by what he heard that he was speechless. There is no point, he thought. The woman is a fanatic. The Canadian CEOs looked at him and at each other. They collected their belongings, rose together, and left the room without uttering a further word to Barb Heinz or her quiet boss.

Once alone, the energy secretary turned toward Barb.

"Are you nuts?" he asked her, looking worried, like he was seeing her for the first time. "They are right that we depend on their oil. And they are right that they can sue us under our trade agreement. The Canadians are required under that agreement to offer their oil to us first, to give us the right of first refusal, before they sell it to other markets.

"You just gave our energy security away by allowing them to sell their oil to the Chinese, who are all over Alberta purchasing oilsands assets and who are impatient to export it to China. That's not in our geopolitical interest. We're not even close to replacing oil with renewable energy."

Barb stood her ground. "We have new, more important global interests," she responded. "We need to show the world that we are serious about climate change. We cannot do that by approving another dirty oil pipeline from Canada. As for the Canadians selling their oil in other markets – I wouldn't bet on it. We'll make it impossible for them to build pipelines to their west and east coasts. We will strand their oil by disrupting their plans to export to other markets."

"Are you suggesting we meddle in Canada's internal affairs, keep them from exporting their products?" the energy secretary asked, incredulous, worrying that Barb had not outgrown her activist instincts despite her new, influential government role. "They have the right to build pipelines in their country where they please," he said. "I am very uncomfortable with this course of action. Canada is our most loyal trading partner and ally."

"Then we need to show our closest friends the error of their ways," Barb responded. "The Save the Climate campaign is endorsed by the highest levels of this administration. We're not backing down." She walked toward the door to show her boss that the conversation was over.

Barb, the energy secretary and their staff walked out through the building's lobby into the street. Mayhem had erupted.

"I thought we agreed with the Canadians to keep this meeting private," the secretary said, wondering why so many Save the Climate activists had stormed the area to demonstrate against the Canadian CEOs and their proposed South pipeline.

"It was. Word must have leaked out," Barb said, grinning. "We helped a little, of course. We'll make the evening news."

The energy secretary realized the woman was going rogue and decided to have a private chat about her with the President. He felt mortified for the oilsands delegation, which was jeered by hundreds of demonstrators armed with signs condemning Canada's dirty oil. TV cameras took shots of the Canadians in suits hiding their faces behind their briefcases and running for cover toward the conference venue.

John Hess, looking rumpled and lost, entered the building last. He straightened his jacket, then headed for the room where he knew Elise's panel was getting under way. He was fuming.

Authoritative and calm, Elise introduced the energy secretary, noting he was her favourite professor during her days at Harvard. The academic praised Elise for her career success and her insightful energy coverage. He spoke enthusiastically about Canada's friendship, the two country's strong energy links, and the many plans under way to better regulate emissions.

Then he pulled out his script, which highlighted government support and programs for renewable energy. Elise managed questions from the floor deftly. The energy secretary responded with pre-approved answers.

He offered no opinion about the demonstrators, the oilsands, or the proposed South Pipeline, to the audience.

"The project is before regulators. We will review their recommendations when they are available and then decide whether it's in the public interest," he said. "But given the strong opposition to the project that we are seeing along the pipeline route and across our country, we may have to organize further public consultation."

Elise thanked him for participating in the conference and concluded the panel discussion. She checked her cell phone and noticed a text from Barb Heinz.

"Do you have a minute?" the climate czar had asked.

Elise ignored the text, left the podium, and got lost in the crowd – mostly Wall Street types looking for investment ideas – exiting quietly through a side door. She had nothing to say to Barb. She had nothing to say to John Hess, either. She saw him standing at the back of the room, looking at her.

The investment part of the conference started. John noticed there were large numbers of empty seats at presentations on oilsands projects and standing-room-only crowds to hear about opportunities in US oil shale. A panel discussion that he participated in drew few spectators. He was disheartened. The oilsands, he feared, were already yesterday's story.

A group of reporters stormed him in a hallway with cameras and tape recorders. They asked him for reaction on the meeting with the energy secretary prior to the conference. John was shocked. The meeting was supposed to have been confidential. He realized Barb had leaked the information to her advantage.

"We heard you asked for a truce on the South Pipeline and that you got the cold shoulder," one of the reporters said.

"We had a productive discussion about the energy flows between our two countries and about new ways to bring Canadian oil to customers," John responded.

"Did you ask for concessions on the South Pipeline?" another reporter asked.

"Why would a foreign company get a break?" a third reporter asked.

"Is it true that you threatened to sue the US?" a fourth reporter chimed in.

"As I said, we had a productive discussion about the energy flows between our two countries," John said, staying calm, as lights from TV cameras brightened his face. "Canada is a trading nation, and we will work with all countries interested in buying Canadian oil. If the US is not interested, there are others who are eager to lock in our secure, responsibly produced oil supplies." He walked away.

John knew the day had been a disaster.

He despised controversy. He hated not being in control. He looked for Elise, but she was nowhere. His oilsands peers had left, leaving him to fend for himself. He knew they blamed him.

What if Elise was right? What if the oilsands had become so toxic they would become stranded, unable to be produced, unable to be transported, unable to attract investment because they had been so disparaged?

Sitting alone in the back of a large but nearly empty room, hearing the laughter in the hallways of conference guests enjoying free wine and finger food, John panicked about his own situation. It looked dire. All his wealth was tied up in his new company, which he had just doubled in size by taking on more debt than he ever had.

His instincts, which had served him so well throughout his career, had failed to warn him that new forces were changing the way oil was valued. Was he losing his touch? Was the climate-change risk becoming a real thing? Were the oilsands becoming the first commodity to decouple from its market value? Would they be needed and worthless at the same time?

He decided he needed to talk to his trusted broker. He needed to protect himself and unload some of his stock to secure his future.

Lost in thought, John Hess didn't notice that a young man dressed in a dark business suit was standing near him, sizing him up.

"John Hess?" the young man asked, approaching. "You look like you could use a drink."

"And you are?" the oilman asked, struck by the young man's exotic good looks.

"Anthony Littlechild. I was told I could find you here."

"Who told you?"

"Elise."

"Ah," John said, his mood lightening. "Where is she?"

"She went back to her newsroom a while ago," he said. "She told me that other reporters from the *Journal* are covering the conference."

"How do you know Elise?" John asked.

"Let's just say she's like my fairy godmother. She wrote an article about me a long time ago," he said, producing from his briefcase a copy of Elise's award-winning story of his difficult adolescent years on a reserve in the oilsands region and his experience as an environmental campaigner. "We are good friends now. I know her children, too. She told me I could find you here and to come prepared."

"You're the hoop dancer?" John asked, surprised and pleased, recalling Elise's story. "I remember the article. I hope it helped you – you know – meet your objectives," he said.

The oilman had been so moved by Anthony's struggle that he made a generous anonymous contribution to a scholarship to fund his law education. But John didn't want the young man to know. He believed charity had to be its own reward. He didn't want to be swamped with other requests. He believed in picking his own miracles.

"It did," Anthony said. "I went back to school and worked harder than was humanly possible. I knew it was my only chance to get off the reserve and do something with my life. I earned a commerce degree, then I went on to Harvard Law. I met Elise's children at Harvard. I work in New York now, for a boutique mergers and acquisitions law firm. It's great experi-ence, but I have bigger plans."

"Let's hear them," the oilman said, standing up and straightening his jacket, glad for the company, and feeling satisfied that his donation had earned such a great return on investment. The two – handsome, tall, and sartorially savvy – cut striking figures as they strolled out of the conference venue into the evening traffic, toward a half-empty bar.

Chapter 50

MANHATTAN, NEW YORK, APRIL 2011

In the heart of Manhattan's Little Italy, Elise entered the Sicilian restaurant where Jordan had agreed to meet her for dinner. The owner, a grizzled old gentleman from Siracusa, recognized her immediately from bygone days and offered her one of his special tables, just off the covered patio. He inquired about her husband, her job, and her children. He hadn't heard about Julien and expressed his deepest sympathies, then looked up and made the sign of the cross, saddened by the loss.

Elise gave him a quick update on her busy life in journalism and promised to visit again. The restauranteur came back with a plateful of cream-filled cannoli, urging her to take it home.

Thirty minutes went by. Elise checked her phone to see if Jordan had cancelled. There were no messages. Disappointed, she was about to leave when she noticed him peering inside the restaurant from the sidewalk, looking haggard, like an aging hippie, in jeans and a loose cotton shirt, his curly hair greying and long.

"Jordan?" She waved, inviting him to come in, concerned by the way he looked.

Elise was still in her suit, complemented by an expensive briefcase and fine leather shoes – the outfit she had picked for the conference – and felt bad she hadn't changed into something more casual. It had not been her intention to one-up her friend.

"Elise. I am sorry. I should have cancelled. I'm not in the right state of mind," he said.

"Of course, you are," Elise insisted.

The restaurant owner rushed to the table and welcomed his other once-regular client.

"Dr. Black," he said cheerfully. He called his wife Bianca over to join the small reunion. "Look who's back for dinner. The good doctor. It's been too long. We need to celebrate," he said, and rushed back to the kitchen.

Jordan took a long, admiring look at Elise. She was as beautiful as ever, he thought, with her ginger hair cut shorter and her face barely touched by age. He was embarrassed by his poor choice of clothes, which was intended for a different audience.

"Apologies for the way I look," he said. "I just left my lawyer's office and finalized my divorce. It's over. Barb was a nightmare right to the end. She's the one who cheated. I'm the one who lost – my assets, my reputation, and nearly my job. And that's the last time I will speak of her tonight."

"Jordan – don't let whatever happened between you and Barb come between us. Let's do a reset and start over?" Elise proposed, hoping to rekindle their friendship. She was worried about her friend. She saw Jordan's hand on the table and held it tight. She wanted him to know she still cared for him.

The restaurant owner came back with two tall glasses of Prosecco and a plate of Parma prosciutto and took their order.

"Elise, I am damaged goods," Jordan said. "I don't know where to go from here. I don't know who to trust. I don't trust myself, either, after making so many bad judgement calls – Barb, Save the Climate, you."

"Me?" Elise asked, shaking her head. "No. Scratch that off your list. You didn't misjudge me. We both had to deal with big changes in our lives and we weren't on the same schedule. We were both swept up by situations that clouded our thinking.

"As far as Barb, don't beat yourself up too much about her," Elise continued, hoping to convince Jordan it was not all his fault. "She's a force of nature. She's been horrible to me, too. The Canadian oilsands industry hasn't been able to figure her out, either. She'll use anyone and anything to achieve her ends, whatever they are. She is uncompromising, ruthless. I have heard she's ruffling a lot of feathers in her new job, too. She'll be yesterday's punchline if she's not careful."

"And before we stop talking about Barb," Elise continued, "you should know that I have taken a huge reputational hit, too. I still have my job, but I doubt I'll get the promotion I have been hoping for all these years. Her campaign has demolished my good name and I need to take a time out. In fact, I'm seriously thinking of doing something new, starting over in a new job, perhaps public relations. I could do boring for a while."

She pulled her smart phone from her purse and showed him the harassing emails in her inbox, the blogs circulating on social media that accused her of shilling for oil companies, and the latest photos of her lunch with John claiming she was conspiring with Big Oil.

"Are you still talking to that oil guy?" Jordan asked.

"I am – but I am not conspiring with him to benefit the oil industry or fraternizing with him. He's a source – and a pretty good one, too. That's all," Elise said, not wanting to disclose more, because whatever had happened between her and John Hess was a mistake and in the past. "He's one of the top oil entrepreneurs in the oilsands sector. I wouldn't be doing my job if I didn't talk to him. Don't believe everything you read online."

Jordan became pensive. He didn't like what was happening to Elise. He'd always admired her dedication to her job and felt responsible for what was happening. "What do you mean that you are taking a time out?" he probed.

"I will be spending the next six months here and in Houston, just to get away from the oilsands campaign," Elise said. "There is a lot happening in Houston in oil shale. We're expanding our coverage there and I will be writing features. But the truth is that I need to distance myself from the oilsands, in any way I can. The campaign is suing me, you know? The activists are following me everywhere. I'm afraid for my safety."

"I knew they were ruthless, but this is ridiculous. You shouldn't be surrendering to them," Jordan said. "You are giving them exactly what they want. They want to sideline you and others like you to suppress real information so they can replace it with their propaganda."

"I know. But I can't keep taking the blows. I still need to work, and I can't keep fighting somebody else's war – especially since the Canadian oilsands industry is doing such a bad job of defending its own interests. Their view is that if they ignore the campaign long enough, it will all go away and they'll resume business as usual," Elise said.

"They're wrong," Jordan said. "The campaign has been a cash cow and will be expanded to other areas. Any sign of weakness emboldens them to push even harder."

The restaurant owner served two steaming seafood pastas with mixed salads on the side, then called his cousin, a violinist, to perform a special song.

Elise noticed that Jordan's mood was improving. She recognized the man she once knew, who was always looking for a way to right a wrong.

"I may be able to help you," he said. "But it means Barb will remain in our lives for a while longer. It's inevitable, and it could get uglier."

"What do you have in mind?" Elise asked.

"I saved many key documents from my time as a director of Save the Climate. You may be interested in a few about their major donors. It's the main reason I resigned. I couldn't live with myself, knowing where their money was coming from. What they are doing is unethical, if not illegal. It's certainly questionable."

"Really? But wouldn't its disclosure get you in trouble? Did you sign a non-disclosure when you left?"

"No. I made sure I didn't. Barb and I were still together then, and she didn't force me. She must have felt guilty since she was obviously sleeping with the tech billionaire. But I was a director, so I am sure there will be repercussions for me. I don't care. The cost of silence is higher than the cost of exposing the truth, in my view."

"What do the documents show? Any big names?" Elise asked, impressed by Jordan's integrity, and downplaying the risks immediately coming to mind.

"Yes. The campaign against the oilsands is funded by people who want to crush new competition. There are Russian oligarchs, the Venezuelan government, Iran, even the Saudis. The usual powerbrokers in the oil world. They support it with money and by spreading misinformation about Canadian oil. There are some clean-energy types who don't want fossil fuels to get in the way of their business plans, some shrewd oil tycoons making a killing buying and refining cheap Canadian oil, and some well-known do-gooders with too much money who feel entitled to remake the world the way they want it.

"There are a few true environmentalists on that list to make it look legitimate, but their contributions are a drop in the bucket. I was one of them. This is not a campaign to improve the environment. It's a campaign to squeeze Canada out of the oil market so the incumbents get to keep as much of it as possible for themselves while the world transitions to new energy sources. The oilsands are the first target because everyone knows the Canadians are easily pushed around."

Elise had suspected much of what Jordan was saying but wasn't able to prove it. "Do you have evidence?"

"Yes. The money is deposited in the bank account of a law firm in Bermuda, which distributes it to various charities in the United States. Those in turn make donations to Canadian environmental organizations, which then deploy them to various collaborators, including Indigenous people, and to the political campaigns of candidates who support the off-oil agenda. The money trail is intentionally complex to hide the identity of the funders, who have been guaranteed anonymity. It stinks to high heaven. The White House is counting on the campaign to show there's big grassroots opposition to pipelines, which justifies their planned rejection of the South Pipeline even if it's met all regulations. I wonder, though, if the government is aware this campaign is supported by foreign, even hostile, powers. I suspect Barb is keeping a lot of those details to herself. I took screenshots of the deposits in the Bermuda account and of the transfers to the various groups," Jordan said.

"Are these illegal contributions?" Elise asked.

"Hard to say. I am not a lawyer. I don't know if Canada has laws against foreign funding of campaigns against their own economic interests. At the very least, it's scandalous that an American environmental charity uses this subterfuge to remake another country's economy. I was very uncomfortable about this when I was on the board of Save the Climate. I had to resign. Barb was so happy with the big cheques that were rolling in, she thought I was crazy."

"If this information becomes public, how do you think she will respond?" Elise asked.

"She'll probably deny it and accuse us of being climate deniers pushing oil propaganda. She'll make sure we're discredited even more, maybe put us on one of her blacklists if we aren't there already. She knows how to turn the truth upside down, how to intimidate. She's the queen of smoke and mirrors. And she will know the documents came from me. But I don't care.

I have nothing left to lose. I would confirm they are authentic if you write about this. I may even be able to get other people to help you out."

Elise's reporter instincts took over. "Forget the time out," she said. "Send me the documents. I'll show them to my editor, I'll make the case and let him make the call. I know he wanted me to lay low for a while – but I'm still in the journalism business and this story needs to be told. And it might even help us on the lawsuit. The campaign might back off if their funders are revealed."

Elise and Jordan left a generous tip, promised the restauranteur they would return soon, and walked in the warm evening side by side.

Elise asked Jordan about his job in Afghanistan and when he planned to return to New York.

"When you do," he responded.

"I want to come back," Elise said. "All this travel and the oilsands' war are exhausting. I love Alberta – I'm thinking of buying a house in the woods for holidays. But I'm ready to come back to New York. I built a good operation there and I want to hand it off to someone else. I want a new challenge. I'm waiting for the right position to open, at the Journal, or elsewhere."

Her words felt like déjà vu – she had expressed similar ones to John. He had been tempting, but she knew he was history. No one wanted to be treated like they only mattered when they were useful. Elise wanted someone she could always count on, a true partner.

"Regardless, I'm spending a lot of time in New York already," she continued. "Simone and Richard are both dating. I want to be around them."

"And I want to be a part of your life," Jordan said. "I know I don't look like someone who deserves a second chance, but I'll take whatever you are able to give me."

Elise reached again for Jordan's hand and looked him straight in the eyes. "I'll take all of you, Jordan," she said. "Let's take care of our careers, but not let them dominate us any more than they have to. All this bad stuff – our worries about our reputations, this manufactured rage, this campaign – only matters if we let it.

"We don't need others' approval to feel good about ourselves," she continued. "We've already done what we were meant to do. We have nothing to apologize for. Let's regroup here as soon as we can and build a life together. This feels to me like it's meant to be, right now. I hope you feel the same way."

"I do, Elise," Jordan said, tearing up. "I love you."

"I love you, too," Elise responded.

They continued to walk on Broadway, between groups of tourists, feeling uplifted by a multi-talented busker belting out a Louis Armstrong tune. They talked more about Elise's kids and about Jordan's clinic.

Then Jordan hailed a taxi, and they climbed in. He had work to do before returning to Kabul, he told her. They hugged and Elise got out first. They promised to stay in touch.

Early the next day, Elise received from Jordan a large email folder. It contained documents about the Save the Climate donors and contact information for former directors and former employees prepared to provide comment and corroborate information.

Elise printed two copies and knocked on Mark Wimhurst's door.

"Good morning, Chief. Do you have a minute?" she asked, peeking into his office.

"Have a seat," he said, pleased to see her. "You look like you've swallowed something big. Spit it out."

"I did – but it means a change in plans," she said, handing him a copy of Jordan's documents.

They analyzed the papers together. There were records of large donations to the campaign from foreign regimes and other big names determined to shut down new oil supplies from Canada, the offshore bank account, the complex transfers to a web of American charities, more transfers to an even bigger web of Canadian recipients.

"It looks like a lot of trouble to hide the identity of the donors," Mark said. "The source is Dr. Black?"

"Yes," Elise said, explaining that he'd taken a job in Afghanistan to ride out the fallout from his wife's affair.

"I'm sorry to hear that. I didn't realize he was so deeply affected," Mark said. "When we spoke to him, he seemed relieved that the whole thing was finally becoming public."

Elise told her boss she had reconnected with Jordan, that they remained close friends, and that an investigation revealing the funders of the campaign could be perceived as a conflict of interest, especially if Jordan was quoted. But she argued the truth needed to be revealed, that the information was too important to ignore, and that *Journal* readers had to be told the full story of the brazen campaign to keep the Canadian oilsands in the ground.

"I agree – but we need to be smart about this," the editor said, pondering the best course of action. "We need to do our homework and ensure that our reporting is thorough and fair to all sides. We need to protect you and the *Journal* from any appearance that we're making these revelations just to bolster our legal case. It might, I think, but that wouldn't be our primary aim. It would be a secondary outcome based on shining a light on the truth."

"That's what we'll do," Elise said.

They invited other senior editors to look at the documents and give their views about whether the project was worthwhile and, if so, how to approach it. The spirited editorial meeting lasted hours. It adjourned with unanimous support for an investigation and a plan of action – including the selection of a team of reporters to talk to Jordan, other former directors, former employees, donors, charities, recipients of funds, government representatives – including those at the White House – and Barb Heinz. A reporter and a photographer would be dispatched to Bermuda to find out more about the law firm in charge of the bank account. Reporters in Calgary would approach all environmental organizations that received funds from Save the Climate and get reaction from those who stood to lose the most from the campaign, such as governments, the oilsands industry, related industries.

When the meeting ended, Mark asked Elise to stay.

"Are you sure you want to take this on?" he asked. "It would be easier for you to avoid the limelight for a while and focus on other, less controversial stories."

"Yes, that would be the easiest way to go – and exactly what these activists want," Elise said.

"I want to do journalism, and I want us to be the medium that readers rely on for the truth – as much of it as we are able to uncover, presented fairly and honestly, even the uncomfortable truth. If we back off, if we allow these campaigns – and believe me, there will be many more, and anything will be fair game – to silence us, to discredit us, and to suppress us in the media so they can replace us and fill the information gap with their own fabrications, we're digging our own grave.

"It's dangerous for democracy, and we can't let it happen," Elise continued. "The Save the Climate campaign represents a hardline fringe of the environmental movement that wants to eliminate oil at any cost, even if it means partnering with foreign regimes that need to keep their share of the oil market for as long as possible. No one voted for these activists. No one vetted their goals or their tactics. They don't want us, the free press, to stand in the way, to scrutinize how they operate, to write about the implications for all of us of not having energy security.

"We're the guardians of the truth. We're the free press. We're the ones who keep people accountable, regardless of who they are. We need to draw a line in the sand. We need to show that we won't be bullied – not by the environmentalists, not by the oilsands industry, not by other fringe groups who want to remake society by shouting the loudest. And make no mistake – the oil guys won't be thrilled about these revelations, either. They would rather dodge controversy because it's bad for their stock prices. You'll see."

And then she added, "I am prepared to put my career on the line over this. If we don't stand up for truth, the whole truth, we stand for nothing. I will resign if this investigation hurts the *Journal* in any way."

Mark, inspired by Elise's words, and worried about losing her, took a mental note to move her to the top of his succession planning list, which he was due to present to the *Journal's* board of directors by the end of the week.

"Very well, then," he said, shaking her hand. "Let's get to work. Will you be returning to Calgary?"

"I can park here until we're ready to go to press," Elise said. "This story belongs in the US as much as it belongs in Canada. Then we'll figure out what to do next. I'd like to work closely with the rest of the team."

Chapter 51
CALGARY, ALBERTA, AUGUST 2011

The *Journal's* multi-part investigation revealed in detail who funded the Save the Climate campaign against the Canadian oilsands, from green industry competitors seeking to grow their business, to foreign regimes interested in preserving their own share of the oil market.

Activists refused to explain their side of the story to the *Journal.* Instead, after publication of the investigation, they doubled down to denounce the reporting, the *Journal's* writers, and all those who were quoted, particularly Dr. Jordan Black, who was singled out for the harshest criticism for revealing confidential documents.

As far as the Save the Climate campaign was concerned, the revelations were the work of climate-change deniers motivated by self-interest to impede important and necessary change.

The oilsands industry cringed about the new dump of bad press and played down the findings. Readers, besieged by so much conflicting information, didn't know who or what to believe. Canadian politicians who condemned the foreign meddling were quickly accused of xenophobia. Investors were still making money off their oilsands stocks and brushed off the new information as questionable 'noise.'

But John Hess read every word, and from his Calgary office made the first of three calls.

"Hi Matthew, how's the brokerage business?" he asked the broker he used for his sensitive trades.

"Never been this crazy," the broker said. "People are selling blue chip stocks, borrowing, and putting mortgages on their houses to load up on oilsands stocks. They think the sky's the limit, they love the dividends, the takeovers, and want to ride it all the way to heaven."

"Great time to go against the flow then," John said.

"What do you mean?" Matthew asked, intrigued by his famous client's contrarian view.

"I'd like to do some portfolio management, sell the Aurora stock held in my Luxembourg account and build up some liquidity, in US dollars, please," he said.

"Is that the numbered company – the one we set up before your divorce?"

"Yes. That's the one. I'd like to liquidate my Aurora holdings and close that account," the oilman repeated.

"It's a big position – could be worth half a billion today. Are you sure you want unload all of it?" the broker asked.

"Yes. Do it in small quantities. We don't want to weaken the stock price or raise flags. Right?" John said.

"Gotcha. I'm on it." They both hung up.

The broker got to work on the oilman's order, and simultaneously sold his own position in Aurora, the hottest of his oilsands stocks. If the boss was selling out, there must be trouble in paradise, he decided.

John's second call was to Anthony Littlechild. He found him in his New York office.

"Hey, Tony," he said cheerfully. "How's the Big Apple?"

"Busy," the young man said. "How's Alberta?"

"Never better," John said. "I have thought about your ideas. I believe they have merit. I'd like to meet with your coalition and offer you an opportunity to get your plan off the ground. Are you available to meet?"

"Yes, of course," Anthony said. "Our group is meeting in Fort McMurray next week. Would you like to join us? We'd be honoured."

"Yes. I'll be there. Let me know where and when – please call me directly, on my private cell phone. I'd like to keep this *entre nous*, okay?"

"Got it. See you next week," Anthony said, and hung up.

His third call was to his executive assistant. He asked her to convene a special meeting of his board.

"What's the topic?" she asked.

"Restructuring. I'll fill everybody in when we meet."

"Sure. How about we schedule it right after our regularly scheduled meeting?" she proposed.

"That works," John responded.

John picked up the *Journal* again and re-read the articles about the funders of the Save the Climate campaign. He counted the bylines on the stories – ten journalists had worked on the project, including Elise, whom he hadn't spoken to since that awkward lunch in Calgary in March.

She wasn't in the city, he knew that much, because he'd dropped into her office and was told she was on a long-term assignment. She didn't return his calls.

John was concerned about no longer being able to influence her to his advantage. She'd given him an edge with her insights and her coverage of the oilsands industry.

He was hurt that Elise hadn't asked him to contribute to the investigation, which she obviously orchestrated with Jordan's help. Now she avoided him, he thought, feeling resentful.

He knew he could have tempered the blow by downplaying the campaign's effectiveness and highlighting the industry's big upside. There was much good news to talk about. So many new technologies were implemented they were changing the industry, for the better. He was disappointed by the responses offered to the *Journal* by other industry players. They were so careful they were ineffective, he thought.

But John also knew that the investigation, by uncovering the ugly truth about the campaign against the oilsands, revealed how far opponents were willing to go to shut his industry down.

No Canadian industry could withstand such powerful headwinds, John realized. He worried that it was game over for him and that his best course of action was to make himself, and his company, as resilient as possible.

He resolved to forget Elise. The malicious rumours circulating about the two of them were affecting his reputation. His inner circle was following every twist and turn on social media and continued to warn him about her.

"You can't trust her," his lawyer told him, again. "She's press. I knew she would sell us out for a scoop." He wasn't wrong, John acknowledged, holding the *Journal*'s printed edition one more time before throwing it angrily into the trash.

In New York, Mark Wimhurst asked Elise to join him in his office. She was about to leave for Houston to coordinate a series of features on the growth of oil shale. As she entered, nervous about getting laid off, he took a final look at the *Journal*'s Save the Climate coverage, which started on the front page and spilled into two inside pages.

"Elise, I wanted to congratulate you for your leadership on this project," he said, surprising her. "It's breaking all records for online readership. We'll submit it for all the usual awards. It's an outstanding piece of work and it should be recognized – though I suspect it won't because it's critical of the climate-change cause, so it's not the type of journalism our industry peers value."

"Thank you," Elise said. "I'm very happy with the way it turned out. The backlash isn't as bad as I expected – other than for Jordan. It's so unfair. I hope he doesn't take it too personally."

"Yes. I hope you get in touch with him and thank him for his contribution. We couldn't have done it without him.

"I have a bit of good news," Mark added. "The Save the Climate campaign dropped us from their lawsuit today. You were right about not caving in. They must have realized that they picked a fight with the wrong people."

Elise was relieved. She didn't care about awards any more. She cared about doing good work, uncovering important information, making a difference.

"I lined up some decent interviews in Houston," she said, grateful her career was still on track, and that she would be away from the crossfire for a while. "They won't be as exciting, but it's a change. The fast money is migrating there. We owe it to our readers to tell them what is going on in oil shale."

Chapter 52

FORT MCMURRAY, ALBERTA, SEPTEMBER 2011

Officially, John Hess was away for a late-summer big-game hunting trip in the North. Unofficially, he was driving to Fort McMurray on a single-lane highway jammed with flat-bed trucks carrying oversized pieces of machinery to build new oilsands projects.

Worried about information leaks, inside and outside his company, he made the eight-hour journey alone, through the yellowing wilderness in the warm, late-summer day, enjoying Jann Arden's ballads on the stereo of his luxurious pickup truck, a recent purchase.

By late afternoon, he checked in at a new hotel just outside of the town of Fort McMurray. A few kilometres north, oilsands mines were teeming with vehicles feeding ore to processing plants, which operated harder than usual to produce oil for the winter heating season.

The oilman entered a conference area in a wing of the hotel. He wore a golf cap, sunglasses, and jeans to avoid being recognized. Anthony Littlechild greeted him in a dark hallway with a bear hug, then accompanied him to a windowless room and introduced him to two dozen Indigenous chiefs representing nations from Saskatchewan, Alberta, and British Columbia.

John felt good about the encounter. He hoped it would set in motion the last big deal of his life, one for the ages.

He recognized a few faces and was delighted to see Chief Anne Proudfoot. He shook her hand and they both smiled. He didn't ask her why she'd abandoned the activists and joined Anthony's team. She didn't ask him why he came to the meeting.

Everyone sat down around a large conference table, settling in for a long night, as a whiff of stale coffee filled the air.

Anthony, looking confident in his dark blazer and jeans, stood up to address the room.

"As you know, John and I had preliminary discussions about a purchase of a big part of Aurora's business by our new Indigenous Oilsands Company – or IOC," he said.

"I have lined up the financing we need from a consortium of US and Canadian banks to make our first big transaction – up to a billion dollars. Our next step is to acquire a selection of Aurora's midstream assets. They will give us a foundation and the credibility to build what I hope becomes the largest Indigenous-owned enterprise in Canada.

"John and I believe a deal involving IOC acquiring parts of Aurora that spin off regular cash, but are not core to the oilsands extraction business, would be a win-win for both sides. IOC would get an ideal foundation from which to grow in the energy business. Aurora would prepare itself for the future. He'll explain why. This discussion is strictly confidential. Please respect that. John, the floor is yours."

John Hess looked around, feeling uneasy, and got up to speak.

He was in unfamiliar territory – away from the slick bankers and big investors who spoke his language, sharks who understood money and how to make it, who didn't care about who got hurt or left behind. They'd been his tribe in the past. They funded his ventures and backed him up when he needed them. Now they barely returned his calls, and when they did, they weren't encouraging. They didn't like the controversy around the oilsands, they told him, even if companies like Aurora were still making money hand over fist, and their stock prices were strong, pushed up by small investors convinced there was still potential for big gains. The oilsands were no longer competitive, they said.

The bankers had a new infatuation – oil shale. They told him those plays were in their infancy, environmental scrutiny was light, there was no organized campaign to shut them down, and they could double their money in a couple of years.

The faces watching John now wore the marks of hardship – weathered, earnest, naïve. He knew they couldn't afford to make a wrong move. For the first time, he wanted them – a team on the other side of his deal – to succeed, even if it meant he didn't.

John knew he was taking a big risk speaking for his entire company, not knowing whether he would get board support to sell so much so soon after closing a major acquisition.

But he believed he saw the future, as so many times before, and it pointed in a new direction – a partnership with an emerging Indigenous enterprise.

There were many reasons. First, Aurora's debt was too large, and he felt it had to be cut with an injection of cash while oil prices were strong. Second, since his last deal, the board was no longer under his control, and he needed new allies, which he believed Indigenous people could become. Third, he needed to throw a wrench in the Save the Climate campaign's relentless assault against his business by breaking its dominance over Indigenous people. Fourth, he wanted his last big deal to be fair to all – the oil companies, the governments, the shareholders, and the Indigenous people who were in the oilsands first.

Speaking from the heart, John laid all his cards on the table.

"I have worked on many deals in my life – deals that made me rich and that I hoped would make me happy," he said. "But I don't enjoy what I do any more. The campaign against the oilsands has made my industry, regretfully, an object of global scorn.

"I know oilsands stocks are hot and most expect big profits for decades to come. I have a different view. I believe that if this campaign continues, our oilsands industry will die, other producers that are conspiring against it will take its market share, and Canada will be poorer and more divided as a result.

"In my view, Indigenous Canadians are the only people with the legal and moral standing to turn this around. I have found in Anthony Littlechild the qualities of an exceptional leader. He is committed to preserving the oilsands as a source of wealth – and especially pride – for all Canadians, and as the cornerstone for our First Nations to elevate their own standard of living.

"The anti-oilsands campaign has been run from the United States with the full but secret support of the current administration. It has found partners in some Indigenous people in Canada and paid them a pittance to sing and dance for its benefit. They've fooled you. They are exploiting your rights and your image. They will abandon you as soon as they achieve their goals, and they are undermining you by taking money from Canada's foreign oil competitors to fund a campaign that suppresses your opportunities to become economically self-sufficient.

"Our Canadian industry was wrong to exclude Indigenous people over the last decade – and for that I apologize, because I am a leader of that industry, and I am guilty. We were too preoccupied with launching our companies, with making them profitable, with getting rich. We were too stuck in our old ways of thinking – ways that made us focus on old financial models that exalted profit and excluded everything else.

"It's time that you take what you deserve, that you benefit as full partners, that you contribute your indigenous knowledge to help us reduce environmental impacts, and that you become the leaders in Canada's economy that you deserve to be.

"Aurora will benefit too because it will reduce its debt and because a partnership with you will enable it to better defend itself against opposition to the oilsands."

John turned on his laptop and explained the main parts of his company – its extraction business, its upgrading business, and supporting businesses that could be sold to IOC – pipelines, storage tanks, maintenance.

Some were built by Aurora, some were acquired, he explained. A deal could involve selling ownership of those assets to IOC, then leasing back services so IOC could collect a steady income stream.

"As you become more experienced in running these assets, you could acquire more and increase your income, diversify your portfolio," John explained. "Or you could build your own, like new pipelines. Your biggest strategic advantage is that the Save the Climate campaign won't dare attack an Indigenous enterprise – even one in the oilsands business they despise."

The chiefs, intrigued by the presentation, struck by John's sincerity, took turns asking questions.

"What happens if oil prices crash?" asked one.

"How do we build the expertise to run these facilities?" asked another.

"What does it take to build our own?"

"How do we build a company that runs efficiently?"

"How do we pick our leadership?"

"How do we build a workforce?"

The oilman answered the questions and offered solutions for all of them.

Some chiefs were skeptical. Others were excited. Late at night, they asked John to leave the room so they could discuss the opportunity between themselves.

Tired from the long day, John went to his hotel room and fell asleep soundly with the windows open, welcoming the crisp air and the melodies of northern Alberta's wildlife.

He got up early the next day, ordered breakfast, and dealt with work issues on his laptop. By noon he packed his overnight bag and prepared to make the long drive back to Calgary, with or without an outcome from the Indigenous group.

Anthony found him checking out and asked him to return to the meeting.

"I apologize for taking so long. We were up most of the night and have come to an agreement," the Indigenous leader said. "We'd like to discuss the highlights."

When John returned to the room, a few chiefs had left, and those who remained were smiling. A proposal to purchase a selection of Aurora's assets was scribbled on a large paper napkin. The offer was for $1 billion, subject to the final approval of financial backers. The $1 billion figure was in red bold letters, underlined twice.

Delighted with the result, satisfied with the number, John explained the long road ahead. Anthony proposed to present an official offer to Aurora's board by the end of the week, then stood up.

"On behalf of our new Indigenous company, I would like to thank you for having faith in us. We are ready to take charge of our future and show Canada what we can do. The oilsands sustained us in many ways in the past and will help us in the future. We won't let foreign activists decide what's best for us. We will rise to the challenge and decide that for ourselves. We believe we have a model that will inspire other First Nations to join us. It's time to resist the resistance."

John offered to help in any way he could and invited the group to make a presentation in person to his board. He asked them again to not disclose that he'd instigated the proposal. He exited the hotel and returned to his pickup truck.

He started the return trip, taking his time driving through downtown Fort McMurray, where he saw hundreds of oilsands workers step off a long line of parked buses. He was proud of those workers. Tough, hardworking men and women who gave all they had to make something from nothing. He headed south, through evergreen forests brightened by the fiery sunset in the wide horizon.

A week later, at the special board meeting called by John Hess to discuss the proposal, Anthony Littlechild, Chief Anne Proudfoot, and two other chiefs entered the boardroom on the executive floor of Aurora's Calgary headquarters. The visitors looked good in their new business suits and shiny leather shoes. The men were nervous. They knew they were taking the first step in a one-billion leap of faith. But Chief Anne felt energized, like she was coming out of the shadows that had held her back.

"Thank you for agreeing to meet with us," Anthony said to the dozen directors in attendance, all older white men. They welcomed him cordially and congratulated him on his Harvard law degree. A couple asked him about his professors.

One politely acknowledged Chief Anne and the other chiefs.

"We are here to discuss an offer for some of Aurora's non-core assets," Anthony said. "A hard copy was made available to you. We've been studying the company for a while and we believe our offer would be mutually beneficial, an exceptional win-win, so to speak.

"By agreeing to this purchase, Aurora would reduce its debt and continue to benefit from the assets by partnering with us. It would gain an immense public relations edge as the first large oilsands company to form an extensive alliance with a consortium of First Nations. We would acquire a business that would give us significant income to start building the first major Indigenous enterprise in the oilsands."

The directors listened intently as Anthony talked about which assets the partnership was interested in, how it would work, why it would help shield Aurora from the anti-oilsands campaign.

But Anthony watched the blank stares and sensed skepticism. He'd seen those looks before, from privileged, comfortable people who claimed they were open to change but fought hard to protect their advantages from outsiders.

"What gave you the impression that these assets are for sale?" a director asked.

"What makes you think you can operate them properly?" asked another.

"What happens if there is a disagreement between our two companies?" asked yet another.

"How do you know the campaign will affect our business?"

Anthony answered all the questions knowledgeably and kept his cool.

Then John, worried by the unsupportive questions, thanked the visitors and promised to let them know if there was interest.

After they left, one of the directors asked John what he thought.

"I think we should seriously consider this offer," he said. "I agree with the rationale they put forward. We need to reduce our debt, and this offer moves us close to our target. Oil prices are cyclical. Today's historically high levels will correct, and we need to be prepared. The campaign against the oilsands is widening and beginning to impact the markets. Oil shale is becoming a formidable competitor, and one of the reasons that they are attracting so much capital is they're not a target of these activists."

The board wasn't convinced.

"Why should we partner with a bunch of Indians?" asked one.

"What happens if the relationship breaks down?" asked another.

"Why them – and not other buyers who have experience running these assets?" asked a third.

John continued his defense of the deal, but he knew his board was not on his side.

One director proposed a compromise. "I accept that we need to reduce our debt – which has been a priority since our big takeover. How about we solicit competing bids? Very quietly, of course. Then we will have met our fiduciary duty to our shareholders and can maybe squeeze a few extra dollars. The Indians will get the assets only if they offer us the most lucrative deal."

The meeting adjourned. John had not anticipated the solicitation of a competing bid. He should have foreseen his board's reaction because that's how he would have reacted, too, in the past, before his industry was upended by the campaign. John blamed himself. He should have known that his directors were too stuck in their ways to accept such a trail-blazing deal.

Chapter 53

Guilt got the better of Elise in the aftermath of her Save the Climate investigation. While she savoured an outpouring of praise for a job well done, both from *Journal* leaders and from readers, she knew Jordan was paying the price.

She did her best to speak with him as frequently as possible over the phone – but felt ill-equipped to console him. The attacks on his reputation on social media platforms were vicious, false, and difficult to rebut without his help.

Elise was convinced the Save the Climate campaign was punishing him for revealing their secrets by planting stories alleging he was involved in inappropriate encounters with patients – all minors – which were then amplified by its army of keyboard warriors. Her media competitors, hungry to promote readership by discrediting the *Journal*, covered the claims as if they were true.

"You need to shut these down and tell your side of the story – prove that the claims are fabricated. Call out your accusers, ask for details," Elise pleaded with Jordan. "Get your hospital to back you up, your former colleagues, your first wife. I can help you. These stories are preposterous. They are planted. They don't pass the smell test."

But Jordan, his mental state deteriorating, wouldn't hear of it. "Look, I know I deserve this, and I knew it was coming," he told her. "I broke their rules – written and unwritten. I did it for the broader good. I wanted people to know how the Save the Climate campaign operates. I feel partly responsible for the way they evolved. I should have done my part as a member of their board to keep it from going down the path they are in, especially in Canada, especially in their crusades against so-called climate deniers. They have no decency."

Elise took matters in her own hands and urged his hospital, her son, his colleagues, former campaign directors, to defend him.

She didn't like that Jordan had given up. She wanted her old Jordan back, the confident surgeon who was her late husband's best friend, who stole her heart in Alberta's Rockies, who mentored her son, who was finally back in her life.

Elise presumed that Barb Heinz was involved in the smear campaign. Her son had been right all along – she was ruthless, and she didn't want her to have him.

But things got worse. Jordan's hospital board, a dozen socialites picked for their wealthy connections and fundraising potential, expressed grave concerned about the scandal. Their circles were threatening to cancel their donations, they warned.

An emergency meeting was called. The board decided Jordan had to be fired, effective immediately. The termination statement would be issued early the next day and include praise for Dr. Jordan Black's decades of exemplary service at the New York hospital and in the Kabul clinic.

The news was delivered to Jordan by the HR department in an email. A separate statement was circulated to staff. All communication was vetted by lawyers.

A day after the announcement, Elise's son, Richard, was organizing a protest to demand Jordan's re-instatement when Elise received a call on her mobile phone from the chair of the hospital's board.

"Ms. Chamonter?" the man asked, sounding contrite, like someone who was coached to manage a crisis.

"Yes?" she said, interrupting a visit of an oil export facility under construction near the Gulf of Mexico, which she planned to feature in a story.

"I'm the chair of the board of Dr. Black's hospital," he said, his voice echoing from a speaker phone. Elise wondered if others were listening in.

"You left me several messages, and I apologize for not getting in touch sooner," he said. "I regret to inform you that Dr. Black died this morning at our clinic in Kabul from a drug overdose. We're planning with the military to transport him back as soon as possible. We're still investigating the circumstances, but it looks like suicide. He left you a note, which I will forward to you as soon as I get it from Kabul. I'm sorry."

Elise's limbs weakened. She collapsed on the concrete floor of the facility as the tour organizers watched. The hospital boss was left hanging on the phone.

Elise was taken to a first-aid station, in shock, her nose bleeding, sweat and tears running down her bruised face.

"Elise is there anything we can do for you?" a company official, an elderly war vet, asked.

"I'm sorry," she said, feeling the sting of her bruises on her forehead, her nose, and her lips. "I just received word that someone very close to me died in Afghanistan."

"Family?" the official asked, holding her arm, feeling her pain.

"Yes, family," she said, without hesitation, sobbing.

She pulled herself together and organized a video call with her children. Richard was at the hospital, Simone at her new TV job. Jordan had been such a constant presence in her children's lives, one way or the other, that Elise worried they couldn't handle another loss.

"What is it, Mom? You look awful – were you in an accident?" Simone asked, alarmed.

"No. I'm alright. I just fainted," she said, trying to stay calm, suppressing her tears. "I have some bad news. Jordan is dead. Suicide, apparently. They are still investigating. He has no family – other than his elderly mom, who has dementia. We'll have to look after *things*."

Richard, who'd been closest to Jordan lately, covered his face with his hands.

"He didn't deserve this – the way he was treated, by the hospital and by Barb Heinz," he said.

"First things first," he continued, trying to hide his grief, taking charge. "You don't look good. You have a large bruise on your forehead. I don't like that you lost consciousness. You need to get yourself to a doctor and get checked. We'll take care of Jordan's return and of the funeral. I'm angry at the hospital. They should have defended him, not fired him. The staff here is outraged by the way he was treated. Wait until they find out that he's gone. Suicide? Didn't they know how fragile he was? We'll have to make things right."

Simone offered to get in touch with Jordan's mom, write his obituary, and handle media calls.

Feeling supported, Elise promised to fly to New York immediately after seeing a doctor. Then she phoned her editor in chief.

"Elise are you okay?" asked Mark, sensing something bad had happened.

"Mark, Jordan … Dr. Black, is dead," she said, unable to stop sobbing.

"Oh my God. What happened? Was it a bomb?" he asked, astounded.

"No. Suicide, most likely. Drug overdose – the hospital is still investigating," she said. "He was in Kabul. They found him in his clinic. He left a note for me, which I should receive shortly. He probably wanted to say goodbye."

Elise told her editor about Jordan's depression, the vicious attacks on his reputation following the *Journal*'s investigation, his unwillingness to defend himself, his recent job loss.

"I saw some of the allegations – brutal," the editor said. "They really went after him. We all know how heartless these smear campaigns are. I am appalled that the hospital terminated him instead of defending him."

"The claims were false, Mark," she said. "Jordan was devastated. He was a brain surgeon, and his contact with patients was limited. Unfortunately, he didn't want to address the allegations. He was in a bad state of mind, and he just didn't have the energy to fight back. He felt he deserved the punishment. Then the hospital fired him to distance itself from the bad publicity. That must have been the last straw for Jordan."

Elise's boss urged her to see a doctor and to let him know when she returned to New York.

Without telling her, Mark mobilized the newsroom to get to the bottom of the allegations against Dr. Jordan Black – who spread them, why, why they were false – and to write an article to celebrate Jordan's life.

Chapter 54

A cold front from Canada was covering New York's streets with fresh snow when Elise read the *Journal*'s moving reporting on Dr. Jordan Black. His handsome face smiled back at her from the front page, alongside a profile chronicling his life of medical achievement, his pioneering contribution to the climate-change movement, his leadership in the establishment of a children's medical clinic in Afghanistan on behalf of his hospital.

The story revealed his struggle with mental illness and his death by suicide immediately following his dismissal by his employer. A companion article exposed the role played by the social media campaign alleging sexual misconduct for Jordan's worsening depression.

The article countered the allegations with extensive, on-the-record interviews with co-workers, former Save the Climate directors and employees, his first wife, Richard, and Elise. All dismissed the charges as false. Reporters tracked down the women who alleged sexual abuse, but they refused to be interviewed. A Save the Climate whistleblower who knew Dr. Black and was distraught about his suicide said the allegations were planted to punish him for revealing confidential information.

There was no official statement from the hospital board, nor from the Save the Climate campaign. Barb Heinz did not respond to requests for comment. Below the fold on the front page, the *Journal* featured her picture and that of the hospital's chair, speaking to each other at a lavish fundraising event. The articles were well written and left the impression that the hospital and Barb had a lot to answer for, without accusing them of being responsible for Jordan's death.

Elise then opened Jordan's sealed letter and read the handwritten content aloud to her children. They had refused to leave her side since her return to New York:

Dear Elise,

By the time you read this, I will be at peace. I took my life knowing that my conscience is clear. My life has been unbearable since my marriage to Barb, though I have been battling depression most of my life. I don't see a way forward given the state of my reputation. I'm handing over my torch to you.

Let me explain. I've always loved Charles Dickens' *A Tale of Two Cities*, particularly Sydney Carton and the nobility of his end. I wanted the same for me. You can do more on my behalf to restore my good name than I could do for myself.

I beg you to stop feeling guilty about the *Journal*'s investigation into the Save the Climate campaign. I made the choice to tell you what I knew. I expected a backlash. Activists are harsh on critics – especially those who break from their own ranks.

I am proud of the journalism you did to expose their ways. I beg you to stick with it. I hope it leads to more public awareness about the danger of extremism. Like so many revolutions, the climate change movement started with a noble cause. But it's turning into a grab for power. Devil's bargains are made. The will of the people is ignored.

As you know, my mother is my only living relative. You, Richard, and Simone are as close as I got to having a family of my own. Julien was the best friend I ever had, and I miss him dearly. He understood my dark moods like no one else.

I have bequeathed to you and your children my remaining properties in New York and in Alberta – a couple of apartments in the city and the log house in the mountains that I built and which I hope you will cherish. I built it with you in mind.

The rest of my estate is in the Black Family Foundation, which I established the last time I was in New York, to support children's health.

I would be grateful if you and/or your children could stay involved as members of the board. It's a sizeable estate, worth about eight hundred million today, the legacy of my family's involvement in oil refining.

I never talked to you about this. I was ashamed of this money and tried to atone by becoming involved in environmental causes.

I know now that I was wrong to judge what my family did. They created a business that served an important need in their time and that paid for my education.

Unfortunately, my ex-wife Barb was aware of these funds and unsuccessfully tried to get her hands on them when we divorced.

My lawyers took every precaution to ensure she never gets another penny – though I suspect she will try. I authorize you to use the funds to fight any legal challenge from Barb or anyone else. My lawyers will get in touch with you to discuss next steps.

Please publicize the existence of this foundation, where the money came from, and invite proposals to receive funds at the earliest opportunity.

Elise, I want you to know that I love you, that I am proud of you, and that I thank you for being the brightest light in my life.

Eternally yours

Jordan

Elise put down the letter and looked at her children. They had a group hug and cried one last time.

"You never really know people, do you?" Simone said.

"Do you think Dad knew all these things about Jordan?" Richard asked, digesting the revelations.

"I suspect Dad did, but he never told me," Elise said. "It might explain why he spent so much time with Jordan. I'm not surprised Jordan didn't want people to know about his family's money. He was not unique in being ashamed. Some of the biggest donors to environmental causes are descendants of oil people."

"It looks like Jordan gave us a lot to think about, with the foundation and all the rest," Simone said.

"Yes," Elise said. "I have to say, I feel a bit better. He explained so many things that I didn't get about him. We'll do what we can to ensure people know the best of Jordan, even if he's no longer here."

A week later, a celebration of Jordan's life was held in one of Manhattan's iconic jazz clubs. Elise, Richard, Simone, and Jordan's elderly mother, who looked happy and unaware of the reason for the festivities, greeted hundreds of people touched by him – former colleagues, environmentalists, politicians, journalists – including a large contingent from the *Journal* headed by Mark Wimhurst.

Elise announced Jordan's foundation. Many in the audience were surprised that the humble surgeon had such a large family fortune. Richard spoke about Jordan's contributions to the medical field and about his clinic in Afghanistan. Simone spoke about the unacceptable cost of character assassination through social media, particularly on people suffering from mental illness.

Despite the circumstances, the mood was upbeat. A live band played some of Jordan's favourite tunes.

Elise was catching up with some of Jordan's hospital colleagues, which had been her late husband's colleagues, when Barb Heinz tapped her on her shoulder.

"Elise, can we speak privately?" Barb asked.

"I have nothing to say to you," Elise responded after moving with Barb to a quieter area. "I'm dismayed you showed up here."

"Look, I'm sorry about all of this. Jordan and I had our differences, but I never thought it would come to this."

"Seriously?" Elise asked. "Why don't you take responsibility? We both know the attacks on his reputation were orchestrated by you. I will never forgive you for that."

"I take responsibility for our failed marriage," Barb admitted. "I should have tried harder. I had nothing to do with the attacks. The campaign is investigating what happened and why. Please give us a chance to get to the bottom of this."

Elise was prepared to forgive. Then Barb got to the point she needed to make. "Look, Jordan and I discussed using some of that foundation money to mitigate climate change. I hope you will honour that commitment," she said.

Elise felt her temperature rise. "Are you out of your mind?" she said. "Jordan had the right to change his mind, and he did. He instructed his lawyers to ensure that not a cent would go to you or your causes. I will honour his wishes to support children's health, and so will my children. I am not finished with you. I will do everything I can do hold you accountable for what you did to Jordan."

Barb remained calm as she uttered her parting words: "I will sue the foundation," she said. "That money was promised to me – to the climate-change campaign."

"You do that, Barb Heinz," Elise said. "I will make sure all the details of your persecution of Jordan are made public, in open court, for everyone to hear."

Barb walked away, regretting the way she'd handled herself. She could not afford more bad publicity. She knew her style was no longer in favour with her political bosses.

A week later, a news release was deposited by Mark Wimhurst on Elise's desk in New York.

"Did you see this?" he asked her, smiling.

"What is it?" Elise said, turning her gaze away from her computer screen.

"Barb Heinz quit her job in the White House to manage Tom Young's presidential run. It looks like he will run on a green agenda – off fossil fuels, renewable energy, big government, and tons of environmental regulations."

"Good for her. She'll finally get to test if voters actually support the stuff," Elise said.

"It seems like a big step down – she's leaving a powerful job for an uncertain one," the editor said. "Plus, everyone knows she's sleeping with the boss – not the best arrangement if you want to be taken seriously."

"True. Should we call our Washington bureau chief?" Elise proposed. "Maybe he knows more about the circumstances."

Elise dialed the number and put her old friend on speaker. "So, what do you know?" she asked him.

"She was dumped – too toxic, too many skeletons, damaged goods," the Washington reporter said. "And my view is that Tom Young doesn't have a chance, even with all his billions. He's the typical wealthy guy who is clueless about what it takes to succeed in politics. How about we do the definitive piece on Barb Heinz – her rise and fall, the final word."

"Works for me," Elise said. "She burned so many bridges it won't be hard to find people to talk."

"Talk to lots – on the record, please," Mark proposed. "A portrait of an environmental activist – the good, the bad, and the ugly."

After a pensive pause, Elise couldn't resist a final thought. "It's too bad we're so divided about climate change. Mitigation is a big deal that will require all of us to do our part. We need intelligent debate; we need the best thinking to prevail – not shaming or cancelling people who have different views."

Chapter 55

CALGARY, ALBERTA, JUNE 2012

Soon after landing in Calgary, on a breathtakingly beautiful June day, Elise drove to the house in the mountains built by Jordan. Memories of happier times, when she took the same TransCanada highway to meet Jordan in Banff, came back. She felt the same sense of anticipation.

She drove by the same foothills, the cow pastures, the Indigenous lands; under the same big blue sky; inhaled the same pure air. When she reached the foot of the mountains, she took a turn toward a new housing development she had never noticed. Tucked behind a forest, her inherited property was barely visible. She parked in front of a large, wood-and-stone chalet surrounded by a thicket of larches and fir. The crystalline water of a stream hurried downhill nearby.

A brawny builder, who had been waiting for her in the large kitchen, greeted her at the door. "Good morning, Ms. Chamonter," he said, shaking her hand and offering her steaming baked goods he had picked up in town and laid out on the kitchen counter.

"I'm so sorry for your loss," he said. "I first met Dr. Black a few years ago when he hired me to build this place. We spoke often on the phone, and I got to know him a bit during construction. He was a good man. This was his retirement dream. I'm glad you get to enjoy it because what he built here is remarkable. He was very involved in all the details. He wanted to replicate something he saw in Switzerland with your late husband."

"Thank you," Elise said, wondering which building had made such a big impression. Then she noticed the snowy mountain peaks through large picture windows that reminded her of their cabin in Jasper. "I didn't know I would inherit it with my children. Jordan and I, we go way back."

The builder guided her through the home's three floors and proudly showed her the main features: the large bedrooms, the library, the main room with a stone fireplace, the modern kitchen, and a media room in the basement. Elise noticed a carved floor-to-ceiling pole. The builder told her Jordan had commissioned the sculpture from an Indigenous artist on the West Coast.

Elise could feel Jordan's presence, and strangely, that of her late husband. She thought about the first time Julien took her on a hike near the Mont Blanc and was comforted by the musty scent of the forest. The same scent embraced her now.

"When will you be moving in?" the builder asked.

"I am not sure," she said. "It's strange. I already feel like I belong here. I talked to Jordan about owning a place in the Canadian Rockies a long time ago. I guess he made it happen."

She took a few more steps around the main room and met the gaze of a deer grazing outside the window. A second deer joined it. Both looked toward her.

"Oh my God, look at that," she exclaimed.

"There's lots of wildlife around here," the builder said. "It's been fun to be in their company while building this place. But be careful about bears. They hang out here, too, and they think they own the place – which they do."

"I made up my mind. I'll move in next week," Elise said, as the deer walked lazily through the backyard. "I want to be here."

The builder handed her the house keys and his contact information.

"Let me know if you need anything – I live nearby," he said. "Issues will come up, such as how to make all the gadgets work. There are many."

He hopped in the SUV parked out front and drove away.

Elise, now alone, envisioned what the house could be – her sanctuary, the part of Alberta that she would always keep.

She took another tour of the house and pictured her children, maybe her grandchildren, sitting around the stone fireplace in the living room together.

After Jordan's death, the Save the Climate attacks against her subsided, despite her newspaper's continuing coverage of off-oil activism and its expansion to new targets, particularly natural gas. Increasingly, it was a market concern – not because people agreed with it, but because they feared the campaign's tactics. Activists were expanding their offensive to large investors and insurers, the same way they had targeted scientists and journalists who didn't support their agenda.

Elise knew that the financial sector was even less equipped to fight back. It handled big sums of money for big pools of funds for big fees – and was easily fired.

The extensive profile on Barb Heinz had few ripples in the corridors of political power, baffling Mark Wimhurst. He began questioning his news judgement, which had carried him all the way to the pinnacle of the news business, he told Elise during one of their phone calls, which were becoming more frequent.

"Anything that doesn't support a certain viewpoint seems to be ignored," he complained. "If we had done the same profile on the rise and fall of a dishonest oil magnate, politicians would have gone wild. Where are all the critical thinkers? Why are they all scared to express their views? Why are we allowing a small minority to dictate the future of our planet? Where are the defenders of democracy?"

"Society is splitting into two major camps at war with each other," he said. "Readership data doesn't lie. Each camp reads information that confirms its biases, which deepens divisions by exposing readers to only one point of view. The *Journal* is being pushed into the conservative camp because we are seen as providing information to rich investors, despite our history of being politically agnostic and publishing news important to market participants."

The days of journalism as the primary source of information were coming to an end, he complained. Social media was disrupting the information landscape with its own offerings – some true, mostly fake – and had scooped the advertising dollars that the news media had relied on to survive. Advertisers wanted eyeballs, and social media delivered them in spades, particularly by fueling and leveraging rage.

"These new platforms are reaching and influencing immense audiences without the reality checks and balances provided by journalism – at least the journalism I know," he told her. "I don't like where we are going. I don't know how we restore what we had." She listened and nodded, grateful for the insights, sharing the concerns. If she could have seen him at the end of the line, in his tidy office, she would have noticed the grief on his face.

The *Journal*'s Calgary operation was unusually quiet when Elise walked in the next day. She had returned to the city after six months of time out from the climate-change campaign. She had a demoralizing task – to re-evaluate the large *Journal* news presence. Production from the oilsands was still growing but there was widespread exhaustion with the attacks. Money was pulling out and moving into US oil shale and offshore plays that had not been targeted. Diminishing investor interest, and the high costs of running the operation, made it a target for downsizing.

Anticipating the move, tired of being shamed for doing their jobs, four employees left letters of resignation on her desk. They loved the *Journal*, they told her, but even straight-forward coverage of the oilsands resulted in smears they feared would damage their reputation forever. They had young children, mortgages to pay, they said.

Two of the journalists had accepted offers in competing publications that were aligned with the anti-oil cause. Another took a communication job at an oilsands company for double the pay. "At least they're paying me well for the abuse," he explained. A fourth accepted an offer to work for a tech publication. Elise wished them well.

She was on a call with Mark Wimhurst to update him on the staff departures when John Hess walked into her office, stood behind her, and tapped her on her shoulder, startling her.

"Oh, hi," she said, not sure how she felt about seeing him. She wrapped up the call with her boss and turned her attention to John.

"Hi Elise," he said. "It's been a while. I was in the neighbourhood and thought I'd check in."

"It's my first day back. I'm just catching up today," she said.

"Then catch up with me," he said. "Let's go for lunch."

Elise searched for a quick excuse to decline but couldn't come up with one. She had a million reasons to be upset with the oilman, but also felt disconnected after such a long absence from Calgary. She almost felt sorry for the once-fearless billionaire, who looked worn out.

"How did you know I was back?" Elise asked.

"A mutual friend told me. I have a scoop for you."

He suggested a new steak restaurant outside the core and asked her to meet there, rather than drive together. "I'll explain when we get there," he said.

Elise didn't argue. They'd been spied on before and she knew she had to be careful.

The family restaurant was in a strip mall – hardly the venue John would have picked in the past. She found him sitting at a table for two, in a separate room away from windows.

"Are you in trouble?" Elise asked him. "Are the activists still on your tail?"

"No. Maybe. I think I am being watched – my board has become less friendly and would love to find a reason to push me out. Talking to the press – you, in particular – would be such a reason. I'm not sure about environmentalists and whether they're still looking for dirt on me. They have dropped that climate-change lawsuit because it was hopeless – but started new ones over other issues with great fanfare," the oilman disclosed. "The claims are frivolous. They are abusing our courts. As for the rest of the campaign, they've become more cautious since your stories about their foreign funders."

"I'm glad someone here read those stories," Elise said. "We worked hard on them. But we got tepid response from your industry. We got zero feedback on Dr. Jordan Black. I expected some appreciation for his efforts to expose who is behind the campaign, but nothing. Not even a letter to the editor. Disappointing."

"I agree," John said. "I'm not trying to find excuses, but you should know our industry is desperately trying to downplay the controversy because it's hurting our ability to raise money. I've seen it at Aurora. We won't be able to grow our production if this continues. We won't be able to build the pipelines we need. But there are many – including some of the directors on my board, unfortunately – who still believe that it will all blow over and that they must continue to make money while they can."

"You know how I feel," Elise said. "This campaign will shut you down unless you find a way to get in front of it. You need to counter what they say, or you will be damaged for a long time. Hiding is not the answer.

The answer is to tell your truth more aggressively than they are spreading theirs."

"Look, I know you are right, but industry doesn't agree," he said. "They think they know best."

He looked at Elise. He was pleased to be with her again. She thought about the first time they met and was, once again, overwhelmed by his presence. He'd done that to her many times before. He captivated her with his energy and attention when he needed her – but ignored her when she needed him.

A young waitress approached them, and they ordered their meals – Alberta beef, baked potatoes, and salads.

"Who is our mutual friend – the one who told you I was here?" Elise asked.

"Anthony Littlechild. He says hi, by the way. We've become friends. We are working on a deal together. That's the scoop I wanted to talk to you about. I'd like to bring you up to date – off the record – until we're prepared to go public."

"Sure," she said. She hadn't talked to Anthony since Jordan's funeral, though she'd heard from her children he was working on an important project in Alberta. She was glad John was involved with him. Perhaps self-improvement was possible, she thought.

John explained to Elise his efforts to sell some of Aurora's assets to Anthony's new Indigenous company, which he saw as an opportunity to deflect the off-oil campaign, doing the right thing for Indigenous people, and reducing the company's debt. A win-win-win, he boasted, hoping she would get as excited as he was.

"Anthony's group had some preliminary discussions with the board to gauge interest. I would have made the deal in the old days. Unfortunately, I don't have control anymore since our latest acquisition. I didn't think I needed it, since I was planning to retire. Big mistake on my part, to give up control.

"I believe this deal would strengthen the company, but I am worried my board doesn't see the full benefit of such a partnership. They're stuck in the past. They don't understand or won't acknowledge the risks to the company of all this activism. They've solicited other proposals. We could end up with a sale to the highest bidder, instead of a sale that protects our future."

"I see," Elise said, feeling flattered that John trusted her enough to tell her his plans, but not surprised the oilman was once again using her to gain an advantage.

"I'm thrilled about Anthony's proposal," she said. "The more I think about it, the more I see that it would benefit your company. Very strategic. The activists are marketing themselves as defenders of Indigenous rights, as we've discussed before. They'll have a tough time attacking a company that is helping Indigenous people become economically self-sufficient. They can't match that."

Elise then asked the question he was waiting to hear. "So, what can I do for you?"

"We'd like you to become familiar with the offer, Anthony's company and its plans, and give it lots of profile when we are ready to go public."

"John Hess. I am not your PR agency," she said. "It's a decent story, perhaps it will play well as a good news piece amid so much oilsands gloom, but I am not sure I'm the best person to write it since I know Anthony personally. I'll have to talk to my editor and get his approval to go ahead. It will get the consideration and play it deserves."

"Fair enough. It would mean a lot to me," he said.

John didn't complain when Elise paid for the meal.

When John returned to his office, a pair of bankers he knew well were waiting for him in the lobby of his company. They were hauling big leather briefcases, implying something was afoot.

"Do you have a minute?" one of them asked him, looking impatient though they didn't have an appointment.

"Only a minute," John said.

"We'd like to discuss a bid for your midstream assets. There have been suggestions that you are entertaining offers. We have an interested party who has an emotional attachment – and the cash to beat anything else you are looking at."

"Emotional attachment?" John asked, frowning.

"Yes. A deep one," said one of the bankers.

Susan Scott walked into the lobby looking lean and tanned, with fuller cheeks.

"Look who's back from the dead!" John said, smiling. He'd always disliked Susan but had to give her credit for bouncing back.

"Yes, alive and kicking – and ready to make a deal," she said.

John invited the group to his boardroom. He had a duty to his shareholders to listen to the proposal.

The former corporate executive explained she represented a group of investors who were consolidating midstream facilities in the oilsands. They asked her to lead the effort because she knew the business, and the Aurora assets in question, which were largely built by her former company, Plains Exploration.

"Go on. I'm listening," John said.

"We'd like to make an offer to the full board," Susan responded. "But we can give you a taste and would like your support – one and a half billion dollars for the assets that the Indigenous Oilsands Company wants to buy – that's fifty percent more."

John Hess was startled. No one knew – or should have known – about the IOC plan. Someone had betrayed him, someone on his board, he realized.

"You are welcome to talk to the board. We are looking at reducing our debt. That's public knowledge, and that's all I will say," John responded.

Susan walked out of the room with a smirk on her face. The bankers followed her.

The oilman's gut told him there was more to the competing bid and decided he needed to make a move to discourage it.

A few days later, IOC issued a news release to announce a $1 billion offer for a portfolio of Aurora's midstream assets. It wanted the market to know it was ready to get its Indigenous enterprise off the ground and had the financial backing to do it.

Elise and her team worked on a lengthy story about the unprecedented proposal from Canada's Indigenous people and its strategy to become one of the oilsands big players, countering the prevailing narrative that they opposed oilsands development.

But a day later, Susan Scott's group announced a bid for $1.5 billion for the same package.

John Hess worried his big strategy to fend off the Save the Climate campaign against the oilsands was taking the wrong turn. He doubted Anthony Littlechild could match Susan Scott's bid. He worried that if Susan won, she'd be back on the scene, or worse, in his company, causing him angst he didn't need.

The board of Aurora welcomed Susan Scott warmly. They had convened at her request so she could present her offer. Most were impressed. She was good on her feet and knew the business.

"Our team has deep pockets and deep expertise, which means they would be better partners for Aurora than the Indigenous group," she concluded.

"But we want something extra for the half-a-billion premium: three board seats – one for me, two more for my backers," she said, looking around the room, confident that she had won them over.

Only John looked away. He wanted to hide his dislike for her.

After she left, directors deliberated on the best course of action.

"Let's ask the Indigenous group if they will match," said one director.

"I have to say, I feel a lot more comfortable with Susan Scott," said another. "She's ruthless, but she knows the business and the assets. We're better off with people who know what they are doing, since they will be transporting and storing our oil."

John came to the defense of the Indigenous group. "We are not desperate to sell these assets," he said. "The deal with Indigenous Oilsands Company is about building our defense against the off-oil crowd. It's about showing we recognize First Nations as full partners. This will become our strategic advantage, which will resonate with investors who are becoming nervous about the risks of the Save the Climate campaign. This deal is not about getting the most money. It's to protect Aurora's future.

"Besides, we'd be fools to give Susan Scott three board seats. She will run the company into the ground, just like she did at Plains," John argued.

"Look, John, you're turning into a Liberal," said another director. "The number-one goal of our company is to make money. We have no business with the Indians, or with saving the planet. Why should we sell to the Indians at a discount to market value? We don't owe them anything. We paid for these assets at fair market value. Our shareholders would want us to sell at the highest possible price."

"You've lost your touch, John," said another. "You're the founder and CEO of this company. You have an obligation to do what's best for shareholders. Get the Indians to match the bid, and they'll win the assets. Otherwise, spare us the sob stories. We're not a charity."

John looked around the room. He knew he'd lost the support of his board – people he'd counted on for years, who didn't see the dark clouds he saw. Now they questioned his leadership.

"Very well, then," he said. "I will ask the Indigenous group if they want to up their bid. I doubt they can raise the money, but we'll see."

The meeting was adjourned. John felt like he was set up and that Susan Scott had finally beaten him. He called Anthony Littlechild immediately and explained the latest.

"Is there room to raise the bid?" John asked.

"We have some room – but not half a billion. That's a crazy amount. We can't make our business plan work," Anthony Littlechild said, exasperated.

"I'm sorry, man. I wanted this to work. I thought the board would see the wisdom of this partnership," the oilman said, apologetically. "Look. I'll make it up to you. Somehow. There's more than one way to get IOC off the ground."

"What do you mean?" Anthony Littlechild asked.

"I can't explain. Watch for next steps."

The next day, John Hess arrived at his office earlier than usual. He noticed in his assistant's diary that a board meeting to approve Susan Scott's bid had been convened, but he was not invited.

Did she forget to tell him? Was his exclusion an oversight? Was it deliberate? He'd been around boardrooms most of his life and knew a bad omen. He was still the CEO, chairman of the board, and the company's single largest shareholder, even if he no longer had a controlling interest.

He decided to show up uninvited and re-enforce his views about the importance of addressing off-oil activism by forging a significant alliance with Indigenous people.

When John walked into his board room, of the company he built, he found Susan Scott at the head of the large table, in *his* seat, surrounded by people he approved as directors.

"What's this about?" he asked, his blue eyes furious.

The entire board was present. The meeting was chaired by his vice-chairman, a recent appointee he didn't know well who'd been recommended by the company Aurora had just taken over.

"Look, John, we don't want a confrontation, but we felt it was best we move forward with this deal without you in the room," the vice-chair said, showing his country-club smile. "There's too much bad blood between you and Ms. Scott. We believe she's offering us a great deal that will help achieve the company's debt-reduction goals.

"On the other hand," the vice-chairman said, "you have lost the confidence of the board by soliciting that crazy bid from the Indians. We know you orchestrated that whole thing. You're out of your mind."

"I am the founder and CEO of this company, and the largest single shareholder," John shouted. "I took the steps that I felt were necessary to ensure its long-term survival. I'm shocked you don't see that the campaign against our industry is threatening our company."

"John, this is not our first rodeo with the anti-oil crowd," the vice-chairman said. "They're a distraction. Conditions have never been better for the oilsands, and growth will continue. We're in this to make money, not to hand over control of our strategic assets to an Indigenous company that has no expertise in the business. They're not like us."

John couldn't believe what he was hearing. He knew the oilpatch behaved like a private elite club. He'd profited from its closed-door policy his entire career. But he didn't expect the bigotry to go that far.

It finally occurred to him that Susan Scott's bid was organized to push him out.

"This looks like a mutiny," he said, as Susan smiled at him from his own chair.

John walked out of the meeting and, once back in the office he'd so carefully furnished, closed the door, and threw some of his belongings in a cardboard box. At the end of the day, after his staff was gone, he picked up the box and left a letter of resignation on his desk, then walked out of his company for the last time.

He was agitated during his drive home, going over what happened, feeling bitter. But he wasn't done. From his home office, he phoned an investment banker who represented a consortium of Chinese businessmen. They had approached him about acquiring a piece of Aurora. He told the banker they could buy his entire block.

A few hours later, the banker told him they scooped the shares at a premium to market – Aurora stock had just set another record high – without blinking. The Chinese couldn't believe their luck, the banker said. They had become the single largest shareholders in the hottest Canadian oilsands play.

By noon the next day, a news release announcing John Hess's retirement, effective immediately, was issued by Aurora.

It included the usual language about his valuable contributions to the company and to the industry, written by the PR department, with comments attributed to the new vice-chairman, who would soon replace John Hess as chairman of the board.

In addition, the news release announced the deal with Susan Scott's group on the sale of Aurora's midstream assets, and her appointment as vice-chair of the board. Susan Scott would lead the search for a new CEO, the announcement said.

The stock rose on the news, until hedge funds got wind of an alarming rumour – John Hess had sold his entire interest in the company he founded to the Chinese.

By the end of the day, Aurora's stock had fallen off a cliff. No John Hess, more Chinese meddling, more Susan Scott, equalled no premium.

Aurora's new chairman, concerned about the stock's freefall, left frantic messages for John on his cell phone, at his house, at his lawyer's, at his broker's.

"John, for God's sake, you didn't have to resign so abruptly," he said. "We could have worked something out and given you a good send off. Why would you sabotage the company you built? What about your staff? They're in shock. We're all in shock."

As an American, he was alarmed by the Chinese purchase. He expected the Chinese would be difficult shareholders who would likely have unreasonable demands, like seats on *his* board.

John wasn't taking calls. He was midway between the Canadian East Coast and Switzerland, napping in his private jet, pondering his next steps.

He was richer than he'd ever been. He knew he needed to organize his affairs. His fortune needed a safe home, and so did he. Switzerland had not been his cup of tea as a place to live, but he admired its banks and their discretion. It would have to do for a while.

Yet he felt miserable. Wealth meant nothing without power. Now that he had no title and no platform, he was just another rich, single, aging guy yearning for love and appreciation – and unable to give any of it back. How did he get maneuvered out of his own company? Did he get the payback he deserved? He did, he realized. He had created the monster that swallowed him in the end.

His thoughts homed in on Elise, as they always did when he needed solace. She'd left him several messages. He was too distraught to answer her calls, too. He hated looking weak, helpless.

He wanted to talk to her, but not now, not until he got his strength back.

Chapter 56

Elise was writing a story on her laptop while waiting for her lunch in one of Kitimat's handful of eateries, a modest fish restaurant overlooking the water owned by an Indigenous family, when she noticed Erika Bernstein shuffle toward her with one of the reporters who'd just quit the *Journal*.

"Elise?" Erika said.

"Erika," Elise said, trying to suppress the dislike she felt for the activist and everything she represented.

"Hi again, Paul," Elise said to her former colleague. "I see you are not wasting time getting up to speed in your new job."

"And you're not wasting time either," Erika said. She was dressed in green fatigues, a black T-shirt, and a knitted toque. "I heard you were here. Let me know if you need anything – sources, leads, our take on the West Pipeline."

"Thank you, but I am good. Who told you about me?" Elise asked, concerned she was being watched by the campaign.

"We have our sources," Erika said. "We have a growing office in Kitimat. This is a small place – everyone knows each other."

"I see you are making a lot of progress," Elise said. "This community is so divided I barely recognize it. I was here many years ago on another assignment. They were hungry for investment. Now they can't wait to chase it away."

"True. Now they know what they are up against," Erika responded. "We have their backs. Too many corporations have come here and made promises, made their fat profits, then pulled out and left the environment in tatters. We won't let it happen again. The West Pipeline will never be built."

Elise smelled trouble and refrained from engaging. She feared Erika was baiting her to say something that could be used against her. She had a job to do, despite the grief she felt from Jordan's loss, which she blamed on the Save the Climate campaign and its leadership, including Erika Bernstein.

Elise thought about the first time she met Erika in Peru. She'd watched her movement mature into a force for change, like a twister clearing a new path across the landscape, leaving destruction in its wake, promising renewal.

The siege of the South Pipeline had been as well organized as any great military operation, Elise acknowledged. The project had been framed so successfully as a proxy for climate catastrophe that no American politician who needed votes from the growing green movement dared to support it. In the end, multiple excuses were made to delay it through the imposition of new hurdles, even though the project had spent billions meeting – even exceeding – all regulatory requirements.

The oilsands' response was to propose a new pipeline. The West Pipeline from Alberta's oilsands to the West Coast would traverse only Canadian lands, and rescue Canada from the irrational, volatile, polarized politics in the US. At first, Elise didn't expect the Save the Climate playbook to work in Canada. And neither did its oilsands industry.

Elise had thought, naively, that the West pipeline would be a slam dunk.

Canadians were supportive of resource development, since so much of their economy depended on it. They were global environmental leaders, respectful of authorities, hostile to American meddling of any kind.

Besides, small coastal towns like Kitimat, located at the head of the Douglas Channel near Alaska, were begging for investment to replace the struggling forestry sector and to reverse declining populations because of lack of opportunity.

Hoping to be welcomed, the West Pipeline picked Kitimat for its proposed pipeline terminal and deep-water port, where big tankers could load bitumen from the oilsands and ship it to markets in Asia.

But views were changing quickly. Led by Erika, Save the Climate campaigners and their agents moved in like guerrillas, spreading dire warnings of environmental calamity if the West project moved ahead, transforming the quiet coastal community into another off-oil battleground.

"Are you doing a story about growing opposition to the West project?" Erika asked Elise.

"I'm looking into it," Elise responded. "I'm still researching the issue. I don't know yet if opposition is growing, or if it's all noise created by your group."

"Let me know," Erika said. "We're raising awareness about the risks.

"I'm sorry for your loss," she continued, trying to address the tension between them. "I met Dr. Black several times when he was on the board. He was a good man."

"Yes, he was," Elise responded. She was not ready to bury the hatchet with Erika. She finished her food and turned her attention to her former young colleague.

"How's the new job?" she asked him.

"It's been pretty good so far," the young man responded. "They're throwing me in the deep end right away, which is what I want."

"Good for you," Elise said. "Hang in there."

She stood up, signalling she was ready to leave.

Then Erika mentioned there was increasing Canadian political support for her campaign against the West Pipeline, and that Save the Climate had plans to fund candidates who shared its beliefs. She talked about Barb Heinz and her success with the Tom Young campaign.

"Who are you targeting here?" Elise asked, sitting back again, intrigued by the campaign's political angle. She turned on her tape recorder.

"We are supporting candidates at the municipal, provincial, and federal level – even at the party leadership level," the activist responded, hoping to secure a quote in Elise's story.

"If they embrace our goals to shut down fossil fuels, we will help them. We have thousands of supporters in this province alone, ready to put an end to this dirty oil pipeline from Alberta. They don't want it. They see it as an investment in an old and polluting industry that doesn't belong in these pristine environments. Look at this coastline."

Erika pointed to the scene outside the window. "Imagine what a spill of bitumen would do to it and to the Indigenous people who depend on fishing and tourism."

Elise turned off her tape recorder and looked outside to take in the area's beauty. Small fishing boats were trawling the fjord. Tall forests claimed every inch of soil, right up to the rocky coastline. A bald eagle surveyed from above, its wings spread wide, looking for food.

"Yes, it's a beautiful place," Elise agreed. "I can see why so many want to protect it. But they can take care of it themselves, without you telling them what to do."

"I know you don't support what we stand for – it shows in your writing. But young people do. They're scared about how far development is going, about how much we are consuming. They're scared about their own survival, and they want to have a stronger voice."

"I'm a mother. I have an appreciation for how young generations feel. I also believe it's irresponsible to paralyze them with fear," Elise responded. She looked at her watch and stood up again. "See you around," she said, and walked out the door.

Elise drove her rented car to a small office building near the shoreline, showed her ID to a security guard, and walked inside.

The leader of the West Pipeline project greeted her in his office.

"Welcome," said the engineer from rural Saskatchewan, shaking her hand. He was a clean-cut, middle-aged bear of a man who rose in the business because of two valuable qualities: his willingness to take tough jobs and his great sales skills.

He was responsible for getting the project approved by regulators, which required studies of environmental impacts, garnering community support, and engaging with governments. Like so many in Canada's energy business, he got the job done, come hell or high water. He'd also lived and worked in harsh northern environments most of his career – certainly longer than the environmentalists who now lectured him about how to preserve it.

Elise noticed the office's walls were covered with blueprints for the planned tanker terminal, the pipeline route, and the tanker route through the channel and into the ocean. "Our economic impact studies show the project would create ten thousand construction jobs and five hundred permanent jobs," he said. "And that doesn't include all the indirect jobs, like restaurants, hotels, retail, you name it. We are negotiating agreements with most of the First Nations along the route. They'll receive more than one billion dollars in benefits over the life of the project."

"But what about the Save the Climate campaign? Aren't you concerned about their mobilization in this region?" Elise asked.

"We are – but we believe that the majority supports the West Pipeline. They don't talk about it because they're afraid of being targeted. The bottom line is that we were invited here by municipal leaders looking for ways to revive the economy, and here we are, working on a project that they have wanted for years," he said. "When this project goes ahead, it will turn this area into a northern economic powerhouse and create more wealth than it's ever seen. In my view, money always wins the day – and there is plenty to go around from the growth of Alberta's oilsands."

Elise was almost caught up in the optimism.

Then she made her next and final stop that day. She arranged to meet with a group of community residents to hear what they thought. She'd picked them carefully. She wanted residents who were representative of the area and were not on the payroll of either side.

She met her freelance photographer/videographer at the entrance of a downtown banquet hall and was happy to see the large turnout: a retired forestry worker, a student, an Indigenous artist, a mother, a small business owner, a fisherman, a municipal employee.

"Thank you so much for taking the time to meet with me," Elise said after the group arranged chairs in a half circle, facing her. She looked sharp but modest, with her red hair in a ponytail and a khaki outfit to blend in.

"Please help yourself to the refreshments on the side table. You all know the photographer, Eric, who lives here and has freelanced for us for several years. Huge talent. As I mentioned to all of you over the phone, my name is Elise, and I am a writer at the *Journal*. We're based in New York, but we have a large office in Calgary, and we are read by the financial community worldwide. As you know, there's big market interest in the oilsands and its growth prospects.

"I'm working on a feature about the West Pipeline. With the South Pipeline on the rocks, the West Pipeline is the big new hope for oilsands production to reach new markets. The battle against this project is intensifying. I want to know where you stand and why. Eric will be shooting photos and videos that we will publish with the piece in print and on our web site."

The high school teacher, a young man in jeans and a casual jacket, stood up and looked straight at the camera, eager to set the tone.

"Thank you for coming here to hear what we have to say. As far as I am concerned, we don't need this project and it should be stopped right now. Our province is facing too much environmental risk, while Alberta is reaping all the benefits. I teach economics, and I reviewed the benefits estimated by the pipeline proponents. They're a mirage. This project would result in a few dozen permanent jobs and make us dependent for decades on a fuel that causes climate change. In addition, the terminal would be so large it would destroy our way of life. We'd have large tankers sail in and out of our narrow channel daily, getting in the way of other traffic and putting us all in danger if there is a spill. Let's build green energy for our future, not dirty oil pipelines."

The retired forestry worker jumped in. His face was wrinkled, his hands calloused. "Look, Joe, it's easy for you to push away investment. You have a secure government union job that pays for your kayaking and fishing. The rest of us need jobs in the private sector. This town will perish without new investment. Look around. This banquet hall is in a mall with nearly no open stores – they've closed because business is so poor. Every second house in this community is owned by the bank. Our population is declining and aging. Kitimat was built by resource companies. It's what we do. It's who we are. The pipeline will give us something to look forward to. As far as your green jobs, they won't happen here. You have been promising them for years. Where are they?"

"They're coming. The government will help us get them off the ground. We need to regulate fossil fuels out of existence and give green energy the chance it deserves," the teacher responded.

The small business owner, a middle-aged woman in a red uniform, put her hand up to speak. "My name is Candace, and I am delighted to be here." She looked at the schoolteacher. "You don't know what you are talking about. We don't have the luxury of waiting for your green energy. No one is going to invest in green energy in Kitimat anytime soon.

"My store is upstairs. I used to do pretty good business here, selling housewares, when forestry and mining were strong. I used to employ five people. Now I work alone, and I'm lucky if a single client a day walks in the door. If things don't change, I'll have to shut down. The environmentalists tell us we need to stop fossil fuels and are chasing business away. Why us? Why are they targeting our little town? Who are these people who come from far away and tell us how to live our lives? What do they really know about what our town needs, what I need? Why don't they pressure their fancy-pant friends in the big cities to stop driving their big cars, going on their fancy holidays, sailing their big boats up and down our coast, to save the environment?" she asked, wiping back tears. "They want to save the environment at our expense, not theirs."

Elise looked at the Indigenous artist, an elderly man with paint on his hands, who was observing quietly. She asked him what he thought.

"We need new jobs," the man chimed in. "But these are not the right jobs. This heavy oil is trouble. I was young when that big oil tanker ran aground in Alaska, just north of here. The coast was a bloody mess. You can't clean up this bitumen. I don't believe the pipeline company. They're no different than the rest. They make lots of promises to get our support, but when something goes wrong, they hide behind their lawyers and we are on our own, left to deal with the consequences. If they contaminate our water, we lose our salmon. We can't live without our salmon."

The municipal employee stood up. He looked nervous.

"My name is Gus. I'm a garbage collector. I worry that if our tax revenue continues to decline, I will be laid off. Something has got to give. Even the union can't protect all of us. The pipeline would save us. If it doesn't go ahead, it will send a message that we're not open for business."

The high school student, a spectacled, pink-haired girl in shorts, put her hand up to speak next. "I hate this place. People are fighting all day, every day, over this pipeline. I'm leaving as soon as I graduate. I don't want a resource job. These industries are too unstable – boom, bust, boom, bust. My dad worked in forestry and was unemployed half the time, and the rest of the time he was drunk. I want a stable job, and I want to stop thinking about this pipeline. I'm fed up with all this."

The fisherman, who was in his fifties, tanned, and impatient to say his piece, pulled a folded map of Douglas Channel from his pocket, opened it and laid it flat on a table.

"See this? It's one of the toughest coastlines to navigate. We deal with heavy fog, nasty snowstorms," he said. "Big tankers won't be able to safely sail in these waters. And if they run aground, it will be catastrophic. We're too far north to organize a rescue and clean-up operation quickly. And what about earthquakes? We're long overdue, and if one happens, that pipeline will break like a toothpick. I'm opposed to this project. These people from Alberta don't know what they are up against. They don't know our ocean."

Elise then turned to the mother, a woman in her mid-fifties. The woman looked at the group and stood up.

"My family has lived in this community for two generations. I have never seen it so divided. This pipeline would bring good-paying jobs and stability. The risks are so overblown it makes me sick. How's the pipeline different from the railway that crosses our mountains loaded with oil? How's it different from mining operations all over the North? How are oil tankers different from the cruise ships that sail up and down our West Coast?

"We need development. We need an economy. This place has never been so depressed. The environmentalists are chasing everyone away – forestry, mining, oil and gas, cruises. They want us to live in a park, and protect the rainforest and the bears, while they enjoy their carefree lifestyles and their tech jobs in the big cities."

The mother pulled her wallet out of her purse and showed the group pictures of her four children. "They're all gone because there is no opportunity here. They're good, hard-working kids. What are they supposed to do? The environmentalists come and go; we have to live with the consequences of their campaigns."

As the debate continued, tempers flared.

"Your children are leaving because of you – you should have held onto your husband instead of kicking him out," the fisherman said.

"You're opposing the pipeline because you want them to give you money," the mother responded.

"Oh my God. Stop," the teenager said, and stormed out of the meeting.

The fisherman jumped in again. "Look, dirty oil isn't going to save anyone. Alberta needs to stop pushing this stuff down our throat. They're filthy rich, and they are squandering their money. For what? Selling their oil to China? When is enough, enough?"

Elise tried to take back control of the debate, but it was too late to end it amicably.

The pipeline opponents left in a rage and slammed the door. The pipeline supporters continued to talk between themselves, like a sad support group.

"I can't believe that we finally managed to attract this project and we are facing this ugly battle," the retired forestry worker said. "I'm very uncomfortable with all this bad publicity. If the pipeline fails, we're dead."

Then the shopkeeper turned to Elise. "What do *you* think?" she asked. Everyone looked at her.

"The debate you are having is happening everywhere," Elise said. "The stakes are much bigger here because you would house the end point of the pipeline and decisions have to be made now. You must choose between having good-paying jobs now – or sacrificing your wellbeing so the world enjoys a clean environment in the future. It's a lot to give up.

"I believe it's possible to have both by ensuring the pipeline is safe and that all risks are mitigated. Pipeline opponents don't want that. They're not in the business of compromise. They see only one solution – eliminating fossil fuels from the planet, starting with the oilsands because they are the latest oil source to come to the market.

"I will cover this issue fairly and represent all points of view," Elise continued. "However, my personal belief is that narrow thinking is wrong. I believe that climate change affects all of us and solutions need to come from all of us. The best ideas need to prevail – not just the ones imposed by a small group.

"Wind and solar energy don't work everywhere. They're certainly not great solutions in cold places like this one, where winters are harsh and distances big. I believe climate change progress cannot come at the expense of our standard of living or our energy security. We need wealth to invest in this energy transition. We need a strong economy and open minds, and to encourage innovators. This shouldn't be a polarizing debate. It should be a unifying debate.

"We certainly cannot single out certain communities – whether it's Kitimat or Fort McMurray, or even Alberta as a whole – to take the fall so others can keep doing what they are doing and claim they won the war on climate change."

The group peppered Elise with questions about her views on the South Pipeline, the oilsands, the Save the Climate campaign. She shared the facts as she knew them. Satisfied that she had heard a variety of views, she thanked the participants. She gathered her things and walked out to her rented car.

Once outside, Elise noticed one of her tires was flat. An ugly line was keyed on the car's door. She looked around but saw no one. She suspected it was the handiwork of one of the pipeline opponents, perhaps even one of the participants in her discussion. Why? she asked herself. They just can't help themselves, she told herself. They must make it personal.

Elise called the car rental company to let them know about the incident. She left the town feeling sorry for the pipeline supporters. Erika Bernstein was right about one thing, Elise concluded. The West Pipeline would never be built.

Chapter 57

CALGARY, ALBERTA, MARCH 2013

Elise couldn't pinpoint the precise moment when the Alberta oilsands became marked as the global climate's enemy No. 1. But she figured the idea of stranding Alberta's deposits became more acceptable when Canadian politicians took up the anti-oilsands cause to bolster their chances of gaining or retaining power. The off-oil politicians spoke about the imperative for Canada to be on the right side of history and establish itself as the world's climate change leader. They downplayed the costs of such a sweeping energy production and consumption transition, or the implications of suppressing a large and historic Alberta-based sector, and all that was connected to it: services, academia, the arts, non-profit organizations, municipal finances, housing, office space, tradition, culture – and Alberta's dignity.

Instead of savouring its success, the Save the Climate campaign pushed even harder. Sympathetic politicians responded with ambitious strategies to fast-track the transition to renewable energy, tighten the leash on oilsands operations, reform regulatory agencies so no more oilsands or pipeline projects would ever be built.

Yet those anti-oil politicians still collected Alberta's oil wealth through heavy taxes and ignored that suppression of the oilsands would have no material impact on the global climate; all the while sowing the seeds of Canada's breakup, as alienated Albertans started to organize to separate from the rest of the country.

Activism against the activists took off too, and confrontations erupted everywhere.

Elise watched as anti-pipeline protests across Canada were met with pro-pipeline protests; social media campaigns by activists were met with counterattacks by outraged oil workers; Indigenous groups disillusioned by unfulfilled Save the Climate promises switched sides and embraced opportunities offered by pipeline and by oil and gas companies. Albertans refused to travel through Canadian provinces that opposed its oil, and international tourists boycotted Alberta because of its dirty oil. Lawsuits on every aspect of the oilsands industry and its products proliferated, burdening the courts.

The oilsands industry, angry about the opposition to the South and West pipelines, created new proposals for more pipelines – the East Pipeline, a second West Pipeline, and a second South Pipeline, to dilute Save the Climate resources.

Meanwhile, oilsands producers loaded more and more of their oil on trains, which had fewer regulatory restrictions, but crossed highly populated communities and generated more greenhouse gases than pipelines.

The destruction of Canadian wealth was in the hundreds of billions because railway transportation was more expensive than pipelines, Canadian oil prices were discounted due to insufficient pipeline capacity, defending projects before regulators in the face of so much opposition increased costs.

While there was no physical violence, the clash between the anti-oilsands camp and the oilsands industry and all it represented was as psychologically damaging to Alberta as a civil war. Feelings of betrayal, shame, isolation, and anger became widespread. Once an economic leader, Alberta lost its confidence.

John Hess's mysterious retreat had ripples far beyond Aurora. If the oilsands were no longer good for the top oil pioneer, Elise heard again and again, they weren't good for the industry's other big guns either, so they took their money quietly off the table and redeployed it abroad.

The changes impacted the *Journal*'s Calgary operation – and Elise's own career plans. Thin trading activity and waning investor interest forced her to reduce Calgary staffing even more. Reporting on the never-ending conflict was repetitive and professionally unsatisfying. She had additional discussions with Mark Wimhurst about returning full time to the newsroom in New York, but there had been no progress. Elise was preparing to jump to a new employer. Other large news organizations that were developing online platforms had responded to her overtures, and she expected an offer soon.

She was collecting a few remaining items from her Calgary apartment to move to her cherished mountain home when her boss phoned her.

"Hi Elise. How's the great white North?" Mark asked cheerfully.

"Hi Mark. Thanks for calling me back. I'd like to resume our discussion about our Calgary operation and plans for the future – particularly my future," she said.

"Yes. I suspected that. I know I have asked you to be patient many times. I apologize for the slow progress, but I think that patience has paid off."

"Really?" she asked.

"Yes, really. The board moves very slowly. But they agreed with me that it's time to put in motion my transition to retirement and to announce my replacement."

"Oh my God, Mark. I heard you were pondering retirement, but I didn't think it would happen so quickly. What's that about?"

"Elise, I have been ready for a while. I'm sixty-seven. My wife wants to go back to London to be with our children and grandchildren – we have a fourth grandchild on the way, and we miss being with them."

"I'm happy for you, for your growing dynasty," Elise said, wishing she'd tried harder to know her boss – her first real mentor – while he'd taken so much interest in her career and in her life.

"The good news is that they want you to replace me," Mark said. "I'll stick around for a while to help get you up to speed, which I am sure you will do in no time. I will stay on as an advisor to the board."

Elise was so surprised she felt faint. She sat down. "I'm shocked," she said. "I honestly didn't know this was in the works. This is amazing news. I'm so grateful for your support."

"Yes. It's good news for everyone," he replied.

"Why me?" she asked. "I have been away for such a long time. Out of sight, out of mind, right?"

"The board knows you well and has great admiration for you and your work. We've been watching you for years. You were the first on my list, and the board accepted my judgement that you have all it takes to do the job.

"They wanted a woman – you'll be our first female editor in chief, and it's about time. You rose through the ranks because of merit, and you have experience with our new social media competitors.

"They wanted someone who knows how to grow the business. You have been loyal to the *Journal* and showed remarkable resilience. Elise, no one else matches your qualifications. I can't think of anyone who is a better fit for the role."

Many thoughts rushed through her head – the start date, her children, her friendships in Alberta, her Calgary staff, her home in the mountains, the future of the oilsands industry. Her other job opportunities. John Hess.

"Look, I know it's a lot to take in," the editor said. "We'll discuss the details in the coming days."

"I'm very grateful for everything you have done for me," Elise said. "I know I haven't expressed it enough. My life has been difficult since my husband passed away. I moved to Calgary to get away from memories. I was prepared to coast for a while, put survival first. I had no idea it would evolve into such a challenging job, such a long-term commitment."

"Things are never what they seem," he said. "You became a better journalist by being away from group think and from office politics. You have been tested in many ways and you came out on top."

"Is this – my appointment – going to be announced?" Elise asked.

"Yes. We will announce it Friday morning. We need an updated photo of you – one that you are happy with. Congrats, Elise," Mark said. "Goodnight."

Elise was so overwhelmed that she wanted to share her news with someone. She decided to wait before calling her children. It was late in New York. She tried one of her Calgary friends, but there was no response. She rarely felt lonely, but this was one of those times. She had no one to talk to about the best thing that had ever happened in her career.

John Hess came to mind again. She knew she owed him some credit for her success, especially during her early days in Calgary, when he shared with her so much information about his industry. She hadn't showed much appreciation to him, either. Elise suspected something awful had happened to him at Aurora, but the details remained unclear. He didn't return her calls after he left Calgary. She had stopped trying. Perhaps she'd judged him harshly without knowing what he was up against.

Even Anthony Littlechild wouldn't talk about him, though she'd heard rumours that John was involved with his company in some capacity. Anthony's Indigenous company was making a name for itself as a consolidator of assets across the oilsands, for a lot less than Aurora sold theirs.

She met Anthony for lunch, occasionally. He shared with her the gossip he knew about. But Anthony was still an outsider, not plugged in like John.

Aurora, on the other hand, was skidding. A CEO who was new to the business was appointed. Susan Scott was vice-chair of the board, but everyone knew she was running the show. Old habits die hard, Elise thought. Some of its talented executives resigned and sold their shares.

Elise thought of Julien. She missed him a lot. She found a bottle of champagne she'd been saving and sat down on her couch. He would have been proud of her. She imagined his face. He kept her company as they celebrated together, like old times.

Two days later, she saw John Hess sitting alone in a private booth, eating dinner at the pub where she first heard his name: O'Reilly. Like her, he was sipping Chianti, perusing his smartphone, looking impatient. He didn't notice her or her group from the *Journal* – or he pretended not to.

Elise and her co-workers were celebrating her promotion and her imminent departure from Calgary. It was dark and after deadline. Wine and beer were flowing freely, a bluegrass band was playing in the corner, powdery snow was falling. Word about the celebration had gotten out. Journalists at other publications were walking in, looking for her. They shook her hand, congratulated her, happy for her big break, aware of her augmented stature and hiring power in the Big Apple. Public relations staff arrived in groups, carrying little gifts for her, picking up liquor tabs.

"Will you be based in New York?" a young female reporter asked. "Big fan. I took a job here because I loved your writing."

"When will you move?" asked a competitor, an older reporter who'd been jealous of Elise.

A public relations executive approached her with a gift-wrapped package.

"From our company. Congratulations and thank you for all you did for our industry," he said. "And don't you dare return this gift – we guarantee it's worth less than fifty dollars. It's a souvenir from an Indigenous nation in the oilsands. Made especially for you."

Another public relations executive handed her a bottle of Scotch. He swore it was the cheap kind – even if it didn't look like it.

"From our team," he said. "I hope your departure doesn't mean the *Journal* will leave us, too."

Elise smiled and promised that her newspaper would be on the scene if there was news to cover.

She was feeling good when she took her leave, just before midnight. She was grateful for the nice send off. She wished she'd heard more kind words when she was on the job, taking so many blows, feeling like she carried the world's weight on her shoulders.

Elise looked around the restaurant before exiting it. John Hess was no longer there. She was disappointed but relieved. She wouldn't have known what to say if they'd come face to face.

Then he appeared suddenly outside the restaurant, through a curtain of falling snow.

"Hi Elise," he said, startling her. He asked her if she needed a ride. Another planned chance encounter, she thought, and smiled.

"You're back," she declared. "How about you walk me to my hotel? I just moved out from my place."

"Sure," he said. "I saw you in there. There were too many reporters, and I didn't want to intrude."

She noticed his skin was tanned, which made his eyes sparkle more in the dark. He looked well rested and was expensively, but casually, dressed.

"I see you're still worried about hanging out with the wrong crowd," Elise said.

"I apologize. I'm in a delicate situation. I don't want to create gossip. I don't want to be hounded by reporters. But I still wanted to congratulate you on your promotion. It's well-deserved and I am very happy for you," he said.

"Thank you, John," Elise said. "I'm ready for a change and I want to be with my children. I have learned to love Alberta and I will continue to spend time here. But my job is done, and it's time for someone else to be in the trenches – someone who can look at the oil and gas sector with fresh eyes."

"Does that mean you will no longer write about it?" he asked.

"That's right. My last piece appears tomorrow. I'll miss the writing – but not the writing about the conflict of the last few years. It's been exhausting, demoralizing."

They were walking side by side, enjoying the spring snow and the barely above-freezing temperature.

John said he missed the good old days in Calgary, building its oil and gas industry, providing employment for so many people. He said he missed feeling good about his business, about saying what was on his mind. He missed his friends. He lived in Switzerland part-time, he revealed.

He told her he was back in Calgary to finish moving to a new place, a condo that was his new base in the city.

"Why Switzerland?" Elise asked. "It's a beautiful place. My late husband was Swiss. The grandparents are Swiss. We spent a lot of time there. But it's a long way from Alberta."

"It is. But it's a safe place and it has mountains. I'll fill you in some day. I have a favour to ask – or a wish I hope you will consider," the oilman said.

"I'm not a writer anymore," Elise responded. "I can't promote your next venture."

"Sorry," he said, looking at her like he'd done so many times before. "This is not about a write-up. This is about you. I'd like to know if I can be with you, with Elise, now that we no longer have to worry about our jobs. I feel we have unresolved issues."

"Like the oilsands?" she asked.

"Like the oilsands," he responded.

He took her face in his hands and kissed her like not a second had passed since they first felt that connection outside the same restaurant many years ago.

Elise didn't resist. It was past midnight, and the street was deserted. She couldn't think of anything appropriate to say. She welcomed his attempt to connect on a new level.

Both were in the autumns of their lives – she in her mid-fifties, he in his mid-sixties. Both had been high achievers. Both were single. Both had complications and obligations. Both had set aside opportunities to explore their mutual attraction because they had put their jobs first.

"Are you getting a strange sense of *deja vu*?" Elise asked him, her heart hoping for more, her head telling her no.

"Yes," he said. "When I heard about your going-away celebration – don't ask me who told me, please – in the restaurant where we first got to know each other, I had to come by and ask you to give me – us – a chance. I hope I don't look too pathetic. I didn't know what else to do. I don't want to lose you."

"John, I'm glad you took the initiative. I was prepared to give us a chance many times, but I gave up," Elise responded. "You had other priorities and hurt me a lot. I feel it's too late now. My days here are numbered. I will have my hands full in New York."

John had anticipated her response. "Elise, I screwed up. You have every right to feel the way you do. But please, meet me here Saturday at six p.m.," he said, giving her a napkin with an address scribbled on it and a key. "I'll take care of dinner."

"I'll have to think about it," Elise responded, unsure what to do.

"I'll wait for you. If you don't come, I'll understand," John said.

When they arrived at her hotel he kissed her again on her fore-head, opened the main door, and walked away through the thickening blowing snow.

Elise decided to see him not because she needed him, but because she didn't.

It wasn't an easy decision. She'd put integrity – personal and professional – ahead of her own feelings since Julien. She was finally able to resolve the irrational attraction she felt for John Hess since the day they met. Deal with it once and for all, she told herself.

It helped that there were no longer rules to break, no gossip to fear, no career implications. No one in New York would care about John Hess. Wall Street had bigger fish to fry, different elites, different gossip. Billionaires were a dime a dozen.

She realized – accepted – that she had been blessed to love three men in her life. Her love for her late husband, Julien, had been unconditional, complete, and uncomplicated. They gave each other everything. They were each other's fans. They grew up together. No one had supported her as much or knew her as much. Their lives had been so connected they'd become one. It was the purest kind of love. The best and longer-lasting love. That's why his loss had been so destabilizing, like the loss of half of herself. That's why she'd found it so difficult to find someone else. The void he left in her was too great.

She'd loved Jordan, too, but for a different reason: They needed each other. But she couldn't meet his expectations and he couldn't meet hers. They were like mismatched gloves. Elise felt they could have come to a resolution, found areas of mutual interest. But his suicide ended it all, and she was hurt that he didn't give her a chance. Jordan had been too damaged to try. Even her attempts to rescue him could not overcome his loss of self-esteem.

And then there was John Hess. Did she love him? Yes. In a strange, irrational way, she acknowledged, because of his intellect and his energy. Did he love her? If he did, it was a private love, a selfish love, more like an obsession, she thought. He wanted her attention and admiration. The big question was whether there was still room for John in her own future.

It was evening when Elise drove to the address scribbled in the white napkin for her Saturday evening date. It was the same napkin John had picked up in a coffee shop during one of their many meetings, with her lipstick smudged on it. He must have planned this for years, she thought, shaking her head.

She'd read about John's new building in the local media – a just-finished complex on the edge of downtown, on the banks the river, that had become the new place to be for the shrinking oil elite. She parked her car in one of the reserved underground spots and used the key he gave her to access an elevator that lifted her to his penthouse. She was thankful for the privacy.

The elevator doors opened on a grand, cream-marbled lobby. Everything looked opulent – the modern furniture, the Indigenous art, the handmade glass lights, the blooming white orchids. He'd recreated the feel of his office, she realized.

"Elise?" he shouted from the vast stainless-steel kitchen.

"Hi John," she said, noticing the dining room table was set for two. He looked younger, in black jeans and white shirt, with his sleeves rolled up above his elbows.

Food prepared by his personal chef was warming up in two ovens. Champagne was chilling in an ice bucket.

"You must have known I was coming before I did," she said.

"I took a chance," John said. "I am glad you came. I would have been crushed if you didn't."

He looked at her with approval. Her red hair was loose, touching her shoulders. She wore a simple black dress with knee-high leather boots and a strand of white pearls she'd bought herself early in her career, before she met Julien.

He touched and admired the flawless pearls, embraced her, and kissed her on the mouth.

She noticed new wrinkles around his eyes, more loose skin on his neck, some extra pounds around his waist.

He noticed she looked tired and tense.

Yet they also both saw the person they first met and for whom they felt a strange, enduring bond.

They caught up, talking about her new job and the rumours on Wall Street, his new life in retirement, his tax issues. They gossiped about people they both knew or read about. Soon they felt comfortable with each other, even with their decades of baggage – some good, so much bad.

John showed her his place – the views of the city and of the mountains, the large cellar stacked with rare wines, his floor-to-ceiling library. They climbed a staircase to the large rooftop terrace and watched a Chinook wind blow in from the west.

"So, this is how the other half lives," she said. "Impressive."

"I'm sure you're not doing too bad yourself," he said. "It's hard to be more elitist than the chief editor of the top financial newspaper on Wall Street."

"How long have you lived here?" Elise asked.

"A couple of months. I'm still waiting for some furniture. I bought the condo from the developer as soon as he got the permits to go ahead. I still have lots of business in the city, and I intend to live here when I am in town."

"And the rest of the time?"

"Geneva, London – New York City?" he asked, looking at her, hoping for an invitation to see her in her turf.

"And are you done with oil?" Elise asked, changing the subject, unable to suppress her reporter's curiosity.

"I'm not sure. I am working with Anthony Littlechild on some interesting deals. Thank you for the introduction, by the way. He's an outstanding young man and I like what he's doing. We've got big plans. We're learning from each other."

They returned to the dining room and celebrated her promotion. Then they dug into their meal, slowly, savouring every bite, feeling years of tension melt.

John took Elise's hand and led her to his bedroom. He stripped away her clothes, she stripped away his, and they kissed and embraced, experiencing a moment so mystical they merged each other's minds.

"I have never felt like this before," John said as they were lying in bed. "I didn't know it was possible."

"Neither have I," Elise said.

"Business changes people, especially at your level," she continued. "You become transactional in everything you do. You don't trust. You feel the need to protect yourself at any cost. You are afraid of being vulnerable. You are afraid of breaking the rules – real and imagined. Loving someone deeply means letting go, trusting, sharing."

John looked at her again, absorbing her wisdom. "How about you, Elise?" he asked. "What held you back?"

"If you are asking me what's held me back from you, I had many reasons," she said. "I sensed you liked me, but also that you weren't willing to fight for me. I felt you picked self-interest over love, which turned me off. I felt you had many other priorities, and that in that long list I was dead last. No one wants to feel that insignificant. No one likes to feel like they're a tool in someone else's agenda. That's how I often felt about you. That you were using me.

"But there were other reasons, too. My late husband and I had a wonderful marriage. I didn't think I could ever love deeply again. A part of me didn't want to move on. I learned to cherish my own company."

"You were not entirely wrong about me," John admitted. "For that, I apologize. If I looked like I was transactional with you, it was because I didn't know how to relate to you. I have always struggled to build relationships, especially with smart women. There was the complication that you're press. I didn't know how to get close to you, make you a part of my life, other than in a professional way. My marriage was a sham. My various affairs – they're not exactly a secret – were to fill the emptiness I have felt all my life. I wish I had children, but I don't. I have many regrets, and not finding a way to be with you is my biggest one."

It was midnight.

Elise prepared to take her leave.

"Stay," he pleaded.

"I want to, but I can't," Elise said. "I'm overwhelmed. I need to think about all this."

"What's next for us?" he asked.

"I don't know," Elise said, her eyes watering, caressing his face, seeing the real John Hess for the first time. "I have a lot of packing to do. I'll have my hands full when I get back to New York. I'll have to measure up because everyone will be watching. I want us to work, but I can't see a way forward."

"The shoe is finally on the other foot," John said. "It serves me right. You in the powerful job, worried about what the world thinks. Me on the outside looking in, ready for love. My timing is awful."

Elise rose, showered, got dressed. John put on a robe. They kissed again.

Elise told him she was flying back to New York mid-week. She asked him whether he was headed back to Europe.

"I need to tie up loose ends here," he said. "I need to talk to some old friends."

Elise nodded without asking questions. She pulled the condo key out of her purse and put it in his hand.

They kissed again. This time it was a long, sad kiss, because they were both aware that they might never see each other again.

"John, you figured out very complicated things before. Fight for me," she pleaded.

Chapter 58

Before dawn on an early June day, John boarded a commercial flight in Calgary, bound for Fort McMurray. He still owned his private jet but left it in the hangar. He was wealthy but reluctant to show it. That was the new Alberta way: displays of oil wealth were no longer desirable.

John could have walked away from the oilsands and never looked back, like so many executives who had cashed out at the top of the market and retired in warmer climates. He could have focussed on Elise and enjoyed the good life. They spoke often – sometimes on the phone, sometimes in person. He flew to New York; she spent long weekends in Alberta's mountains. He liked being around her and wanted to make up for lost time. They kept their relationship private.

John liked that Elise encouraged him to look at his life, at himself, from a new perspective. His departure from Aurora had left too many things unsaid, too many said too much, she told him. Questions lingered about what happened – why he handed over the company to a new group, why he cashed out so abruptly, why he abandoned the industry he helped build. He didn't want to run away anymore. He wanted to be proud and to be judged on his record. He wanted the oilsands to survive and thrive. He wanted Aurora to do well – even without him. He wanted a good legacy.

John entered the aircraft's cabin and took an aisle seat beside a tall man bent over his computer. He didn't miss those stressful days – always on the road, always working, always anxious about the next operational setback and the next market trend. The flight was packed with oilsands workers. There were many Newfoundlanders returning to Alberta after a two-week break. They were loud, tired, half drunk, happy. Work in the oilsands supported extended families in their depressed province. John had employed many and loved their humour. They worked hard under the harshest conditions. Alberta's oilsands' industry could not have been built without them, he thought.

"John Hess?" his seat mate asked.

"Jim? Jim McKinnon?" John replied, barely recognizing him. He looked older, his hair thinning, his face tense. "How are you? Still working at Aurora?"

"Yes. Still there," Jim said. "Running oilsands operations. But it's not the same place since you left."

"Sorry to hear that," John said, feeling guilty that his departure had let people down – people who'd supported him again and again so he could succeed. "You're good at what you do. You must be in great demand."

Jim shook his head. "Things are not well in this industry," he said, confirming what John already knew. "Our costs are out of control. No one is hiring. We are producing too much oil. Pipelines are full and we can't get it to market. Something's got to give, and it's not going to be OPEC. Aurora is in over its head. Our board is lost. And to top it off, this anti-oilsands campaign is pounding our stock price and scaring away investors. It's not a pretty picture.

"I'd like to pack it in, but I can't," Jim continued. "My retirement savings are tied up in Aurora stock."

John wanted to share with his former employee how he was pushed out the door, that he'd foreseen at least some of Aurora's problems, that the new team had refused to accept the obvious. But he couldn't. He wouldn't. He was proud. He would not betray his own company, even if it had betrayed him.

"Everything goes in cycles," John said, hoping the old cliché would reassure his former employee.

"What are you up to these days?" Jim asked, sensing John's reluctance to talk about his old workplace. There had been rumours that he'd been pushed out in a palace coup. He didn't believe, at first, that John Hess could be outmaneuvered. Eventually, he accepted them.

"I'm helping some friends. Have you heard of Indigenous Oilsands – IOC?" John asked.

"Of course. They're taking over Fort McMurray and stealing our workforce," Jim said. "Anthony Littlechild is a smart guy – getting up to speed fast. We should have partnered with them, not Susan Scott. We're paying dearly for that mistake."

"Yes. Anthony is doing a great job. Stay tuned because he's just getting started," John said.

The conversation turned to Susan Scott. Jim reminded his old boss he'd left Plains because of her, which put him in a difficult position at Aurora. John nodded but didn't reveal his own challenges. He didn't like badmouthing people, especially executives he'd worked with. Whatever happened in boardrooms stayed in boardrooms, he believed.

They gossiped about companies they both knew, stock prices, political events.

The sun, which had been up for much of the late-spring night in the northern region, brightened even more by the time they landed at Fort McMurray airport, which was newly expanded to accommodate the growth in traffic. The two men exchanged contact information and walked together through the terminal.

John was about to exit to pick up a rented car when he recognized Chief Anne, Anthony, and another Indigenous man he didn't know. They approached him like old friends. He hadn't expected a welcoming party. He was thankful for the gesture.

"Welcome to Fort McMurray," Anthony said, hugging him enthusiastically, leading him to a new black SUV waiting nearby. "We can afford to drive you now."

The Indigenous driver took the wheel, Chief Anne sat in the front passenger seat, and John and Anthony sat in the back. The scene would have been unthinkable a few years back, John thought. He felt more valued than he'd ever been.

They quickly got down to business.

"I'm nervous about the glut of oil piling up in the world," said Anthony, who had become IOC's President and CEO.

"Oilsands production is growing, oil from US shale is soaring, and the old guard in the Middle East is threatening a price war to protect its market share against the new entrants like us," he continued, looking at John. "If our industry stumbles, our Indigenous company could fail – or at least fail to become the Indigenous force I envisioned."

"I am worried too, but there are ways to protect yourselves until it blows over," John responded. He'd helped IOC informally with mentoring and strategic advice. He knew Anthony needed more of him now, and he was prepared to listen.

John was pleased that IOC had made big progress. It owned tank farms, pipelines, and other businesses that provided services to oilsands developers. It employed thousands of people – some Indigenous, some from all over Canada, some from around the world. Anthony was a media darling. IOC's story was encouraging other bands to embrace resource-related businesses. Young Indigenous men and women were enrolling in university, inspired by his success.

After losing the Aurora opportunity, the upstart had pursued the acquisition of similar assets in other companies. It took longer to assemble a good portfolio, but banks keen to tap the Indigenous economy had been supportive. The assets generated good and stable cash flow.

When they arrived at IOC's just-completed headquarters near Fort McMurray, John gave it an approving look. The log building had a sunny atrium and was surrounded by forest. Indigenous art from local bands was displayed throughout. A plaque credited the government for its generous support. John Hess's financial help was left unsaid. He'd paid for most of the building, but as in the past, he asked to remain anonymous. He was proud that he'd contributed to the success of the new company. He wished Aurora had seen what he saw in these Indigenous people.

"We are proud of our new home," Anthony said. "It's become a meeting place and a tangible example of what we can do when we take charge of our lives."

John was led to the largest boardroom. A dozen Indigenous men and women were already waiting. They were the same people who had supported the establishment of IOC when he was still in charge of Aurora.

"Nice to see you again," said one who was wearing long braids. "You kept your word."

"All this couldn't have happened without you," said another who was sporting a cowboy hat and an ill-fitting business suit.

John smiled and nodded.

Anthony called the meeting to order. "Thank you for travelling here today. We asked John to join us for an update on our progress – and to thank him in person for all his contributions. We wouldn't be here without his financial support and especially without his guidance. It's the reason we would like to formalize his role."

Anthony turned to his mentor. "John Hess, we'd like you to be the chairman of Indigenous Oilsands Company," he said. "We know it's a big commitment. You don't have to decide now. Please think about it."

"I'm flattered and surprised," John said. "I'll consider it, for sure. I need to weigh the implications, such as whether I can dedicate the time." John had had no expectations – yet the idea intrigued him. He promised to respond quickly.

"There are at least three reasons we need someone of John Hess's caliber to guide us through the next phase of our company," Anthony continued, hoping to sway him to agree.

"The first one is that more and more Indigenous communities want to join IOC and share in our success. They see the benefit of what we do and would like to be involved in even more ambitious projects. For example, there's appetite for owning pieces of one or more of the proposed oilsands pipelines, or in developing of our own oilsands leases.

"The second is that we need to prepare for a downturn. The oilsands boom is showing some cracks. It could destroy everything we have achieved if we don't make ourselves resilient.

"The final reason has to do with the environmental lobby. It's the toughest one to address. They are standing in the way of our success. We believe it's time to look for a compromise. In their quest to suppress the oilsands, they are suppressing our aspirations to improve our lives. We need a negotiator like John Hess to help us find a way forward."

The young Indigenous CEO invited Chief Anne to provide an update on discussions with new Indigenous partners. She'd been his most capable executive at IOC. Like all other chiefs around the table, she supported John's chairmanship.

Chief Anne spoke proudly of the Indigenous leaders who'd contacted her, wanting to find out more about the company and its plans.

"Indigenous communities are waking up," she said. "They're abandoning the Save the Climate campaign and looking at what we do because we offer hope and a way toward financial independence.

"In contrast, the anti-oilsands campaign binds them to a new form of dependence that rewards a few who are paid to be their props in a cause that they have no input over. I speak from experience. We're the true environmentalists, the ones who have been stewards of our lands for millennia. But we need prosperity to achieve our full potential. We cannot be left behind again. We can participate in the resource economy and use our traditional knowledge to protect the environment and manage the risks at the same time."

The other Indigenous leaders nodded and applauded.

"How many bands are prepared to join IOC?" John asked.

"We're in discussions with about fifty right now. The challenge is to bring them onboard without diluting existing partners too much, but we are working on that."

The discussion moved to ensuring IOC's long-term financial future.

John suggested increasing the company's lines of credit. Anthony raised the possibility of a public offering.

"Imagine that," he said. "We could raise capital in the public markets and keep acquiring assets on behalf of our Indigenous partners."

"Another option is to find a partner," John said. "Just because Aurora didn't work out, others might see the merit."

They agreed to hire advisors to explore all options.

Anthony knew the final topic would be contentious. He argued that IOC needed to lead discussions for a compromise between the oilsands industry and the green lobby.

Chief Anne was skeptical. "They will never compromise," she said. "They will take anything they can negotiate from our side and then continue with their hard line on the oilsands. The campaign is a cash cow. They can't give it up."

John jumped in. "It's a difficult move, but as a responsible company, we need to look at all our options – even painful ones. I despise what the Save the Climate campaign has done to our business, our country. How it's fueled divisions and conflict and destroyed our reputations – personal and corporate. I hadn't thought about looking for a compromise until Anthony raised it. That's why I like him. He thinks outside the box.

"The reality is that we won't have the luxury of ignoring the campaign much longer – especially if there is a downturn. We are businesspeople, and we need to protect our company. We have great assets, but we need the rest of the oilsands industry to be resilient, too, because we store and transport their oil. I think the prudent path is to open lines of communication with the activists, see if there's room for a middle ground. Industry tried that in the past but failed. Environmentalists might be more open to a compromise if the idea comes from Indigenous people."

Before the week was over, after agreeing to become IOC's volunteer interim chair, John made the long drive with Anthony across the Canadian Rockies to Vancouver for a meeting with Erika Bernstein and her lawyers. Along the way, they stopped to visit bands interested in becoming partners.

The retired oilman watched with admiration the camaraderie between members of different First Nations and listened to their stories – some about poverty and dependence, some about business triumphs. Much turned on the effectiveness of their leadership, he thought, just like in the rest of the world. They invited him to their tables and offered him their food. They asked him questions and offered their views. He welcomed their sincerity, the commitment to the community.

The next day, John and Anthony entered the modern boardroom overlooking Vancouver's harbour that housed the law firm that advised the Save the Climate campaign.

John Hess sized up the other side. Erika Bernstein and her legal team looked like they smelled blood. They read the same news he did. Oil company shares were melting down, and oil prices were dropping, because OPEC was restless over the increasing amount of oil coming from Canada's oilsands and oil shale fields in the US.

"Welcome to Vancouver," Erika said. "Anthony, it's been too long. I have followed your career with interest. I am delighted with everything you have done for Indigenous people in the oilsands area. Mr. Hess, your reputation precedes you. We welcome this opportunity to look at any points of inter-section between our goals and yours."

John focused more closely on Erika, the woman who more than anyone had brought his industry to its knees. Indirectly, she'd brought him to his knees, too. He would still be leading Aurora if activists like her had not disrupted his business.

She struck him as a natural leader who pushed hard and didn't hesitate to get her hands dirty. Like him, she got things done. He liked her direct-ness, even if he knew he shouldn't. Barb Heinz, in contrast, was a politi-cian, always looking out for number one. In another place, another time, Erika would have made an excellent corporate executive, he thought.

John hoped the activist would see merit in collaboration. Working alongside industry to achieve common climate-change goals, instead of demanding its destruction, could accelerate progress instead of bogging it down in conflict over whose agenda should prevail.

"Thank you for agreeing to meet with us," John said. "As you know, Anthony and I have big plans for IOC. Our new company has made a posi-tive impact on Indigenous communities in the oilsands area, and we see opportunity to bring new partners under our umbrella. We're here to talk. What would it take for you to leave our industry alone?"

"We are prepared to accept current oilsands production levels, but no more growth," Erika said. "We want to see producers reduce greenhouse gas emissions to zero. We want you to stop building new pipelines. Longer term, we want to see a plan to phase out the business altogether."

John couldn't believe the audacity. Erika's starting point was unrealistic, he thought.

"The oilsands industry is unable to stop projects already under con-struction – you're asking them to lay off tens of thousands of people who are working on new projects right now, and to squander billions in invest-ments," he said. "We have a duty to our shareholders to complete our plans. If you had your way, the economy of Alberta – of Canada – would col-lapse. There is room to achieve your environmental goals, over time. The industry is working hard on new technologies to reduce environmental impacts. That's how industry can continue to produce and reduce emis-sions at the same."

The activist dug in. She made it clear the Save the Climate campaign's goal was to stop – not rehabilitate – the oilsands. "We need to transition to green energy now," Erika insisted. "We cannot allow the oilsands to continue to grow. The oilsands need to stay in the ground."

"Green energy cannot replace fossil fuels for decades," John argued, becoming angry. "You're unrealistic. Besides, every barrel that you suppress in Canada will be produced elsewhere in the world to meet demand. You're just moving production to other jurisdictions that have lax environmental regulation, that will weaponize their oil when it suits them."

Anthony Littlechild, worried the conversation was getting stuck in the same old views, decided it was time to put Erika in her place. "Look, Erika. We're here to look for a solution that works for all of us. If you kill the oilsands, you kill the best chance Indigenous communities have to be self-sufficient in an industry that values them. Dozens of Indigenous leaders are knocking on our doors and begging to join our company because they see a way to lift themselves out of poverty. They are prepared to go public with their stories about how your campaign is manipulating them. Be careful, because without the backing of our people, you have no campaign. You're an American messing with Canada's resource economy, funded by foreign money that wants to shut down competition from Canada, who takes advantage of Indigenous Canadians – just like you took advantage of me."

Erika looked at him and paused. She was calculating the cost of Anthony's wrath to her cause.

"Indigenous people have diverse views," the activist responded. "Many support our campaign here on the West Coast."

"You're finally telling the truth – that Indigenous people have diverse views," Anthony said. "Why are you telling the world that Indigenous Canadians support your campaign? You're ignoring those of us who want to be partners in resource development. The oilsands have been good to our community. We need this industry to thrive, so we can thrive. Forget your ultimatums. We can play hardball, too. We can disrupt your campaign, too. Imagine how that will play out, Erika Bernstein."

Feeling cornered, the activist softened her stance. "Let's continue this discussion," she proposed. "I'd like to get input from the campaign. I suggest you meet with the rest of the industry and produce a list of areas where you are prepared to reduce your environmental impacts."

John and Anthony left the meeting feeling optimistic. The campaign had opened the door to a compromise.

Chapter 59

Winter was at its peak and Fort McMurray was in agony. Another frigid front was blowing in from the Arctic, and the first major oil-price shock since the commercialization of the oilsands was lashing it from the Persian Gulf.

Feeling as powerless as he did during his miserable childhood on the reserve, Anthony Littlechild called an emergency meeting of his board to discuss options.

"Can we afford to keep all our staff?" he asked John, hoping for reassurance from someone who had survived previous OPEC-ordered oil price wars. "I can't believe we're having to tighten our belts so soon after finally generating enough revenue to take care of ourselves."

John, who'd flown in from Switzerland to attend in person, was nervous. He'd been through many highs and lows in his career. The secret, he said to Anthony, was to hope for the best but prepare for the worst, because markets could be irrational longer than companies could remain solvent.

"We've got a good financial cushion, but we should implement a hiring freeze and cut salaries to preserve cash," John said to the board. "If this war is short, there will be opportunities for cheap acquisitions, and we could cherry pick good assets and come out ahead. But it could drag on and we must do everything we can to ensure our survival, particularly that we have enough cash and access to credit to see us through. The good news is that most of our assets generate revenue. These price wars are rough. We're at the mercy of OPEC, but markets eventually take care of themselves. As they say, the best cure for low oil prices is low oil prices."

"How vulnerable is the oilsands industry?" Anthony asked him.

John had watched the Saudis, bolstered by their new Russian friends, declare the oil-price war in late November. They said they were fed up with losing market share to new entrants. As they had done before, they flooded the market with their cheap oil, causing world prices to collapse. Their unspoken but well-understood goal was to push enough of the new competitors – Canada's oilsands, US shale and deep-water projects in other parts of the world – into bankruptcy so they could restore their grip over Western consumers and their governments.

"Among the upstarts, the oilsands are the weakest," John explained. "The Save the Climate campaign has contributed to making Canada's oilsands more vulnerable to oil shocks by raising its costs, destroying our reputation, and scaring away investment. You may recall that Middle East oil kingpins were identified by the *Journal* as funders of the anti-oilsands campaign. Perhaps this price war is about finishing the job."

The declaration of war had the harshest impact on his industry he'd ever seen, John continued. Bank loans were being recalled. Spending plans were halted. Production was shut in. Projects were put on hold. Layoffs, from Calgary to Fort McMurray, Peace River to Red Deer, were making the news – first a trickle, then a flood. Tens of thousands were losing their livelihood. The green industry was too young and too small to absorb so many unemployed. Jobs in oil services and other sectors were disappearing. Malls were deserted. Restaurants were empty. Office buildings were vacated. Housing prices fell. Holidays were cancelled. Suicides spiked.

Alberta was collapsing like a wounded soldier.

"I'm disappointed that there is no sympathy for our suffering in the rest of the country," John continued. "It's like Canadians' generosity and openness toward each other have been replaced by division and blame. That has been Save the Climate's true legacy."

Chief Anne said Alberta government revenue was shrinking so much that sweeping cuts to services were announced, fueling outrage from government workers. With provincial and federal elections due shortly, she had heard rumours that the Save the Climate campaign was funding candidates who supported its green energy goals.

"Could environmentalists form government in Alberta?" Anthony wondered, shocking himself for asking the question, given the province's long history of supporting oil.

"It's a long shot – but not impossible," John said. "People are divided. They're scared of unemployment. They're tired of this campaign, of being shamed for what they do – I know I am."

"What could a government backed by the Save the Climate campaign do to our industry?" Anthony asked.

"They could regulate us to death," John responded. "They could raise our taxes. They could make it impossible for us to grow. They could stop construction of new projects."

"Don't people see that killing the oilsands doesn't solve climate change and destroys our economy? Demand for oil will grow for decades once this price war is over. Other producers will fill that void," Anthony said. "No other oil-producing country is being pressured to sacrifice its energy security for some impossible-to-achieve broader climate good."

"That's right," John said. "But it's obvious that the activists' real goal is power. They want to suppress Canada's most important industry because of its political influence. By making it weak, they get to fill the power vacuum with their own people and to remake Canada into what they want. Climate-change activism has become the direct pathway to taking over government. The minority has figured out how to impose its agenda on the complacent majority. He – or she – who controls the climate, controls the land."

The meeting adjourned. IOC directors were concerned. It was their first exposure to a severe downturn. There was unanimous agreement to keep all jobs for as long as possible, to cut costs. A long list of ideas for discussions with the Save the Climate campaign was taking shape.

John was about to leave the IOC's building and walk to his hotel when Anthony chased after him to hand him a message.

"John, it looks like your old pal at Aurora wants to talk to you," he said, handing John a piece of paper with a phone number scribbled on it.

"Aurora's chairman?" John asked. "He must be desperate. Thanks for delivering this. Good night – and don't lose hope. We'll overcome this." He patted his protégé on his back.

John put the piece of paper in a pocket of his parka, pulled up the hood, and walked out into the dark and snowy night. He knew he had minutes to get to his hotel before his skin froze and his lungs burned. For most people, such harsh cold meant unbearable pain. He embraced it, like a deep cleansing.

John walked into the warm hotel lobby, found his room, and dialed the private number. He knew he didn't have to. He'd closed that door and was thankful he sold Aurora's stock when he did.

"John?" his old rival said at the other end of the line.

"Yes, this is John Hess. I'm returning your call."

"John, we have been trying to get in touch since your *departure*," the chairman said, sounding sheepish. "We heard you remained involved with Anthony Littlechild."

"That's right," John said. "He's done a great job and he'll come out on top, as I expected."

"He sure did. Are you in town?" Aurora's chairman asked.

"Not today," John responded, enjoying the man's discomfort. They'd been civil, once, if not friends. He suspected an ask would come next.

"John, first, I'd like to apologize for the way things *ended*. We made a terrible judgement call. With you gone, the market abandoned us. We need to save what's left. I heard about your new role at IOC, and about your preliminary discussions with the Save the Climate campaign."

"I'm just helping out. Anthony is leading those discussions. They're his idea and you need to talk to him," John responded, trying to disengage.

"I have been asked by the largest companies in the oilsands to talk to you," the chairman insisted. "We believe you are the best person to represent all of us in our negotiations with the campaign – the Save the Climate campaign. In fact, Erika Bernstein suggested that you should be the face of industry because you are trusted and respected all around. They also like that you have a leadership role with the Indigenous company. Erika said it would make it easier to sell a truce to their own base, if they can show they are compromising to help the Indigenous economy."

John couldn't believe what he was hearing. Aurora's chairman was finally acknowledging that he'd been right along – that the only way for the oilsands to survive involved Indigenous inclusion, ownership, and leadership.

"I'm pleased that you are finally seeing what I saw. I wish you'd figured it out when I proposed it and made Aurora a leader by embracing Indigenous participation," John said. "You and I wouldn't be where we are today."

The chairman agreed, and once again begged John to forgive him.

John accepted the offer to meet and discuss next steps. He knew negotiations would be difficult. He knew there was nothing in it for him, financially. But the alternative – doing nothing – was unbearable because it would be the end of the industry he loved.

Gratified by the vote of confidence and the opportunity to give back, John looked outside his hotel window and noticed the night sky had cleared. A full moon illuminated the town. It would be a good night for northern lights, he thought, and decided to stay up to see them shine.

Chapter 60

CALGARY, ALBERTA, MAY 2015

Elise tuned into the mid-morning press conference from the *Journal's* soon-to-be-closed Calgary office. She was back in her messy old digs. She was alone – just like she was when she first moved to Alberta. She barely knew the Canadian province when she applied for the far-away correspondent job. Yet the rich experience had put her on a path to the powerful, fulfilling, happy life she now enjoyed.

Elise was so emotionally attached to the city she called home for fifteen years – its shining glass towers, its fearless oil pioneers, the big blue skies, the pure mountain landscapes, the crisp air, the generous people – that she had wanted it to thrive and fulfill its mission to supply the world with its bountiful energy. She continued to visit her mountain refuge as often as she could, sometimes with her children, sometimes with John.

Her new job was demanding, but not as stressful as being on the front lines of journalism. She loved the new pace and she felt good about being back in the newsroom, making decisions about expanding coverage of new innovative businesses, offering new trading platforms, diversifying into new niche information products.

But her new job also involved making tough choices. Canada's energy sector was stumbling so badly – as the sacrificial lamb of the Save the Climate campaign, as the easy target of the Middle East oil price war, and because of new Canadian regulation – that the *Journal* could no longer fund it.

Trading activity, advertising, and subscriptions had shrunk sharply. The oilsands had become yesterday's embarrassing industry, all over the world. The activists had won. There was no point spinning a story that no investor wanted to read. *Un-investable.* That's how market commentators were describing Canada's oilsands companies.

She believed that the reckoning had just begun for Alberta. Governments with anti-oilsands agendas had been elected by Canadian voters disillusioned with oil's booms and busts, tired of the conflict, terrified about climate change. Foreign companies that had fuelled the industry put their oilsands operations up for sale at fire-sale prices, or abandoned proposed projects, or moved capital and employees to other jurisdictions.

Elise, too, decided to redeploy her resources to other areas. The news conference would help her gauge how fast she had to move out.

The bit of unofficial information she had gleaned from John wasn't encouraging. He had told her that secret negotiations had taken place between the new anti-oilsands government, industry, and the Save the Climate campaign to *reform* the oilsands sector.

Elise had kept the intelligence to herself but dispatched her last remaining reporter in Calgary to cover the event before he too was re-assigned to the *Journal*'s Houston office, where the oil shale business was still thriving.

The screen of the *Journal*'s large TV filled with a close-up of Erika Bernstein, in her new capacity as senior climate advisor to the newly elected provincial premier. Standing behind her were John Hess and two other oilsands company leaders, representatives of three environmental organizations, Anthony Littlechild, and two other Indigenous leaders.

"Thank you for attending this important announcement about the future of the oilsands," Erika said, looking all business in a pant suit and silky shirt.

"Today we are announcing the terms that will govern the oilsands' industry of the future, the centrepiece of our Green New Deal. They were finalized yesterday, after months of intense negotiations between industry, led by John Hess, who is here today, environmental organizations, and Indigenous leaders led by Anthony Littlechild, who is also here today. I negotiated for our new government."

She proudly listed the highlights: Industry emissions would be capped to discourage production growth; an onerous tax on carbon would be introduced; proposed pipelines would be subjected to new climate-change tests and more extensive public hearings, which would make new permits difficult to obtain. And the knockout punch: Alberta, owner of the world's second-largest deposits of oil, would implement a quick transition to clean energy.

Erika Bernstein invited John Hess to speak.

The former oil executive wore a casual shirt over khakis. His hair was greyer and longer than usual. His face wore his defeat. He was like a general who had accepted a harsh surrender to salvage what was left of his army.

"Today, we are announcing a historic agreement to bring much-needed peace," he said. "Our companies are in unbearable distress from low oil prices, over which we have no control, and from years of relentless attacks from environmentalists against our industry. Our companies are in such grave danger of insolvency they appointed me to lead negotiations for a compromise, so we can start an orderly transition to new energy sources. The terms you just heard involve aspects of our business that we can change, such as cancelling investments in growth projects, improving our environmental performance, and cooperating with our Indigenous partners.

"This agreement will further increase our costs. It will be harsh for our largest companies and could be fatal for our smaller companies, which have less flexibility to adapt. For that, I am sorry. It's the best we could do, given the aggressive demands to reduce our emissions imposed by our new government. Unfortunately, the new terms will result in more workforce reductions because of our inability to grow, but, we hope, the preservation of what we have already built.

"On a personal level, I want to thank all those who helped me build the most enterprising, hard-working, and innovative oil industry that the world will ever see. I regret that we were not given the opportunity to take the oilsands to the next level, to continue to create wealth for investors and for the people of Canada, and that we will not have the money to innovate to make our oil the most responsibly produced in the world.

"But I respect the will of the people who elected our new government with a strong mandate to transition away from fossil fuels. I wish you well."

John moved back from the microphone and Anthony stepped forward.

"I want to thank John Hess for his leadership in these difficult negotiations, and for guiding our Indigenous company to become the important player in the oilsands that it is today. John has been a Canadian pioneer and deserves our gratitude," he said, pausing as he looked admiringly at the oilman.

"The growing involvement of our people in providing services, transportation, and storage to oilsands companies provides motivation for governments to ensure this industry continues until it's replaced by new energy sources, which we plan to participate in," Anthony said. "Meanwhile, we will do our part to ensure the environment is protected. We call on our brothers and sisters across Canada to talk to us about participating in the energy economy and become our partners."

Questions and answers followed, moderated by Erika Bernstein.

Elise noticed that John was no longer in the room. She expected he didn't want to say more than he had to, or to participate in a group photograph to benefit the environmental cause.

Minutes after the end of the conference, Erika Bernstein phoned her.

"Elise," the activist-turned-government-leader said, sounding concerned. "I heard from your reporter that you are shutting down the *Journal's* Calgary operation. Our new government would like to have a word with you."

"You heard right. Congratulations on your election, and I'd love to hear from the new government," said Elise. "But this is my last day here. Unfortunately, we had no choice but to shut down our bureau. This office has been bleeding money and people. With so many oil companies getting out, it doesn't make sense for us to keep this operation."

"We need you to reconsider," Erika said. "Investors around the world need to know about our energy transition here in Alberta, how we are developing a model for others to follow."

"Sorry, Erika," Elise responded. "It's too late. You are going to have to get your message out through other channels. The *Journal* is done here." Elise hung up before Erika could respond.

Elise knew she'd allowed her personal dislike of Erika Bernstein to influence her business judgement. Perhaps the *Journal* could have kept a presence to document the planned energy transition.

But Elise felt Erika needed to feel the consequences of her disruption. She was convinced that without a thriving oil industry, built over decades of risk-taking and expertise, involving much of its population, Alberta would struggle to re-invent itself in an image imposed by outsiders, with skills it didn't have, without oil money to pay for it, all the while resenting that any advance in reducing its carbon emissions would make no difference to the world's climate.

Then John showed up, unannounced.

"This feels like old times – although you're in the fancy suit, and I'm suited for a street fight," he said, looking relieved. He kissed her, thinking about the first time they met in the same office.

Elise had flashbacks, too, of those first moments together. They'd come a long way – attraction, loathing, estrangement, betrayal, and closeness again. So much of that evolution had to do with the push and pull of their careers and of the oilsands business that had bound them together.

Now both were moving to a new stage when the rest of the world mattered less.

John Hess was no longer married to oil. Elise had achieved as much as she could in journalism. Her children were grown up and successful. They could finally be themselves and stop caring about what others said or wanted from them.

"You took off fast from that news conference," she said. "Didn't you want to bask in the glory of your historic deal? Get your picture taken for posterity?"

"No, thanks," John said. "Erika Bernstein doesn't own me, and I don't want to have anything more to do with her. I know that industry will deliver its end of the bargain – they have no choice given this government will be in charge for four years. They must protect their shareholders in any way they can. But I'd be shocked if she does. She'll put all our concessions in her pocket, and then demand more. Change the goal posts. That's been my experience, anyway. There will be nothing left of our industry when this government is done."

Elise hoped he wasn't right, that the oilsands industry would weather the setback and bounce back stronger.

She had to ask: "Was it worth it – to accept such painful terms from the Save the Climate campaign? Will Alberta's sacrifice, perhaps Canada's sacrifice if it leads to the breakup of the country, improve climate change?"

"Of course not," John said. "We're too small to make a difference. This is all symbolism. It's about creating a template for suppression of fossil fuel industries that, in time, will be deployed elsewhere – until people wake up and resist rules that put climate policy ahead of everything else. There's got to be a better way, more thought put into this, real cooperation, and technology.

"The same energy transition could have been achieved by allowing people to continue to produce the oilsands while funding climate change solutions through innovation. Or by ramping up production of natural gas, which is the best transition fuel. It's true that necessity is the mother of all invention. But innovation takes money, especially at scale. Anti-oil activism has made us poorer, weaker, divided. It will keep us from moving forward."

"It sounds like the business still needs you," Elise said.

John smiled. "I'd rather be on the sidelines for a while."

They were interrupted by loud noises in the street below – people chanting, beating drums, honking horns. They walked to the window to see what was going on.

Oil workers in business suits and coveralls, men and women, young and old, were walking out of office towers to join a demonstration against the new government's green agenda. It was a rare sight. Industry didn't like its employees to engage in protests of any kind.

"Erika Bernstein's announcement must have been the last straw, an acknowledgement by industry that their detente has been a failure," Elise said. "It looks like Canada's oil and gas workers are taking matters into their own hands to protect their jobs."

"They should," John said. "Industry did fail them. They're on their own. I doubt that governments will rescue them."

The demonstration spilled into every major downtown street. It was joined by roughnecks in their pickup trucks, restaurant and coffee-shop owners, real estate agents, artists and social workers, hotel maids and chefs, taxi drivers and shopkeepers, chanting: "We love Canadian oil and gas!" or "Build that pipe!" or "The world needs more Canadian oil!"

Some waved effigies of Erika Bernstein and called for her head.

The boldest called for Alberta's separation from the Canadian federation so the oil-rich province could make its own decisions about the future of its industry, rather than cave to pressure from the central government, or other provinces, or other countries, or foreign activists, to meet aggressive targets to mitigate climate change that no other country had volunteered to meet.

As it grew, the boisterous crowd marched in front of shuttered stores and empty office towers and stopped outside the imposing government building, so Erika Bernstein and her government could hear and feel their pain.

John Hess shook his head.

"Guess what makes the news today? Not her big announcement," he told Elise. "The rebels are facing rebellion. Her plan to remake Alberta into something that isn't – a green wonderland for the world to emulate – won't be a walk in the park after all. She'll find out soon enough that it takes money to run a government, and oil to run an economy."

Elise nodded. "Erika Bernstein hasn't figured out the difference between activism and leadership," she said. "Activism is power by pressure. But it takes leadership to create a following. Without people buying into her vision, she won't be able to create the new green economy she wants to replace the old one she crushed."

The biggest blow to Erika Bernstein's plan came from the environmental lobby. By the end of the day, the off-oil activists Erika had nurtured and funded refused to accept her deal with the oilsands industry. They issued a flurry of statements pledging they would continue the fight to shut down the oilsands until their last breath. Industry's acceptance of harsh terms had made them bolder in their fight for climate justice, not more compromising, they said.

More news releases announced the start of new campaigns against other energy sources, industries, and infrastructure – natural gas, big hydro, big mining, big banks, big tourism, big retail, big fashion, even population growth – and any other human activity they felt degraded the planet. Elise read a few before unplugging her computer.

"These threats – they're scary for investors," Elise said to John. "I doubt many will stay to see who wins. There are too many opportunities to make money elsewhere, with less grief."

"This industry has had more than its share of booms and busts," John said. "We know how to deal with those. This movement has a different measure of value that I don't understand. I did the best I could. I feel bad for those we're leaving behind."

"As do I," Elise said. "But I fought the good fight. Someone needs to take it from here and find new ways to move forward that address these new challenges."

Elise locked the door of her old office one last time and together they walked in the deserted downtown, heading for O'Reilly.

They found it closed. A For Lease sign was posted on the door.

"They're gone, too," John said. "They had a big business crowd. They must have taken a hit from this downturn."

Then he looked at her like a man on a mission. "It's still early," he said. "I know a restaurant out of town – a real landmark. Let's drive there."

They drove south in his pickup truck toward the US border and found a back-county road through cow pastures and ranches, wellheads and pump jacks. Ian Tyson's *Four Strong Winds* serenaded them on the radio, making them feel like the fearless cowboys who had roamed the prairies long before Alberta was a place.

They arrived at the lonely steakhouse on a cliff just as the sun started setting, and Alberta's pure sky spit flames of pink and orange above the mountains.

After they were seated and ordered their meals, John kissed Elise's hand. "Elise, when are you coming back?" he asked.

"Soon," she said. "You are welcome to come to see me, too."

"And then?" he asked. "What's next for us?"

"A new beginning," she said, feeling lighter, like the wind was at her back. They enjoyed their meals, tuned out the world and into each other, and then Elise asked the waiter for the cheque.

Final words from the author

The Canada Project is a work of fiction inspired by true events. They include, in chronological order:

1921 – Dr. Karl Clark, a chemist, joined the Scientific and Industrial Research Council of Alberta and experimented with ways of separating oil from the oilsands using hot water and a chemical reagent.

1963 – Sun Oil of Philadelphia invested $240 million in Great Canadian Oil Sands, the predecessor of Suncor Energy. Chairman Howard Pew believed the investment would reduce US dependence on offshore oil.

1964 – Syncrude Canada incorporated with four owners: Imperial Oil, Royalite, Atlantic Richfield Canada, and Cities Service Athabasca.

1995 – The National Oil Sands Task Force announced improvements in fiscal terms to encourage oilsands development. The initiative involved cooperation between all levels of government in Canada, developers, trade unions and suppliers at a time of weak employment and economic growth.

1997 – Oilsands pioneers Suncor and Syncrude phased out bucketwheels and conveyor belts that were prone to breaking down, and replaced them with trucks and shovels, reducing costs. Suncor announced Project Millennium, a $2.2-billion expansion to double production. Syncrude announced $6 billion in new investments, including a new upgrader, the new Aurora mine, and other improvements. Their goal was to profitably produce enough oil to supply half of Canada's oil needs and to replace a growing share of the oil imported by the US from the Middle East and other producers like Mexico and Venezuela.

2000 – The Ladyfern natural gas field was discovered in northeast British Columbia by Murphy Oil. The discovery, one of the largest in Western

Canada, set off an exploration rush that caused land prices to soar, drilling activity to escalate, and the field to quickly deplete.

2001 – Militants associated with the Islamic extremist group al-Quaeda launched attacks against the United States. Two airplanes flew into the twin towers of the World Trade Centre in Manhattan

2003 – Activism against the oilsands ramps up.

2004 – Facebook was created.

2006 – Twitter was created.

2008 – A coalition of US and Canadian environmental organizations expands the campaign against the Canadian oilsands. It involved raising the negatives, raising the costs, slowing down and stopping infrastructure, and enrolling key decision-makers.

2014 – OPEC, led by Saudi Arabia, unleashed a price war against new sources of oil, including the oilsands, to protect its share of the global oil market.

2015 – Alberta elected its first left-of-centre government. It introduced a climate-change plan that imposed limits on oilsands emissions and a path to transition to green energy.

2015 – Four large oilsands companies – Suncor, Canadian Natural Resources, Shell, and Cenovus – agreed to cap emissions in exchange for environmental groups backing down on opposition to export pipelines. The agreement followed months of secret negotiations between the companies and four environmental organizations.

2015 – The Keystone XL pipeline from Alberta to the US Gulf Coast was rejected by US President Barack Obama.

2015 – The Northern Gateway pipeline from Alberta to the west coast of British Columbia was cancelled by Canada's Prime Minister, Justin Trudeau.

2015 – An exodus of companies and investment from the oilsands contributed to the loss of 100,000 jobs and plunged Alberta's economy into a protracted downturn.

2017 – The Energy East pipeline project was abandoned after the Canadian government imposed new climate change criteria.

2021 – A public inquiry into allegations that an anti-Alberta energy campaign was organized by foreign interest groups to landlock Alberta resources found that $1.28 billion in foreign funding flowed into Canadian-based environmental initiatives between 2003 and 2019. The inquiry, appointed by the Government of Alberta, said the amount was likely significantly underrepresented. The amount included $925 million in foreign funding reported by Canadian charities for "environmental initiatives," and $352 million in foreign funding of "Canadian-based" environmental initiatives, such as anti-pipeline campaigns, that remained in the US.

2021 – Stephen Guilbault, a Quebec environmentalist who helped lead the campaign against the oilsands, including working as a director and campaign manager for Greenpeace, was appointed federal environment and climate change minister.

2022 – Alberta's oilsands industry achieved record production of 3.5 million barrels a day as oil prices climbed back above US$100 because of global underinvestment in fossil fuels, Russia's invasion of Ukraine, and demand growth following the COVID-19 pandemic.

2022 – No new oilsands projects are planned.

Acknowledgements

I am grateful for the guidance provided by the exceptional team at FriesenPress Publishing Services on all aspects of publishing *The Canada Project*.

I'm indebted to my husband, Ioan Dobre, a geophysicist, for always being my first and most loyal reader, and for providing advice on technical aspects of the oil and gas industry; and to my children, Charlotte and Julian, who helped with suggestions and encouragement.

I'm grateful that Carol Howes, my friend and former colleague, shared her sharp editing skills so generously; and that Donna Kennedy Glans, my friend and fellow writer, helped with general feedback.

I am thankful that thousands of people, from Indigenous people to oil industry CEOs, politicians to roughnecks, engineers to communicators, environmentalists to academics, trusted me to tell their stories in Canada's *Financial Post*, where I worked as journalist specializing in energy for most of my career. I retired in 2018.

Claudia Cattaneo